The Homesteader

She, too, had a hard time keeping her mind on her teaching and would rather be back at the farm watching the windmill go up—watching Trace as he moved about hoisting things into place—seeing his muscles ripple in the sun when he got too warm and took off his shirt.

Her thoughts shocked her. What was wrong with her? She shouldn't be thinking of Trace like that. She raised her head up from the textbook at her desk. She looked around her classroom to see that all the students were doing their studies and none had caught her in her daydream.

At last, she gazed out the small window to where the sun shone across the wide-open valley. It was hard not to think of Trace in a romantic manner with him sleeping just inches above her at night. It was difficult to fall asleep at bedtime; no matter how tired she was, knowing he was up there—above her. She felt a tingling in her inner thighs, inside her skirt beneath her desk. *No. He is just helping out. Soon, he'll be on his way to live his own life—and we'll be better off for having known him. It wouldn't pay to get involved with a drifter.*

She tried to shoo the sweet thoughts that buzzed like flies above a sticky dried-apple pie, away from her mind. But, just like the pestering insects, her musings persisted.

What They Are Saying About
The Homesteader

Ms. Kelso has written a wonderful story filled with love, romance, tenderness and the true meaning of how a family should keep that closeness intact throughout any obstacle. She gives her characters emotions and feelings that stir the heart and make you want to read more. The Homesteader is a page turner that is hard to put down. I look forward to reading more of her books.

—Cherokee Sanders,
Coffee Time Romance

Mary Jean Kelso's *"The Homesteader"* is a touching story of the old west, one where the bad guy has a heart that melts when he stumbles across a woman in trouble. He finds himself indebted to a lonely widow woman, and the three children she has taken on to raise as her own.

—JoEllen Conger
Queen of Candelore
Rite of Passage

Other Books From The Pen Of

Mary Jean Kelso

Goodbye Is Forever: March 2006

When Lynne Garrett goes to visit historic Virginia City, Nevada, she unwittingly acquires a beautiful jeweled scarab necklace that embroils her in a complex scheme to save a stranger's life—by endangering hers.

To Mary Haughney

Best wishes

Mary Jean Kelso

5-17-05

Dedication

To my maternal grandmother,

Mary Ellen (Molly) Hall Warren Klapp,

a New Mexico pioneer, homesteader and school teacher.

And my paternal great-grandfather,

Samuel Jennings,

a Texas Ranger

Also to Matt Edenso—

who showed me what happiness is.

Acknowledgement:

With special thanks to my first readers:

Ray and Tina Powell

and

Robert MacMillan.

You help keep me on track.

Also, my appreciation goes to

Candy Goodness and Jessica MacMurray

for their editorial input.

One

"Get off my rocks!" Molly Kling called out.

"What are you talking about, lady?"

"I said, get off my rocks!" Molly lowered the rifle and felt the trigger against her finger. Lead zinged inches from the man's left leg.

Her arms and fingers ached from holding the horses in check during the long drive from her homestead to the mountain, but her aim was steady.

No man was going to take what she had come for.

Now, the man stood. He stared at her in disbelief.

She didn't know if he was surprised to see a woman out here in the backcountry without a man, or startled to be staring down the barrel of her rifle.

"What's the matter with you? Are you crazy?" He glanced at the flat shale chunks protruding from the clay bank beneath his boots. "What are they, gold or something?"

"Better than that. Those rocks are going to be the foundation for my house."

"Hold on, now. Don't get antsy with your rifle." The man raised his hands in front of him, waving his palms toward her.

"I said, those rocks are mine. I claimed them for my house. I drove all morning through the heat and dust to get them. I'm tired, I'm hot, and I'm not giving them up. Now, get down off my rocks or the next shot will draw blood."

"And I said, hold on. I'm unarmed. Can't you see that?"

Molly lowered the rifle and looked at the man's waist where she would expect to see a gun belt buckled. There was none.

"Now, will you listen to reason?"

"You're on my—"

"Look, lady—" he paused, as if considering the term then went on, "—my horse threw me back there over the ridge. I'm on my way to look for work around Albuquerque. I'm hungry. I'm tired and I'm sore. And I don't want your damn rocks!"

Molly bristled at his swearing. She considered his comment, squinting against the bright sun. They were alone with no lawman to arrest him for his vulgarity.

He dropped his hands to his sides while Molly decided his fate.

A scrubby tree a few feet taller than the man shaded him. He looked ragged, dirty, and disheveled. His hair hung in filthy strands to his shoulders, framing a square jawed face, with an unkempt beard and mustache.

She had seen many men with a similar appearance when she lived near the coal mines in Oklahoma. She found they were often stragglers meandering from one job to another. Or they were outlaws waiting to jump the first miner that let his guard down on his way home with his pay in his pocket. She had lost her own husband to one of these lurking opportunists. Now, she was left struggling to make a home for herself and her three stepchildren.

Out here, even a hundred miles from any coal mine, the man could only be trouble. She made out that, perhaps, some of the dirt could be attributed to being thrown from a horse. The man's face bore dust, not the black grime of a mine. Not having any saddlebags, guns or bedroll would bear out his story, as well.

"I ain't had a meal in some time." The man stared at the picnic basket.

"Haven't had," Molly corrected out of habit.

Molly relaxed the hammer on the gun. She lowered the barrel, but kept the rifle nearby.

"That's our lunch." She tossed her head toward the picnic basket where the children huddled behind her. She thought about the food.

Surely, she had packed enough food she could share a sandwich with a hungry stranger. But she would not let her guard down.

"Rosie, please get the man one of those sandwiches we made," she instructed her stepdaughter.

"Yes, Ma."

The man stepped in rigid jerks down off the rocks and slid along the hillside until he approached the buckboard. He stopped and waited patiently a few feet away.

Molly noted the stiff way he moved from his perch on her rocks and his efforts to work the kinks out of his legs.

"Your horse do that to you?"

"Partly." He watched Rosie dig into the woven wicker basket.

Rosie picked up one of the large sandwiches and apprehensively held it out toward him. The stranger stepped forward and took the food.

He shoved the sandwich into his mouth. Tearing a large bite off with his teeth, he savored the taste. The roast beef had been cooked in the coals of a campfire and the edges were burnt. The meat's center, nearly rare, felt tender and moist on his tongue. The bread, rough sliced, but not more than a few days old, held the chunks of beef together.

He ate as if he couldn't remember when he had tasted anything better.

The food disappeared as though he hadn't seen a meal in months and Molly no longer doubted that part of his story, either. She moved, tentatively, down from the buckboard. She kept her rifle at her side, the barrel pointed at the ground.

"You work the coal mines?" She still remembered more than she wanted to about the mines.

The man finished choking down the sandwich and looked at the water jug next to the oldest child. He traced the outline of his lips with the tip of his tongue.

Molly nodded. "Give the man a drink, Andy. I imagine that was kind of a dry morsel."

Andy lifted the jug and held it out to the stranger.

The man took a swig and lowered the jug. He wiped his mouth with the back of his dirty sleeve.

"Good water, Ma'am. Cool, too."

"First thing we did was hire a couple of drifters to dig a well." She didn't want to provide too much information. "I asked if you were a miner."

"No, not much of a one, anyway. I tried it for a few days. That's where I was coming from when my horse and I got into an argument. He wanted to turn back and eat buffalo grass and I wanted to get on into the nearest town. He always was ornery." The stranger shook his head and looked at Rosie, then back at Molly. "Name's Trace. Trace Westerman."

"I'm Molly Kling. These are my kids, Rosie, Andy, the eldest, and Seth, the baby."

Seth scowled at Molly.

"Ma, can we eat now, too?" Rosie tugged at the basket's handles.

The trip had been long and hot across the vast Estancia Valley and Molly gauged the angle of the sun. She judged it was nearing noon, anyway. They would have to hurry if they were going to get the rocks and get back before dark.

"Grab the quilt and spread it out in the shade. We might as well eat. Then, we better load the rocks and head back home."

"I'll help. In return, maybe you can give me a ride toward town."

"Closest town to us is Moriarty. Not much there. Estancia is a bit larger, but it's farther on south from our place. Albuquerque's a good piece on west of us."

"So you're homesteaders?"

Molly nodded.

"It's unusual to see a woman homesteader. Don't you have a man around?"

"Don't you worry about that. I filed on the claim, myself. The children and I are managing."

"Didn't mean anything by it, Ma'am. Just, like I said, it is quite unusual."

"Do sit down, Mr. Westerman. I'm sure we have enough food to share the meal with you."

She watched him cross his ankles and bend his knees to squat as he lowered himself at the edge of the patchwork quilt. He kept his body on the grass.

"And you, Mr. Westerman, do you have an avocation?"

She watched as he crunched the shell in his large fist. She sat on the edge of the quilt, as did the children. Through her skirt, she felt the comfortable shape of the rifle's wooden butt against her thigh. Ever since her husband was killed, she never trusted men.

"Are you a married man, Mr. Westerman?"

"No, Ma'am. Never hankered to take on a woman. I've been a rancher, mostly." He'd had enough to do running his own ranch and making a place for his parents to live. What did he need with a wife and, of all things, kids? Now, that had all changed. He certainly didn't need any complications to his latest challenge—that of tracking the vicious gang that destroyed the life he had known and loved so well.

The children finished their meal and ran to explore the intriguing mountainside.

The man watched the youngsters as they played tag across the meadow below the picnic site.

"Are you averse to children, Mr. Westerman?"

The question seemed to surprise him.

"Trace. Call me Trace. No. It's just—that kind of family life's not for me. Seems hard enough to take care of myself, much less kids that don't know nothing or do much."

"These children are my stepchildren. I took on the responsibility gladly. I don't know what I would do without them. Really, Mr. Westerman—Trace—kids are nothing less than little people."

"Maybe, but I know nothing about them and don't care to learn."

Pressing the man further about his business seemed a dead end and Molly stood, crossed her arms and cradled the rifle across her bosom. Her long brown skirt whipped in a sudden breeze and she lifted her head to smell the air for rain. Although the moisture would be welcome, she hoped any incoming storm would hold off until they were back home.

Rosie ran back from the game of tag and began picking up the picnic remains. She folded the bright quilt and put their things in the buckboard.

Molly smiled, smugly. *See,* she wanted to say, *how helpful and well mannered they are.* But, she kept her silence. One had a right to his own opinion.

"This homesteading—are you just starting out, then?"

"We're new at it." Molly thought, fondly, about the land to which she had laid claim. The ground held not one stone—not even a rock for a boy to throw. Fine talcum-powder loam that formed a crust when it dried after a shower and could be turned with a stick to plant pinto beans made up the entire 160 acres. A cover of low-growing prairie grass, and a few rattlesnakes—that was the extent of their domain. But, the pigs she planned to get would make short work of the snakes and the beans would soon be in their furrows. There were no trees there, either. The lack of trees led the family to make their first journey to the mountain. It seemed to have everything that their homestead did not.

With the meal over, their conversation ended.

Molly watched Trace push himself up from the ground. He moved to a squatting position. At last, he stood and stepped as if he were walking on sharp stones.

"How about it, boys, are you ready to get those rocks loaded? Let's let the womenfolk take care of things here. I got a feeling your ma's going to be a whole lot more comfortable holding that gun on me than she is packing rocks."

Fine. You're right, I will. "Only nice flat ones, now," she called after them as they moved to the pile to dig the chunks out with their fingers.

Molly began to relax a little as she watched them work. They dragged the chunks from the outcropping and stacked them in smaller piles to put into the back of the buckboard.

Soon, she could see a rhythm take shape as the three of them moved to get the job done. She began to feel herself lulled into a sense of security. *Don't let your guard down,* a little voice inside her head warned.

"Best turn the team and buckboard around before we load it," Trace called to her.

She nodded. That had been her plan before he showed up, anyway. She certainly didn't need a man telling her how to do what should be her work. She felt her Irish pride surge inside her and her cheeks warmed with anger. But, then, he was the one laboring away for her sake. She would cooperate. She just didn't care for the way he seemed to be giving orders and she didn't intend to be bossed around by some stranger—especially a man.

"Yes, that's exactly what I planned to do."

She spoke to Rosie. "Get into the back of the buckboard before I turn it around so I know where you are. I don't want to risk running over you."

Rosie did as she was told.

Molly could still hear the rocks thumping onto the pile as she turned and put the rifle at the foot of the driver's box, then climbed onto the seat. She called to the team and rippled the leather straps across their backs as she held the reins tight and edged the horses in a slow circle on the sloping hillside.

Not very far below her were large trees and she would have to arc around to get the buckboard turned without backing the horses up—a next to impossible task.

"Hang on tight, Rosie."

Rosie clung to the upper sideboard of the wagon as the whole box tilted precariously.

Molly directed the horses out of the circle and aimed to straighten the buckboard and pull back up alongside the growing rock pile from the opposite direction.

Molly glimpsed Trace standing above the rock pile with his hands on his hips. He looked her way with disapproval. Well, she'd like to see him do any better! She adjusted her bottom to the slant of the wooden seat. She heard the picnic basket and water jug tumble behind her. The noise startled the horses and they gave a jerk and lunged forward.

Molly saw a ravine off to her right. If the horses bolted and the wagon rolled, which now seemed a good possibility, she and Rosie would both surely die.

"Whoa, Jake. Whoa, Big Boy!"

The team, mismatched in size, tugged toward the side of Big Boy, the larger horse. He pulled on the downhill side and his strength snapped the buckboard forward sharply, jack-knifing the doubletree connection against the wagon frame. Molly struggled with all her strength to keep the horses in check.

"Hold 'em," Trace yelled as he ran toward the wagon.

What did he think she was trying to do? She clenched her jaw and struggled to straighten the mess out.

Suddenly, the wagon tipped on its side, tossing Rosie from where she clung to the higher sideboard. Molly heard Rosie scream as the child flew through the air behind her. Molly slid down the seat of the buckboard still trying to hang on to the reins. She felt the heavy wagon following her.

Oh, God, it's going to crush us.

"Where's Rosie?"

She heard a loud *W-h-u-m-p!* When she looked up, she saw the wagon braced against a tree. The tree kept it from rolling completely over on top of her. She scurried out from underneath the wagon box and scrambled to her feet, still searching for the little girl.

"Where's Rosie?"

Rosie was gone.

The rifle was gone.

She saw Trace and the two boys running to another tree some fifty feet below her.

"Over here," Trace called out.

"Seth, see about Ma," Andy ordered the smaller boy who had been trying to keep up with them.

Feeling faint, Molly slumped against the tree trunk next to the wagon. Then, with a surge of energy, she started toward Seth. She ran on with her legs quaking until she met him.

"Rosie?"

Seth turned and pointed to where Trace and Andy knelt beside the girl.

Molly, with Seth close behind, broke into a run.

"Oh, no! Oh, God, let her be all right."

She dropped beside Trace and saw that Rosie lay still.

"Is she dead?"

"She's breathing. I can't find anything broken." Trace continued to look at Rosie's arms and legs, turning them gently with his big hands.

"What about her neck? You always hear it's the neck that snaps. Oh, God, Rosie, I'm so sorry." Molly fought back tears.

"I don't think we should move her until she comes to. That way, she'll move what she can, on her own. I felt the bones in her neck and didn't feel anything unusual." Trace looked at the girl. He had worked with many newborn calves and colts on his ranch back in Texas, but his small expertise of veterinary medicine was insufficient here.

Rosie lay flat on her back in the grass appearing to simply be asleep. Trace and Molly knelt beside her, waiting for her to stir. Andy and Seth stood nearby, the blood drained from their faces, leaving them ashen. They stared in fear and disbelief.

What would she do if Rosie didn't wake up? *It's my fault. My fault. My fault.*

"I should never have brought these children up here. What kind of mother am I? They should be home tending to chores and chasing each other in the pasture."

"It was an accident. It could have happened to anybody." Trace stood. He shook his head, "There's nothing I can do here. You watch her while I see what I can do about straightening the wagon out. If she comes to, holler. Don't let her get up until I get back."

Molly nodded.

Trace motioned for the boys to follow him and they went over to study the situation with the team and wagon.

The horses were nosing at grass, trying to nibble it between the harness constraints. They snorted and darted their eyes about warily.

"Well, at least they didn't run. I can see I'll have to unhitch them and move them uphill to try to right the wagon. You boys see if you can find some large sticks to help pry the top over, if we need to."

While the two boys looked for heavy limbs to help set the outfit upright, Trace examined the undercarriage and found that nothing had broken. The wagon, with its downhill sideboard leaning against the tree trunk, sat with the wheels on the uphill side nearly horizontal. The rims of the two wheels braced against the mountain cut gashes into the dirt.

Trace unhitched the horses.

"Whoa, boy."

The horses fidgeted.

Trace patted them lightly on their necks and spoke encouraging words to them. They shook their manes and watched this new person carefully. There was nothing in his manner to distrust and they moved as he directed them. Finally, they were free of the tilting wagon and the man tugged forcefully on their reins. Trace moved them uphill, away from the wagon, where the grass was lush. He secured them to a tree and went back to contemplate the best way to attach the harness to the wagon box and drop it back onto all four wheels.

He walked around to the downhill side of the wreck and saw the picnic basket. It lay crushed and with the lid ripped off. The water jug sat nearby, having narrowly missed a tree trunk and rolled onto a heavy clump of grass. He picked the water jug up. Leaving the distorted picnic basket behind, he walked uphill to the rock pile. He placed the jug where it would be safe until he got the rig back together.

Molly sat further downhill from where Trace left her belongings. She stroked Rosie's forehead. Molly's lips moved.

He didn't know if she was comforting the child or praying.

She was probably doing a little of both.

He reminded himself there was nothing he could do to help the little girl and set about the task at hand.

The bright colors of the patchwork quilt drew his attention as he moved toward the wagon bed. It had caught a corner on the metal strap of the driver's seat. Molly might be glad to have it to cover

Rosie. He reached to disentangle it and found the rifle lying beneath the section draped onto the grass.

He picked the rifle up by its barrel and leaned it against a tree. He would check the sights later, in case the fall had bent them off kilter. For now, it would be out of harm's way when he started to upright the wagon. He folded the quilt and laid it beside the rifle butt.

When he straightened up, again, he saw the two boys far below, near the cliff, and whistled.

They looked up and he motioned them back to him with his arm swung high. He made sure they turned toward him before he put his attention to the job of righting the wagon. He was right. Kids took a lot of watching. They knew nothing and they didn't think things out.

At last, Andy and Seth reached the wagon with two large tree limbs. By then, Trace had hooked Big Boy's harness straps through the gap between the sideboards and secured them to the top board.

"I wanted to be sure we got a hold on the highest part," he told the boys. We don't want the thing coming down too fast, either. Don't want to break something and be stuck here." He studied the situation, then led Big Boy forward until the lines were snug.

"You boys take the sticks around behind the wagon. No, wait." Trace grasped each boy by the shoulders and positioned them where he felt they could lend the most assistance. Indecision tore him between whether to hold the horse's lead himself or put the strength of his shoulder against the wagon and trust that one of the boys could control the horse. He analyzed the dilemma momentarily.

"Andy, you stay here and keep the horse still." When the boy got a good grip on Big Boy's halter, Trace said, "Now hold on tight, but watch what I'm going to show you. You may have to trade places with me."

Trace picked up one of the sticks the boys had brought. He tossed it to Seth. Then he picked up the other one for himself. He didn't expect much help from the five-year-old but by giving him a place to stand, hopefully, he'd be able to keep him safe.

"Seth, you get next to the tree. If anything moves your way, get behind it. Understand?"

Seth looked scared, but took a stance, ready to help. He nodded back at Trace.

Trace lodged the other stick into the ground beneath the wagon bed. He put pressure against the frame and began to apply leverage against the box.

"Hold him steady, Andy. As I move the box, edge him up the hill, slowly. I want the wagon to come down gently."

Andy nodded.

Seth jabbed his stick into the dirt, copying Trace's action. He wedged it against his part of the wagon, too. He stayed next to the tree, on the opposite side from Trace, and pried with the stick with all his might.

The wagon moved in slow motion. It hung in the air for a short time, balanced against the strength of Big Boy's pull and the momentum of Trace and Seth's push.

Trace's foot slipped and he started to slide downhill.

"Whoa!"

"You all right, Mr. Westerman?" Andy called as Trace regained his position.

"Yeah." Trace kicked sod and dirt with his foot. "I've got a good toe hold, now. Walk him carefully, Andy. One step at a time."

Suddenly, the wheels dropped. The entire wagon bounced up and down like a canoe in rapids. Gradually, the bounces settled and the box was still.

"That does it!"

Trace moved to take control of Big Boy. Andy brought Jake alongside and helped Trace re-hitch the team.

Trace climbed into the driver's seat and moved the wagon to the rock pile.

It all looked so simple, now. Molly watched Trace climb off the buckboard, then turned her attention back to Rosie.

Trace walked back to where the gun and the quilt were. He picked them up and moved toward Molly and Rosie.

Molly, so intent on watching Rosie, didn't see Trace approach. She jumped when he spoke.

"You lost this." Trace held the gun out to her, butt first.

She took the rifle and laid it down arm's length away from Rosie.

"I brought the quilt. Thought maybe we better cover the girl up with it."

"She hasn't moved," worry quivered in Molly's voice. "Thank you." She took the quilt from him and unfolded it.

"What do we do now?" Molly looked up at him, searching for answers.

Two

Trace studied their situation.

Rosie lay still as a stunned bird.

They couldn't leave her there. Yet, if they moved her, it could kill her. There were no obvious signs of any broken bones, but no one knew what was going on inside her body. *Were there internal injuries?*

Trace had enough to worry about without getting involved with this family. All he wanted to do was get on with his hunt for the gang of thieves and killers that had struck his ranch. Helping the Klings would set him back—far enough back to lose the trail he'd followed from Texas to the Oklahoma coal mines and, now, to New Mexico.

But, he had no choice. This family needed him and a man just couldn't walk out on people who needed his help—not if he wanted to continue feeling like a man instead of a no good, low-down, egg-sucking skunk. He scolded himself for even thinking about abandoning the Klings.

What he had to do to settle up with his own past would have to wait until he could untangle himself from these new responsibilities he was about to take on.

He reached a decision about the girl. Now, it was up to Molly to either agree—or show him just how stubborn she could be.

"Well, it's getting late. I reckon we should let the rocks be and load Rosie into the wagon."

Molly nodded. The important thing now was to get help for Rosie. Molly fussed with the quilt. She tucked the bright colors of its patches beneath the girl's arms and around the edges of her body.

"How are we going to do that without hurting her more?"

"Guess it's a chance we're just going to have to take." Trace saw the worry in Molly's eyes. "I'll pick her up and carry her to the wagon. I'll be careful, I promise."

Molly nodded. For Rosie's sake, she'd just have to trust this man that had wandered haphazardly into her life.

"There's a doctor in Moriarty. If we can get her to our homestead, I can send Andy on to get him."

Trace scooped his strong arms under Rosie's body. The quilt draped beneath her as he felt her light weight against his forearms. Rosie's tiny frame weighed only a fraction of that of a newborn calf out on the range. He was used to carrying the squirming animals to safety. The child lay limp against him and he wished for some movement from this little body. Careful not to let her neck drop, in case it was broken, he rose to his feet, feeling the tug of his own sore muscles.

"You drive," Molly said. "I'll stay in back with Rosie. Andy can tell you how to get to the place." Without waiting for an answer, Molly climbed over the tailgate. She laid the rifle against the side of the wagon, taking care to keep the barrel pointed away from everyone.

Andy hoisted himself onto the passenger seat. Seth settled into the corner behind the driver's seat. Molly sat in the opposite corner. Trace placed Rosie on Molly's lap so she could brace Rosie against the jolting of the buckboard.

Poor baby. Fear continued to grip Molly's stomach.

Trace climbed onto the driver's seat and took the reins from Andy.

There were distinct wheel tracks ahead of them where the buckboard had come in earlier in the day. He called to the team and popped the harness strap. They ambled toward the ruts and home.

They rode along without talking. The only noise was the creaking of the wagon wheels and an occasional "clink" as one of the metal rims struck a rock in the path.

Seth, frightened that his sister would die, clung to the wagon's sideboard and fought back tears. Molly knew he thought he was too big to cry. But, occasionally, a wet drop of water rolled down his cheek, clearing a path through the dust on his face.

Soon, they were off the mountain and several tracks etched the flat land ahead where settlers and homesteaders had crossed paths as they traveled the valley floor.

Molly heard a quiet discussion between Trace and Andy as the boy pointed out the way to their property.

"Go down the main trail, there, where the ruts are deepest. We're straight down the center of the valley, then to the right. We have quite a ways to go before we turn, though."

The drive seemed to take forever. The storm Molly had smelled earlier in the day was forming in a huge black thundercloud off to the west. She feared it would catch them before they got home.

Rosie lay still on her lap and Molly wondered if the child would ever wake up. She saw Trace glance back. She shook her head to indicate that there had been no improvement. He turned back around and concentrated on his driving.

They were nearing the turn to the roadway. Andy raised his arm to point out the small cluster of supplies sitting in the middle of their otherwise barren land.

"Where are the buildings? A cabin? A shed? Something?" Trace looked back at Molly.

"I told you, we're just starting out."

A longhaired white dog, mottled with variegated gray markings, bounded toward them.

Andy called to it.

"Ho! Crazy Leg!"

The dog jumped and dodged at the wagon, trying to touch Andy's outstretched arm, as they made their way off the main tracks onto the trail to the homesteader's encampment.

"Funny name for a dog," Trace commented.

"Yeah. He was a runt," Andy said. "My pa said his one leg was bent wrong when he found him. Try as he could he never did get a splint to straighten it. Crazy Leg kept chewing the sticks off. So we just gave up and called him that."

Trace pulled the reins to turn the buckboard right. From there he could tell the homesteaders didn't have much. He had expected to see a makeshift shack or a shelter of some kind, but no buildings were in view. He wondered just what, besides the dirt, these people possessed. He didn't know how little there was until they neared the campsite.

Some hundred yards away from where he turned he made out an adobe oven, coarsely fashioned after those of the Navajo. A campfire bed, where a tripod supported a black kettle above it, stood like a sentry over the family's nearby pile of possessions. What few supplies they had were apparently secure beneath a canvas tarp not far from the cooking area.

As they approached the edge of the campsite, Andy said, "We need to stop here a minute."

Before the buckboard came to a halt, Andy jumped off and ran ahead with the dog. He picked up the end of a rope and moved it to one side, then motioned for Trace to come on. As soon as the wagon moved past, Andy walked back across the road and dropped the rope across the trail behind them.

Trace wondered what Andy was doing.

Andy hopped back up on the wagon.

"We pull up alongside the tarp," Andy spoke as if he had practiced this many times.

Trace nodded. He urged the horses in the direction Andy pointed.

Chickens scattered ahead of Big Boy and Jake, squawking as they rushed to their roost in a small coop built out of scrap wood and tin sheets. The crinkled tin roof had seen better days. It appeared as if it had blown in from another homestead during a windstorm.

To the left, Trace saw a gelding in a rough corral. Strands of barbed wire were woven around crooked sticks stuck in the earth to keep the midnight-black horse with its white jagged marking across the forehead confined.

The sleek animal neighed to the approaching team.

Opposite the flimsy corral, across from the fire pit, there was a low wooden water trough next to a hand-dug well. The well was surrounded by whatever the family could find to keep the animals, and kids, from falling in. A wooden bucket with a rope handle sat upside down on the corner of the trough. Alongside were more pieces of tin cut into windmill blades and stacked neatly.

"What was the rope for, back there?" Trace asked Molly as he slowly moved the team to park the wagon where Andy instructed.

"We managed to get enough rope to circle the campsite. Someone once told me it would keep the rattlesnakes out."

Trace chuckled beneath his breath. He didn't want to hurt her feelings, but he wondered at the magical powers of stringing a rope to discourage snakes.

"Guess they don't like to scrape their bellies on it." He doubted it helped, but, if it made Molly feel better, who was he to tell her different?

Once Trace stopped the wagon, Molly began giving orders.

"Andy, get Comet and go for the doctor."

How glad she was they had arrived! Help for Rosie would not be far off now.

Trace notice Molly sat stiffly as though every muscle in her body was either stiff or sore—or both. He figured her legs were probably cramped from holding Rosie tight on the long ride home.

"As soon as I get the team unhitched, I'll come and get the girl."

He dropped to the ground and went to disconnect the trappings that kept the horses in line. He let the long wooden shaft separating them ease to the dirt.

With the horses free of the wagon, he moved to Molly's side and reached over to lift Rosie off Molly's outstretched legs.

He felt the warmth of Molly's thighs, through her thin skirt against his arms, as he lifted Rosie from Molly's lap. He avoided looking at her face for fear of embarrassing her—or himself—as he felt a sudden stirring within his body.

"This is home. It isn't much, but it's going to be ours once we've proved up on it." Molly rose from the wagon bed and stretched before she reached down to retrieve the rifle.

Andy lifted the tarp off the pile of their worldly goods and removed Comet's bridle. He also took out a bedroll and tossed it beneath the buckboard.

"I'll lay that out. You go on. Maybe you can get ahead of the storm." Molly gazed in the direction of the black cloud with concern. She already had one child in trouble and here she was sending another out into danger—what kind of mother was she? She had no choice. Trace was too new to know the way. And she needed to stay with Rosie. She would just have to trust Andy to be careful.

Trace's words jarred her away from her thoughts, "You mean, you live here under the wagon?"

"For now. That's why I was after the rocks. I wanted something to set the stringers for the house on."

Trace stood with Rosie in his arms while he waited for Molly to get the bedroll open, then bent to lay her down. The child had yet to stir, and, he was becoming less hopeful that she would.

Trace settled Rosie on the bedroll and straightened up from beneath the wagon.

Andy rode Comet bareback out of the makeshift corral. The animal pranced about, eager to run.

"Hurry, Andy. Darkness is gathering and the storm's coming in. I don't need to worry about you, too."

Andy waved and kicked his bare heels into the gelding's sides. Clods of the soft dirt splayed behind the horse as they reversed the path Trace and the family had just traveled. Comet made a short jump over the rope around the camp and they were off.

"Seth, get the firewood, please. We'll get some soup on, in case Rosie is hungry when she wakes up. In the meantime, Trace, would you help me pull the tarp over the wagon?"

The sound of the gelding's hooves faded in the distance.

"You go ahead and stay with Rosie. I'll pull it over."

What kind of woman was this? He unfolded the large dusty white canvas tarp. Stubborn, he had assessed her, at first. Maybe she was simply doing what was necessary to survive. It looked to him, as if she had a good start on doing just that. A man had to admire a woman like Molly Kling.

Molly crawled beneath the wagon bed. She hung the rifle across some nails she had driven there and bent up into hooks, specifically for the gun. It wasn't a gun rack over a mantle, she had thought at the time, but it would work until she had an indoor fireplace and a mantle for the purpose. She sat down on the dirt next to Rosie. The bright patchwork quilt still covered Rosie's small frame. Molly huddled beneath the buckboard. She remembered receiving the quilt from her mother-in-law the day she married Rosie's father.

That all seemed so long ago. Now, she recalled happier times in Oklahoma before her husband was killed—murdered, really—for his small pay from the coal mine.

She had tried to stay near the children's grandparents. It had been her plan that they would help each other. But, God had another plan and both Kling parents followed their son shortly after that. When the bank claimed their farm for back payments, Molly and the children had to move on. The Widow Kling and her charges packed up what little they could haul and headed west. After weeks of meandering, Molly heard of a teaching position in New Mexico.

There, they could file claim to a homestead. The possibility of a job and a home had seemed too good to be true.

Molly shook her head. It had been some time since she had let herself think about those painful events in her life. She didn't want to remember them now. She distracted herself by checking, again, for the hundredth time, on Rosie. She noted the color in her face was good and it gave her hope she would soon awake.

"Any change?" Trace tugged the canvas until it slid over the top of the wagon bed and down to the ground on three sides. He lifted the front section of tarp on the long side of the wagon and folded it back so he could still see Molly and Rosie beneath.

Molly shook her head sadly. With nothing else to do but wait, she watched the preparations for the night, which were going on outside her small domain.

Beyond the wagon's sanctuary Seth dropped wood into the ashes of the fire pit.

The wood made a dull thud until the last piece struck a chunk of one of the few rocks with a sharper sound. There, a small piece of shale lay on each of the fire pit's four corners. A small pile of the rocks sat beside the other supplies.

The family had gathered some loose shale that they had found on a previous trip to the mountain.

"I'll light the fire." Trace moved away from Molly, toward Seth.

When Trace approached him, Seth was carefully positioning the dry pieces of twigs and small limbs beneath the sticks of wood he had piled until they were leaning against each other in the shape of a teepee, ready to ignite. The wood, too, had come from the mountain. Trace surveyed the homestead as far as he could see in the fading light and saw no sign of a tree or branch, except for those used as makeshift fence posts for the corral.

Trace pulled a small glass vial containing dry matches from his vest pocket, removed a wooden stick and struck it against one of the rocks.

Seth watched in wonder.

"We have a flint for that."

Trace cupped his hands to shelter the flame from the threatening breeze. He held the match against the small handful of dry moss Seth had prepared for his spark.

Within seconds the flame roared up the center of the pile of sticks, throwing light across the yard and beneath the wagon.

Molly spoke from the shadows.

"I have an oil lamp we could light, if you think we'll need it."

"Let's wait 'til the doctor gets here. Might as well save what oil you have until it's necessary."

Trace lifted the heavy kettle from its hook above the fire before the flames could heat it up. He set it on one of the rocks and went to the water trough where he picked up the bucket and flipped it upright. He grasped the short rope tied to the handle and he walked to the well. He dropped the bucket down the hole until there was a splash. The water filled into the pail and he raised it to the top.

With the first bucketful of water, Trace washed up the best he could. He made sure his hands were clean. He scrubbed his face, heavy with beard.

He refilled the bucket and, careful not to spill the water over the sides, walked back to the campfire. He rinsed the pot, then poured it half full with fresh water.

He set the water over the fire to boil.

"There's a coffee pot and some grounds under the tarp. I think we both could use some coffee. It's apt to be a long night." Molly looked sadly at Rosie, willing the child to wake.

Trace followed her directions, searching in the right-hand corner of the tarp-covered storage.

"There's some dried beef in a crock, there, too. We can cut it up for the soup. Wish I'd started some beans. I would have, but I knew we weren't going to be here to keep the fire going and to stir them so they wouldn't stick."

"That's all right. We'll manage. You just stay settled there. I'll come up with something."

He found an onion, a bit worse for age, but salvageable, in a canvas bag and potatoes beneath that sack. Eyes were growing on the potatoes but the flesh was firm. Onion, potatoes and dried beef—he searched for salt to improve the flavor.

"No, salt?"

He had stopped calling her "lady" or "Ma'am" when the wagon rolled. It seemed their troubles had bonded them in some strange way, and the formalities were no longer necessary.

"It's probably buried somewhere near the bottom. The beef is quite salty from its cure. We probably won't need more." *What did a man know about cooking, anyway?*

Trace lifted the end canvas and flipped it back up on the wagon so he could drop the tailgate for a worktable. He laid the beef on a tin platter he had found in the pile of dishes and whittled away at the meat, cutting it into small pieces. He peeled the onion and potatoes, rinsed them off with water from the bucket, and tossed the skins out across the trampled yard for the chickens to find in the morning.

When he had all his ingredients chopped the way he wanted them, he took the heaping dish to the kettle. He used a stick from the pile of firewood to lift the top. Inside, the water was starting to boil and he dumped the chunks of food into the hot water.

Seth sat silently warming himself by the fire, as the evening had taken on a chill. Crazy Leg snuggled close to the boy. Both of them seemed resigned to sparse meals and having to wait for them. Their eyes sparked with interest as they watched the promise of something to eat become a probability.

"There's bread in one of the crocks. I bake several loaves at a time when I have enough wood to fire up the oven. If I don't protect it, the chickens find it and peck it to bits."

Trace filled the coffee pot and set it in the edge of the coals where it was soon boiling away, filling the air around the camp with an aroma that caused all their stomachs to rumble for food.

Trace searched out three blue enamel cups and filled each with hot coffee. He cooled Seth's by diluting it with fresh water. He added a couple of spoonfuls of lumpy sugar from a jar he'd pulled out from next to the salt he had finally found.

Trace got the rest of the bedrolls and tossed them under the shelter for Molly to unroll. There was one extra, larger than the rest. He lifted the tarp and dropped it into the box of the buckboard.

"I'll sleep up here, under the tarp, near the back where I can keep an eye out for trouble."

"Why would there be any trouble?" No one ever bothered the family on their homestead, save for a drifter now and then, looking for work. An occasional coyote or skunk tried to capture a chicken sometimes, but she didn't expect any real trouble. *Was Trace running from something? Would he be dragging his troubles in on them?* She was so concerned about Rosie, she had put the thought of what this stranger might be running from out of her mind.

Was he an outlaw? Had she accepted his help too quickly? But then, what else could she do?

"Are you expecting trouble?"

What if he was a wanted man? Was he running from the law? She made a mental note to check with the local sheriff the next time she went to Estancia or Moriarty. *Don't be so suspicious,* she told herself. But, he did seem extremely cautious for a man whose only problem was that his mount threw him. She warned herself not to let her guard down again.

"Don't worry. There's probably nothing out there to cause condern. It's just unfamiliar territory to me. A man's always careful when he's in a strange place."

She hoped that was all. Uneasiness seemed to permeate the air, now that Trace's words dredged up the threat of danger.

The night wore on and Seth began to tire.

At last, Trace checked the soup and found it done enough to eat. He had added plenty of water to provide broth for Rosie, should she wake up.

He took one of the large circular loaves of bread from the crock. He held it firm and cut it into chunks with a hunting knife he'd taken from the kitchen supplies. Then he filled blue and white speckled enamel plates with food for Molly and Seth. The heat of the food radiated into the rim of the metal plates. He used care not to slosh the soup over the sides and scald his fingers.

He set a plate beside Seth's bedroll.

"Come on and eat before you fall asleep where you are, Seth."

Seth rose, rubbing his eyes from sleepiness and campfire smoke, and shuffled to his bedroll.

Trace found an old crockery bowl near where Seth and Crazy Leg had sat. Its edge was cracked and one side was split halfway down. It showed evidence of having held food for the dog and having been licked clean, except for the cracks and chips that Crazy Leg's tongue had avoided. Trace put a bit of the soup and a chunk of the bread in it for Crazy Leg.

"Keep away 'til it cools," he warned the dog. *Dumb animal probably doesn't understand,* he chastised himself for talking to a dog. Crazy Leg sniffed the bowl and stood back whining while he waited for it to cool.

Seth scooped up a spoonful of soup and tasted it. It wasn't as good as Molly made, but he didn't complain. His stomach was more than ready for nourishment, his body more than ready for rest.

Finally, Trace took a plate for himself and went to lean against the buckboard while he ate. The bread was hard and dry, but it sopped the soup up just fine.

Trace and Molly ate in silence.

When they finished, Trace put more wood on the fire and added more water to the remaining soup to make up for evaporation.

The first drops of rain pelted against his face as he stacked the few dishes out of the way to clean in the morning. A few more drops sizzled against the kettle, into the flames, and against the hot rocks beside the campfire.

Crazy Leg finished his food and crawled alongside Seth under shelter before the downpour hit.

"We'll have to shake Seth's bedroll good in the morning. The dog's got fleas, but it's impossible to keep the two of them apart."

"Storm's gonna hit. Hope it doesn't rain hard enough to put out the campfire."

"I hope it doesn't delay the doctor. How long has Andy been gone?" She was just working up to a good case of worry when she heard the sound of a horse's hooves pounding across the property.

Trace hid in the shadows of the supplies.

Molly reached for her rifle. If he was that jumpy, perhaps she should be prepared, too.

They heard the sound of wheels turning in the soft dirt. The doctor's small buggy, pulled by a single bay mare, stopped near the campfire.

"Molly Kling?" The doctor studied the outline of the wagon in the firelight.

"Doctor! Thank God you've come."

He climbed down from his black-hooded carriage.

"I met Andy on the road this side of town a ways. He said you had some trouble here."

"It's Rosie. She got thrown from the wagon. She hasn't woken since."

Once Trace knew it was the doctor, he moved from the shadows.

"This is a fellow we came across up on the mountain, Doc. He helped bring her home."

"Doc Landry, here." The doctor reached a hand out to Trace.

"Trace Westerman. Thanks for coming." The downpour hit as Doc Landry bent to crawl beneath the wagon. Trace reached for the oil lamp he had placed beneath the wagon and struck another match. He lit the wick and replaced the chimney providing a soft glow for the doctor to work.

"Well, let's have a look." Doc Landry hunkered under the buckboard. He was used to treating patients wherever they were. A family scratching a living out of the spoils of the earth was nothing new to him.

"Hmm," he said, examining Rosie. He tapped her stomach and lifted her limp hand, then let it drop. He ran his fingernail up her bare foot and watched her leg for a reaction.

"What do you think, Doc?" Molly was unable to keep quiet any longer.

"Well, obviously, she's had the wind knocked out of her. May have hit her head. Could be she collapsed a lung. Maybe a concussion. Hard to tell at this point. All we can do is keep her warm, dry, and wait for her to wake up."

Disappointment registered on Molly's face in the lamplight. She had hoped for a miracle.

"Isn't there something you can give her?"

"Not right now. I am going to leave you some powder for when she does come around. She's apt to have quite a headache."

"But, she will wake up, won't she, Doc?"

"Now, Miz Kling, you know all I can do is give you my best guess on that. Talk to her. And wait. That's all you can do."

He lifted the canvas that kept the rain out and looked toward the campfire and his buggy. The rain drops splattered and fried as they came down on the cook pot and the flames. He hated to leave their little nest to make a run through the wet.

He turned back to Molly. "I'll come out again tomorrow to check on her. There's nothing I can do here tonight. I best head for home before the mud gets too deep for Nellie to pull the buggy along the road."

Just as the doctor turned to crawl out from beneath the wagon, Rosie sat upright and screamed.

Startled, Doctor Landry slammed his head on the side of the wagon.

The shriek sent a chill up Molly's spine.

Trace poked his head beneath the wagon.

Molly grasped the girl by both shoulders and stared at her. What had caused this sudden change?

"Andy! Andy!" Rosie called out with her eyes wide open. Fear distorted her face.

Molly clutched her tight.

"It's all right, Rosie. We're home." Molly tried to comfort the girl. She began rocking her slowly back and forth, making what she hoped would be soothing sounds.

Doc Landry crawled back down alongside where the girl sat. He motioned for Trace to hold the lamp higher. He checked her eyes.

"Ma, Andy's been thrown."

"Whatever are you talking about?"

"There was thunder and lightning. Comet reared up and threw him. He's lying on his back in a gully along the road. I can see him."

Molly looked around her. Andy was nowhere nearby. She looked at the doctor for an explanation. How could it be? How could Rosie know if something had happened to Andy?

"There was a bolt of lightning shortly after we parted. I didn't think much about it, knowing the storm was coming. I had just hoped to beat it here. Andy was right behind me at the time. I thought he'd pass me before I barely got started. I was so intent on getting here, I didn't pay any attention to if, or when, he did. Thought sure he'd beat me here. He surely should have been here by now." Doc Landry turned his attention back to Rosie.

"Do you hurt anywhere, young lady?"

"Shhhh," Trace said. "Hear that?"

"What is it?" Molly's voice was barely audible.

"Rider coming in."

"It must be Andy."

Trace handed the lamp to Molly for her to hold in her free hand while she clutched Rosie against her chest with the other.

Trace straightened from where he squatted beneath the wagon. His eyes searched the darkness for the animal that was trotting toward the camp.

The doctor's horse whinnied.

The approaching animal answered back.

Big Boy and Jake, now enclosed in the corral, added their chorus.

Comet came into the firelight and headed for the corral. His reins were tangled in his mane.

He was alone.

There was no sign of Andy.

Three

Trace stood for a second staring at the gelding. The animal was barely visible in the firelight, blending as he did, into the night.

Comet stamped his front hooves and blew air through his nostrils while he waited beside the corral gate.

What the hell was wrong with all these animals? First, my mount throws me in favor of a good meal, and gets me in this mess. I already had enough on my mind! I could a done without this family's problems on top of my own troubles. Now, this!

And the girl! Now that she's awake, she's seeing things that aren't even there. He didn't know what to make of that.

He looked up at the sky. A full moon broke through a hole in the clouds. He'd heard of strange things happening on a full moon. Animals, and people, got restless.

Trace reached for Comet's mane to untangle the reins.

He had no idea where to look for Andy, but he felt he must go. He didn't hanker to leaving a young boy, possibly injured, to fend for himself on such a stormy night.

Doc Landry walked up behind him.

"At least the storm's lettin' up, some. I can pretty well tell where we were when the lightning started. Maybe I can be of some help finding the boy."

"What do you make of it, Doc? Ever heard tell of someone wakin' up and knowin' something's happened?" Trace hoisted himself onto Comet's wet, steamy back. He felt the dampness soak through his

30

pants. *We're all going to be lucky if we don't get pneumonia.* He shrugged the discomfort off and concentrated on preparing to search for Andy.

Comet blew his nostrils, again. He had completed his day and it was time for oats and to join the team in the corral. Somehow, this stranger apparently didn't know the routine. Comet yanked his head sideways against Trace's directions.

"Whoa," Trace said as he heard Doc's answer.

"It happens. There's things medicine sometimes can't explain."

"Guess I'll just have to accept that. Right now, I gotta go look for that boy."

"I'll follow you. When you get to the main road, turn right. If you don't find him after about three miles, wait for me to catch up. We'll be getting close to where I last saw him."

It would help if he knew where he was going. But, he had never been in this part of New Mexico before and he had no idea of the lay of the land. He needed a guide.

Trace kicked his boot heels into Comet's sides and held on. If he hadn't been able to stay on his own horse with its saddle on, how the heck did he think he was going to fare any better riding this one, bareback? His mount had run away and no amount of chasing after him had gotten his ride back. He'd have to be very careful with this one or he knew he would be afoot again—this time in a nasty storm.

"Andy's a smart boy," Doc Landry called out to Trace as he rode away. "He can take care of himself." His words were as much to reassure Molly as to encourage Trace.

Then, under his breath he said, "If he's not hurt. If nothing else, he's probably soaked to the bone." Doc Landry figured it was prudent he went along, not only to point out the way, but in case the boy was injured.

Trace, astride Comet, far outdistanced Doc Landry's slower horse and buggy. They moved swiftly along the road. Trace called Andy's name out as they traveled. If he wasn't dead, or injured too badly to answer, he'd surely hear them coming.

Trace listened over Comet's heavy breathing and staccato hoof beats. He approached what he estimated to be near the spot Doc

Landry described. If Andy wasn't there, he would walk Comet and wait for Doc to catch up.

It was time to slow down and search more thoroughly. He could hear Doc's buggy far behind him, its trappings jingling as the doctor hurried Nellie along.

What was that? A noise caught his attention. But, it wasn't a voice. It was the pounding of more hoof beats. It sounded like a small stampede coming his way from the direction of town. Riders in a group that large, riding that hard, could only mean one of two things: outlaws or a posse. Either way, it meant trouble to a man alone in a location unfamiliar to him.

Trace didn't have time to deal with outlaws—or the law, for that matter. And, he didn't have time to warn Doc Landry, either. He moved Comet off the road and urged him toward a swale he hoped would be far enough away, and deep enough, to hide them in the dark of night.

He hoped the group of riders, not expecting to see a lone rider on the road, would not suspect that he was there, watching. Right now, he wished he had Molly's rifle, although he was outnumbered. He counted six figures, dark shadows in the night, on horseback.

The group slowed as they approached Doc Landry's buggy. Then they stopped, clustering around Nellie and the buggy.

There was a quick flare of a match as it illuminated the buggy driver's face.

Trace held his breath. He strained to hear their words.

"Whatcha doin' out here this late, old man?"

Trace heard the voice ask clearly in the night air that had stilled between storms.

"Had a call," Doc answered. "Why aren't you fellas bedded down for the night? It's a heck of a night to be out."

"We're looking for someone. Maybe you've seen him?"

"Doubt it. You fellas the law?"

A burst of uproarious laughter echoed through the night.

"We look like the law?" The lead man asked.

Doc Landry didn't answer.

Trace sensed the doctor felt himself in deep trouble. And, if these men were who Trace thought they were, he was. He would recognize the one voice anywhere. It was that of the leader of the gang he had been tracking. But, there should be nine men, not six. There had been nine when he first ran into them. Three had been Mexicans. Where were they? He heard no Spanish tonight. He studied the dilemma. With Andy highest on his mind, he was in no position to confront the outlaws, now. Nor was he armed to handle the situation.

"So, you're a doctor. Don't 'spose you've got any money on ya?"

"Nope. Most of my patients can't afford to pay much. Usually I'm lucky if they keep victuals on my table for me. I'm not in the business to get rich."

Trace heard the doctor's voice crackle nervously. He edged Comet toward the road. It was becoming obvious to him that he was going to have to intervene, even if he didn't have a gun. What he would do, he hadn't figured out yet.

"No? Didn't figure you would have."

Trace heard the distinct click of a six-gun cocking.

"Ah, leave the doc alone, Snake. We might need him someday," said one of the other riders.

Snake! That was definitely a name Trace knew. He was right about recognizing the voice. He bristled at the man's name. Snake was the one Trace wanted to get his hands on! But he wasn't prepared to take them all on—he had to find Andy. How was he going to get Doc out of this?

Before Trace could race in, hoping to startle the rider's horses, and miss being shot in the process, Doc Landry slapped the reins against Nellie's back and called out, "Giddy up—Go!"

Nellie responded with a quick burst of speed and left the other riders trying to scatter their animals out of the way of the buggy wheels.

A shot rang out in the dark.

"You old cuss!" The leader called after the buggy. "Next time, I won't miss. Next time, I'll shoot first before you have a chance to get away."

Trace hoped the man, unprepared and off guard, had missed his target.

"Come on, Snake, let's go. Leave the old man alone," another man's voice spoke.

"Who's the ramrod of this outfit?" Snake snapped back.

Trace heard low grumbling, but the men regrouped and started on down the road away from town.

Once there was enough distance between them, Trace turned Comet to follow the buggy that was diminishing in the dark.

At last, Doc Landry reined Nellie up and Trace approached the buggy.

"You all right, Doc?"

"Have to admit, they shook me up a bit. Where were you?"

"I was watching. I was getting ready to come in when you pulled your get-a-way."

"Some of the towns I've worked in, you had to be fast to stay alive. I trained my horse not to hesitate when I yelled. 'Course, the mud slowed me down a bit. How about you?"

"Don't think they even saw me. Take it from me, they're a mean bunch. I didn't want to tackle all of them, alone, if I'd had a gun— much less riding naked," Trace said referring to his lack of having a gun.

Doc nodded. "I see your point. If I were you, I'd get armed. Well, this is about where I last saw the boy."

"You stay put, Doc, I'll see what I can find."

Trace knew, even though the rain had stopped, it would be well into daylight before things started to dry out. He might need the doctor to take care of Andy and, if he was under the buggy cover, he'd be better able to tend to him there where they would be dry.

Trace moved Comet ahead slowly, calling out Andy's name and identifying himself.

At last, he heard a shrill whistle.

Comet perked up his ears.

"Andy, that you?"

Finally, Trace made out the form of the boy stumbling toward him in the dark. He nudged his knees into Comet's sides to urge him forward and meet Andy.

"Yeah. I hid out when I heard that pack of horses coming."

"Good for you, Andy. You hurt anywhere?"

"My arm. It twisted behind me when I hit the ground." Andy stood alongside Comet. He reached up and rubbed the horse's nose.

"It's okay, boy, I'm not mad at you."

"Give me your hand on the side that doesn't hurt. I'll hoist you up behind me."

Andy reached up and did his best to jump high enough to reach Comet's back, but didn't make it.

"Here, next time you jump, I'll pull harder. I know the other arm probably hurts like heck, but don't fight me. I'll get you up."

The boy couldn't be more than eleven or twelve, Trace thought as he whipped him into the air and he lit, lopsided, behind him. Light as a feather, not much more meat on his bones than his sister, Trace assessed. Comet probably hadn't even felt him on his back when he bolted in terror at the thunder and lightning.

Andy repositioned himself behind Trace.

"Did Doc get there? How's Rosie?"

"She's doin' just fine. You did a good job gettin' the doctor headed to your Ma's place. Doc Landry is down the road a piece. We'll get him to take a look at that arm before we take you home. You're mighty wet." Trace felt the moisture from the boy's clothes against his back.

Trace deposited Andy on the seat alongside Doc Landry, beneath the protection of the buggy's cover. He dismounted and waited for Doc to examine Andy.

The doctor lifted a heavy woolen lap blanket off the seat beside him. He placed it over Andy's shoulders. Then he began to check out his arm.

"Does it hurt here?"

"Ow. Yeah!"

"How about here?" Doc asked as he felt with deft fingers in the dark.

"No. Is it broke, Doc?"

"It doesn't seem to be. Think it's probably a bad sprain. I'm going to put it in a sling for a few days," he said as he opened his worn black leather bag and felt around in it. Inside, he had some pieces of clean flour sack he kept for such purposes.

"Now, don't use that arm for a few days. I'm going back out to see your sister tomorrow. I'll give that a better look in the daylight."

"Maybe I should drive him back," he spoke to Trace who was standing nearby.

"It's been a long night for all of us. You better go on home, Doc. Besides, if that wild bunch stopped along the road behind us it'll be easier for the two of us to get around them, than for you and your buggy to get through. This time, Snake might keep his promise."

"You're probably right." Doc Landry moved his arm and brought out a shotgun.

"Here, you take this. As you can see, I wasn't totally unprotected. Had it on the seat under that lap robe all the time. Had my finger on the trigger, too. I'm sworn to mend the injured and cure the sick, but I gotta stay alive to do it."

Trace, mounted on Comet again, edged closer to the buggy and grasped the cold steel of the double-barrel shotgun.

"Thanks, Doc. But, are you sure you won't need it?" Trace settled the shotgun across his thighs. Andy stood up in the front of the buggy and swung his leg over Comet's back behind Trace. He wrapped his good arm around the man's waist to hang on.

"You can keep that robe until I see you tomorrow, Andy," Doc said.

As Andy settled on Comet, against Trace's damp back, he was glad it was dark and difficult to make out the features of each other's faces. He wouldn't want anyone to know how close he was to bawling with relief at being found. Being alone in the storm with an arm that hurt like the dickens, sure could make one want their Ma and the safety of their own bedroll.

He didn't blame Comet for rearing like he had. He had been as scared as Comet. Next time he'd be smarter. Next time he had to run an errand, he'd think ahead to the possibilities. He should have known a storm like that would bring thunder and lightning. He should have known to grip the reins tighter, or twist his fingers in Comet's mane, and the reins along with them.

"I'm only about a half-mile short of my place. I'll hurry," Doc Landry told Trace. "You go on, get the boy home and in bed."

"Say, Doc, did any of those outlaws ask about me?"

"That Snake character asked if I'd seen anyone."

"Thanks for not telling him I was there."

"For one thing, I figured it was none of their business. Secondly, I figured you had a better chance of getting out of there and finding the boy if they didn't know about you."

Trace turned Comet around so they were facing each other and headed in opposite directions.

"Thanks, again, Doc."

"I don't know what your troubles are, son, but I figure a man that would help a family like the Klings can't be all bad."

"See ya tomorrow Doc. Get a good night's rest."

"You, too, Trace—Andy."

Gently this time, Doc Landry snapped the reins on Nellie's back and clacked his tongue to get her moving.

Trace nudged Comet in the ribs with his boot. They began plodding along toward the Kling place. He was sure he could retrace the direction he had come from, even in the dark. If he had to, he'd give Comet his head and let him lead the way. Although, this time, he'd be prepared and keep a close eye out for Snake and his bunch. Right now, all he wanted was to get himself and Andy into a warm bedroll.

It wasn't long until he felt Andy sag against his back as the boy fell asleep. Trace smiled to himself. It had been a long time since anyone had depended on him.

He rode along, tired and cold and—happy. Yep! If Molly would let him stay for a while, he wouldn't mind working for her and the kids, for his keep, until he could get himself situated. At some point, he'd have to go after Snake and his gang. He couldn't regain what they had taken from him, but maybe he could, at least, bring them to justice.

He felt Andy slip to the side behind him and reached back to push him up into riding position.

Ahead and off to his left, he could see a pinpoint glow of Molly's campfire. With each step Comet took, it looked bigger and more inviting.

He was off the road, now, and angling across the property. Soon, he'd have the boy, and himself, in bed. His muscles ached for relief and he felt an old bullet wound in his hip complain from the ride and the cold. He wanted to raise up and re-situate his backside, but refrained for fear of dislodging Andy. He would tough it out.

Suddenly, a shot rang out.

Comet jerked his head back.

At attention now, Trace gripped the shotgun lying across his lap as Andy came out of the fog of sleep.

"What was that?"

"Shhh," Trace warned him. "It was a pistol shot," he explained in a whisper.

Ahead, by the firelight, he could see Molly fighting to hang onto her rifle as one of the outlaws gripped it in his hand.

Two others were uncovering the supplies and rummaging through them. Crazy Leg barked and jumped at the man struggling with Molly over the rifle.

They heard a yelp, then silence.

Trace slid Andy to his feet to stand beside Comet.

"Here, you take the reins and walk Comet out of sight. Stay out of the way. Don't let them see you. I've enough to worry about with your Ma and the other kids there, understand?"

"Yeah."

Trace grabbed Comet's neck with one hand and slid off the horse, dropping down next to Andy.

"Now, go! And, don't come in until I let you know it's safe."

Like Trace, the outlaws must have seen Molly's campfire from the main road. Looking for someone to rob, they caught Molly off guard after the long, hard, day she had been through.

Now, she was putting up a fight and would get hurt if he didn't get there fast. He dropped to his haunches and studied the surrounding area ahead of him.

Gradually, he crept toward the camp.

One of the bandits stood not more than twenty feet ahead of him. He guarded the entrance to the campsite. Trace crept up behind him. Before he could call out, Trace swung his arm around and pulled the shotgun barrel tight against the man's throat. He tugged the gun barrel against the man's flesh until he lost consciousness and slumped to the dirt, dragging Trace down with him.

Carefully, Trace rose to his feet and crawled the next few yards to the makeshift chicken coop. There he took cover and counted the bandits again.

After taking the guard out, there were only three. *There were nine back at his ranch in Texas. Then there had been six out on the road to Moriarty. Where were the other two men now?*

There wasn't time to puzzle over that. If he didn't act quickly, Molly or the kids might get hurt. He stood and blasted one barrel of the shotgun into the air above the bandits' head.

Snake released his grip on Molly's rifle. She stumbled and regained her footing. She moved from behind the campfire closer to the buckboard, and held her rifle on the men scavenging in her household contents.

"Leave the stuff alone," she said.

They held their arms in the air and backed slowly away from her supplies.

"That was just one barrel. Get out of here before I squeeze off the other one. Pick up your other man on the way out."

"You again," Snake spit out from near the firelight. "I told you last time, I'd kill you if I ever caught up with you. There ain't room for you and me both in this new country."

Molly bit her lip to keep from correcting the man's English.

"You know what? You're right. Since I intend on staying, you best be going."

Trace heard a snap behind him. The two missing men appeared.

"Put that shotgun down," one of them commanded.

When Trace turned, the firelight glinted off two six-guns—one in each of one man's hands. He was sure the other outlaw had his guns drawn, too.

"Snake, a man can't even go out into the rabbit brush to leak without you getting yourself in a fix," the other man ribbed the leader.

Trace dropped the shotgun to his side.

"I said, all the way down. On the ground. Then, kick it away," the man said. "Move on up next to the woman, over there."

Molly had ignored the order to Trace and still held her rifle on the men she was watching.

"Guess you didn't hear me, putting the gun down went for you, too, woman," the fellow instructed Molly.

As Trace moved toward the side of the fire pit, next to the wagon where Molly stood, the two men and Snake followed. The one who had spoken to Snake moved his foot around ahead of him. He searched for the shotgun as he pointed his pistol toward Molly and Trace.

"Damn," he said through gritted teeth. "I can't find the damn shotgun. Too dark to see where it dropped. Oh, well. Leastwise he's away from it," the man moved into the firelight closer to the flames.

"That heat feels damn good after riding out in the wet. Maybe we should tie 'em up and spend the night right here, Snake. What do you think?"

Molly bristled.

"I think you're getting too smart-mouthed for your own good. Jest you remember who runs this outfit, Slade. We stay if I say we stay. Got that?"

Snake reached down and picked up a stick and lifted the pot lid. "Now, that's right invitin'. I'll consider your suggestion, Slade."

"Woman, get over here and dish us up some of this succotash or whatever you call it," Snake ordered. "It'll be daylight soon," he told his men, "I'll decide what to do then, when we can get a good look at what's here for the taking."

Molly glanced at Trace. Worry etched her face. He nodded for her to go ahead and feed the men. If for nothing else, it would buy them some time. Maybe Andy had walked Comet off and headed for help.

Maybe he'd come up with a way, himself, to turn the tables on these guys. He did not intend to let Snake and his bunch get the better of him this time. Maybe he could figure something out. He needed time—as much or as little time as it might be.

One of the men took Molly's rifle from her and laid it on top of the buckboard's canvas cover out of Trace's reach.

"Bob, you go see about Zeke. Bring that rope we found laying in the road back there, too, so's we can use it to tie these folks up."

"Why don't we jest kill 'em and get it over with?" Slade questioned the leader again.

"Well, now, guess that's why I'm in charge. We kill 'em after lettin' the doctor get away, who do you think the law's going to come after?"

The men fell silent while they considered the family's fate.

Beneath the buckboard Seth slept peacefully. He shivered, as the warm spot where Crazy Leg had slept before the intruders approached cooled.

Now, as Seth stirred, Rosie stared in wide-eyed fear. She watched the long shadows these horrid men cast from beside the campfire. Molly had told her to remain quiet, and she did. Molly hoped the men wouldn't notice the children hidden in their meager shelter.

Four

Andy tied Comet to the backside of the corral and slipped up behind the outlaws while they held Trace at bay. He hid in the dark near the team, careful not to expose himself to the gang.

He had understood Trace well when he told him not to interfere, but he wasn't about to let these thieves take over the place or hurt Ma and the other kids.

At first, he thought Trace could handle them. Not many people would go up against a scattergun, he knew, but that was before the two outlaws crept up in the dark behind Trace and made him drop the gun in the mud.

Now, Andy lay flat on his belly in more mud nearby. With the men's backs toward him, he eased himself forward with his elbows. The pain of his right arm made him want to cry out, but he gritted his teeth to keep from making any noise. Doc Landry would never recognize his sling. Andy only hoped, when the doctor arrived tomorrow, he'd still be alive to show it to him. Andy lay on his sore right arm and slipped his left arm out to pull the heavy shotgun back from where it lay, where Trace had dropped it in the muck.

He edged his way back beside the chicken coop next to where Crazy Leg had taken refuge when Snake kicked him. The dog was smart enough not to go back for more and cowered there in the shadows.

Andy seethed with anger at Snake for hurting Crazy Leg. He reached down and scratched the dog's muzzle, trying to provide a bit of comfort to the injured animal.

Crazy Leg let out a low whine of pain.

"What was that?" The man who had disarmed Trace asked.

"Just the damn dog," Snake said. "I kicked him out of the way. Must have knocked the wind out of him. He acted like I got him pretty good," Snake said with no remorse.

Andy held his breath and waited quietly until the bandit's attention turned back to the group near the campfire. Then, leaving the shotgun hidden alongside the chicken coop, he crawled to the makeshift gate of the corral and opened it. He hoped that the blast from the shotgun, when he set it off, would startle the horses enough to make them rush out and confuse the men.

He slipped back next to Crazy Leg, and braced his back against the low wall of the chicken coop. There he rested momentarily trying to figure out which barrel Trace had already fired. He didn't want to break the gun down and look at the shells. That would cause too much noise when he had to snap it back together. He would just have to take his chances.

Andy knew, as he prepared to shoot with his right arm in a sling, he was going to have to aim left-handed. He also knew his left shoulder was going to take a beating from the kick of the gun butt. If he survived to see tomorrow, both of his shoulders were going to hurt like crazy.

With the shotgun, he was sure his aim didn't have to be accurate. He would just have to keep the barrel steady and point it where the buckshot wouldn't spray across Trace and Molly. He only hoped they had built the chicken coop solid enough to keep him from sliding backwards on his rear end clear across the rest of the barnyard.

Andy watched Molly dump a small amount of food onto plates she took from a pile of dishes on the ground nearby. She handed each man one of the plates, but was still short two portions and looked about for more dishes. She saw the split bowl and considered that for a moment.

"That looks like a dog dish to me," one of the men who had been rummaging in the supplies spoke up when Molly was near enough to hear him but away from the other men. He found two more plates in the pile of supplies.

"Here, use these," he spoke quietly. "Don't know what you'd had in those others, but I prefer my food on a clean plate," he told her low enough so Snake, busy wolfing down his meal, didn't hear.

Molly noticed the man was young, probably not but five or six years older than Andy, and cleaner than the rest. He spoke with a more refined vocabulary and didn't seem to fit in with this bunch. She moved to put food on the plates and was a bit more generous with his.

He was near the buckboard, away from the rest of the men, when she handed him the food.

The young man nodded a thank you as he saw that his plate was fuller than the rest.

Beneath the buckboard, Rosie's appetite had returned. She smelled the food and her stomach grumbled. Yet, she dared not expose herself.

Molly set a chunk of the dry bread on the young man's plate. He moved the plate aside, on top of the pile of supplies, for the food to cool.

"Eat up, Tommy, boy," Snake called to him. "You gotta take what you can get, where you can get it."

"He's new at this," Snake spoke out of the corner of his mouth to a man next to him. "He don't have the stomach for it yet. He'll toughen up," he talked as if defending his reasons for taking on the young, inexperienced drifter.

Turning to speak to Slade, Snake didn't notice when the young man bent and set the plate on the ground and pushed it with the toe of his boot beneath the buckboard next to Rosie.

"Tom," he said nearly inaudibly. "It's Tom." He looked at Trace as if to see that Trace understood it was important he be known by a man's name instead of a boy's.

Trace, standing closest to the young man, heard his words and saw his action. He was puzzled. This guy was so unlike the rest of the gang. Why was he so different?

Rosie took the plate apprehensively, pinching its hot edge between her thumb and index finger. She pulled it toward her and wasted no time gobbling down the meal. Only when she finished eating did she realize the man's giving her the plate also meant he, of course, knew she was there beneath the wagon.

Molly moved back alongside Trace. She hoped that by standing in front of the buckboard, they could keep the two smaller children hidden from the rest of the gang. Since the younger man knew they were there, and hadn't reported it to Snake already, he probably wouldn't expose them.

Andy waited for the man he had heard Snake call Tommy to walk over to the other marauders so he could fire at all of them at once.

Time was ticking away in his head. He became alert to every sound and every breath he, and Crazy Leg, took.

Finally, unable to wait any longer, when the young outlaw didn't move, Andy decided he must act. If he were going to surprise them, he'd have to do it now.

He took a deep breath, positioned himself with his back solid against the metal of the chicken coop. He pulled his knees up midway to his chest. There, he balanced the gun barrel on the little dip between his knee caps and raised the butt of the gun to his left shoulder.

Carefully, he swung the shotgun in the direction of the campfire and the outlaws standing there. He only hoped one shotgun blast could take out four men. Trace would have to handle the one next to him and Molly.

He quietly cocked the gun.

Slowly, evenly, and smoothly, he pulled the trigger in anticipation of the gun's kick.

Click.

"What was that?" Snake shrieked. "One of you bastards cock your gun?"

Before he could say more, Andy pulled the trigger on the second barrel.

KaBoooooooooom!

Buckshot flew through the air, bouncing off the cook pot and splattering into flesh like rocks into overripe melons.

The blast came shortly after the misfire and there had been no time for Snake to investigate what he had thought was one of his own men cocking their gun.

"Ow!"

"Hey! Where'd that come from?"

Chickens squawked. The outlaws' horses reared and broke free from their tethers squealing in fright at the blast. The team rushed from the corral and split at the campfire as they stumbled through the maze of confused men.

"What the hell?" Slade called out, fumbling for his guns, while he clutched his leg in pain with one hand. One of his six-shooters fell in the mud.

"Get the horses," Snake shouted as their mounts ran past them. "Let's get outta here!"

There were no apparent mortal wounds. None of the men, although stumbling and grasping body parts, collapsed.

The young man, Tom, still standing next to the buckboard, looked toward Trace and Molly with shock on his face. Unhurt, he hurried to follow the others.

"See ya!" He spoke quietly over his shoulder to Trace as he turned away.

Now, what the hell did that mean? Trace wondered in all the pandemonium. Who had fired the shot? And where the hell was Andy? He had told him to stay put. Obviously, if he was behind the blast, he had disobeyed his orders.

Molly took cover under the buckboard with Rosie and Seth while Trace squatted nearby on the side away from the chaos.

Where the hell was Andy? Trace searched the darkness toward where the shot had originated.

He smelled the acrid odor of gunpowder as it hung in a heavy cloud. He saw that Molly's cook pot had several dents in the side, but none of the liquid spilled out onto the flames. The wooden bucket hadn't fared so well and water squirted out of a hole in the upper side. The flames evaporated the liquid where it sprayed and the droplets sizzled on one of the rocks. The pail would still be serviceable. They would have to be careful not to get it too full or they would have water running, as if from a spigot, on the one side.

What had that young outlaw meant when he had whispered that he'd see them? The mystery was lost on Molly. She was happy to see the men departing, leaving her supplies intact.

Andy ran up to them, barely able to keep the heavy shotgun's barrel holes out of the mud as he came. Both shoulders hurt and he didn't know which one ached worse. Doc's shotgun had slammed his left shoulder so hard it was sure to be black and blue for days. Relieved that the family was safe, he felt the price he paid in pain was worth it. He'd have the doctor look at that one tomorrow. At least it appeared as if there would be a tomorrow.

Suddenly, Molly was clutching him to her in a tight hug. "Thank goodness you're all right," she said as Andy winced at her grasp around his sore shoulders.

She released him and turned to Trace, "Do you think they'll come back?"

"I doubt it. Not tonight, anyway. Come daylight, they'll be less able to sneak up on us. I'll rig a warning device up before nighttime tomorrow. At least, if they show up again, we'll have your rifle and a shotgun." He didn't bother to tell her there were no more shells for the shotgun. Neither she, nor Snake's gang, needed to know that.

"There's a pistol on the other side of the fire. I saw one of them drop it," Andy said.

Trace moved to look for it. Without ammunition for the shotgun, he could use a six-shooter. He only hoped there were bullets in it. He might need it later on, when he went to settle things with Snake and his bunch.

Trace returned with the gun. He wiped the sloppy mud off it as best he could with his fingers. He slung a glob into the air and wiped the rest on his muddy pants.

"Thought I told you to stay put," he reminded Andy.

"I know, but I couldn't see how you and Ma could get out of that one."

"Well, this time, I'm glad you didn't stay out of it. I was about to have to take on that young fellow and, wiry as he was, I wasn't sure how I'd fare. You did good, Andy. You earned your rest," Trace said. "You better get into your bedroll. Here, I'll take Doc's shotgun. You get in those covers and warm up. I'll round up the horses."

Andy gladly handed the shotgun over and moved toward the buckboard.

As the boy walked away from him, Trace wondered how Andy's shoulder was where the gun had thumped it. His own shoulder was tender from the first blast. Despite the resulting bruises they would both have, he was glad they'd had the gun. He could see no other way they could have gotten out of their predicament. He only wished Doc had given them some spare shells for it.

Trace wondered what tomorrow would bring as he walked away from the campfire in the direction the team had fled.

The animals had wandered only a short distance away and were grazing calmly on the low grass. Standing between them, Trace took a handful of mane on each horse and led them back to the corral.

Molly put more wood on the fire. Although exhaustion overtook her, she wanted the firelight to be able to see if the bandits returned. With Trace and Andy having been soaked, they could use whatever heat they could get to dry out.

Andy had already peeled out of his outer clothes and climbed into the dry bedroll. He was fast asleep before Trace latched the horses in the corral.

Trace approached the campfire where Molly stood holding the palms of her hands over the flames to warm herself.

"You best get yourself to bed," he told Molly.

"I will. Tomorrow's Sunday so maybe we can all rest up a bit. Normally, the kids and I go to church, but we'll be thankful for our blessings right here. Thank you for coming to our rescue—more than once, today. You saved our lives."

"Andy had a bit to do with it, too."

"I know, but I don't know how we would have managed without you. For someone who doesn't like kids, you sure went out of your way for them today."

"Didn't say I didn't like 'em. Just never had any reason to deal with 'em before."

"Well, I'm sure, we're all grateful."

As exhausted as she was, it was difficult for Molly to calm down and set her mind at ease enough to go to bed. She poured them each a cup of coffee. Trace accepted the cup and sipped the hot liquid. The pot had sat alongside the fire all evening, the liquid thickening into a bitter brew. Trace thinned it with water from the pail. He noted that the water level had finally fallen below the hole. As he poured a dash of liquid into his cup, he saw that the buckshot had gone on through the backside of the pail as well.

"We're going to have to either plug this pail or pull up a short supply of water. Andy really did a job on this one." He spun the rope handle of the bucket between his thumb and fingers and chuckled.

"I'm thankful it didn't penetrate my cook pot." Molly looked at the dings in the side.

Trace nodded, the firelight illuminated his tired face and muddy clothes.

"We were lucky tonight. If Andy hadn't gotten the shotgun, we'd all have been goners. It doesn't pay to mess with that one called Snake. He has no conscience. He'd just as soon shoot someone as look at 'em."

"What do you know about those men?" Molly sat warming herself beside the fire. *Had he been one of them himself?* she wanted to know, but was afraid to ask. Which side of the law was Trace Westerman on?

"I've had a run in with them before. Actually, a couple of times now. Thought sure they were going to kill Doc on his way home. Then, Andy and I got here to find them trying to take over your place. That one that stood back and gave the food to Rosie—Tom—he's a new one."

"He was strange. He seemed too polite to be an outlaw."

"First time I ran into them was in Texas—quite a ways past your mountain." Trace nodded in the direction of where he had met Molly and the kids. "Most of the pack that was with him, then, were the same ones here tonight—except Tom. Snake must have replaced one of the others he had with him before."

"Texas? Is that where you were coming from when you lost your horse?"

"Yeah, by way of Oklahoma. It's a long story—too long to get into tonight." He hoped she'd quit asking questions soon. He didn't plan to share his entire history with her, leastwise not now.

Trace stood up.

"Think I'll turn in." He popped the cylinder open on the six-shooter and found it loaded. He spun it and snapped it back together. If any more trouble showed up tonight, he'd be ready for it. Trace tucked the six-shooter into the waist of his pants.

"Good night," he said. If she wanted to sit here until daylight, she was welcome to do so. But, he knew the rooster was going to crow too early to suit him in the morning and he didn't relish answering any more of her questions. All he wanted to do, now, was get himself stripped and into a dry bedroll.

"Good night," Molly called after him as he looked back at her forlorn figure near the campfire.

"I'll be crawling under there with the kids, soon, too."

Trace was proving to be a remarkable man. She watched him lift the tarp to settle in the back of the buckboard. Rain water ran from the top and down the side.

Crazy Leg sidled up to her at the campfire. She reached down and petted the dog on the shoulder and he curled up at her feet.

"You had a rough night, tonight, too, didn't you fella?" The dog rose and sat on his haunches. She poured water into his bowl and sat it beside him.

The dog lapped a couple of drinks, as if to pacify her; he had already drunk his fill from one of the puddles the hard rain had formed. Crazy Leg then turned and made his way back to snuggle in beside Seth.

Her family was settling down. She could hear the chickens still grumbling in their coop as they tried to reposition themselves after having their sleep disturbed by the sudden explosion of the shotgun. She hoped the excitement didn't throw them off their laying schedule. Eggs were on the breakfast menu, along with baking powder biscuits, and lard gravy.

Would her own life ever settle down? How much more turmoil could she stand before she lost her mind? Today, she felt, could have made her walk around in circles mumbling to herself like a lunatic in the state asylum at Las Vegas. She hated to think what might have happened if they hadn't come across Trace. Where would she and the children be now? Would Rosie be dead up on the mountain? They truly owed Rosie's life to Trace. Without his help, she felt sure they would all be stuck on the mountain with a wrecked wagon and a lost child. Now, with the attack by Snake's gang fresh in her mind, she felt she could never repay Trace for saving them.

Her mind ran its worry pattern around and around inside her head until, finally, she too decided dawn was coming much too early for her to wait up for it.

She took her place beside her family and waited for the worries to turn off inside her head and for peace to let her sleep.

She lay there staring up at the bottom of the buckboard, knowing Trace was inches away from her. It had been a long time since she had slept that close to a man and thoughts of her husband wafted through her mind. She shook them aside.

She listened intently for any sign of danger, but all she could hear was the children's breathing beside her, Trace's heavier breathing above and the dog's light snore from where he kept Seth warm.

She should feel safe, now. Instead, she wondered, what next?

Five

When the rooster crowed Molly stirred. She wondered if it had woken the children. When she saw them begin to wiggle about in their bedrolls, she whispered, "You can sleep in today. Get some rest. You all need it."

It had been an exhausting night and, although Seth had slept through most of it, none of the children were eager to get out of bed.

Crazy Leg nudged Seth in the ribs and the boy dropped his arm around the dog's neck. Rosie remained snuggled in her bedding. Andy pulled the cover over his head and burrowed deeper into the bedroll.

The boards above Molly's head creaked as Trace rolled over in the wagon bed above them. She crawled out from between the kids to get breakfast started.

She stretched as she came out from under the wagon. Trace sat up. He pulled the tarp back from the wagon's sides and tugged his boots on. His chest was bare and he had already gotten into his still-damp pants, his only pair, from the previous night. His shirt, too, would be a mess, she was sure, but she had nothing to offer him in the way of clothing. Andy's shirts were too small and they had not packed any of her late husband's garments when they left Oklahoma. They hadn't seen a need for them. Molly had chosen to sell everything they didn't have room in the wagon to haul. Most of her late husband's things, including his clothes, had gone at auction.

"Good morning," Molly said.

"Morning." Trace's voice was still thick from sleep.

The day was promising to be a pretty one. After the storm, the sky had cleared and the sunrise along the horizon was unbroken by rain clouds. One could see for miles in all directions and she didn't detect any sign of Snake's bunch anywhere in sight. Maybe he had decided to leave them alone.

Molly made her way to the chicken coop. Eager to be turned loose, the chickens burst through the small door, scrambling over each other in their haste. They rushed to scratch for anything they could find to eat. They were soon busy pecking at the peelings that Trace had tossed out for them the night before.

Molly squatted beside the tiny chicken coop door to reach in for the few eggs that were already there. She had no doubt the activities from the night before had cut down on the hens' production. She would just have to wait to see when it would pick back up.

She had no way to keep more eggs than they could use for very long and sold what extras they got to the General Store in Moriarty. With another mouth to feed and fewer eggs, she would not be making that trip soon. That was a small price to pay for all Trace had done for them. She was glad to have him around here. Her uneasiness about his background nagged her occasionally, but she was sure the good in him must outweigh the bad.

Back at the buckboard, Trace placed the partially full water bucket on the tailgate. He put the coffee grounds in the enamel pot, preparing it to sit in the coals that remained from last night's fire, while he went to bring more wood.

Molly, having carried the eggs carefully in a pouch she fashioned out of the front of her skirt, put them into a bowl. She set the bowl on the tailgate, using it as their makeshift counter.

She found the wash pan and poured water in it to wash her hands. She then searched out a second, larger, bowl and took it to a strong wooden barrel where she kept flour.

She removed the wooden lid from the barrel and scooped the flour into the bowl. She took it and a can of lard back to the tailgate. The flour the storekeeper had sold her in Oklahoma was getting old. She ran her hands through it to remove the weevils as best as she could, tossing them to the chickens before adding the other ingredients.

A flurry of red feathers and a cacophony of squawking burst forth from the birds. When they had cleaned up all the bits of flour and bugs, they returned to work some more on the peelings. They pecked the larger pieces and shook them in their beaks until they broke them into edible chunks.

Molly opened the lard can and smelled its contents to make sure the grease wasn't rancid. She removed a glob to add to the flour. Salt, baking powder, which she cautiously sealed back up to keep the moisture from ruining it, and sugar finished the mix. Without milk for moisture, water would have to do. Soon, she had a thick dough she worked in the bowl with her hands until she squeezed off bits between her fingers and shaped them into small rounds, then pressed them flat on two sides between her palms.

The fire was ready. She dropped a dab of lard into the kettle to melt and coat the bottom and sides of the pot before positioning the biscuits in it to bake.

Molly hoisted a heavy black skillet and set it alongside the campfire on one of the rocks. Another dollop of lard went into that to cook the eggs.

Back at the counter, she washed the eggs and broke them into the bowl. She stirred them to blend the yolks and whites before carrying them back to the cast iron skillet. Once they were done, she removed the fluffy clumps of egg to the large bowl again. She melted more lard in the frying pan and added flour for thickening. When the mixture browned, she poured water into the skillet to make a poor man's gravy.

The coffee aroma stirred Crazy Leg from his bed. He knew, with that smell, food wouldn't be far behind.

One by one the children followed the dog and Molly filled the plates Trace washed and handed her. All, including Crazy Leg, had plenty to eat.

"Mighty good, Molly," Trace complimented her. "I'll go out later and see if I can plunk a sage hen or rabbit for dinner."

"Some of the farmers have been calling this, 'The Year of the Rabbit,'" Molly said. "Hear tell there seems to be a rotating overrun of one animal or another through here. Rabbits one year, mice another. The farmers say some years you have to stand guard over your crops with a stick to beat the things off and save enough for harvest."

"Andy's been pretty good at trapping us a few meals," Molly said. "My laying hens are trying to set and none of them are old enough to put in the pot without feeling it's a waste. If we get desperate enough, sometimes we have to sacrifice one. I'm going to let some of them start building up eggs in their nest for setting. Once those chicks mature, we'll probably have so much chicken we'll get tired of eating it."

Trace doubted that they would ever have food so abundant they would get tired of chicken, but he knew it would be much better if they could vary their diet with something else. Besides, hatching and raising the chickens was going to take time.

"I saw deer tracks up on the mountain near your rocks. Maybe one day, soon, Andy and I can go hunting."

Andy looked up, excited.

Rosie and Seth had kept silent, filling their mouths with food and listening to the conversation. Now, both of them looked at Trace with interest.

"Do you mean you're planning to stay?" Molly asked.

"I thought, maybe, you could use a hired hand for a bit. I'm in no rush to move on. I'd work for my room and board."

"Well, with you helping supply the food, too, that doesn't seem like much of a fair deal for you." Actually, the "room" part was laughable, since the bedroll on a hard wagon bed couldn't be considered much of a place to bunk.

The kids looked at each other, holding their breaths, while they waited for the grownups to strike a deal.

"I figure you could use the help. And, I got the time. Besides, I want to stick around and see if Rosie has any more of those 'dreams' of hers." Trace winked at Rosie.

In all the excitement, no one had told Andy about Rosie's flash of intuition.

Andy looked at Rosie with questioning eyes.

Molly broke in before Andy could ask his little sister what Trace was talking about.

"We'll go into that later. For now, we'll just have to wait and see how Rosie does."

Seth, having finished his food, picked up a stick and called for Crazy Leg to follow him.

The dog bounced away, then whined when his paws hit the ground and he felt the painful jar in his ribs. Reminded of his injuries from the night before, he slowed down and walked beside the boy.

"You be careful, you hear?" Molly called after the youngster.

"Yes, Ma."

"We'd be more than happy to have you stay a while, Trace," Molly turned her attention back to their previous conversation. "But, you've got to let me pay you something. I make a small salary teaching school down the road. It isn't much, but I wouldn't feel right if I didn't give you something."

"I'll stay, if you'll promise not to drag that rifle around with you all the time. It scares the bejeebers out of me."

"What's 'bejeebers'?" Rosie asked, her tongue stumbling over the unusual word.

"Never mind," Molly said.

Molly ducked her head. He was joshing her. It had been a long time since she'd had anyone with whom to share a joke. She knew she was lowering her guard. Not that she trusted him wholeheartedly, but he had proven himself to be a man who would look out for the family. How could she watch him save their lives and not trust him? Still, a tiny nagging doubt flickered in her mind. She sensed there were things he wasn't telling her. Was there something that she might, someday, regret not knowing?

"Don't worry, Molly, we'll work something out. In the meantime, maybe I can look at Andy's rabbit trap. If we can catch dinner with that, we can save the bullets in the six-gun."

Andy looked at Rosie and smiled. Maybe her getting thrown from the wagon would bring them some good luck for a change. They sure could use it. Trace was fast becoming a hero to him. Better than any he had read about in the dime novels his aunt from back East had sent to him. He was real. And he was here. There was no doubt in Andy's mind that Trace was sent to be their personal Guardian Angel. Hadn't he already saved all of their lives? Not once, but twice for him and Rosie. Whatever trouble was following Trace Westerman, it was far outweighed in Andy's mind by the good he had already done.

"If you're finished eating, what say we go look at that trap, Andy? If your arms aren't too sore."

"The right one feels better. Today, I think the shoulder I braced the shotgun with, hurts worse than the one I landed on. The trap's close enough we can walk," Andy was unsure if he could handle the lift up onto Comet's back. "I haven't set the trap in a few days 'cause we were busy with other things."

Molly picked up the dishes and set about cleaning up the clutter from breakfast.

"You two go on, I can get this."

Andy, wanting to be sure Trace would remain, asked, "Then Trace can stay, Ma?"

"Trace can stay. Lord knows, we need the help."

Molly removed the remaining biscuits to put them away for the noon meal. She was glad to see there were enough left over for that. Then, with any luck with Andy's trap, they'd cook whatever he caught for dinner. Another chicken might be spared, if an animal wandered into the snare.

Andy went to get his pocketknife and a length of rope. Trace waited, emptying his coffee cup and handing it to Molly.

Off in the distance, Crazy Leg began to bark.

Rosie stood up from where she sat near the fire. She was stiff and still. She stared across the field, looking in the direction Seth and the dog had gone, but unable to see them.

"Crazy Leg's got a snake pinned in an old prairie dog hole, Ma."

"What? Rosie, are you sure? How do you know?"

"I just see it, Ma, in my head."

Molly glanced at Trace with a concerned look.

"Come on, Andy." Trace drew the six-gun out of the waist of his pants. If Rosie sounded the alarm, they better pay attention. Trace and Andy began running toward the dog's persistent barking.

"Stay here," Trace shouted to Molly, who had started to follow. She hung back with Rosie, the two of them clutching each other in concern for Seth.

Not far off Trace and Andy saw Seth standing behind the dog while Crazy Leg barked and snapped at the hole.

"Seth, get away," Trace called out.

When they reached the dog, Seth stood waiting for them to catch up.

"Crazy Leg's got him down in that hole."

"What is it?" Andy demanded.

"Ol' rattler was too fast for Crazy Leg, today. Before he could catch him and snap his head off, he made it down the hole," Seth said matter-of-factly.

"Seth, Ma's told you not to mess around when you hear a snake!"

Trace held the pistol out. He'd have to use one of the precious bullets. With the snake striking its head out at the dog and nothing for Crazy Leg to grab onto, he was sure to get bit, if Trace didn't shoot.

"Get back, Crazy Leg," Trace ordered.

The dog looked at him with disappointment. He tucked his tail between his legs and walked back to Seth whining at the loss of his game.

"It's Crazy Leg's job to get rid of rattlesnakes," Seth informed Trace.

"Not today. Hold him there, Seth," Trace said.

When the rattler struck again, Trace pulled the trigger, killing the snake.

"Give me that stick, Seth."

Trace reached down with the stick and pulled the snake from the hole to make sure it was dead. He dropped it on the ground. He could see where the bullet had hit. He pulled his knife out and cut off the head. He carefully kicked the head back down the hole and filled the hole in behind it, packing dirt on top, with the heel of his boot.

He picked the rest of the snake up and handed it to Andy.

Andy looked at him in confusion.

"Dinner. Hasn't your Ma ever cooked rattlesnake stew before? Tastes just like chicken."

Andy wasn't too sure about that, but he headed back to camp with the meat.

Trace expected to hear a scream when Andy reached camp and presented Molly their booty.

"Seth, you best stay closer to camp, you hear?" Trace spoke to the younger boy.

"Yes, sir."

"You can have the rattles, Seth, when we clean it." He reached down and scratched the dog's head to make amends for taking its prey.

He sensed staying with this family was certainly going to present a challenge.

Andy came running back toward them.

To Trace's surprise, he hadn't heard a scream. Perhaps he had misjudged Molly, after all.

"Can we go see my trap, now?"

"Yeah. But, I think we better take these two with us to keep them safe."

They reached the rabbit trap. Andy had fashioned his contraption out of old rags cut and braided into flat rope, then woven and tied to form a loose net. A stick lay alongside to hold the funnel-like tube open at the large end.

Andy poked the stick in the dirt and positioned the fork in the top of it to hold the front of the trap open. He tossed a small handful of oats into the back of the trap. Andy's theory was, when the animal went in to eat, it would knock the stick down and get entangled in the net.

"Not a bad idea. How's it been working?"

"I've caught a rabbit and a couple of sage hens in it."

"Andy, you amaze me! Your Ma's lucky to have a man like you around."

"Well, after Pa and Grandma and Grandpa died, she had to have someone to look after her."

"I'd say you've done right well. You, too, Seth. Let's go back and see what we can do to help the girls."

Seth whistled for the dog and they went back to camp to give the rabbit trap a chance to work.

Having Trace there certainly made life interesting, Molly had to admit to herself as she saw the three of them approaching. She'd had guests bring something to the supper table before, but never a rattlesnake. For certain, he'd have to show her how to cook it. But, she'd be darned if she'd give him the satisfaction of letting him know his contribution disturbed her. She hated snakes. Rattlesnakes were the worst to her. She had almost turned down the land claim when she found they were natural creatures to the area. Only the family's desperation kept her from moving on. Since then, she had done everything in her power to eradicate or, at least, keep the snakes at bay. She might cook one for Trace but she wasn't about to eat it.

Rosie rushed to meet the boys.

"I was right, wasn't I? It was a snake. I told you so." She was thrilled with her newfound powers and, although the visions came sporadically, they excited her. It was a new gift and it was fun seeing the others' reactions.

Trace moved to the campfire where Molly had let the fire die down as the day warmed. She would save what wood she could, knowing when they got low they would have to make another trip to the mountain. She was willing to go, but the next time, she wanted those rocks! Any wood would have to be piled on top, if the buckboard could hold the weight.

They had to have a house before winter. It didn't have to be fancy. Even a frame structure of boards and siding and nothing on the inside would be better than living under a wagon. She wanted a roof over their heads and a real cookstove. Maybe, with Trace here to help, it really could happen.

"What's your plan for the day?" Trace asked Molly when he saw that she had everything cleaned and put away, except for the snake stretched out on the tailgate of the buckboard.

The bedrolls, including his, had been shaken and left in the sun to air. The mud from last night was nearly dust already as the thirsty earth sucked the moisture down and left the top crisp like baked sugar crystals on a pie crust. There were raw scrapes across the earth where the chickens had scratched and moved on.

"Well, we need to take care of the horses. We usually fill the trough and bring them out for water, then turn them out to pasture where the grass is better. The land is lower on one corner and the rain doesn't soak in so fast. The grass gets taller and makes a better feed. The horses will stay close. The neighbors have a fence that keeps them from wandering onto their property and I figure to fence the rest off and grow beans on the piece that doesn't provide such good grass. The boys take them out there. They'll come back on their own when they get thirsty."

"I'll go with them. I might as well learn the lay of the land if I'm going to be helping out around here."

"Rosie and I'll see to the chickens. I've got a few broken bowls and things around we fill with water for them to help themselves. Last night's rain probably put some in, but we'll make sure they're full."

Molly stood with her hands on her hips surveying the surrounding campsite.

"Then, I guess I better sort and re-stack the supplies. The way they were rummaged through, it's next to impossible to find anything." She was just grateful to still have them, even in disarray.

Trace looked around, too. In the daylight, he could see that there was plenty of work to keep him, and probably several men, busy if Molly was to get her place in order and be in a better shelter by winter. He thought about a house- and barn-raising—but that was off in the future.

Once the horses were in the pasture, he planned to come back to the well and with Andy's help, begin to construct a windmill so the water would pump into the trough without someone having to toss and retrieve a partial pail of water to fill it.

For now, he and Andy, who was swinging the pail lightheartedly, went to fill the trough the hard way.

"Rider coming in," Andy stopped and called out at the sound of the horse's hooves against the hard packed earth on the trail leading into the homestead. The pace was slow and steady, not a threatening pace and it didn't alarm him. Soon, he saw it was Doc Landry's buggy.

The doctor drove at an unhurried pace and all of them were relieved that he appeared not to have anyone following him.

Shortly, he pulled up at the fire pit.

"Whoa, Nellie," he called to the bay. "Howdy, Folks."

Rosie rushed up to greet him.

"My, aren't you doing well this morning," Doc Landry said as Rosie stopped to pet Nellie.

Trace and Andy approached from dumping water into the trough and Doc Landry saw Andy's sling soiled beyond any possibility of getting it free of stains.

"What on earth happened to you, Andy? Did you fall off Comet again?"

Trace spoke up, "We had some trouble here last night, Doc. If it hadn't been for your shotgun, you might be tending to dead bodies this morning."

"That gang lay in wait for you?"

"No. They beat us here and were ransacking the place when we arrived. I thought I had them where I wanted them with your shotgun, then two of them snuck up behind me out of the dark. If it hadn't been for Andy, here, getting the shotgun where they made me drop it, well, there's no telling what might have happened. You best take a look at both his shoulders this morning, Doc. I'm afraid your shotgun gave him quite a jolt."

The doctor walked to the buckboard and sat his worn black bag on the tailgate. He saw the snake's body lying there and raised his eyebrows in surprise. What it was doing there was none of his business, he figured. He opened his bag to get a new sling for Andy.

"Hope I'm not going to have to put two of these things on you. You'd look pretty helpless with both wings strapped to your sides. Let's see the new damage first."

Andy allowed Molly to unbutton his shirt and remove the sleeve. She gasped aloud when she saw the massive bruise on Andy's shoulder.

Doc Landry touched the bruise gingerly. "It'll probably be sore for a couple of days. Tomorrow, it'll probably be green, then yellow. It'll go away gradually."

Molly untied the sling from Andy's shoulder and took the shirt off his arm. She folded them while she awaited the rest of Doc Landry's diagnosis.

"I'll get you a clean shirt. This one certainly needs washing." She cringed at the sight of even more bruises.

"You pulled some ligaments in your right arm. That's going to take more time to heal. It'll probably be sore longer, too. Keep a sling on it so the arm stays immobile and it'll heal faster. Try not to wallow in the mud with it this time," Doc Landry said dryly as he positioned a new sling on his patient.

"You might want to wash up that other sling," he told Molly, "so you can change it later. I'm sure he's not going to be able to keep out of the dirt."

Molly nodded. "Thanks, Doc. What about Rosie?"

"She looked fine to me. Is she having any problems?"

"No. She did have another one of those spells this morning, though. She warned us about a snake in time for Trace to go kill it. What do you think is going on?"

Molly didn't want anyone thinking her child was strange. They went back to school tomorrow. It wouldn't do for Rosie to have spells there. If Rosie was ill, she wanted her cured. If Rosie's visions were evil, she wanted to know. So far, Rosie had only seen things that were happening to the family and that had been helpful. But, she was concerned about Rosie's unusual knack because she, nor no one else, understood it.

"I wondered about the snake over there—" Doc said thoughtfully.

"Some places, down Texas way, rattlesnake is a delicacy," Trace told him with a smile.

"Look, Molly, consider it Rosie's gift—a blessing unless it's proven not to be," Doc went on. "So far, everything's been fine. Maybe it will go away. As long as Rosie isn't frightened by what's happening, let it be."

"She seems to be enjoying it," Trace cut in, remembering her early morning taunting of the boys.

"Well, I best be on my way."

"Andy hasn't had a chance to look for your lap robe, Doc. It got lost in the turmoil last night." Trace told him as they prepared to walk to the buggy. "We'll be sure to get it to you just as soon as we can." He pulled the shotgun out from beneath the buckboard seat and handed it to the doctor. "It's no good now, Doc. It's empty."

The doctor chuckled.

"Tell you the truth, I'm glad to see Old Bessie. I don't mind wandering around in the daylight without her company, but come nighttime—well, you never know what you're going to come up against."

"We were mighty glad to have her last night."

"If I ever loan her out again, I'll try to remember to send some extra shells with her."

"You better keep your eye out, Doc. Andy nailed a few of those fellows with the buckshot. Could be some of them might have to come see you, if they can't take care of it themselves."

"Thanks, Trace." They were nearing the doctor's buggy where Rosie stood petting Nellie on the nose. "Like I said, before, if you need me, just send someone. Rosie, dear," Doc Landry pulled a sack out of his bag and handed it to the child, "you take this to your Ma and tell her I said each of you children are to take one of these twice a day until it's all gone."

Rosie gleefully snatched the bag and ran to Molly.

"Hard Rock candy. I wanted everyone out of earshot. I've got something important to tell you."

Trace nodded, waiting with curiosity for Doc to go on.

"There was a man in the sheriff's office this morning when I checked on a prisoner's condition in the jail. I think he was looking for you. He didn't say what it was about and I didn't catch who he was, but I definitely heard him mention Trace Westerman."

Trace mulled the information over.

"Don't worry, I didn't say anything."

"What'd he look like?"

"He was a big moose of a man. Mean looking, too. If I'd been the sheriff, I'd a got out the wanted posters and seen if he was on any of them. He was dressed fancy though, like a tenderfoot."

Trace nodded.

"I'll be staying around here for a while, Doc. I'm going to try to help Molly and the kids get some things done. Until I raise enough money for a horse and some gear, there isn't much sense in me going on—not on foot, anyway. This is as good a place as any to hang out for a while."

"The Klings sure can use your help. As far as I know, nobody knows you're here, except those outlaws. With any luck they're out of the territory by now."

"I hope you're right, Doc."

Doc snapped his black bag shut and laid it and Old Bessie at the foot of the bench seat in the buggy. He climbed in.

By now, Molly and the kids had discovered what the "medicine" was and the children were already enjoying their first dose.

Doc waved to them.

"Thanks, Doc," Molly called out.

"Thank you. Thank you," came a chorus from Seth and Rosie.

"Yeah, thanks," Andy added as if he thought he was too old to enjoy hard candy.

Doc smiled and nodded to them. His job wasn't always this pleasant. A serious look crossed his face as he spoke to Trace.

"Mind my words, Trace. That guy was a strange one. You watch your step!"

Trace nodded. He knew the man Doc Landry described. He had been avoiding him for some time. He still wasn't ready to meet up with him. The time just wasn't right. Yet.

Six

Trace watched Doc circle the buggy in a wide arc and head back toward the road. The buggy wheels churned the soft dirt until it puffed out in tiny dust clouds.

He walked on to the corral and took bridles from a post nearby, where Andy had hung them in preparation for moving the horses to pasture.

"We'll lead them out with those, then take them off when we get there," Andy said as he rushed up to help.

"Trough's full enough," he added, taking the bridles from Trace and sorting them out for each horse. He knew which fit each animal and he gave a low whistle to tell Comet to come forward for his.

Comet moved between the team and edged his way along while the other horses flung their heads from side to side in protest. They all knew the results would be water and food and the team resented the single horse getting ahead of them.

"Whoa, Big Boy. There's enough for all of you," Andy tried to calm the anxious animals.

The horses were getting a late start to pasture this morning and the delay agitated them.

Trace held the bit up to the smaller horse's mouth. Jake bared his teeth and refused to let the metal bit slip past his teeth. Andy led Comet aside and tied his reins to the corral. He went back to put Big Boy's bit in his mouth and help Trace with the stubborn animal.

Trace was attempting to force the sorrel to open his teeth by squeezing his fingers on the outside of the animal's mouth behind the rear molars.

Andy stuck his hand in his pants' pocket and reached up beneath the horse's lips. The animal's tongue came out and curled against Andy's index finger as it licked it clean. Andy quickly jammed the bit in place.

"I always get just a dab of sugar before I come out in case one of them acts like that."

"Boy, what your Ma must find in those pockets when she washes. You could might near have your breakfast out of your pockets what with the oats for the rabbits and, now, sugar. Gotta give you a hand though. It worked." Trace's voice was laced with admiration.

He had to admit, this boy had some new ideas about doing things. He had always done everything the hard way. It was difficult for him to believe there was an easier way to get things done.

"I remember seeing my Pa doin' that with honey, back home in Oklahoma. I know he always kept a little jar of it in the barn, 'for persuasion,' he said."

Trace noticed a far away look in the boy's eyes and he knew he missed his father something fierce. As must Molly miss her husband. It was hard thinking of Molly as a married woman when he had known her as a widow—a woman he could easily be interested in.

His mind was playing tricks on him. He shouldn't even be thinking about the woman as anything more than a stubborn homesteader trying to make a living on a hard land. But he was.

She was a striking woman. She was tall, nearly reaching his height, and almost willowy. Life had etched hard lines on her fair-skinned face, as had the long exposure to the elements. He had never seen her laugh but he bet, when she did, she would be like a young woman again. He liked the way her long red hair dropped from its bun during her endeavors around the place. He liked when the wind caught her hair and her skirts and bounced them playfully, causing her to clutch at the wayward strands with one hand and the skirt with the other. He liked how the sun would glint off her hair's highlights—or the slightest hint of gray.

Trace thought about her brown eyes, not so dark that you couldn't see deep within them, but layered with overtones of brown hues with each circle getting smaller and darker until the pupils were black.

He had never known a woman like Molly. In fact, it had been a long time since he had gotten close to a woman at all.

Having never been married, he wondered what it would feel like to have a wife and kids to come home to each night. Working for Molly wouldn't be the same as having a family of his own, but he guessed he'd get the chance to get a feel of it. So far, it had been a whole lot of work and downright dangerous. If he saw this job through, he'd have really accomplished something.

Trace and Andy walked the horses past the buckboard to the water trough, passing Molly busily brushing and braiding Rosie's hair. The animals drank their fill, sucking the water noisily up through their lips as if they were going to drain the trough dry and pull the bottom up from the ground. They shook their manes and bobbed their heads when their thirst was satisfied. Andy and Trace led them away and headed for the pasture.

Trace walked in front of the team, holding the reins of both horses in one big hand, while Andy led Comet. Andy winced when the horse jerked his head, or crowded him in a rush to get to the grass. He felt his shoulders twinge in pain with each jerk or bump.

Once they reached the pasture, Andy removed Comet's bridle.

"They'll stay here until they get thirsty, then they'll come back into camp for water," Andy said as he helped Trace remove the other bridles. "It's simple enough to lead them to the corral by their manes then. They know we usually have a bit of oats to give them in the evening."

Trace looked at Andy. He had the routine down pat. He would be a good ranch hand one day.

Back at the well, the two of them refilled the trough.

"Soon you won't have to do this," Trace said as he straightened his back and pulled his shirtsleeve across his brow to clear the sweat. "When we get the windmill going, it'll keep the trough full on its own."

Andy splashed another partial pail of water into the trough.

"Of course, it wouldn't take us so long, now, if you hadn't put two holes through the sides of that bucket."

It was Trace's way of letting Andy know he had done a good job protecting them the previous night. The pail had been the only casualty on their side. Andy had tried to push sticks through the holes to plug them. He broke the sticks off and that worked for a while. But, if the water didn't get to sit in the bucket long enough, the twigs didn't swell up, the next pail full of water forced the sticks out the sides and he had to start all over again. When they finished filling the trough, he would ram bigger sticks in and let the pail sit, full of water, to try to stop the flow.

At last, the trough was full enough so that Trace and Andy could concentrate on something else.

Trace showed Andy how he planned to build the windmill. He told Andy what boards he would need as they looked over the pile of timbers and lumber Molly'd had brought in from a sawmill.

The wood was rough cut, but strong and a good grade of lumber.

She must have spent most of her money on materials, Trace thought as he examined the timbers in the pile. He found several long stringers lying beneath shorter pieces. He sure hoped Molly had ordered enough for the windmill and the house. Sure as she hadn't, he was going to catch heck for using these.

He looked up to see her approaching. The sun, behind her, showed through the sides of her shirt and skirt and between her legs as she walked. Her body blocked the sun's rays and exposed her form as he had imagined—willowy.

He averted his eyes. She surely wouldn't like his appreciation of her feminine shape, if she caught him looking. He reminded himself to search for the hunting knife to cut his hair and shave his beard with while Molly was at school the next day. It was time he really cleaned up. He waited to hear Molly's outrage at his selection of timbers.

Well, it's better I find out now if these timbers are going to get me in trouble, than after the damage is done, he thought.

Molly stopped nearby and watched the selection process.

Trace picked out four timbers and walked their length, measuring them in footsteps.

69

"I'd say they're close to thirty feet," Trace said to Andy, trying to keep his mind on the work at hand rather than on Molly's figure.

"Thirty-two is what the man at the mill told me."

Trace saw Molly's eyes rove over the remaining timbers. He knew she was mentally counting to be sure there were enough for the house. She probably didn't have the money to buy more.

"Building materials are hard to come by. Even if you can afford them, the demand is so high there's a waiting list at the mill."

Trace picked up one of the sticks Andy had broken off trying to mend the bucket. He knelt down and cleared a place in the dirt with the edge of his palm. He drew a plan to show Molly and Andy how he would build the windmill frame.

He needed four strong, long, timbers, one for each corner. He planned to bury the ends of each in the dirt to anchor the corners. Trace gouged the stick into the ground to show them where the uprights for the tower would go.

"Andy, see if you can pull out some of those shorter planks. We'll need something to attach to all four sides, every few feet up, for bracing. I'll start digging the corner holes where we'll set the uprights. We'll have to use the team to drag them next to the holes and help us raise them."

Trace began to pace off the footage he wanted to mark the square that would surround the well. At each corner he dug his boot heel into the dirt and kicked some of the fine soil aside to mark the spot to dig.

Molly watched with interest. In the background, she could hear Seth and Rosie playing tag and Crazy Leg barking as he jumped between them and joined the game. She was surprised Rosie showed so little sign of her ordeal. Kids were resilient. She wished, as an adult, she could bounce back as quickly from her own trials. The noise the two children made told her they were fine and she could relax and talk, for a bit, with Trace and Andy.

"Like I said earlier, tomorrow's school. I'll excuse Andy from coming, so he can help you here. I'll take Seth and Rosie on Comet with me. That way, you'll have the team—and the little ones will be out of the way in case a beam should fall."

"Good idea. We'll be most of this afternoon lining things out, anyway."

Andy grinned at the prospect of getting a day free from school.

"There's a blacksmith in Moriarty that will put the wheel together. He's so busy he gave us a pattern for the vanes and offered to adjust the price if we'd cut them out ourselves. They are kind of rough because we didn't have the right tools, but he assured me he'd smooth the edges and bend the ends so they'll bite the wind good. He's fashioning the tail shaft, too."

"If you and Andy get through with the team tomorrow, I can take the wagon the next day and haul the blades on to town after school."

"Good. We should have the frame in place and braced enough to keep it up. We can go ahead and add the sideboards while you're gone that day. What about Andy's schooling, though?" Trace didn't want to interrupt the boy's book learning.

Andy looked at Trace with dismay registering on his face.

"I'll catch him up, at night, after supper. Since I'm the teacher, that won't be any problem. He'll still get his lessons."

Andy hid his disappointment. He had hoped to skip school all together.

"Good," Trace said. He had never had a formal education. As a child, he grew up too far out in the wilderness to reach a schoolhouse. He had learned his lessons from nature and to read, write and do arithmetic from his mother. Anything else, like geography, he learned a limited lesson from wandering the newly opening world of the West. He'd been as far as the Texas/Mexico border on the south and Missouri on the north.

He had crossed Oklahoma and traveled through New Mexico, following cattle drives along the Chisholm Trail, and other cattle trails, until he tried a short stint of coal mining to sustain himself while he searched for Snake's gang.

It was dirty and disgusting work and he soon found his lungs were made for breathing air, not black dust. He had left that behind and wandered toward Albuquerque to see what job opportunities were available.

He'd never picked up the habit of smoking or drinking, unlike most of the men he had run into. Neither appealed to him. His biggest vice was trying to mind his own business—and not liking it when others wouldn't let him. Snake had crossed that boundary beyond anything Trace could ever forgive. He'd have no peace until the scum was brought to justice. The conflict last night, while terrifying, had ended better than Trace's first encounter with the villain.

Trace smelled the fresh wood cuts as he and Andy moved the boards apart looking for the smaller braces. It reminded him of a time before Snake came into his life. It was a time when he had a ranch of his own. He was deep in his own thoughts when he heard Molly raise her voice, "Trace, I asked you if you wanted a noon meal."

"What? Sorry, Molly. No, I'm not hungry. That big breakfast did me fine. How about you Andy?"

Trace slipped back into memories of his ranch along the Pecos River in Texas while he waited for Andy to give Molly his answer. Looking out across the land was too much like his pasture where his own cattle had grazed. Except for the lack of trees, at certain times of the year the land could be the same. In Trace's mind he revisited happier days of riding herd on his stock. The next flash of memory shook him.

One hot autumn night, Snake had ridden in with eight other men. They rounded up most of the herd and headed to Mexico in the dark. By the time Trace heard the cattle lowing, it was too late for him, his Pa, and the few ranch hands they had to stop them.

He'd ridden hard all night trying to catch up, but when Snake couldn't move the cattle across The Rio Grande quietly, he spooked them with gun shots in the air and raced for the border.

Trace winced at the memory. He came back to the present as he heard Andy answer Molly's question.

"I'm fine, Ma."

"We'll have an early supper, then." Molly picked up a dipper alongside the pail and got a drink. Soon, there would be water a-plenty flowing into the trough. She couldn't help the little stir of excitement that gurgled in her stomach. It was one more step in getting a real home going—one more step toward proving up on the land and having a place of their own.

Leaving the men to their work, Molly went back to finish restacking and organizing the supplies.

They worked on into the late afternoon until, at last, Trace called a halt to their project.

"We better take a break and get the meat ready for Molly to cook. Why don't you go see if you've caught anything in your trap?"

He headed back to the buckboard while Andy went to check his trap for game.

Trace was just finishing skinning the rattlesnake and cleaning it when Andy walked up carrying two sage hens by their feet. He raised them into the air with his left arm to show the family with pride.

"Well, that changes the looks of things," Trace said. "We can clean those and have fried bird. Bet once all the meat's rolled in flour and browned pretty you won't even know which is fowl and which ain't."

Molly frowned in Trace's direction.

Rosie turned up her nose, "Ain't eatin' no snake," she said, pouting.

"I'm not," Molly corrected her. "The proper phrase is 'I'm not eating any snake. Thank you.' We don't use the word ain't."

"I swear, the girl is as stubborn as her Ma," Trace teased Molly.

"Thank you, but I'll have sage hen as well."

"If you two aren't the pickiest things," Trace grinned as he cut the rattlers off the skin. He handed them to Seth.

"Too bad you don't have a big cowboy hat, Seth. We could dry the skin and make a fancy hatband for you like the ones they wear down Texas way. Maybe next time." He was sure there would be a next time. From what he saw of the land, he'd not be surprised if, at certain times of the year, it wasn't crawling with them. He'd have to teach Seth, and the dog, not to mess with them for sure. And he'd want to remind Andy and the girls. He knew the snakes took more to attacking than running, especially when they first came out of hibernation or when they were shedding their skins.

"Well, if you won't try it, there's just going to be more for the rest of us."

Andy cringed, but was curious and thought he just might taste it. After all, he couldn't look less a man in front of Trace. Seth was satisfied with the rattles. He had decided he'd wait until he was either older to taste it—or much hungrier.

Trace butchered the sage hens and cut them up in pieces. He had no doubt they'd be a little tough and taste gamy.

With the meat cut up and clean, Molly placed it in an old whiskey barrel she had devised as a cooler. She poured cold water midway up the barrel and suspended the big bowl full of meat partially into the water by cradling it inside an empty flour sack. She closed the lid on the edge of the sack to keep the bowl from falling and filling with water.

Come suppertime, she'd fry the meat and dig potatoes out from beneath the coals where they were already baking.

"When you cook the meat, the drippings would make mighty good gravy," Trace suggested. He knew she wasn't a woman to waste anything. That was obvious from the way she found a use for whatever presented itself.

"It would really be better if we had milk to make it out of. Tomorrow, I'll stop on the way home and pick up a pail of milk and some butter from a neighbor. I've traded eggs to the woman while her chickens were molting, on the promise of a spring supply of milk products when her cow came fresh. The calf's two weeks old by now and she'll be saving some for us. With the three of us riding Comet, we can't carry much." She would take some biscuits and some leftover sage hen, if there was any, in the pail to school for lunch. Although the lard pail was small, it had a lid that snapped on tight and she hoped they would be able to get the milk home without spilling it along the way.

Since dinner was already planned, along with a surprise, she would save the drippings for real gravy the next night. There wasn't time in the morning to spend doing much cooking before leaving for the schoolhouse.

Trace and Andy went back to work on the windmill frame. Seth stood around shaking the rattles and causing Crazy Leg to jump and yip until Rosie, tired of their game, threatened to toss the rattles into the fire. Molly shook her head at their bickering and set about making a dried apple pie to bake in the big pot for their surprise dessert.

Tonight, they would celebrate. It had been a long time since they had enjoyed a real treat, but the progress they were soon to make put Molly in an optimistic mood.

Supper was ready at dusk and Trace and Andy, having washed up at the horse trough when the horses came in, walked the animals to the corral. Andy drug out a gunny sack half full of oats and portioned out enough for each horse into their feed boxes.

When Trace and Andy came toward the campfire they were wiping their hands on the back of their pants and looking forward to supper.

"Sure smells good," Trace said as he approached.

Molly had moved the cooked food to the tailgate of the buckboard. She had even found a bolt of gingham she had bought for dresses, to use as a tablecloth. She wasn't about to have time to sew the fabric into clothes between now and winter. It could serve both purposes. She'd just wash it up and put it away for when she needed to cut new school dresses for Rosie out of it. If they were very careful, perhaps she'd be able to store it, again, none the worse for its use.

If Trace was going to work so hard, the least she could do was feed him well, and try to make things pleasant. She justified her actions to herself feeling a bit like a schoolgirl.

Rosie had picked wildflowers of deep blue and goldenrod to put in an old bottle she used for a vase. The flowers, having grown close to the soil, had such short stems she had needed to fill the bottle to the top with water in order to keep them fresh.

"Very nice, ladies. I don't know when I've been served a nicer looking spread," Trace said.

Andy looked at Molly with a bit of curiosity tweaking his mind. He couldn't remember a time when she had fussed about like she had this evening since her and his father were first married. Come to think of it, he hadn't seen her draw her rifle out all day, either.

Molly began handing out the enamel plates and cups stacked alongside the food.

Molly smiled, for the first time, at Trace.

I was right, Trace thought, *the brightness of her mood erased the lines formed by years of hardship.*

"Help yourselves. You can fill your plates and then go sit by the fire." She gave the younger children a look to let them know they were to wait until Trace and Andy had served themselves before dishing up their food. The two of them had put in a hard day's work for the family's benefit—they deserved respect and a full stomach, she had told the younger children earlier. Her stern look reminded them to be patient.

When Trace and Andy moved to the fire, Molly helped Seth and Rosie get their food. Then, she served herself and took a place across the fire from Trace. Andy sat nearby on the ground with his back leaned up against the tarp covering the supplies. He balanced his plate with his right hand while he picked up the hot food with the other one free of a sling. There was little conversation as they ate. Molly sensed they all were quite tired and that it would be a short evening before everyone turned in for the night.

Trace was sore, and he suspected Andy must be even worse off than he was. There was school in the morning for the younger children and Molly had kept herself busy all day so as not to feel guilty about not helping on the windmill.

Crazy Leg ate his food. Trace suspected the dog's portion was mostly snake. Molly hadn't objected to cooking the meat, but he hadn't seen any of it on anyone else's plate except his and Crazy Leg's bowl. Amused, he turned his attention to devouring every bite.

Crazy Leg licked his bowl clean, then stretched out on his belly with his chin on his paws and his nose toward the fire, dozing contentedly while he waited for Seth to go to bed.

When they had eaten their fill, Molly uncovered the dried-apple pie and the aroma of cinnamon, cloves, and nutmeg filled the air. She watched with pleasure as they all eagerly dug into the sweet fruit treat.

They ate until no one had room for any more.

Tonight, life was good. Molly hated to disturb the group as they so enjoyed themselves, but the time had come.

"Rosie, you and Seth best get to bed, now."

"I think I'll crawl in, too," Andy said, "as soon as I close the chickens up." He knew they were already roosting, but it wasn't safe to leave the small door open to nighttime predators. If anyone was going to eat one of the hens, it better be the family. He left to complete his chore before settling beneath the buckboard to rest his sore body.

That Trace sure does know how to work a fellow, Andy thought as he courted sleep. He guessed it was just as well. The busy day had kept his mind off his injuries, except when he bumped against something or pulled the wrong way.

He couldn't quite figure out what was up with Molly, though. She hadn't acted so fussy in most of the time he had known her. It had been a long time since he had seen her smile. The last time, he remembered, was before his Pa died. She had taken on a serious no-nonsense way about her once they were on their own. This new attitude bothered him, and he didn't understand why.

Seven

When Molly and the children returned home the next afternoon, the four uprights for the tower of the windmill reached high into the bright blue sky. Braces, temporarily tacked crosswise from one timber to another, formed an "X" on each of the four sides. The beams stood on end, reaching upward some distance, tapering inwards toward the top as they went.

Molly rode Comet up to the water trough and admired the structure. Seth sat between her and Rosie, one arm around Molly's waist and the other hand clutching the wire handle of the lard pail in his fingers.

Rosie, behind him, released her hold on Seth and began petting a half-grown kitten she carried across her leg.

"It looks wonderful, Trace," Molly said as she slackened the reins in her hand to let Comet drink from the full trough. Molly relaxed and let him take in the cool water as it ran down his throat in a soothing, dust-cutting stream.

While Molly and the little kids had been at school, Trace had dug the corner holes as deep as he could dig with the posthole digger he had found in the jumbled pile of tools.

He had slanted the inner side of the holes toward the well, slightly, with a shovel to get the angle he wanted to bring the upper end of the tower closer together. Each bottom corner post was eight feet apart. The plan was to fasten the beams four feet apart at the top. He wanted enough space on top to attach a small platform all the way around, to kneel on to set and make repairs on the wheel, the gear, or the tail shaft.

"Whatcha got there, Rosie?" Andy asked when he saw the calico cat.

Crazy Leg whined softly beside Andy. He wasn't sure what to make of this new addition to the farm's menagerie. Rosie held it in her arms to keep him from chasing it. His tongue hung from his mouth and he panted in anticipation.

"Mrs. Smith gave her to me. She said she was a right good mouser. And, you leave her alone! Do you hear me Crazy Leg?" She looked at the dog with scolding eyes and he ducked his head, whining louder and watching the cat from the corner of his eye.

Molly knew it was important for the children to have pets. With Rosie's recent experiences, she wanted her to have something to love. Rosie could use the gentle attention she would get in return. Molly didn't really care to have another mouth to feed, but the neighbor promised Rosie all the milk the cat could drink and, if she caught mice that might get into their food supply, she would certainly earn her keep.

"Shucks, I end up dumpin' a lot of milk out to the hogs, anyhow," Mrs. Smith had told Molly to persuade her to let Rosie have the cat—and to accept more milk in the future. She knew the family could use the food and the children needed the milk. She planned to see that what she sent was more than sufficient to keep the cat happy. The children could drink the excess. She also sensed Molly was too proud to take anything, unless she felt she had, in some way, paid for it.

"Go ahead, you'll be doing me a favor taking an extra cat off my hands. She's always wanting attention and underfoot when I'm trying to do something. What she needs is a nice little girl to keep her occupied."

So, Mrs. Smith and Molly had struck a deal and Rosie got the cat.

"I'm going to call her Callie," Rosie told the group with pleasure as the cat pressed the top of its head against Rosie's open palm and purred contentedly.

Crazy Leg watched the cat with interest. As long as she was on Rosie's lap, he wouldn't dare make a move. He would have to wait for a time when Callie was on her own four feet.

Trace reached up and lifted Rosie, with Callie still clutched in her arms, down off Comet's bare back. Then he lifted Seth, swinging his light weight in the air carefully so as not to knock the lid off the pail and spill the milk. At last, he folded the fingers of both his hands together and formed a step for Molly to slip her foot into and swing down from the horse on her own. She carried a small flour sack with her as she dismounted.

"Thank you. I'll start dinner right away. I imagine you're both hungry."

She called after Seth, "Careful with that pail. Don't let the dog knock it out of your hands!"

Crazy Leg bounced up first at Seth, then at Callie in Rosie's arms.

"Yes, Ma."

"Get away, you dumb dog!" Rosie shrieked. "Ma, make Seth make his dog stop." She wrinkled her face up as she turned to Seth.

"Crazy Leg! Stop!" Molly shouted, instead.

Sufficiently scolded, Crazy Leg ran on ahead scattering chickens as he went.

That night, the biscuits and gravy were richer due to the added milk. Molly made plenty of biscuits to see them through breakfast and the noon meal the next day. What biscuits they didn't smother in gravy, they slathered in melting, oozing, finger-licking-good butter taken from a bowl inside the flour sack Molly brought home.

The children drank the milk by passing the pail back and forth between them. Rosie sat it aside when enough remained for Callie's evening and morning meals. Molly and Trace drank hot coffee sweetened with sugar and tanned with the heavy cream from the top of the milk.

"Ma, can I have some of that?" Seth pleaded.

Trace waited for Molly to nod that it was fine for him to fix Seth a cup.

"Yes. But please dilute it, Trace."

He poured a fourth of a cup of coffee and filled it to the top with water and the remaining cream to make it very weak. He scooped a couple of spoonfuls of sugar into the tepid liquid and handed it to the youngest boy.

As far as he could see, a kid shouldn't be hurt much by such a drink. Yet, had Molly not provided the recipe, he would have given him the liquid straight out of the pot with a little water added to cool it.

"Next time we bring milk home, I'll make you some Cambridge Tea," Molly promised. She had drunk the hot water dashed with milk and sweetened with sugar, herself, as a child. It had been a tradition, when her mother sat down at their hand-hewn kitchen table to partake of her own tea, to provide the special treat for Molly.

She reminded herself that it was usually girls, not boys, who had tea parties and wondered if Seth would enjoy the drink as much as she had.

The recollection of those times filtered through Molly's mind like a hummingbird approaching a blossom and then darting away.

She couldn't catch a hummingbird in her hand and she didn't want to dwell on memories that brought back the pain of losing her mother, no matter how sweet the reminiscences were.

Molly made plans for the next day as they finished their meal.

"If you think the two of you can keep the fire going tomorrow, I'll put on a pot of beans in the morning." She looked directly at Trace.

"We should be able to. I plan to get the sideboards up on the tower and work on the platform. Andy can't climb up there with his bum arms, but he can send supplies up to me with a rope and a pulley, once I get it attached."

"Good. I'll put them to soak tonight before we go to bed."

When supper was cleared away, Molly set about preparing the dry beans for several meals in advance. She sorted the pinto beans, picking out, and tossing aside, any rocks or bad beans. She washed and rinsed them. Finally, she added enough water to cover them a couple of inches deep to soak overnight.

The next morning, Andy hitched up the buckboard while Trace revived the fire.

Molly checked on the beans, rinsed them again, and added more water before attaching the pot's handle to the hook above the fire.

"Don't let it get too hot." She feared the beans would stick to the bottom of the kettle and burn. She didn't want dinner to go up in smoke. "And add water, if they need it."

"We'll check on them. I'm not much of a cook but I do believe I can keep beans from scorching," Trace said.

"Don't worry, Ma," Andy told her as he held the team steady. He and Trace had loaded the rough-cut metal blades into the back of the wagon the day before and Molly now put hers and the children's noon meal behind the seat of the buckboard. She secured the rifle beside her feet and prepared to hurry the horses on their way.

Rosie, still with Callie in her arms, reached to climb aboard.

"The cat can't come," Molly told her sternly.

Rosie turned with a pout on her lips and quickly deposited the cat on top of her bedroll.

"You leave her alone, like I said." Rosie shook her index finger in Crazy Leg's face.

Crazy Leg cocked his head sideways and stared back at her. He appeared as if he were wondering what was this animal he couldn't chase?

Seth scooted up beside Molly as Rosie returned.

"Seth! That's my spot. I was there before I had to put Callie down. Move!"

Seth sat in silence.

"Your dog better not bother my cat while we're gone. He does, and he's in big trouble."

Seth turned toward her, behind Molly's back, and stuck his tongue out in defiance.

"Maaaa! Make him move."

Rosie climbed on the seat and tugged at Seth's sleeve.

"Seth, move." Molly spoke briskly. The day was starting out badly. It always seemed when the children bickered in the morning, the day didn't get any better. Molly sighed. She just didn't feel like dealing with their petty arguments today. She cracked the reins across the team's back and started them toward the schoolhouse.

Seth and Rosie stopped fighting and hung on to the seat railing of the buckboard with both hands.

~ * ~

At the schoolhouse, Molly wrote the day's assignment on the chalkboard. Already, the weather was getting pleasant enough that they had quit building a fire in the little pot-bellied stove in the corner of the room. The children were having difficulty keeping their attention on their lessons. Maybe spring fever was why Rosie and Seth were fighting so much lately.

Rosie didn't understand why Andy could stay home and she and Seth had to go to school with Molly. Every time she broached the subject with Molly, Molly was unwilling to listen to her argument and certainly wouldn't entertain any discussion of it in front of the class. She didn't want all of her students rebelling.

As sorely as they needed to get their farm in shape, she needed the small salary she earned as schoolmarm just as badly in order to accomplish that dream. Rosie and Seth would just have to suffer along with her other students.

She, too, had a hard time keeping her mind on her teaching and would rather be back at the farm watching the windmill go up—watching Trace as he moved about hoisting things into place—seeing his muscles ripple in the sun when he got too warm and took off his shirt.

Her errant thoughts shocked her. What was wrong with her? She shouldn't be thinking of Trace like that. She raised her head up from the textbook at her desk. She looked around her classroom to see that all the students were doing their studies and none had caught her in her daydream.

At last, she gazed out the small window to where the sun shone across the wide-open valley. It was hard not to think of Trace in a romantic manner with him sleeping just inches above her at night. It was difficult to fall asleep at bedtime, no matter how tired she was, knowing he was up there—above her. She felt a tingling in her inner thighs, inside her skirt beneath her desk. *No. He is just helping out. Soon, he'll be on his way to live his own life—and we'll be better off for having known him. It wouldn't pay to get involved with a drifter.*

She tried to shoo the sweet thoughts that were buzzing like flies above a sticky dried-apple pie, away from her mind. But, just like the pestering insects, her musings persisted.

As she stared out the window, she imagined Trace placing the proper boards on the windmill structure. She imagined him precisely measuring them and making sure the uprights stood high enough to catch the wind that blew across the vast valley without trees to block its path. She tried to concentrate on the mechanics of the structure—not the man. The windmill didn't have to be very high. The twenty-five feet Trace had set it would be plenty. After all, there was nothing to stop the wind. And nothing to stop her from daydreaming.

She smiled to herself and looked away from the window, trying to concentrate on the job at hand and leave the hired man in her mind to do his work.

She reminded herself that she had to do her part by taking the pieces for the wheel to the blacksmith several buildings down the road.

A nagging notion crossed her mind. She had promised herself she would check with the sheriff the first chance she got, to see if Trace was a wanted man. Now, she wasn't sure if she cared to find out or not.

She felt a twinge of embarrassment at the idea of her possible betrayal. After all Trace had done for them, she would like to let her suspicions go. Her common sense refused to allow her to ignore the fact that she knew little about the man.

Why had he had run-ins with Snake and his gang before? Was he staying at her place to hide from something?

The day seemed to drag on until she was finally able to pick up her hand bell, a few minutes early, and announce the end of the school day. In her mind she justified the premature dismissal with the children's, and the teacher's, inattention to their work.

"Hurry and get into the wagon," she told Seth and Rosie as her other pupils scattered for home. She wanted to deposit the parts for the windmill as soon as she could. Trace would have the structure ready soon and she didn't want him to be waiting for the mechanical parts. She was determined that the construction wouldn't be held up on her account.

She reined the team up in front of the blacksmith's shop.

"You two stay here while I talk to Mr. Hughes. Don't touch the reins! You hear me?"

Rosie and Seth nodded in tandem.

The last thing she needed, right now, was a runaway team with two kids in the wagon. She also did not want to lose the parts for her windmill.

"Afternoon, Mrs. Kling," Mr. Hughes greeted her.

"Afternoon. I brought the pieces for the windmill."

"Are you ready for me to put it together so soon?"

"Yes, well, we've been working really hard to get the tower ready."

"Heard you had a hired hand out there. Also heard you had some trouble."

"Nothing we weren't able to handle," she assured him and avoided discussing Trace.

"Josh, you go retrieve them parts from the back of Mrs. Kling's wagon for me, will ya?"

Josh, the apprentice, nodded his agreement and moved to pick up Molly's treasured windmill blades from the bottom of the buckboard. She watched as he dropped them gently onto the dirt floor in a corner.

"When do you think you'll have the wheel ready?"

"I know you're in a hurry to get water flowing, Mrs. Kling. Guess I can set something else aside and work on that for you. It should be ready Friday, if we don't run into any problems or get overloaded with some emergency work."

"Thank you, Mr. Hughes. We've waited a long time for this. It would be nice to have plenty of water when summer hits and the days get hot." She daydreamed about the vegetable garden she hoped to raise to supplement their meager diet. She could plant some things soon, if she had sufficient water to irrigate.

She climbed back onto the seat of the buckboard and drove the team on down the dirt street. When she approached the General Store she pulled alongside the hitching rail and got down.

She tied the team to the rail and, again, instructed the children to stay put.

"Don't you even think of getting down from there." She didn't want to take them into the sheriff's office with her. She didn't want to risk the chance that they would, innocently, tell Trace where they had been—what they had seen. In fact, she hoped they would busy themselves looking at the things in the General Store's window and not notice which door she entered.

She moved past the General Store and walked down the wooden sidewalk behind the wagon until she came to the jail. There, she quickly moved inside and out of sight of Rosie and Seth.

"Afternoon, Sheriff."

The sheriff sat behind an oversized wooden desk with his feet resting on its top. At the sound of Molly's voice, he sat up straight, skidding the back legs of the chair across the floor in a screech, nearly tipping over as he tried to get up.

"Afternoon. What can I do for you?"

"I'm Molly Kling. We have a homestead outside town."

"I heard tell."

"I was wondering if I could look at your wanted posters?"

"O' course. Heard you had some trouble out at your place. You looking to identify some of those varmints?" He gave no excuse for not following up on the rumor and checking the Kling place after the raid.

"Yes," she lied to keep from telling him her real reason for wanting to look through the posters.

He reached into a drawer on the right side of the desk and hauled out a sheaf of worn, dirty sheets of paper. He slapped the stack onto the top of the desk and picked up his coffee cup to move to the pot perking on the stove nearby.

"You let me know if you recognize any of those fellas."

Molly picked up the stack of papers and walked to the window where the light would be better and where, she hoped, she could keep an eye on Rosie and Seth.

The children were occupying themselves with a vigorous discussion. At least, the reins were secure at the hitching rail and they couldn't cause too much trouble right where people were passing them by on their way to and from the General Store or Baker's Mercantile.

Molly moved each poster from the top to the bottom of the pile as she studied one sketch and description after another carefully. When she reached the first one she had looked at, again, she was relieved not to have found Trace's face or description in the pile.

"Are these all you have?"

"That's it. Didn't find who you were lookin' for, there?"

"No." She was glad Trace was not wanted in Torrance County.

"Thank you, Sheriff." She moved to leave the dusty, cigar-smoke-smelling sheriff's office.

"Let me know if I can be of any more help."

Outside, on the boardwalk, she saw that Seth and Rosie were in a full-fledged argument, now. Their voices were shrill and people along the street looked at them with curiosity. They began to fling their arms and legs in each other's direction.

Molly lifted her skirt front enough to allow her to hurry to settle the children down. It wouldn't do for the schoolmarm's kids to be raising a fuss in the middle of town. People would surely think she couldn't handle a school full of children if she couldn't manage her own.

As she approached the wagon, Seth caught his big toe on the trigger of the rifle. He looked down. Although there was normally no bullet in the chamber, it was still loaded from the night Snake and his bunch terrorized them.

The shot rang out before Molly reached the team. The horses reared and jerked their reins. In their fright, they nearly fell backward onto the children. Instead, the bouncing tumbled Seth and Rosie over the seat back and into the bed of the buckboard.

Rosie screamed. Seth's face drained white with fear.

"Whoa! Big Boy! Jake!" Molly tried to calm the team.

The horses jerked the reins hard enough to uproot the hitching rail and tore off down the street as fast as they could go. The wooden poles for the hitching rail slung from side to side across their chests, scaring the horses even more.

For an instant, Molly stood staring after them in disbelief.

"Someone, stop them! Please, someone do something!" A sense of helplessness overwhelmed her as she watched the children and the buckboard disappear around the corner.

Molly ran down the boardwalk following the horses. How she hoped no one was shot. Seth had looked so pale. Had the bullet hit him? Her heart pounded in her chest while she ran until her sides ached, trying to catch a glimpse of the runaway team and the frightened children.

She heard the horrified sounds of people screaming and horses clattering their trappings as they rushed to get out of the way of the racing team. The sheriff came up behind her, in the street, riding his horse. He soon out-distanced her as he pursued the team.

"Grab 'em, Josh!" she heard the sheriff shout as she came around the corner and could see the buckboard, again, churning up a cloud of dust as it sped toward the outer edge of town.

Mr. Hughes and Josh, having heard the oncoming commotion, stood in the roadway when the horses reached the blacksmith shop.

The team reared at the sight of humans ahead and disagreed on which way to turn to avoid running over them. Their indecision provided a momentary opportunity and, at the sheriff's shouted instruction, Josh jumped for Big Boy. He hung on with his arms wrapped around the horse's neck. He ran alongside. He soon threw his right leg up over the horse's back and began to tug on what strap of rein he could reach.

With Big Boy slowing, Jake did, too. At last, Josh had the animals down to a walk. He kept them at that pace until he turned them around the other direction. He slowly let them calm down before he pulled them to a complete halt to remove what remained of the hitching rail. The worn poles were firewood, now. Josh tossed them aside.

Molly ran up to the buckboard and lifted Rosie and Seth down.

"Are you all right?" She looked each over for bullet wounds and found nothing. The color was returning to Seth's face and tears began to pour down both his and Rosie's cheeks. "You scared me to death!"

"Are you goin' to whop me, Ma? Billy says he gets whopped when he's done somethin' bad." Seth's sobs were erratic now, and

Molly felt so sorry for the little boy she couldn't have given him a whipping, even if she had wanted to do so. She was just thankful they were both all right.

She shook her head and clutched them both to her sides.

"How can I thank you, Josh? That was a brave thing you did."

"It wasn't anything, Ma'am. I just happened to be where I could help. Glad to do it."

"Mr. Hughes, can we leave the horses here while we walk back to the General Store and see what damage there is?" God, she hoped no one was hurt. She didn't want to frighten the children further with her fears.

The sheriff climbed down off his horse and walked beside Molly, leading the animal behind them.

"I'm sure sorry about this, Sheriff. Hope nobody was hurt."

"Everyone on the street managed to get out of the way of the horses. Had a little snarl of buggies and riders there for a while, though. You know, runaways aren't that unusual around here."

"Maybe I ought to look into getting some different horses."

"Don't think it would have made a bit of difference, Mrs. Kling. I think any team would have reacted if a rifle went off right behind their tails."

When they reached the General Store discussions were taking place among the storeowner, in a long white apron, and people on the sidewalk out front.

The storekeeper was inspecting the barrels of goods outside the store.

"The bullet went clean through that barrel of crackers, right through the wall, and into a bale of sheep's wool waiting to be shipped to Albuquerque. If that farmer hadn't already sheared the sheep, that bullet would have sheared it for him," the storekeeper exaggerated in awe to the sheriff.

"Anybody hurt, Harold?"

"Nah. Not unless you count people's nerves, thinkin' they were in the middle of a gun battle. We ain't had one of those around here for a long time."

"Ma," Seth tugged at Molly's skirt. "Ma, that's what Rosie and I were arguing about. She said she saw one of those men, she told me about, that was at our place the other night. I said she was lyin'."

"I told him, he wouldn't know if I did or not 'cause he slept right through all the trouble. Then he started wiggling around on the seat and caught his big toe in the rifle."

So that was what started all this. Molly shook her head. The cracker barrel reminded her of the pail Andy had hit at home.

"I'll gladly pay for the damage, sir," Molly told the storekeeper reluctantly. She knew she owed him something, but she had little to offer.

"Ah, no one was hurt. My wife was startled, but she'll get over it. The wool shouldn't be damaged too badly and I'll plug the wall and the cracker barrel. I'm just glad your kids weren't injured."

"I promise I'll never leave them alone in the wagon again." Molly gave a stern look to Rosie and Seth. "Thank you. Thank you so much. You're very kind." She would see that she bought all her supplies there in the future, unless the storekeeper didn't have what she needed. Then, she'd have to go on to Baker's Mercantile. She was sure the story would reach Mr. Baker, too. So, she'd have to keep her word and take the children in with her, wherever she went.

"Well, Harold, looks like you got things under control here, then. I'll get back over to my office."

"Ain't had this much excitement in town in a long time," Molly heard someone say as she and Seth and Rosie turned to go back to the blacksmith's shop.

On the way, Molly asked, "Which one of those men did you see Rosie?"

"She lied, Ma," Seth broke in.

"Seth!"

"No, Ma, I didn't lie. It was the one that gave me his food, Ma."

"Are you sure, Rosie?"

"Sure as can be. He even winked at me as he walked by. I didn't say nothing 'cause I knew who he was and I was afraid they'd hurt us. But it was him, sure as anything."

Molly was worried. If Rosie had seen the younger man, then Snake was surely somewhere close by—along with all his other henchmen. They would have to be watchful going home.

When she reached the buckboard, the kids scrambled onto the seat and sat like statuary. Molly removed the rifle and checked the breach, releasing the spent bullet casing. She did not reload it, for fear something might happen to set it off again, but she did take two bullets from a heavy canvas bag she kept tied tight to the wagon bench and slip them into the pocket of her skirt.

She was prepared in case Snake raised his ugly head along the road home.

Eight

The days and nights came and went. Days, the windmill tower grew as if by magic while Molly and the younger children were away. Nights, Molly was more and more keenly aware of Trace's nearness.

Trace, pleased with his accomplishments, was content and found Molly in his mind both day and night. Although he told himself he didn't need the complications of a woman in his life, especially one with three kids, his dreams at night completed what thoughts his daydreams didn't. He awoke more than one night with an ache in his groin, thinking about the woman asleep just a few feet away.

At last, it was Friday—the day Mr. Hughes had promised to have the pieces for the windmill ready. Trace and Andy would have the structure complete today. They would be ready to set the wheel and tail shaft Saturday. Everyone could be home to see the wheel turn free in the wind high atop its perch.

The weather had remained unusually warm for early spring and the day dawned bright and clear. The weather promised to be unseasonably hot; the night had held some of its warmth over, and the day's temperature started high.

Everyone was eager to get on with the day, so the wheel could be brought home for Saturday's installation. Breakfast was cold biscuits without a campfire. They drank the leftover lukewarm coffee from the night before.

Molly had neglected to tell Trace about their experience in town on Tuesday. She didn't want to concern him with her troubles when he had the windmill to finish. As she mulled the incident over in her mind, she debated if or when she should tell him.

"Figure I'll build a small well house at the bottom to keep the food cool," Trace said, breaking her stream of thought.

How smart of him to think of that! Molly had been concerned about getting the water flowing. She hadn't considered the possibility of an insulated structure, over the well, to serve another purpose.

"That is a wonderful idea, Trace. We certainly could use a way to keep the perishable goods longer. The Smith's have their whole tower enclosed as a well house. Not that I'd want that," she hurried to add for fear that too much of her precious lumber might be used for that instead of the house for which she longed.

With Rosie playing with Callie and Seth eating in his bedroll while Andy fetched the team, it seemed like a good time to tell Trace about the runaway team, so Molly filled him in.

When she finished, Trace sipped the last of his coffee and put the cup down, considering what Molly had told him.

"Why didn't Rosie 'see' the accident coming?"

"I don't know. She hasn't had any more of those visions the past few days that I know of. When she did before, it was about someone else, not herself. Anyway, thank goodness, it all worked out and no one was injured."

"I wondered why Seth has been so quiet lately. He must be trying to stay out of trouble with you."

"I only told you because we're going to town to get the parts today. Since Rosie swears she saw the man Snake called Tommy, I'm a little concerned that we might run into that gang again. Rosie insisted she saw him and that he winked at her. Anyway, no one bothered us on the way home." Molly finished her story, relieved that she had not seen the rest of the outlaws.

"Tom. That's what the fellow said when Snake called him Tommy," Trace told her, concern edging his voice. "You be careful."

"I will."

"Something's broke a hole in the barbed wire at the back property line. I noticed it when Andy and I went out to check one of his traps.

We walked the back line while we were there, checking to see there weren't any more breaks in the fence."

Like any good rancher, Molly thought.

"Since we didn't have any tools with us, I figure we'll walk out there later today and fix it if the neighbor hasn't already taken care of it."

Molly nodded at the talk of necessary, but mundane, work required to keep a place up. She'd much rather Trace and Andy spent their time on the windmill, but she knew other tasks were important, too.

"Don't worry," Trace told her as if reading her mind. "We'll be ready to set the wheel tomorrow. The pipe's already in and ready to be hooked up. You'll have your water no later than Sunday, I promise." Trace smiled, amused by her eagerness.

Andy returned with the team. Seth crawled out from under the wagon with Crazy Leg. Rosie sat on the buckboard seat, with Callie on her lap, while Andy hitched up the team.

Crazy Leg eyed the cat with curiosity.

"Put the cat down. I shouldn't have to tell you that every time, Rosie," Molly said as Seth climbed onto the seat next to Rosie.

"Don't take my place," Rosie ordered Seth. She claimed the spot next to Molly as her own. That put her in the center where she felt more secure behind Molly's elbow when she pulled the reins or snapped them smartly on the horses' backs. Rosie could crowd close to Molly's side and, after the wagon crash, whether it protected her or not, she felt safer. After her recent experiences, the buckboard was not her friend.

"No fighting today. Did you get the lunch pail?"

"It's behind the seat," Rosie answered.

Molly glanced back. The pail sat in the center of a round of rope Trace had put on the deck to use to tie the wheel in.

Crazy Leg stood next to Andy and Trace as Andy handed Molly the reins.

"Like I said, be careful." Trace knew better than Molly how mean and dangerous Snake and his bunch were. If they hadn't shown themselves on Molly's way home the other night, it was probably because they were up to something more devious than chasing or challenging a woman and a couple of kids. That didn't mean they wouldn't try to make their move tonight. To keep from worrying Molly further, he didn't voice his concerns.

On the ride in to the schoolhouse, Molly noticed the wind was picking up.

By the time everyone went outside for morning recess, a warm breeze was blowing steadily.

Molly was eager to end the day and get to the blacksmith's shop.

At last, the school day was over and Molly rang the final bell, letting the children rush from the stifling atmosphere of the small building into the freedom of the schoolyard as they left for home.

She brought the wagon around and picked up Rosie and Seth and headed for the blacksmith's shop with anticipation churning in her stomach.

"Afternoon, Mr. Hughes." Molly jumped from the buckboard onto the ground.

"You're right early, Mrs. Kling."

"Ma says first thing she's going to do when the water flows is take a bath with her clothes on," Rosie chatted at the burly man.

"Rosie!" Molly felt her face flush.

"Can't say as how's I blame you, Ma'am. I don't take to pulling buckets of water and carrying them myself."

"We brought some rope—" Molly hoped he wouldn't dash her excitement by telling her the wheel wasn't done.

"Good. We got her finished. But, I think it's going to be a mite wide for your buckboard." He studied the size of the wagon box.

"Josh, you want to bring Mrs. Kling's parts out here?"

Josh soon arrived with the tail shaft and placed it against the sideboard.

When he rolled the wheel out, Molly could see it was going to take the two of them to lift it into the back of the wagon.

Josh rolled it up alongside the tailgate. It stood on the ground at the bottom and reached high above the end of the buckboard.

"Hold 'er there a minute," Mr. Hughes instructed.

They heaved the wheel carefully into the back of the wagon.

The wheel looked like an oversized wagon wheel with a heavy rim on the outside encasing the thin tin blades along its inside edge. Each vane had three inches of lip overhanging the steel rim and Mr. Hughes had curved them to bite the wind. He planned on it turning even when very little breeze blew across the flat countryside. The wheel was so large it hung over the side of the buckboard two feet. Mr. Hughes wrapped the rope around the hub and tied it tightly to each corner of the buckboard.

"There. The wheel ain't going nowhere, now." He stood back and surveyed his work.

"Ma, he said ain't," Rosie whispered to Molly.

"Shush."

Molly paid the man and slowly drove the team away from town.

There was a smile on her face and she burst into song once they were on the road alone. The children looked at her in surprise, but joined in quickly. Today was a most joyous day. Molly sang praises to everyone, and everything she could remember, that had been good to her and the children. Despite their hardships, she was glad they had come to New Mexico to make their home.

As they rode along, Rosie gradually became quieter until she sat, silent, while Molly and Seth sang on either side of her. Molly bumped her with her elbow to encourage her to join back in.

But something was bothering the girl and Molly didn't know what it was.

Rosie felt uneasy, as if someone was watching them—or following them. Rosie glanced worriedly behind them.

She saw nothing.

"What is it?"

"I—I don't know. Just, I feel kind of—kind of strange."

"We're not far from home," Molly turned and smiled at the girl, trying to ease her concerns. Up ahead, their front property line came into view. They would soon see the windmill derrick off to their left.

Despite her effort to maintain her joyous attitude, Molly felt Rosie's apprehension creeping in on her own good mood.

"It's Callie, Ma. I know—it's Callie."

She turned to Seth. "If that dumb dog of yours has hurt my cat, you're going to get it!"

"I'm sure Callie's fine. She can run from Crazy Leg, if he did take a notion to go after her. Why—why she could climb up the windmill tower and lay on one of the boards holding it together or on the platform Trace built at the top. There's no way Crazy Leg could get her there."

Molly began straining her eyes, looking for trouble—looking for Callie. She was eager to know what Rosie sensed was wrong. She couldn't see Trace or Andy anywhere. *Was one of them in trouble?*

They were going to fix the fence sometime today. Perhaps they got a late start and hadn't returned from the back line.

Rosie screamed.

Molly shot a look in Rosie's direction, then followed the girl's gaze to the windmill tower.

There, hanging from a length of rope slung up over an untrimmed horizontal timber, was Callie.

Rosie screamed again. "Is she dead?"

Molly snapped the reins on the horses' backs. She forgot, for the moment, about the load behind her. Luckily, Mr. Hughes' knots held and the wheel stayed on as the wagon lurched across the uneven terrain.

Trace and Andy heard Rosie's scream as they were walking back from repairing the fence. They both burst into a run. Crazy Leg raced ahead of them.

Callie hung, upside down, tied by her hind legs, swinging from the top of the tower. She yowled in anger and irritation. No matter how hard she swiveled her body, she was unable to swing herself close enough to the platform to sink her claws into the boards and pull herself free.

Molly tugged on the reins, pulling the team to a halt in front of the well.

What had gone on here? Who would do such a thing?

Rosie wailed as the three of them rushed off the buckboard and Molly contemplated what to do.

"Hush, Rosie. She's alive. Just—uncomfortable. We'll get her down—some way." Molly studied the distance up the tower and shuddered. Heights didn't appeal to her. Could she overcome her fear and climb the sideboards to release Callie?

If this was somebody's idea of a joke, it was cruel. She only hoped she could get the cat loose before she injured herself, if she hadn't already.

Trace and Andy came huffing up alongside the rest of the family. They had seen the cat as they ran.

Trace gasped to catch his breath. Andy looked at Rosie, then up at Callie. He moved toward the tower and put his left hand on the next horizontal board. Then, he remembered his right shoulder and stopped to remove the sling.

"No," Trace said. "I'll do it." He muttered to himself. It was probably all his fault anyway. Obviously, this was a warning from Snake. He visualized the outlaw smirking with pleasure at his prank. If he hadn't stayed to help Molly and the kids, maybe Snake wouldn't be bothering them. But, now that they had run Snake off, he was probably lying in wait to catch Trace off by himself—or get to Molly and the kids when he wasn't around them. They would have to be even more vigilant.

Trace pulled himself up from one board to the next until he reached the platform. He knelt there and reached far out over the timber to the rope. He doubted Snake, or any of his men, had climbed the tower. He and Andy had only been gone a short time. One of them, probably, had tossed the rope up and over the stub of timber while they were off guard. They must have tied the cat to one end and hoisted her into the air from below.

How they had managed to wrap the end of the rope beyond his reach was a puzzle he didn't care to solve. It was a mean thing to do to the cat—and the child. But then, he was sure Snake knew he could get to him by hurting one of them. Right now, all he wanted to do was get the cat down and calm Rosie.

Trace released Callie from the rope, holding her away from his body by the scruff of her neck. Callie, stilled by his grasp, worked her paws feebly in midair in search of something solid in which to cling.

He dropped the rope to the ground and tried to soothe her before climbing back down. He needed to figure out some way of doing it without getting scratched.

At last, he removed his shirt and tied Callie inside it. He tied the sleeves together to slip the crook of his arm through and have his hands free while he worked his way back down to safety for both of them.

"I think she's just scared." Trace handed the bundle to Rosie. "Take care, or she'll shoot out of there like a bullet when you untie her."

"Thank you, Trace." The experience had shaken Rosie to the core. She was frightened for Callie and, in some way she didn't understand, for herself.

Trace turned to Molly as Rosie and Seth headed back to their pile of personal belongings where Rosie could unwrap Callie in familiar surroundings.

Andy stood nearby.

Molly looked at Trace. "How could that happen?"

Trace shook his head. "Andy and I were out at the back line, repairing that fence I told you about. Crazy Leg was with us. Snake, or one of his men, must have come by and seen an opportunity to get into some mischief. I'm sure it must have been a warning to me. He'd like nothing better than for me to ride on and leave you and the kids open to his thievery or whatever else he has in mind."

He didn't tell Molly, but he worried that next time it might be one of them Snake went after. Trace sensed the outlaw wouldn't give up until the two of them finally faced each other and only one of them walked away—leaving the other one dead. He didn't need to worry Molly more with that, either.

Trace moved to the back of the buckboard and studied the wheel.

"Looks mighty good," he said, trying to change the subject.

"Trace! This was no innocent prank." Molly spoke in frustration as she followed him.

"I know. But, if it wasn't a warning, he'd have hung Callie by the neck—not the legs. I don't think he meant to kill her. He probably wanted to scare us—a little."

"Well, he did that!"

"We'll have to make sure someone is in camp with a gun at all times. We can't give him a chance to get in here again. We'll have to be on guard." He looked toward where Rosie sat petting the cat and talking soothingly to it. Seth had taken Crazy Leg over near the corral to avoid making Callie any more nervous.

Everything appeared peaceful. Even Comet was coming in from the pasture and heading toward the water trough for a drink.

"We best get this unloaded so we can get the buckboard set up for the night. Don't worry, we'll be more careful in the future."

Molly gave Trace an uncertain look. But she stood back out of the way while he and Andy untied the big wheel. They rolled it carefully over alongside the pile of lumber and settled it at an angle against the wood. Trace picked up the tail shaft and laid it aside. Then, he took the rope and coiled it into a neat roll.

Molly walked over to Rosie. All the joy was gone from her day and she no longer sang. She left the team for Andy to bring around to the corral. She uncovered the supplies, wondering what she might find there—or what might be missing.

Everything seemed in order. Whoever had hung Callie from the windmill frame must not have had time to do any more damage for fear Andy and Trace would return. She suspected that if it was one of Snake's men, the coward wouldn't confront them alone. It took the whole gang to have enough gumption to face someone.

"How's Callie?" Molly asked as she reached down to pet the cat's soft fur.

The cat purred in Rosie's lap.

"She seems all right." Rosie looked up with tears in her eyes. "Who would do such a thing, Ma? Who would hurt a defenseless kitten?"

"I don't know, Rosie, but I want you to promise me you will be very careful, no matter where you are. All right?"

"I promise."

"Keep an eye out for Seth, too."

"I will."

Molly set about figuring out what to fix to go with the beans for their evening meal while Trace and Andy took care of the horses.

She checked the biscuits for mold and smelled the beans to see that they hadn't soured. Trying to distract herself from the horror of the day, she thought about the well house Trace had promised. It would make her work easier. It would keep the perishable food safer, longer.

Whenever memories of their frightening homecoming crossed her mind, she reminded herself of the better things that were happening, like the windmill and the well house. She crowded the bad images away as best she could.

She had settled into a feeling of security with Trace about the place. She had let her guard down—something she reminded herself never to do again. Complacency had no place in their lives right now.

She looked toward the horizon and saw the sun setting in the west.

Tomorrow, they would set the wheel for the windmill. The next day promised to be warm as stillness clung heavy in the evening air. It was one of those calm evenings that had a special feel about it—like you could breathe comfort from the atmosphere's very essence.

It should have given her peace of mind, but it didn't. Instead, the threat of Snake's gang hung like a weight in her heart and she tried not to show her fear.

Somehow, she knew, the danger was not over. For some reason, Snake was out to get Trace by any means he could—even if it meant hurting others around him—and she didn't know why.

Nine

Saturday dawned bright and clear.

Rosie stirred, but stayed in her bedroll. Seth snuggled closer to Crazy Leg. The adults, and Andy, were eager to start the day and to finish the windmill.

Molly filled the coffee pot and set it to brew. Fresh coffee would spur them on their way.

When the meal was ready, they wasted little time eating. Trace finished his coffee as he walked toward the well. He drained the last drop of liquid from the enamel cup as he stood surveying the job ahead.

Trace directed Andy as they worked, preparing the parts to be hoisted to the platform at the top of the derrick. Trace used the pulley that had pulled the boards for the platform up to lift the parts to the top.

Once the younger children arose and ate breakfast, Molly kept them, and their excited pets, out from underfoot while Trace and Andy moved about below the tower.

She realized now that Trace had not trimmed the overhanging board on the windmill, where they had found Callie hanging, for a reason. He was using it to help guide the heavy parts in place.

Andy stood below the tower, carefully pulling the rope while Trace, standing on the platform, guided the tail shaft. Trace tied off the rope and pulled the shaft cautiously around to the other side of the windmill's platform. He lifted it into position and set it in its brackets.

It took a few minutes for him to tighten the bolts that would hold the gear head and shaft in position for the next important piece.

Finally, he dropped the rope back down to Andy, who tied it to a harness Trace had fashioned on the wheel to keep it moving in an upright position. If it swung and dropped forward in transit, it could cause him to fall from his lofty perch—or the wheel could careen out of control and injure Andy.

He hoped to avoid either incident, but the risks were real.

Molly stood by the buckboard with an arm over each of the children's shoulders to keep them firmly in check. She watched with interest and awe.

It seemed to take forever for the wheel to slide up the 25-foot-high beams. When it reached the platform, Trace tied off the rope. He twisted the other end in his gloved hands as he tugged with all his might to move the wheel into position. This piece he wanted, because of its size, to swing directly into place and attach to the gear head before he released the rope. Once it slid onto the shaft jutting from the headgear, Trace tightened each bolt. When he finished, he removed the rope and dropped it back down to Andy. Trace attached a long shaft to the wheel that was hooked to a brake below it. He could slow or stop the wheel from the ground with the mechanism. For now, he locked the brake so the wheel couldn't turn in the wind until he was ready to pronounce it finished and release it with ceremony.

He turned and flexed his muscles like a circus strong man in the direction of Molly and the children.

Rosie giggled at his antics. Seeing the wheel in its rightful place, at last, made Molly happy. Seeing Trace so blatantly proud and lighthearted excited her, too. Molly grinned broadly. She released her grip on Rosie and Seth and waved at Trace.

Trace moved behind the wheel and attached the tail vane to its horizontal shaft. This would act like a rudder in the wind, steering the wheel to take advantage of the best breeze.

At last, Trace trimmed the odd board and let it fall. Any future work on the windmill could be accomplished from the platform. He climbed, cautiously, back down the tower.

It seemed to Molly that the day was passing fast and she was beginning to think they would not see the windmill wheel turn until the next day. It was afternoon and the sun was angling toward the west. The weather had gotten hotter and, standing near the buckboard without shade, Molly was uncomfortably warm.

Beneath the tower of the windmill, the bracing and uprights created some shade for Andy and Trace to work. One of the first things she was going to do, now that they would have plenty of running water, was plant some shade trees. She would get some fast-growing poplar starts from Mrs. Smith. She would create a shaded area, perhaps around the house site. She didn't want to plant anything that would grow big enough to slow the wind so necessary to operate the windmill.

Molly scanned the open land all around her. The windmill was, certainly, the tallest, most impressive structure she could see. There were no trees within miles—nothing to stop the air from circulating, blowing as a breeze in summer and a blast in winter.

Finally, Trace waved his arm in the air, motioning for the rest of the family to join him and Andy.

With everything ready, he was eager to demonstrate the wonders of wind power for pumping water.

Rosie dropped Callie to the ground so she could stay behind, if she chose. Seth and Crazy Leg burst full speed ahead. Rosie raced to catch up. Molly ran behind them trying to keep up with her kids.

When they reached him, Trace described each mechanical piece to them and warned the children to keep their distance.

"Not only can the mechanism be dangerous, but, until I get the well house built around the base of the well, and the hole encased, I don't want anything falling in—especially a youngster or one of their pets."

"Yes. Yes," they all agreed.

The mechanics were boring to Molly. She wanted to have it work, not know how or why. She just wanted Trace to turn it on. She felt like a child that wanted to jump up and down and beg for the promised treat. She restrained herself.

"Be patient," she told the children, but the advice was as much for her as it was for them.

"But, how's the water going to get here?" Rosie asked.

Impatiently, Molly attempted to stop the child's inquisitiveness, "Rosie—" Molly began.

Trace interrupted. "Wait," he said as he looked about the base of the water trough and the legs of the windmill tower. Then, he reached down with one free hand and pulled a dry reed out by its roots and broke the stalk off.

"Suck on this. Feel the air?"

Rosie nodded as she sucked on the tube and then blew her breath back through it and felt the air against her open palm.

"If you put the end in the water trough and sucked, you'd get water."

Rosie rushed to the tank to try.

"It's the same thing." Trace pointed to the pipe descending into the well. "The wind will cause the wheel to turn and the suction will bring the water up, much like you did."

Rosie walked back to join Molly and Seth while they watched to see this miracle occur.

"Are you ready, Andy?" Trace placed his hand on a long metal shaft with a lever attached.

Andy nodded.

"Everybody stand back a bit."

All of them, except Trace, backed up toward the water trough waiting for the wheel to turn and pump the water into the container.

Trace released the brake and stepped out from beneath the tower to watch the wheel as it began to turn. All eyes were skyward as the squeaks and grinding noises held their attention.

"It has to work the grease into the gears before it smoothes out," Trace assured them.

Gradually, the wheel turned. Slowly at first, then faster. The tail shaft adjusted itself, so it shifted the wheel into the wind, as it should. The blades sliced the air and the wheel picked up speed. At last, the wheel ran smoothly and quietly.

"Listen to that, Molly!" Trace said proudly.

"What?"

"The quiet whir. That's what lots and lots of grease does."

"But where's the water?" Rosie asked.

"Patience, dear Rosie. Patience," Trace said with an air of drama.

Suddenly, water gushed from the pipe where Trace had tied it, temporarily, eight feet up in the air. It squirted everyone including a surprised Crazy Leg, who yelped with shock and ran for drier places.

Molly yelled.

Rosie shrieked.

Seth leaped into the air and stomped his bare feet in the forming mud.

Chickens squawked and ran to peck at the new puddles created where the water splattered.

Andy slipped in the mud and sat down hard on the ground, laughing. Trace took Molly in his arms and waltzed her around the water trough, her hair and clothes dripping wet. She loved it. Never in her life had something been so important to her as her family having water—plenty of water.

Trace was soaked through now, too. But neither he, nor Molly, wanted to stop this happy dance.

"If Indians do a rain dance, this must be our well dance." Molly laughed. "If anyone sees us, they'll think we're crazy."

She looked up at Trace with gratitude.

He looked down at her and saw the happiness and the fun and her soft lips saying "Thank you" and he kissed her. It was a quick kiss. He wanted to kiss her long and hard and as wantonly as any man could, but he restrained himself because of the youngsters nearby.

She kissed him back with abandon. She was momentarily oblivious to the children, and anything else in the world except Trace's mouth on hers.

When he pulled away with a slight look of embarrassment she understood and brushed her hair from her face.

Out of breath, and soaked to the skin, Trace led Molly to a spot in the sun and let her sit down.

The children were all staring at them and she glanced around uncomfortably. Then she held her head high and relished the moment that had been, it seemed to her, a long time in coming.

Molly looked up at the metal vanes slicing through the air—gray wings against a deep, deep blue sky. It was beautiful. It was wondrous. It was a miracle.

Trace went to the well and reset the brake to stop the windmill from turning while he adjusted the pipe so the water would run into its proper place at the trough. He then released it again and the water flowed like magic.

"No more dragging a bucket up the well," Andy said with relief. Building the windmill had been hard work, but the payoff would be worth it. He picked up the bucket and set it under the pipe. He watched it fill. Still shocked at Molly and Trace's kiss, he headed for the buckboard with the water. The chore gave him an excuse to get away and think about what had happened between the two adults in his life. Their actions confused him and, although he was entering puberty, he didn't think much about girls yet.

Crazy Leg raced up to Andy with Seth right behind him.

"Andy," Seth asked, "does this mean Ma and Trace'll be getting married?"

"Nah," Andy hoped it didn't mean Trace wouldn't have time in his life for him, now. He'd seen it happen with the older boys in town. They'd be pals, then one of them would get a girlfriend and she was all they could think about, talk about, and want to be with anymore. He set the pail of water on the tailgate of the buckboard and stared off toward the pasture. He sure hoped that didn't happen with Trace. He untied his sling and removed it. He winced in pain when his shoulder tried to support his right arm. If it hurt bad enough, maybe it would take his mind off what had happened.

Rosie seemed to pay no never mind to Trace and Molly's kiss. She came up behind the boys and retrieved Callie from where she lay stretched out in the sun on the seat of the buckboard. The girl snuggled her face into the cat's fur and smelled the warmth it had soaked from the sun.

In the distance, Andy could see the horses coming in from the pasture. At least he wouldn't have to drag the pail up and down to fill the trough tonight. By the time the horses reached it, the trough would be overflowing with water and Trace would probably set the brake on the windmill to cut its flow until the next time it was needed.

That night, at supper, everyone was dry and everyone, except Andy, was happy. The discussion around the campfire turned to the construction of the house. With the windmill up and running, Molly was beginning to believe in the possibility of building the house. It would feel so good to be sleeping in a real house instead of on the bare earth beneath the buckboard—so good to be cooking in an honest-to-goodness kitchen on a real stove and eating at a real table with four legs and chairs to sit in.

Trace assured her that before summer was out, she would have her four-walled two-story house with the bottom floor partitioned for a kitchen and parlor and the upstairs divided into three bedrooms.

He would make it happen, if it were at all within his power.

Molly smiled at him across the campfire as the flames danced light across his strong features. She still felt the warmth of his kiss.

For Molly, it seemed hard to believe that he had really kissed her earlier this afternoon. *Was it all a dream?* The water was real—the refreshing shower in the midst of the hot afternoon sun was real, and the kiss had been real, too. It had not been one of her many dreams that woke her part way through the night. Trace had kissed her. Had he done it because he had feelings for her, or simply because he was so excited about bringing the water in? Self-doubt filled her. She saw herself as plain and, while not ugly, not pretty, either. She had felt fortunate when her husband had courted her. But then, the man was looking for a mother for his children having lost his wife the year before to an unknown illness.

Molly had always felt that, while there was affection between them, the spark of excitement wasn't there. The marriage was more for convenience than romance, and she had so craved the thrill of being truly loved. At this stage in her life she hungered for the spark of desire.

Andy completed his chores and went to put the bedrolls under the buckboard. They had finished the windmill a day ahead of plans. There were no rocks brought down from the mountain to start the foundation of the house they talked about, and he wondered what tomorrow would bring.

He felt his shoulder gingerly with the fingers on his left hand. It was still tender. He tucked his right thumb into the waist of his pants, providing some support for the arm. He supposed that perhaps he had removed the sling a bit too early, but he was frustrated, not only by the possibility of losing Trace's attention, but also because he was tired of waiting for the shoulder to heal. He decided, even if he slept without the support of the sling, the shoulder might feel better in the morning. If it didn't, he guessed he'd have to ask Molly to replace it for him.

Rosie and Seth went to bed shortly after Andy turned in. Trace and Molly stayed by the fire, discussing house plans until late into the evening. With the next day being Sunday, there was no rush to go to sleep.

Andy heard their voices talking quietly until he could no longer keep sleep at bay.

When he awoke the next morning, the plans were set. He and Trace would go to the mountain on Monday. Molly and the youngsters would ride Comet to school. He and Trace would load slabs of shale until they felt the wagon could hold no more.

Plans for the foundation were well underway and Molly moved about with a lively step as she made breakfast.

"If you don't mind, I'll take the rifle with me. Maybe we can get some venison while we're up there," Trace said.

"Venison would be a welcome change."

"I'm worried about leaving the camp unprotected, though."

"I know," Molly agreed. "But what can we do? The kids and I have to go to school and you'll need Andy to help you on the mountain. Maybe, just this once, we can take a chance. I'll let Rosie take Callie with her to school. Once won't hurt." Molly hated breaking the rule she had set with Rosie about leaving the cat at home.

She would hate it even worse if something happened to Callie while they were gone.

"What about the dog?" Trace asked.

"I doubt very much anyone would mess with Crazy Leg. He'd probably run anyway if someone tried to get hold of him."

Trace didn't want to mention the possibility of someone shooting him.

"I know it's a risk. But we've left him here alone before. He's supposed to guard the place," Molly said.

"If you're sure you want to chance it, I'll give you the six-gun to carry with you." Trace didn't want her going anywhere unarmed.

Sunday became a day of celebration and the homesteaders took a break from the heavy-duty work. Except for the normal chores to see that the animals were cared for and meals were fixed, most of the day was spent relaxing.

Monday was uneventful for Molly and her pupils. She and the youngsters rode Comet home bareback. A saddle would have been more comfortable for her. She told herself it was just as well they didn't have one. The three of them wouldn't fit on the seat anyway, and putting Seth in front of the saddle and Rosie behind it would have been too uncomfortable for a long ride.

Molly had a way of reasoning a disadvantage into an advantage. It was a good thing because it seemed many came her way. She had been lucky to get the job teaching school when they first arrived. The income had kept them going. She counted her blessings.

She was blessed that Trace had come into their lives. She thought about his trip to the mountain.

Today, the rocks she had so desperately tried to keep Trace from stealing would be coming home with the man she had, at first, distrusted. Life was ironic.

Molly hurried Comet home in anticipation.

Trace and Andy were not there yet. She set about doing her chores and getting the evening meal started.

She was edgy at being alone on the property with only the innocent youngsters by her side. She felt safer when Andy and Trace were there.

As the sun set and day and night began to seam together, she worried that Trace had not gotten the buckboard off the mountain in time to get home tonight. Would she have to spend the darkened hours on her own?

She fed the children and half-heartedly ate her own meal. After dark, she jumped at every pop of the fire, or snap of a twig she heard. If the chickens stirred in their coop, she was on her feet and reaching for the pistol. A hoot owl that had taken up residence under the rim of the chicken coop roof, called out and she jumped in fear.

She told herself that she had spent many nights alone with the kids, but that didn't ease her tension. That was before Snake had raided them. She shook the memory away. If they weren't back by the time the fire died down, she'd go to bed. It was foolish to wait up when she had school to teach tomorrow. She knew she would get little rest until Trace and Andy came home.

At last, she heard a team coming in, heard the buckboard creaking under its heavy load. It had to be Trace and Andy. Still, she listened intently until the team came into view near the fire.

Molly rushed to Trace's side.

"Thank goodness, it's you. I was getting concerned."

"It took us longer than we realized. Then, on the way off the hill Andy spotted a deer. It isn't very big, but it should be enough meat to hold us for a while. Leastwise, it'll be a change of taste."

"Tomorrow night, we'll have some nice venison steak to fry. And guess who we found up there?" Trace motioned with his thumb toward the back of the buckboard where the shadows concealed his find.

"Who?"

"My horse." Trace was glad to have the cantankerous animal back. He had tied him to the back of the buckboard and led him home, rather than ride him. He was a handful for Trace to handle before he went wild. Now, there had been no way he would put Andy on him with his sore arm and he had to drive the team for the same reason. But Trace was happy to have retrieved him.

"Of course, he had the saddle half tore off of him. My rifle was still in the scabbard, but the leather's going to take some repairing to be usable again. Danged horse! I took the saddle off and tossed it into the back with the rest of the stuff."

"I'm surprised he survived, what with the cougar and coyote up there. I wouldn't want to wander around there at night." Molly said.

"My saddle bags were still there. Guess nobody saw him, or he wouldn't let anyone get close enough to take anything off. As it was, I had to rope him with the rope I took to tie the cargo down. Had to tie him to a tree for a while. That helped make us late, too. But, I got my gear off him. Now, maybe I'll have a change of clothes." He was tired of having to wear the same dirty outfit. Or having to strip during the day and scrub his one shirt and pants, then hope they dried before Molly got home at night. More than once he'd had to rush to put damp clothes on when he heard the horses coming.

Andy said nothing. The jarring of the buckboard had tired him out. His arm, back in its sling, had taken offense at the jolting of the wagon. He was glad he had asked Molly to retie the sling this morning. He was sure he would be near tears with pain in his shoulder, if he hadn't. Perhaps he hadn't been so smart to take it off. Trying to get Molly and Trace's attention with his injury had backfired and the pain was his alone to bear. Now, all he wanted was some rest.

Andy steadied himself with his left hand to drop from the wagon.

Trace watched the boy land on the ground. It was obvious he was hurting. He saw Molly look at Andy with concern.

"It's been a long day for him," Trace told Molly. "Andy, you best get in your bedroll and get some sleep. I'll unhitch the team and put away the horses."

"Guess we'll have to sleep under the stars tonight, Molly," Trace said.

"I've already got Seth and Rosie settled down for the night. Figured, when it got dark, you wouldn't have time to unload the wagon until morning."

"Guess you and the kids will have to take Comet tomorrow. Sorry."

"Don't apologize. That's fine." Molly put her foot in the spoke of one of the rear wheels and lifted herself up to look in the back of the buckboard. She reassured herself the rocks were there, along with a small gutted deer and Trace's mangled tack.

She could smell the metallic tinge of deer blood.

"There should be enough rocks in there to form a single outline to lay the stringers on."

Molly nodded her approval. "I know it must have been a long, hard day for you and Andy. You better be getting some rest yourself. I'll unhitch the team while you hang the meat."

"I'll take that ornery horse of mine to the corral myself. He needs some work to calm him down before I trust him to anyone else."

Molly had hitched and unhitched the horses on so many occasions it took her less time to complete her job than it did for Trace to finish his.

Trace sent his horse through the corral gate. Comet snorted and nipped at the new horse's neck. A stranger to the other horses in the corral, he met with disapproval from the team as well.

"Here! Stop that!" Trace swatted Comet on the rear.

"Big Boy! Jake! Behave yourselves! I'll get them all some oats," Molly said. "Perhaps that'll keep them busy for a while."

They separated the horses by placing the grain for each a distance away from the other.

"I hope that does it." Molly was concerned the animals might fight and knock the flimsy wire fence down.

"Tomorrow I'll inspect the corral and see if I can make it stronger. I'm sure Flapjack will bolt again if he gets the chance to break free. In the meantime, we'll have to hope for the best."

"You call him Flapjack?" Molly asked as they walked back to the buckboard.

"Yeah. He was the bunkhouse cook's horse until we lost most of our livestock and what wranglers were left took off. I traded the chuck wagon for him and I've regretted it ever since."

"Maybe he'd behave better if you gave him a nicer name."

Trace chuckled. *Now, what kind of sense did that make?*

"No problems here today?"

"Everything was fine. Callie slept most of the time at school. Crazy Leg was happy to see us when we got home. There wasn't any sign of anyone being here."

"Good. And, if you think it'll help, I'll think about renaming my horse."

Trace reached into the wagon and lifted the deer to his shoulder.

"The rest of the stuff can wait 'til morning. There isn't much that can happen to that saddle to hurt it any worse." Trace took the saddlebags and his rifle in his other hand and slung them up out of the buckboard.

He dropped the saddlebags next to his bedroll by the supply pile, and walked toward the only structure on the place tall enough to hang the meat out of the reach of Crazy Leg, Callie, and any stray predator that wandered by it. The windmill was becoming the focus of their existence as they depended upon it for so many things.

Away from the light of the fire, the moonlight was bright enough to allow Trace to see his way about easily. He could hear crickets nearby and knew many wild creatures would appreciate whatever moisture they could find from the overflow of the water trough next to the well.

With water such a necessary commodity, it was also one of the most difficult things to come by in the dry New Mexico country. Anywhere it ran, spilled, or sat, new life was drawn to it. New grass took hold in clumps where the dampness held along the bottom of the trough and at the base of each upright on the windmill where the moisture seeped down.

Trace leaned his own rifle against the corner of the tower as he set about getting the deer ready to hang.

Molly brought a length of clean, white muslin for him to wrap around the carcass. The cloth would discourage the flies that were sure to gather there in daylight from spoiling the meat. Trace tossed a rope up over the second horizontal rail on the tower and pulled the carcass up to hang like a ghost in the night. He hoped none of the young ones saw it before he had a chance to explain what it was and what it was doing there.

After Rosie's scare with Callie, Trace worried that he might upset her if she saw the latest addition to the tower.

"I'll wash the cavity out in the morning. Then I'll skin it and butcher it, hopefully before Rosie catches an eyeful of it."

Molly held the bucket of water and poured the liquid over Trace's hands as he washed up. A chunk of lye soap, which he had used to scrub his clothes, sat on the edge of the trough and he applied that to his palms and rubbed his hands together. Once he rinsed the soap from his hands, he let Molly fill his cupped palms once more and scrubbed them across his face.

It felt good to get some of the grime off. Tomorrow, when Molly and the kids were gone, he'd fill the trough and climb into it for a real bath. Then, if his clothes were presentable, he would at least, again, feel clean.

He expected the things in the bags to smell musty from being confined in the leather pouches while the horse did who knew what. But, that was a small price to pay for having a change. He would empty the bags once he reached his bedroll and put the clothes out to air. In the morning he would inspect them for damage before he bathed and put them on. Molly was probably getting sick of seeing him in the same old thing. At once, he realized it was important to him what Molly thought about his personal grooming.

"You must be exhausted," Molly spoke close to his elbow as she set the pail on the edge of the trough next to the soap.

"I am, a bit."

He took the few steps to pick up the rifle and returned.

"Let's head for bed," he suggested.

Ten

Trace saw Molly's face register shock in the moonlight. Before she could raise her hackles and put him in his place, he tried to explain.

"I didn't mean anything disrespectful, Molly."

"I certainly hope not!" Her morals stopped her from entertaining the enjoyable possibilities her mind had played with at idle moments.

He slung the rifle over his shoulder and they walked the rest of the way back to their individual bedrolls in silence.

Trace spread his bedroll on the ground.

As he wrapped himself in the warmth of the scratchy blanket, he thought about his words and Molly's reaction. Someday, he'd like to ask her to bed and mean it in the way she mistook him then. He lay awake listening to the night noises—the crickets chirping—the far-off yodel of a coyote...

What was wrong with women, anyway? Molly hadn't recoiled from his kiss. She had, in fact, seemed to enjoy it as much as he did. But, when he slipped up and innocently said something suggestive, she practically ran backward trying to avoid him.

He stared at the bright stars directly overhead, but no matter how hard he tried to keep his eyes open, the lids kept drooping shut. Someday, perhaps, they would share the night. He was keenly aware of Molly's closeness that might as well have been as distant as the stars above him. But, even if he had taken Molly to his bed tonight, he was too tired to do anything about it. Her virtue would have remained

116

intact. He was so exhausted after the long day that he soon sank into the deep velvet of an undisturbed sleep.

Molly had to will herself to go to sleep. Even when she did, she slept restlessly and she knew she would be tired the next day. Trace's words spun round and round in her head. He had no idea that she'd like to be engulfed in the warmth of his strong arms right now, feeling his heart beat next to hers. But, she had the kids to think about, too. She must remain proper for them. Her morals must be kept in check. She hoped Trace would understand. Molly tried to sink into a deep sleep as thoughts about the next day's chores skirted her mind. She hoped her pupils would be easy on her tomorrow. Thank goodness school would end soon for the summer. There would be more time to help with the house, plant and tend a garden, and do all the things it was so necessary to do.

At last, she slept.

~ * ~

While Molly was at school the next day, Trace bathed and changed his clothes. He scrubbed his dirty clothes with lye soap, rinsed them, and spread them out to dry on the short grass. Then he and Andy used Big Boy to drag the remaining thirty-two-foot beams to the house site.

He laid four of them out, positioning them straight to what he judged to be accurately east, west, north and south, creating a 32-by-32-foot square of timbers flat on the dirt. Trace and Molly had talked about facing the front of the house to the south and putting a side door to the west so, when the winter wind blew from the north, it would hit an unbroken flat of wall that would keep some of the cold out. The east side would be protected against a storm blast from that direction, as well, with only a kitchen window and two of the upstairs bedroom windows on that side. With the front door to the south and the side door to the west, they planned for milder winds when either door was open.

Eventually, newly planted trees would grow large enough to form a windbreak for the house.

It sounded good, in theory, and it made sense to face the kitchen to the east in order to get the morning sun instead of the afternoon heat.

Once the boards were laid out straight, the horses were hooked up to the buckboard and it was driven closer to the house site to be unloaded. Trace and Andy began selecting the flattest rocks from the buckboard that they would set beneath the timbers.

Around noon, Trace left Andy to work with the rocks and went to butcher the deer still hanging in the shade of the windmill. Rosie had been busy, and still sleepy-headed, when it had come time to leave for school. Fortunately, she paid no attention to the windmill's treasure.

Now, Trace lowered the carcass swiftly, cleaned it, skinned it, and quartered the meat. He sliced a few steaks from one of the sections, then wrapped all of the meat up in the muslin and secured it in a cool spot by the well.

As he left, he whistled to Crazy Leg, who had been standing by, watching with curiosity.

"Come on, now. You leave that alone and come back with me." He had to turn a couple of times, slap his leg, and call the dog repeatedly, before Crazy Leg, reluctantly, came away from the meat.

It had been a busy day for Trace and Andy. When Molly, Seth, and Rosie arrived home that evening, Trace and Andy had the outside perimeter stringers in place on the rocks, and cross beams in position. Trace was just finishing nailing the framework together with large spikes fashioned at the blacksmith's shop. Making the spikes had been one of Josh's first assignments on his own, Molly had told Trace. She had opted to get the spikes from Josh, rather than special order the big nails through the General Store and have to wait until the shipment arrived.

The next day, Trace planned to start nailing the sub-floor diagonally across the timbers for strength.

As usual, when she came home, Molly stopped Comet alongside where Andy and Trace worked on their current project. She appraised how much they had accomplished with enthusiasm. Their days of sleeping under the buckboard truly seemed to be numbered.

When she studied the layout of the house before her, the surface it covered seemed small against the vast expanse of wide-open land. She knew the beginning of the house was larger than most that stood in the nearby towns, although it would be no mansion. She could hardly contain her excitement at the construction underway.

Supper tonight called for another celebration.

"We've brought fresh milk and butter for our evening meal," she told Trace when he stood up, stretching backwards to straighten his stiff muscles.

"Mrs. Smith has an early garden she protected from the frost and we even got some fresh greens." It had been a long time since any of them had tasted something newly picked from a garden. Wilted greens fried in bacon fat and venison steak would be a pleasant change.

~ * ~

The next day, Trace had the sub-floor nailed onto the stringers of the house and began framing the walls. Some of the lumber was poor quality and he set those boards aside for use in other spots. It felt good to be working with the wood and building something with his hands. Andy was becoming quite an apprentice, learning at Trace's side.

So far, the young boy had not seen any change in attitude toward him after Molly and Trace's brief encounter at the well. Perhaps adults could handle fancying each other and not cut other people out. After all, the boys he had known in Oklahoma were inexperienced lovers. Maybe it might be different when you were older. In the meantime, he would just enjoy working with Trace.

At night, by the campfire, Molly now insisted that he study in order to pass the year-end tests she must give him. He would have to go to the schoolhouse one day soon and take the tests. He hoped he passed so he wouldn't make Ma look bad as a teacher, but his mind hadn't really been on his studies.

Trace insisted that he keep up with his lessons in order to stay home and work with him. Trace seemed to think a formal education was awful important. But, the life lessons he was garnering were practical, too. Both might give him a better future. Right now, he just wanted to be a kid living on his Ma's farm and not worry about coming of age and having to fend for himself. That was scary.

Andy handed Trace a board before continuing his thoughts. It was fearsome to think about a time when he would have to get out on his own. The thought of eventually getting married and becoming responsible for someone else was even more frightening. Maybe it would be easier not to grow up so fast. Maybe he could stay on and help Ma run the farm, then he wouldn't have to try to figure out his own survival.

"You got a problem there, Andy?" Trace asked as he saw the boy struggling to keep his mind on his work.

"Nah—just thinking." He didn't want to tell Trace about his fears of growing up and becoming a man. There was nothing anyone could do about it. You grew up, that was all there was to it. He guessed that was better than not growing up. After all, being alive beat the alternative.

"Something troubling you, boy?"

"Nah. I'm fine." Andy attempted to perk up and moved to get more lumber.

Trace studied the boy for a moment, then shrugged. He guessed it was just being a kid—sometimes when they reached a certain age, people say they get peculiar.

The framing was coming along well. Although the walls were lying flat on the sub-floor, there were four sides. The north wall would be solid—no windows or doors. Holes for windows and doors on the other three sides were in place. Molly would like a front porch for shade in the summer and shelter in the winter. But that would have to be added on later. Right now, his concern was to get the main section of the house up, sided, and a roof on it.

He could see he was going to need help to raise the walls. Andy, with one wing still tied up, wouldn't be much good at lifting the weight. He supposed he could use the team and fashion some sort of pulley system to pull the walls in place, but it might be easier, and faster, if he had some other men to assist him.

Trace considered his idea for a few minutes while he reinforced the openings for the windows and doors.

A house raising was what they needed, he told himself. He was sure there must be some men in town who would be glad to give him a hand to help the schoolteacher that taught their kids.

While Trace worked, he formed an idea. Tomorrow, while Molly was at school, he would ride Flapjack into town and see if he could form a crew to help him get the walls up and braced.

That night, after dinner was over, the chores done, and everyone in bed beneath the buckboard, Trace lay looking up at the stars. He spoke to Molly where he knew she lay below.

"Been thinking, Molly. I need to take that saddle of mine in to have it repaired. That crazy horse is bad enough to ride with a saddle. Returning bareback, he's going to really be a piece of work—but I think I can handle him."

What was Trace leading up to? Molly wondered.

"Anyway, I figured Andy and I could take the day off. I'd take the saddle in and Andy could go with you and take his test."

The little kids were asleep, but Andy heard the conversation and grimaced. He was not looking forward to taking the test and had hoped to stall it off so, maybe, Molly would give him an oral exam at home and be done with it. There would be no such luck, now, unless Molly objected to Trace's plan to go into Moriarty on his own.

Andy listened intently for her response.

"What about those hoodlums that were hanging around town? They may still be there."

"It'll be broad daylight. I can take care of myself."

"I didn't mean you couldn't—just, well there were several of them and there's only one of you."

Trace chuckled. How did she think he'd survived before he met her? He'd had a short lapse of time between having his mother to worry about him before he heard that same tone in Molly's voice. Besides, hadn't she even threatened to shoot him, herself? It was funny, now, to think about the day she'd held the rifle on him. She'd been like a feisty hen protecting her nest.

"Andy does need to complete his work so he can pass to the next grade. And, the school year is running out. If you're going to ride your horse, he can ride Comet so he can come home, right after he finishes his test, and watch the place."

"Comet's so used to being ridden bareback I didn't figure he'd take well to being saddled to take it in for repair. Just warn Andy to watch for anything unusual when he comes home."

"I will."

"Is there anything you want me to pick up while I'm there?"

"No. Just be careful."

"I will."

The next morning, Trace saw the family off in the buckboard. He was in no rush to get an early start, so he inspected the work he'd done the previous day. Then he made sure everything was secure before heading out.

Callie lay on the tarp soaking up the early sun. Crazy Leg followed Trace about as he satisfied himself that the farm would be safe while he was gone. The time between his leaving and Andy's return should be short. He hoped their vigilance would avoid more trouble.

Trace went to the corral where he threw his tattered saddle blanket onto Flapjack's back, then the damaged saddle on top and, sticking a bent knee into Flapjack's side, pulled the cinch tight. At least the cinch was strong and, except for cosmetic rips in the main part of the leather, the stirrups and their attachments needed the most work. He was careful to position his toe in the strongest section of the right-hand stirrup and swing up into the saddle.

Flapjack backed up nervously and turned in a circle.

"Don't give me any trouble, today." It was Friday. If he could get a crew arranged today, Molly could be home to see the house go up tomorrow. He had too much to do to argue with a cantankerous horse.

Trace rode Flapjack over to where his saddlebags and rifle lay on top of the tarp near Callie. It was a good thing no one had found his horse—or maybe he was just so danged ornery no one could get next to him. All the money he had to his name was still there inside the one saddlebag, where he had hidden it, when he had unrolled his socks to look.

When he pulled the saddlebags away, it disturbed Callie and she looked up, barely raising her head sideways and opening one eye. Trace could see her belly moving up and down in a purr.

"No, I'm not going to stop and pet you. Not only am I dealing with kids these days, they've got me talking to animals, as well." *What difference did it make?* He kind of enjoyed both the kids and the animals. "Go back to sleep, Callie."

He placed his rifle in its damaged scabbard. He tossed the saddlebags behind Flapjack's shoulders in front of the saddle. He tucked the narrower piece of leather, between the two pouches, tightly beneath the saddle blanket and Flapjack's back. There, his weight on the saddle would keep the bags in place.

"You leave the cat alone, Crazy Leg." The dog moved to follow as Trace turned Flapjack back toward the trail out to the main road.

"No. Stay! Guard the place!"

Crazy Leg sat back down on his haunches and looked from Trace, riding out, to Callie lazing in the sun. It was the second time lately he had been left home alone.

What mischief could he get into? Trace rose in the saddle and looked over his shoulder in his direction.

Crazy Leg found a soft place in the dirt and turned in circles until he was satisfied with the spot and lay down. He put his head on his front paws and listened to Flapjack walk slowly away.

Trace rode toward town, following the road with vague familiarity. It was strange to be off the place and he studied the landscape along the trail with interest. He recognized different landmarks from the night he'd looked for Andy, and studied the route so he would know it better in the future. It was good to know if there were places one could race a horse across the valley, if trouble arose. It didn't pay to get caught where you couldn't escape if someone took a notion to rob you.

He looked behind him and saw no one. The windmill stood tall, breaking the horizon with its height and Trace was proud. It looked pretty darned good standing up there—looked like someone was making a permanent home—carving a life out of the raw land.

He felt a warmth of pleasure as he remembered kissing Molly. She sure could grow on a man. But, she was, he suspected, newly widowed and, although they had never discussed their pasts, he sensed it was going to take some time before she would be ready to love another man. That was all right. He was in no rush. Things were looking up, though. He had his outfit back. It was all his necessities. Molly was a good cook. He had a job to keep him busy. He had a place to stay until he was ready to face Snake and his gang on his own terms.

The thought of Snake turned his mood dark. He was irritated at himself that he had let what had started out as an upbeat day become darkened by his past. He tried to lighten his mood at the same time Flapjack decided to try to lighten his load.

Flapjack bucked suddenly and, if Trace hadn't been resting his hands on the saddle horn so he could clutch it quickly, he might have been thrown into the dirt alongside the road and left like before in the dirt.

Darned horse! Trace cursed under his breath and held on.

"What got a burr under your saddle?" he yelled.

Flapjack continued to buck, coming down out of the air onto the hard packed ruts so that all four hooves clumped together in a tight space forming his back into a hump. When he didn't loosen his rider from the saddle with that trick, he reared onto his hind feet and kicked his forefeet into the air before coming back to earth with a bone-jarring slam.

Trace hung on, trying not to lose his grip on the saddle horn. His body felt as if his ribs and lungs had been thrust up into his throat then jerked back down in place.

Flapjack reared again, and came down hard, then spun in a circle and twisted his back like someone tweaking a handsaw and letting it spring straight.

At last, Trace was dizzy and Flapjack winded.

Trace was mad and it was a toss-up which one of them was the more disgusted.

"You ornery son-of-a-gun! I ought to sell you and let someone else put up with you. If I'd had any choice I wouldn't have let Cookie stick me with you in the first place!"

Flapjack laid his ears back and Trace could tell he wanted to bite him, so he yanked the reins to keep the animal's head, and teeth, away from his knee.

"That'd be too mean a trick, to knowingly dump you on anyone else!"

Finally Flapjack stood, blowing heated air through his nostrils and trying to catch his breath. His sides heaved in and out.

"Bet you regret that little show and dance, now, don't ya?"

After a bit, Flapjack was rested enough for Trace to urge him on toward town. Trace knew he dared not trust the cranky horse again. Obviously, the animal could turn on him at a whim. He didn't plan to give him another chance.

Up ahead, Trace could see the schoolhouse off to his right, and the little town of Moriarty further on, in the distance.

He was glad he'd soon be able to get down off the bad tempered horse, ease his weary legs and rest his saddle-beaten rear end.

Trace rode down the main street of town slowly, getting a feel for what was available to him and looking for a tack supplier. He searched for a livery stable, knowing that, if the proprietor didn't work leather, he could probably tell him someone who did.

In a nearby alley, between two saloons on his right, somebody scurried away, like a rat in the shadows.

Trace caught the movement out of the corner of his eye, but dismissed it. *Probably a townsman in a hurry,* he thought. He had his own business to attend to and he planned to be back to the farm before dark.

The street was crowded with wagons and riders. Horses lined the hitching rails in front of the saloons and the boardwalks were abuzz with activity. He followed the street to its end and saw a livery sitting off to the right, some distance away from the store buildings. The owner had a few horses inside a corral with posts not much sturdier than the ones back at the farm.

Trace dismounted and approached a man sitting on top of a wooden slatted barrel. He was whittling a stick into a whistle, cutting pieces of wood away, notching the mouthpiece, testing it in his lips, then carving some more. Trace watched him for a moment.

"Howdy."

The man nodded acknowledgment, sizing the stranger up with a glance.

"Can you tell me where I can get some tack repaired?"

"Well, I hear Josh, down at the blacksmith's shop, used to do that before he started working with Hughes. We hain't got much of a selection around here what with the town being so small and all. Now, over in Estancia, you might find someone. Sure as you go on into Albuquerque, or up to Santa Fe, you'd find someone either place."

"Thanks. I hadn't planned to travel on today."

"If it's nothing fancy—no delicate toolin' or anything, Josh's your best bet around here."

"Good. I'll look him up."

Trace turned to leave and decided he would walk Flapjack, rather than put his sore muscles back up into the saddle. Leaving the saddle for repair and riding him back without a saddle had no appeal since the animal had given him such a hard time on the road.

Perhaps, if he got his business done in time, he could catch a ride back to the farm with Molly and the kids in the buckboard. In the meantime, stretching his legs and flexing the muscles in his butt cheeks would be refreshing.

At the blacksmith's shop, Josh was happy to take the saddle for repair.

"We're real busy here, but I'll take it home with me tonight and work on it evenings after I'm through here."

"Good! By the way, the work you did for Mrs. Kling on the windmill parts came out just fine. It's up and running and the most admired piece of work on the farm."

"So, you're the stranger that's been helping Mrs. Kling out over there?" Mr. Hughes said. "Heard she had a hired hand out at her place."

"Well, she needed the help and I needed a short-term job. It's worked out well for both of us, I'd say."

"Josh, here, had to repair a bullet hole in Doc Landry's buggy cover 'bout the time we heard she had a man at her place."

"Yeah. Well, we had a bit of trouble and Doc happened to be on the road at the time. It's all taken care of, though." Trace hoped he sounded convincing. He didn't mention Callie's hanging experience. Now, he hoped, maybe the trouble had gone away.

126

"How about, I leave the horse and all," Trace asked, turning to Josh.

Josh nodded. "I suppose that'd be all right."

Trace reached for his saddlebags and rifle.

"Don't ride him, though. He's a mean one and he'll throw you, if he gets the chance. His name's Flapjack."

Josh walked up to Flapjack and rubbed his nose with his rough fist. Flapjack nuzzled Josh back as if to make a liar out of Trace.

"They're as fickle as a woman," Mr. Hughes laughed.

Trace was happy to be shed of Flapjack for the day. They needed a short break from each other. Maybe the animal would have a better disposition when he got him back. Let Josh sweet-talk him for a while, he didn't care.

Trace agreed to a fair price with Josh and slung his saddlebags over his shoulder. He headed down the street in search of one of the local homesteaders who could help him put a crew together for Molly's house raising.

He walked past several stores, stocked with the normal supplies needed by the locals, and past a barbershop offering haircuts, shaves, and hot baths. He was approaching one of the saloons when he heard a clatter of spurs behind him.

Two men stepped up on either side of Trace and one remained in back, breathing down the collar of his shirt. The one behind him pressed a pistol barrel in his back and reached to take his rifle away.

The one on the street side spoke. "Don't make no fuss. Take a right turn into this alley, here."

The voice was cold and hard and Trace felt a chill race through his veins.

He thought, all of a sudden, that he wouldn't make it back to the schoolhouse and Molly any time soon.

Eleven

"Now," the voice said, shoving Trace into a corner where two buildings came together too closely for him to escape. His back was against the wall and his three assailants faced him without any attempt to conceal their identity.

"Now, you're going to get what you deserve for interfering with us at the woman's place," one of Snake's henchmen, Slade, said.

Trace recognized the voice of the man that had walked behind him as that of the one who left his six-shooter behind at the farm.

"What's this?" Slade asked when he saw the butt of the pistol sticking out from Trace's waistband. "My gun, I do believe." He removed the weapon and hefted it in his hand.

Trace remembered all three of them—Slade, Zeke, the man who had been on guard, that he had chokes on the farm, and the younger man, Tom, who had befuddled him and Molly with his generous actions.

Slade whipped his hand up letting the metal on the six-shooter land squarely on Trace's right cheek.

Trace felt his knees buckling, but he fought to stay upright. Tom slugged Trace in the stomach and Trace looked at him in surprise. The blow had barely fazed him; as the younger man had pulled his punch back, keeping his fist from landing hard.

"We'll teach this gun-thieving coyote a thing or two," Slade said and stepped back to let Zeke land a punch from the left.

"That's for jumping me the other night."

The blows were taking their toll on Trace.

"Your turn, Tom," Slade said.

Tom stepped up and swung again, leaning in close as he did.

"Go down," Tom ordered in a whisper.

Trace dropped to his knees and Tom raised his foot to kick Trace's head. Trace rolled with the kick and flattened in the dirt.

"Come on, I think he's had enough," Tom told the other two.

"I don't know. Some of these homesteaders are pretty hardheaded. Maybe I better boot him a few times in the ribs and break them so's he'll be out of commission for a while," Zeke said.

Tom leaned over and lifted Trace's head by his hair. "Nah, he's out." Tom glanced back toward the main street. "We better git. I think someone saw us!"

The three of them hurried back up the alley to a spot where they could squeeze between buildings and get away.

Trace lay there for a time, both trying to ease his pain and to make sure the men were gone before he moved.

He was confused. Why did Tom try to keep the others from hurting him? Why did he soften his blows?

He started to get to his feet, but the licks the other two had gotten in had been hard and he sank back down.

The next time he tried to get up, it was dark.

He was stuck without a horse and without a ride back to the farm. Molly would be worried now, with good reason.

The next thing he knew he heard footsteps and someone lit a match and held it in front of his face.

"I thought I heard something back here," the sheriff said. "What you doin' sacked out in the alley?"

"I got jumped. It wasn't my plan to get beat up."

The sheriff helped him to his feet, holding the match until it nearly burned his fingers, before shaking it out.

"I think you better come along with me." He didn't smell any liquor on Trace, but he obviously wasn't in any shape to stay here. He'd take him back and decide whether to throw him in a cell or not once he got a good look at his condition in the light of the kerosene lamp at his office and once he heard his whole story.

~ * ~

Molly cooked supper and waited for Trace to return. Surely, it didn't take this long to turn a ripped saddle over for repair.

When Trace didn't get back at dark, they ate their portions of the meal and saved the rest for Trace.

After chores, Molly sent the children to bed and remained by the fire, keeping Trace's food warm and waiting for his return.

When, hours later, she had to admit that perhaps he wasn't coming back this night, she finally went to bed and lay there going over in her mind all the possible reasons he had not returned.

She hadn't taken him to be a drinking man, but he had been away from civilization for some time—maybe he had gone for a drink.

What if he found her cold and aloof because she was not someone to jump into another person's bedroll at the slightest suggestion? What if, thinking she didn't care for him, he had gone to one of the saloons? What if he had had a drink, or many drinks? Perhaps he was lying drunk along the road. Perhaps Flapjack had thrown him again. She had told him to rename that darned horse. But, would he listen to her? She remembered that Trace had planned to ride bareback on the return trip. That would be an even more hazardous ride than with the saddle. Then, her mind turned to the drive seemingly knowledgeable people said was more powerful in men than women. What if, finding her cold and resistant, he had gone to a saloon and taken up with one of the girls there?

How could she blame him? She hadn't been very quick to respond to his advances. She regretted that now.

If he ever came back, she would let him know how important he was to her.

Near daybreak, Molly finally slept and when the rooster crowed she awoke exhausted. Reluctantly, she got up and set about doing chores while she let the children sleep longer.

She walked to the site where the house was beginning to take shape and looked at the work Trace had done the day before yesterday.

Where could he be?

She tried to figure out what to do.

If she went into town looking for him, and found him in an embarrassing situation, she would never forgive herself. On the other hand, if she didn't go and he was lying along the road somewhere, she wouldn't be able to live with that, either.

Molly walked to the windmill and released the brake, letting the wheel slowly pick up speed as the morning breeze caught in its blades. The water began to flow into the trough.

Finally, she knew what she had to do. She had to go look for Trace, even if the outcome was something she would rather not know.

Andy was awake and stirring about, now. Molly returned to the buckboard.

"Where's Trace?" Andy asked.

"I don't know. He didn't come back last night."

Andy heard the edge in Molly's voice.

"Do you think he's all right?"

"I-I don't know."

Just then Rosie crawled out from under the wagon carrying Callie in her arms and walking in a daze.

"Go back to bed, Rosie," Molly said. "You look like you're sleepwalking."

Rosie looked at Molly as if she didn't believe what she was about to say. "Ma, I saw Trace. He's hurt. Some men beat him up," Rosie said, awed by the vision.

"Rosie, listen to me carefully. Where was Trace?"

"I don't know. It was a shady place—between some buildings. I saw that nice young man's face, too. But he was hitting Trace as much as the others, maybe more. What does it mean, Ma?"

"I don't know Rosie, but I'm going to find out. Lay back down for a while longer. There's some cold venison and biscuits for breakfast when you get up. Andy, stay here with the children."

"Let me go! Please," Andy said.

Molly thought for a minute. If Rosie was wrong and Trace was in the company of another woman, perhaps, for Trace, it would be less embarrassing if Andy was the one who found him.

On the other hand, she reached for her rifle, if he was in trouble she wasn't above shooting one of the bastards if she had to do so.

"No, I'll go. You protect the kids."

Andy rushed to get Comet's bridle for Molly. Trace had ridden Flapjack out. If he had been thrown again, he could ride double with Molly on the trip home.

On the way to Moriarty, Molly ran the horse as hard as she dared. It was early in the morning yet, and the temperature was cool. Comet enjoyed the exercise.

When Molly thought she had kept the horse at the fast pace as long as he could endure it, she slowed him to let him rest, then kicked her heels into his ribs to run again.

At last, she reached the schoolhouse without seeing a sign of Trace anywhere on the road.

She raced Comet on to the first business in town, Mr. Hughes' blacksmith's shop. There, she saw Flapjack tied beneath a small tree, bare of his saddle.

Molly dismounted, dropping Comet's reins to dangle free, and entered the blacksmith's shop where Mr. Hughes and Josh were hammering and turning a large length of iron on top of a big anvil.

They did not hear her approach because of the noise from their hammering and the bellows blowing on the hot coals. Finally, there was a break between blows on the iron and Molly was able to get their attention.

"Mr. Hughes, I see Trace's horse outside. Do you know where he is?"

"Mrs. Kling!" Mr. Hughes dropped his hammer to his side. "I saw him yesterday, when he brought his horse and tack in for Josh to work on his saddle. Ain't seen him since. How about you, Josh?"

"No. I just figured he went back out to your place to wait for his tack, Mrs. Kling."

"Well, he didn't get there and I'm worried."

"Maybe he stayed at the hotel—or one of the saloons," Mr. Hughes said.

Molly didn't like what he was insinuating.

"I'll check the hotel. That could be where he is. Thank you."

"If he comes by, we'll tell him you're looking for him." Mr. Hughes offered.

"Thank you."

In order to search more thoroughly for Trace, Molly decided to walk Comet the rest of the way. She watched carefully as she passed open lots and new construction sites. If she saw something unusual, she moved to inspect it—a scrap of cloth, a bit of metal, anything that could possibly provide an indication of Trace's disappearance.

At the first hotel she came to, she tied Comet to the post that held up the porch. She took her rifle, being careful to keep the barrel pointed at the ground and her fingers away from the trigger, and went inside.

At the desk she asked to see the guest register.

"Sorry, Ma'am, we don't usually give out the names of our guests," the clerk replied.

"But, this man is missing—"

"Perhaps if you could describe him, I could tell you if I've seen him."

Molly complied, describing Trace as best she could.

"No, can't say as I've seen anyone like that come in. You might check the saloons. Sounds like he'd fit the description of one of the cowhands that came in off the Abilene Trail or Chisholm Trail. There're quite a few cowpunchers in town this week."

Molly dreaded approaching the saloons, but seemed to have no choice. There was another small hotel, but it was at the far end of town, past the saloons. She decided to take the buildings as she came to them and hoped she'd find him before she ran out of possibilities.

She left Comet tied and walked down the boardwalk, figuring she'd have to come back on the other side of the street anyway, if she hadn't found Trace by the time she reached the last building on this side.

When she reached the saloon, she hesitated at the swinging doors. She could hear the clinking of glasses, the tinkling of a piano, and the sound of rough voices rising and falling inside the dim room.

Molly pushed one of the swinging doors aside and peered in.

Trace was nowhere in sight. Of course, that didn't mean he wasn't in one of the upstairs rooms—in the arms of some woman. She knew it would do no good to ask the bartender if he were there. He'd surely protect the identity of his customers—or lose them.

The next saloon was even more crowded and, this time, she pushed the door open and entered when she couldn't see beyond the people.

A women in a fancy dress flitted from one customer to another. A few men sat playing poker and drinking. She made her way to the far end of the bar and studied the faces of the two men standing there.

"Something I can do for you, lady?" The barman poured a glass of beer for a greasy older man at the end of the counter.

"Yes, I'm looking for someone. His name's Trace Westerman. Have you seen him?"

"Can't say as I have. The name's not familiar. If they come in here often, I remember at least the first name."

"He was new to town. Yesterday was the first time he'd been here."

"Well, I usually 'member a stranger, too. Can't say as how I seen any but two yesterday. One short and fat, the other one of them was a black man. Now, those two were unusual enough, I remembered them."

"Thank you."

"Now, I don't mean no disrespect, Ma'am, but women like you put a damper on my business. The men tend to think they better get home before the wife comes looking for 'em."

Molly nodded. "I'm leaving."

The bartender scrubbed a towel inside a beer mug and watched her go.

There was some buzz between the men at the bar about going home.

"A round on the house, fellas?" The barkeeper tried to shift their interest back to their drinking.

The noise in the bar grew louder as the men slapped each other on the back and decided home, and what they needed to do there, could wait a bit longer.

Molly walked into Baker's Mercantile, but neither the owner, nor his clerk, recalled seeing Trace. She tried the General Store with the same results.

"Did hear they had quite a ruckus out back in the alley last night, though," Harold, the owner, informed her. "I never got involved—jest stayed out of trouble and kept my nose in here."

"What went on, do you know?"

"Not really. Heard the sheriff took someone off to his office. Don't know if he kept him or not."

Rosie had said Trace had been hurt in a dark place. When she peered between two store buildings, the alley was narrow and nearly blocked at the end where the siding of both buildings came close together. Could it be where Rosie thought Trace had been injured?

Twelve

She headed for the sheriff's office. Maybe the person he took to his office was gone by now, but the sheriff should be able to tell her if Trace was involved.

She hesitated. What if Trace was wanted and the sheriff had arrested him? She hadn't seen him on any of the posters, but new ones could have come in since then. She didn't want to think of Trace in jail. What would she do if he were an outlaw? She was too fond of him. How could she ever forget him, if he were a criminal? Her heart didn't know the difference—it only knew to thump and lurch when he was in sight.

She walked into the sheriff's office apprehensively.

"Mrs. Kling, isn't it?" The sheriff paused midway between the stove and his desk when he saw her.

"Yes."

"What brings you in, today?"

"I'm looking for someone. He may have gotten injured here last night."

The sheriff raised his eyebrows. "Well, I'm sure if he did, I'd know about it."

Molly described Trace for what seemed like the hundredth time.

"Yep. I saw him. He'd been beaten up some. I came across him late at night and brought him back here."

So far, he hadn't said anything about Trace being a wanted man.

"Where is he now?"

"Back there in one of my cells."

Molly's heart dropped. *So Trace was wanted by the law.*

"Like I said, he was beat up and by the time I found him he wasn't doing too good. I brought him back here. We talked for a while then I put him up in one of the cells for the night." The sheriff got up from his chair and nodded for Molly to follow him.

She went timidly, embarrassed that Trace was in jail. She had never cared about someone who was outside the law before.

The sheriff stopped at a cell with an open door and single wooden and canvas cot inside.

There, still asleep with his face turned toward the wall, was Trace.

Molly looked at the sheriff. Her eyes questioned his but she didn't want to ask anything for fear of the sheriff's answer.

"Hey, fella, wake up," the sheriff called, banging his fist on the iron of the cell door. "You've got a visitor."

Trace stirred with great effort.

"That little tussle he got himself into last night kinda wiped him out. I decided to let him get a few hours rest before he headed home. Didn't figure anyone would give him any trouble in here."

"Trace?" Molly was anxious to know the extent of his injuries.

Trace rolled toward her and slowly hung his legs over the edge of the cot.

"Oh. Hello, Molly. Guess I didn't make it back last night. Ran into some of the fellas that gave us so much trouble out at your place."

Molly saw the scrape up the side of Trace's face. One eye had a large black crescent-shaped bruise beneath it.

"Trace!" Molly said, shocked.

"It isn't as bad as it looks." Trace hoped his words rang true because the injuries sure felt bad enough. He winced as he started to stand up from the cot.

"The sheriff was kind enough to let me sack out here last night. Didn't figure it would be too smart to try to get back to your place in the dark, on foot, and not in my best form."

"We went over some of the wanted posters last night," the sheriff said. "He was able to pick out two of his assailants, but one of them wasn't there."

"How are the kids?"

"They're fine. Rosie was worried about you."

"Oh," Trace understood Molly's implication.

"Good for Rosie. 'Spose that's why you're here."

"Well, I figured something must have happened. Maybe you should go see Doc Landry."

"I'll be all right. In a few days I'll get over being sore. I don't think they broke any of my ribs or anything. The sheriff found my saddlebags next to where he found me." Trace was relieved that he hadn't lost his money.

"Why don't we get something to eat over at the hotel and then head back out to the farm before the kids come looking for both of us?" Trace turned his attention to the sheriff.

"Thanks, Sheriff. I'll let you know if we have any more trouble with that bunch," Trace situated his hat on his head.

"Trace, you better watch yourself. You could have been in a lot worse shape than you are. I'll be looking for Snake and his gang. Meantime, if you aren't going to let Doc take a look at you, you better take it easy."

Trace nodded and reached to pull his saddlebags off the floor next to the cot.

"You've got nice accommodations, Sheriff. I highly recommend them—especially for Snake and his gang. I hope my rifle shows up."

"I'll keep watch for it."

Trace ushered Molly back into the office, away from the jail cells, and out the front door into the sunshine.

They walked back to the hotel where Molly had tied Comet. Intent on finding coffee to help soothe his aching head and eliminate the cobwebs, Trace was unaware of Molly jerking to a stop beside him.

"Trace!"

He stopped short and turned around.

"What is it?"

"Comet's gone! I tied him right here to the post of the hotel and he's gone."

"You were probably upset when you got into town. Maybe you tied him in front of some other building."

"No. It's not likely I would misplace a horse. I tied him right here." She looked and saw a still fresh pile of horse manure where Comet had been tethered.

This day was not getting any better.

"I told you, I tied him right here. Now, what do we do? How do we get back to the farm—on foot?"

Trace studied the activity up and down the street. The horse was nowhere in sight.

Where was Comet?

Molly stood in the street staring at the post where she had tied Comet.

"Darn! Darn! Darn!" She blurted out in frustration at this latest complication in her life. Why would anyone steal her horse? Well, Andy's horse, anyway?

She kicked the dirt several times, like a child throwing a tantrum, fighting the urge to sit down right there in the street and cry. She wasn't a woman prone to tears. She found out long ago that they did her no good. When you were through with the bawling and feeling sorry for yourself and wiped your face, the problem was always still there. If tears couldn't dissolve the problem, what good were they? She kicked her foot again and again, until the dust from the toes of her boots sprayed over the last sign of Comet—the pile of road apples he had left in the street.

She turned her back to Trace and stared out across the town. Her fury blinded her temporarily until she could scrub her sleeve across her eyes and clear them.

At last, she turned back to Trace.

"What do I tell Andy? He loved that horse. We all did. It's my fault. I should have walked him along with me."

Trace could find no answer for her.

"Who'd ever think we'd have horse thieves, here, in Moriarty? Anybody that knows us, knows that horse is ours!"

"Could he have gotten loose on his own?" Trace immediately regretted broaching the possibility that she might not have tied Comet securely in her anxiety to search for him. He didn't want Molly's anger to turn on him. He'd never seen her lose her temper. She had always been in control and, in fact, apt to handle a problem with the rifle in her hand instead of letting go of her emotions.

She looked at him with disbelief.

"That's Andy's horse. I tied him to that post you're leaning on—tight. He wasn't going anywhere unless someone took him."

"Well, I guess we better report the theft to the sheriff, then."

"Then what? Look at you. You're in no shape to walk all the way home."

"We'll figure something out. I guess we'll have to see what we can do about a ride. There's a livery at the end of town. We could rent a carriage."

"Yes, and besides having to pay cold, hard cash for that, we'd have to get the buggy and horses back to town. That means another trip in with the team, now that Comet's gone." Molly's practical mind kicked into gear.

"Maybe Doc Landry'll be headed out on a call. Maybe we can catch a ride with him. You should let him look at you anyway, Trace."

"We could go get that sorry animal of mine and ride him double, bareback."

"I thought he was hard enough to ride with just one person in the saddle, let alone with two and without a saddle."

"He is. He also tried to shake me off on the way to town. But, he is mine and we wouldn't have to come right back to town. Frankly, I'm too sore to stand here discussing the problem any longer."

"I saw Flapjack tied down at the blacksmith's shop when I first got to town. Why don't you start down there and I'll go to the sheriff's office."

"I've got a better idea. If you've already eaten breakfast, why don't I go in here and get something—at least some coffee. Then, when you get back, we can go on to Mr. Hughes' place together."

"I'm sorry, Trace. You must be really hurting and I forgot you hadn't eaten. You go ahead. I'll report Comet missing, then meet you here."

"Are you sure you don't want something?"

"All I want is Andy's horse. I haven't had breakfast, either, but I'm too mad to be hungry." Molly slung the rifle up over her shoulder and Trace watched her stomp back up onto the wooden sidewalk and head toward the sheriff's office.

Trace sat down at a table with a plain white cloth on it and ordered his food. When the woman who ran the place sat a full plate in front of him, he held her attention momentarily.

"Do you know if anyone saw the black horse tied outside this morning?"

"My boy. He's nearing twelve. Horses are all there is in life, to hear him tell it."

"I wonder, could I talk to him?"

"I suppose," she said, curious.

Trace had finished eating his meal and the woman was pouring his second cup of coffee when the boy showed up.

"Son, this man has some questions about that black horse you were admiring earlier."

The boy looked at him with a hint of fear showing in his eyes.

"I didn't take him, mister. Jest petted his head a bit."

"I didn't think you had taken him, son. I'm sure Comet enjoyed your company. Anyway, did you see the lady that tied him up there?"

"You mean the schoolteacher? No, I seen her riding him to school. I know he's Andy Kling's horse."

"That's right, you and Andy would be about the same age, wouldn't you?

The boy nodded.

"Andy lct me pet him before. I didn't think it'd do no harm."

"It didn't. But now, Comet's gone and we're looking for him."

"I saw a fellow untie him and get on him. I was just coming back into the restaurant to wash dishes for Ma when I heard the horse whinny. I looked back and this mean-looking man was climbing on him. I ran out the door and hollered at him, but the man raced away toward the edge of town. He headed north toward Santa Fe. I knew it was Andy's horse so I ran out to try to find the sheriff. He wasn't at his office and I couldn't go into the saloon where someone said he was, 'cause Ma wouldn't like it, so I came back. That's where I was when Ma first started looking for me—I was lookin' for the sheriff."

"You've been a big help. Figure I know who took Comet." Trace thought about the direction the rider had gone. It was exactly opposite of the location of Molly's homestead. Obviously, he planned to get as far away as he could as fast as he could.

"Was it one of the same guys that beat you up?"

Trace raised his hand to his face. He gently felt his bruises self-consciously.

"Probably was. They've been giving us some trouble."

The boy picked up Trace's empty crockery plate and headed toward the kitchen.

"Thanks," Trace called after him. "You've been a big help."

"Sure hope Andy's gets his horse back soon, mister. That man sure looked mean."

"I hope I do, too. Comet means a lot to Andy. He means a lot to all of us." Andy was going to be mighty upset when he found out Comet was missing.

Trace paid for his meal and went back outside to wait for Molly. He was surprised she hadn't returned already. But, if the sheriff wasn't at his office, he knew she would hunt until she found him.

She was mad, and he didn't blame her.

At last, Molly walked up to Trace where he was leaning against the post to the hotel.

"Any luck?"

"No," she said with sadness tingeing her voice. "I sure hate to go home without that horse."

"I know." It was like losing one of the family and Andy was going to take it hard. Funny how he'd become so attached to Andy and the other kids—how he'd do anything to keep them from being hurt.

"As soon as I get to feeling better, I'll come back and look for Comet."

"I only hope Andy will wait. If someone doesn't go soon, we'll probably never see him again. The sheriff wasn't much help. He said he'd watch for him, but not to expect any miracles."

Trace nodded. He didn't tell her the reason he was in no rush to search for Comet. Besides his insides feeling as if they were shredded, he figured Comet was long gone. A horse thief usually didn't stick around in the area where the animal was familiar to people. Stealing a man's horse was a hanging offense where he came from. A stolen horse was usually ridden hard out of the area or resold down the road a piece. As fast as Comet was, he might find him in a race somewhere. Anybody that knew horseflesh would surely see that he could be a winner.

"Well, the boy in here, one of your students, saw the fella that took him."

Molly perked up.

"Sounded like one of Snake's bunch."

"Them again! When are they going to leave us alone?"

"Maybe after I'm gone."

Molly looked at him. *Just what did that mean?* She certainly didn't want him to leave.

Trace slipped his arm around Molly's waist and she resisted a temptation to put her head on his shoulder. It wouldn't do for her to act improperly where someone who knew she was the schoolteacher might see her.

"Guess it's a ride on my ornery cuss, then." The two of them started for the blacksmith's shop.

When they arrived at the shop, Flapjack stood out front flicking flies with his tail and seeming content with his current life.

Josh was inside cooling metal in a big tub. Molly heard the sizzle from the hot iron being dropped in the water as Trace went up to the young man.

"Don't suppose my luck would be such that you'd have my saddle ready?"

Josh looked at him in surprise. "No. I thought I had a few days."

Josh studied Trace's bruised and swollen face.

"Who beat you up? You don't look in any shape to ride, anyway."

"I'll be all right if I can just get some rest. You can take all the time you want with the saddle. Right now, Mrs. Kling and I need the horse to get back out to her place."

"Well, the saddle's in worse shape now than when you brought it in. I had to tear some of the seams apart to repair the leather right. Goin' to have to replace some of it completely."

"That's fine, Josh. I guess we'll just have to ride him bareback." Trace didn't like the chance they would have to take, riding Flapjack double, bareback, but it was necessary for him to get back to Molly's place and rest so he could search for Comet.

Building the house would have to wait, for now. It was a big setback. Trace knew if he didn't give himself some time to heal he'd get even further behind schedule. He couldn't afford any permanent damage to his body, if the house were to get done before winter. Molly had too much for him to do to be laid up too long. Let alone the pleasures she might offer down the road a ways—

Josh wiped his hands on his pants and set the piece of metal aside. He walked to Flapjack and rubbed his nose.

"Guess you're going home for a bit, fella."

Flapjack nickered back. The two of them had bonded instantly and neither was happy to be separated.

"I'll get back in, soon, to see if the saddle's ready." Trace had reached his limit and needed to get on Flapjack while he could still stand. He untied Flapjack and walked him to a wooden box where he and Molly could get on more easily. Trace dropped his saddlebags over Flapjack's shoulders.

"Andy's horse was stolen. Watch for it, will you Josh?"

"Stolen? Of course I'll let you know if I see it. You sure you can make it to Mrs. Kling's place? You look pretty bad."

"I'll make it." Trace was beginning to feel more and more punk as the day progressed. Even before Josh mentioned his condition, he wondered if he was going to pass out from the pain and leave Molly to deal with him and Flapjack. He fought the pain. He hoped he'd feel better once he was on Flapjack and Molly was situated behind him.

Trace climbed onto Flapjack's back.

"You better wrap your skirt behind you good to cushion yourself from this critter's hide," he told Molly when he felt Flapjack's hair prickle his inner thighs through his pants.

Molly handed her rifle to him, then climbed on behind him.

"You ready?" Trace handed the rifle back to her before gripping the reins firmly in his hands.

"You behave yourself, now," Josh told Flapjack as he held his palm up to his lips and shoved a lump of sugar in the animal's mouth. "I'll have more sugar for you when you come back, if you do."

"Sure hope he understands that." Trace wasn't in the mood for another toss off Flapjack.

"Let's go," Molly said as she laid the rifle across her lap between them.

Trace turned Flapjack south and headed back to the homestead.

With the extra weight on his back, Flapjack seemed to sense the need to remain firmly on all four feet. He plodded along, resigned to his job.

They were nearly halfway home when Trace slumped into unconsciousness and Molly reached around him to take the reins from his hands. She helped his body ease along Flapjack's neck and draped one of his arms on each side. She gripped her arms around his waist, trying to keep him from falling off.

She wanted to hurry Flapjack, but feared to try. As long as she could keep them both on his back, timing probably wouldn't make much difference.

She had to get Trace home and let him rest. The beating had taken all his energy. It was going to take some time for him to recuperate. She only hoped there was no permanent damage inside his body.

When they reached the farm, Molly saw Doc Landry's buggy parked next to the buckboard.

What a lucky break!

Rosie and Seth came bounding toward them, eager to see about Trace.

"Is he dead, Ma?" Seth asked.

"No, of course not." Molly was angry at the possibility and didn't want to worry the children.

Both Andy and Doc Landry came running from the watering trough where Andy had been showing the doctor how the windmill filled the trough.

Molly stopped Flapjack as close to the buckboard as she could.

Doc Landry and Andy lifted Trace down while Molly steadied him and tried to keep Flapjack calm.

"What happened?" Doc asked.

"Some of that bunch that was here the other night got to him."

Molly dismounted. Andy and the doctor laid Trace on the ground. Andy quickly rolled Trace's bedroll out in the open while Doc held Trace up by the shoulders. Molly helped them stretch Trace onto his bedroll.

The doctor examined him while he explained his presence to Molly.

"I came by on my way back from the Millers'—they had a new baby last night. Anyway, thought I'd stop and see how things were going. Obviously, not too good, it looks like."

"There's more bad news, Andy. They stole Comet."

"What? I'm going after them!" Andy jerked to his feet, clenching his fists.

"No!" Molly jumped up to grasp him so he wouldn't make a break for Trace's horse and ride to town.

"Wait, Andy. There's nothing you can do right now. Whichever one it was, he took off toward Santa Fe and there's no way you could catch him now. Let Trace get better and then let him handle it."

Andy jerked roughly away from her. He stomped off toward the pasture.

"Trace's got some bruised muscles around his ribs, Molly. I can't find anything broken. He's probably just exhausted from the beating he took." He raised Trace's eyelid where the crescent bruise bloomed. "Another fraction of an inch and he most probably would have lost the sight in that eye."

Lying flat on his back, now Trace was beginning to come around.

"Welcome back," Doc Landry said.

"What are you doing here? How long have I been out?" Trace's head was fuzzy, he presumed if Molly had sent someone for Doc Landry it must have been quite some time.

"I just happened to be here when you two rode in."

Trace tried to sit up.

"Better stay down a while. You're going to be fine. Just give yourself a few days to rest up."

"Say, that's some windmill you put up there. Andy's right proud—as he should be."

"Poor Andy. That horse meant everything to him." Molly dug her toe into the soft ground while she puzzled what they should do about the boy—and Comet.

"That's a hard problem to solve. Probably isn't much can be done about it. I'll keep a lookout in my travels. Of course, if I run into that bunch again, I'm apt to do well to survive it myself."

"Why can't the sheriff do something?" Molly wondered aloud.

"He's gotta catch them first. You can button his shirt back up, Mrs. Kling. I'm through with Trace for now."

"Well, I made sure I pointed out their wanted posters to him. All except for that one called Tom. Strange, he didn't have one for him," Trace said.

Trace leaned up on his elbow. He winced at the pain his movement caused.

"Another strange thing—it was like he was trying to save my life when the others were beating on me. He pulled his punches and told me to drop. Then he told the others I was out—when I wasn't yet."

"Rosie knew he was there. It confused her that he was hitting you when he'd been friendly toward her." Molly bent to re-button Trace's shirt.

"I can do that." Trace moved to dress himself, then dropped back.

"No, you can't. Just let me take care of it."

"So, Rosie had another one of her spells. I figured that's what you meant when you said she'd known about the beating."

"Yes. It was as if she were still asleep, only with her eyes open. She insisted you were in trouble. That's why I went looking for you."

"Good for Rosie. Where is she now?"

"She followed Andy. I hope she doesn't upset him any worse than he already is."

Seth stood nearby, inspecting Flapjack.

"Seth." Trace noticed him dangerously close to the animal. "Get away. He's a biter. I don't want him taking your ear off!"

Seth turned toward Trace and started in the direction of Molly, Trace, and Doc Landry.

Having had his chance to bite disrupted, Flapjack lowered his head and butted Seth in the behind, lifting him high and sending him tumbling head over feet.

Molly jumped up and rushed to help Seth up from the ground where he sprawled in front of them.

When he was back on his feet, dusting his pants off and looking surprised and embarrassed, Molly made sure he wasn't hurt before she lectured him.

"Trace told you to stay away from that horse before. You have to listen or you're going to get hurt, Seth!"

"If I'd been alert, I'd have expected something like that since he didn't toss us off on the way home." Trace let his body relax back against the bedroll.

"I think just Seth's pride is hurt, this time," Doc diagnosed. "Well, I better get on home. I'll put my two cents in with the sheriff when I get there. Chances are, like you said, Trace, Comet is out of the county by now."

"If we can keep Andy reined in, I'll go after those thieves myself, as soon as I have the strength back to do it." Trace hated being incapacitated, especially at such a critical time.

"You better be careful. You need to take a posse with you. Maybe the sheriff can loan you a few men or deputize someone," Doc Landry advised.

"As bad as I want Andy's horse back, I don't want you hurt worse—or killed." Molly frowned. The last thing she wanted was anybody hurt, again.

"You rest up, there, Trace. Next time I see you, it'll probably be in town."

Molly walked with the doctor toward his buggy.

"Thank God you were here, Doc."

"Glad to help, Mrs. Kling. You just keep him down a few days, if you can do that. I figure he's going to be wanting to move about by tomorrow. If you can keep him quiet that long, I'll be surprised."

"I'll do my best, Doc."

They walked to the buggy parked between the new construction and the campsite.

"Looks like your house is coming along."

"Trace's been a really big help. With him out of commission, the kids and I will figure out a way to get the walls up. It can't be too difficult if we use the team and I can drive the nails through the sills, if I have to. I hadn't expected to have much help before Trace came along, so I figured to do most of it myself, anyway."

Doc nodded. "A person does what they have to do. Leastwise, you got a start."

"Thanks, again, Doc. I don't know what we'd do without you."

"We'd all be a lot healthier if this Snake fellow would take his gang and hightail it out of here. Take care, now, Mrs. Kling."

The doctor called out to his horse and started Nellie around the short circle to go back to the main road.

Molly stood for a minute with her hands on her hips and looked at the structure before her. It was too late in the day to get started on it, now. Besides, she didn't want Trace forcing himself up to help her, like she knew he would. He needed to rest.

The house would just have to wait for another day. One when she didn't have an unhappy boy because he's lost his horse and an injured man lying in camp trying to recover.

Sometimes, life just keeps punching you down like bread dough, Molly thought. She didn't know what she could do about it—except to struggle. Would there ever be a day when she didn't have to fight for her own existence, as well as that of the children?

"Ma," Rosie called out. "Ma, Andy won't come back."

Molly looked out across the pasture and saw the boy standing there with Big Boy and Jake.

"Leave him alone for a bit, Rosie."

There were hard lessons to deal with in life. Would this one be too much for Andy? He'd lost his father and now his horse. How much heartache could a twelve-year-old boy take?

Thirteen

When the evening meal was ready, Molly sent Seth to get Andy. She knew losing Comet would only compound the boy's grief over losing his father. Comet had been the one thing his father had been able to give him, and Andy treasured the horse twice as much after his father was killed.

How she wished she could undo the events of the day. How she wished she had been able to ride Comet home, instead of wondering where he was and if he would ever return. She hoped Andy would come in for his meal and allow her to talk to him about his loss.

Andy approached the campfire remorsefully. He didn't want to eat, but agreed to take a plate of food to Trace. When Molly came over later, with a plate for Andy anyway, he reluctantly accepted it.

Molly noticed that, when she approached, the two of them had ceased their conversation. Perhaps there had been some man talk going on. If Trace was able to console the boy any, she wouldn't risk any progress he had made by sticking her nose in.

Instead, she sat down beside them and remained quiet as they finished their food.

"Ma, can I have some more fried potatoes," Rosie asked. "With gravy, please."

"Of course. Anyone else?"

Crazy Leg sat on his haunches and barked.

"Not you, Crazy Leg. You've already had twice as much as you need."

"I'll take more," Seth said.

"No, thanks," Andy told her. His appetite was just not there and he had choked down what little he had eaten. He scraped the remainder of the food from his plate into Crazy Leg's bowl.

Big Boy and Jake were at the water trough and Andy used that as an excuse to leave the group, "I've gotta get the team into the corral."

"No, thanks, Molly," Trace said. "I think I overdid it this morning, trying to get back here. I don't have much of an appetite tonight, either. Andy, you watch Flapjack when you go into the corral. He really got Seth earlier."

"Sure, Trace." Andy's tone was lackluster. He didn't much care what the other horses did, all he cared about was Comet and where he was.

Molly finished dishing up second helpings for Rosie and Seth.

"I swear you two are growing so much lately. No wonder you're wanting more to eat." She was glad she had the food to give them in the quantities they wanted. They had seen leaner days and she didn't want to go there again.

Molly sat back down next to Trace, and leaned her head back against the buckboard wheel. They both sat watching the children eat their dinner as the flames of the campfire flared irregularly into the air when pitch pockets blew in the wood.

"We're going to need to make a trip to the mountain for firewood again, soon," Trace said to make conversation.

"When you're feeling better. I don't want you rushing things. We'll manage."

"Maybe a trip up there would take Andy's mind off Comet for a bit."

"You talk like Comet's never coming back!" Molly looked at him in shock. "We'll find him, again, won't we?

"We'll sure try. But, I have to warn you, the chances are slim that we do."

"Why do you think this Snake's bunch is giving us such a hard time?"

"Well, it's a long story. I told you I'd had run-ins with them before. Snake's wanted for murder and cattle rustling down along the

Pecos River in Texas. He knows he'll hang, or be put away for a long time, if he's ever caught. I could testify against him and he doesn't like that idea."

"When my husband was killed, I had to attend the trial of the man who did it. I wouldn't let any of the kids go, because I thought it would be too hard for them. Anyway, the only witness had an accident shortly before the killer came to trial. His horse rode off a ridge in the dark. Neither the man nor his horse survived. The Judge had to let the killer go—'no hard evidence,' he said."

"It's a heck of a shame." Trace shifted his weight to his left elbow and looked up at Molly from where he lay.

"Snake killed my parents. I saw him. He raided my herd and when my Pa and I tried to stop him, he shot my Pa. My Ma ran out with the shotgun to try to stop Snake from hurting us and he shot and killed her, too. Just point blank shot both of them right before my eyes. I swore I'd get him one day. I want to be the one to bring him in. The timing just hasn't been right, yet." Trace looked off in the distance, past the dancing fire.

Molly wondered if he was seeing his Texas ranch in his mind.

"I'm so sorry to hear that."

"I'm sure if it hadn't been for Andy that night Snake and his bunch stopped here, we'd all be dead, too. Guess, now, he's decided to taunt us a bit before he comes back in for the kill. I'm sorry I brought all this trouble down on you."

Molly felt a chill run up her spine.

"If Snake was in this territory, anyway, he must have seen we weren't prepared to put up a fight to protect what little we had. We were probably a prime target for his bunch. It may not have anything to do with you."

"Not until I went up against him and he recognized me that night."

The chill gripped Molly tighter.

"Rosie, Seth, get ready for bed," Molly called out. She wanted them safe and warm in their bedrolls. She heard a tapping off in the distance and looked at Trace.

"Did you hear that?"

"Yes. Sounded like something rapping against the windmill in the breeze."

"Some folks say when you hear hammering in the night, it's nails being driven in your coffin." She reminded herself to be sure the rifle was loaded when she turned in for the night. Trace was in no shape to protect them. She would have to be the one to keep watch.

"Andy, if you're finished with your chores, best get to bed," she called to the boy. The eerie tapping left her uneasy. The only way she would know all of the kids were safe was if they were all in their respective places.

"Yes, Ma." His voice was faint and came from somewhere near the chicken coop.

~ * ~

Back at Snake's camp, Tom, Slade, and Zeke had rejoined the band of outlaws. Zeke rode Comet into the light of the campfire, leading his own horse behind him. He had taken the saddle from his horse at some point along the trail, and put it on Comet's back. The horse, used to being ridden bareback, didn't like it. He was being uncooperative and stubborn and had already suffered several beatings before finally arriving at the campsite in the mountains near Santa Fe.

"Where'd you get that?" Snake asked Zeke.

"The woman tied him up and walked away. I waited until she couldn't see me and took off with him. Ain't he a beauty? And he's fast, too."

"Spose you're planning to race him, too," Snake sneered to show the man how dumb he thought his actions were.

"Betcha he'd win! Easy money!"

"Don't go gettin' no bright ideas. Last thing we need is you getting out in public with a stolen horse. Everybody around Torrance County knows that horse belongs to the schoolteacher's kid. You'll bring the law down on us, for sure!"

"Well, maybe I won't race him. Maybe I'll see what ol' Reyes'll give me for him when we meet up with him and his *vaqueros* again."

Tom stood back listening to the discussion about the horse. He felt sorry for the animal. The horse certainly wasn't used to the abuse Zeke had been giving it.

"Had us an interesting time back there in Moriarty," Zeke added.

"Did you check out the bank like you was supposed to?" Snake asked.

"Yeah," Slade said. "There's cattle drives going on all around the place and the cowpunchers are coming into town to get supplies and get drunk. The bank should be heavy with cash right about now."

"Good."

"B'sides that, we beat the crap out of that Trace Westerman, too. Would a kicked him to death, but Tom, here, said he'd had enough," Zeke reported.

Tom stayed out of the conversation. He knew Snake wouldn't be too happy with him for letting the Westerman fellow off easy. He watched some of the men settle into their bedrolls and get ready for the night as he tried to avoid direct interaction with Snake.

"Grayson, don't get too comfortable," Snake spoke to one of the men, "you got first guard duty."

Zeke was removing his saddle from Comet's back. He dragged it near the campfire, planning to use it to support his head and shoulders while he slept.

"Yeah, we'd of finished him," Slade continued, "But Tom stopped us. You'd of thought they were some sort of kinfolk, or somethin', the way Tom eased us out of there."

"That right?" Snake asked. "So, you's soft on him? You and that fella go back some, Tommy boy?"

Tom stood his ground and kept silent. He sensed he was about to be exposed and he prepared himself to draw his gun, if need be.

"You're from down Texas way, too, aren't you?"

Tom made no comment.

"I said, where you from? Around the Pecos way like Westerman? Couldn't be you were there when his folks got in the way, now, could it?"

Tom felt his left hand wanting to flash toward his pistol, but he still held his tongue. Arguing with a maniac like Snake would get him nowhere.

Slade walked up to Snake and handed him Trace's rifle. "Here, use this. When they find him with Westerman's rifle nearby and a bullet in his heart, Westerman'll get the blame and no one'll even come lookin' for us."

Snake took the gun and flipped the barrel up toward Tom's chest, lifting the flap up on his shirt pocket, near his heart, with the tip.

The weight of the long gun's butt lifted the barrel up, so that a fired bullet would either go over his left shoulder—or into it. Tom reached for his pistol. Before his hand touched the butt a shot flashed behind him and he dropped, face down in dry twigs and dirt.

"Now, what'd you go and do that for, Zeke? I wanted the pleasure," Snake said. He stuck his boot out and nudged Tom's body with his toe. "Get this piece of crap out of here. Toss him on that horse Zeke stole, Slade, and make sure wherever you dump him, the rifle stays there, too."

Slade grasped Tom's body under the armpits, and Zeke took his legs, moving his feet to either side of his waist so he could carry the load easier. The two of them drooped the body over Comet's back and Slade mounted his own horse to lead Comet away in the direction from which they had just come.

"And don't come back until you're sure he's where whoever finds him thinks Westerman done it!" Snake ordered.

~ * ~

"Trace, wake up!" Molly shook Trace without concern about his injuries.

It was early in the morning hours. She had no clock to know what time it was, but the rooster hadn't stirred yet and everyone was asleep.

"What's wrong? You're hurting me, for cryin' out loud!"

"Andy's gone! I had to get up and I checked the kids before I laid back down. Andy's gone!" She shoved his sling toward Trace as proof the boy was missing. "He must have taken this off so he'd have both arms free when he left."

Trace tried to rise, through the grog of pain and cloud of sleep. He lowered his head for a moment. The world spun around and he didn't know if he could get to his feet or not. He tried sitting up again, more slowly. Then he reached for his boots and pulled them on.

"He's gone after Comet, I just know he has." Molly's voice rumbled in his ear as Trace tried to clear his head.

"How'd he go? On foot?"

"No. He took Jake. I woke you up because I'm going after him. I can't let him go out there alone and I couldn't leave you wondering where we were."

"No. How'd you go? Take Big Boy?"

"If I have to. You're in no shape to go."

"Well, I'm not letting you go after him alone and someone has to stay with the kids."

Trace tried to stand and had to clutch the side of the buckboard to keep from falling. Yesterday was a nightmare. He must have been running on adrenaline alone when he left Moriarty with Molly. The soreness that had set into his muscles was slowing him down. He felt like a creaking, rusty pile of junk. If his muscles were aching, what else might be bruised inside? He had to do this. He had to go after that foolhardy kid. He righted himself on his feet at last. Andy was gone and there was no one else to look for him. He wouldn't turn anyone else loose on Flapjack.

Once erect, he was able to fake a fairly natural walk and get to his horse. If he could get on him, he would have to hang on and let the horse go toward town. If he didn't see Andy by then, assuming he was still able to sit horseback, he'd have to go on toward Santa Fe. That was the way the boy at the hotel dining room had said the man rode out.

"Trace, you can't do this." Molly's voice was a coarse whisper behind him as he bridled Flapjack.

"Stay with the kids, Molly. I'll make it," Trace promised as he mounted Flapjack.

What else was she to do? Molly wondered.

"Trace, be careful." Molly worried that he was unfit to ride. She worried more that something dreadful would happen to Andy, if someone didn't go after him.

"Here," Molly ran after Trace as he started out, "take my rifle. You can't go unarmed!"

Trace stopped the horse.

Knowing what he was heading into, Trace had to agree. "But—"

"Don't worry about us. I'll keep a sharp, long-handled shovel handy. If anyone tries anything, I'll let them have that."

"I believe you will." Trace was feeling better, now that the fog was clearing from his head and he held himself straight, hoping his stature would lessen Molly's concern about him. He leaned, stiffly, over from the waist and placed a brief kiss on the part in Molly's hair.

"Don't you worry," he said through clenched teeth and tightened lips.

~ * ~

Andy aimed Jake in the direction of town. The horse, unused to having a passenger on his back, was unsure what was expected of him.

Andy had one goal on his mind—find Comet. Trace had said that the outlaws were somewhere toward Santa Fe. He figured he'd bypass Moriarty and head straight for the hills to the north. He didn't think the outlaws would get too far off the main road, if they wanted to be able to come and go as they had been.

He hoped Ma and Trace would sleep late so they wouldn't know he had left until he had gotten a good head start before someone came looking for him. He guessed he should have taken Trace's boots so he'd be less inclined to chase after him. But, then, that probably wouldn't have stopped him.

Periodically, Andy reined Jake in, whistled his special code, and waited for Comet to answer with a nicker or whinny. He knew he was probably too far away from the outlaw's camp for Comet to hear him unless the horse had managed to get away from them and head home. Andy knew if Comet could get loose, he would do just that—head for the corral and his ration of oats.

After all, they were family. You didn't abandon family.

He peered over his shoulder and saw no one. He felt reasonably sure he was miles ahead of Trace or Ma—whichever one would come.

He skirted the town early in the day—avoiding the possibility of being seen by someone that might recognize him. Once at the north end of town, he urged the horse into a trot as they rode toward Santa Fe.

No matter how many times he stopped and whistled, he got no response from Comet. At noon, when the sun was high overhead, he dug some jerky out of his pocket and chewed on it as he rode along.

He stopped to rest alongside the road and took a swig of water from an old canteen Molly had stored in the household supplies. The well water was sweet and refreshing and Andy was soon ready to ride on.

He spent the rest of the afternoon along the trail, stopping now and then to listen for voices or sniff the air for the scent of smoke that might mean a campsite was nearby. Occasionally, a single rider passed him. When someone came from behind, he moved aside, into the brush, before the rider caught up, in case it was someone looking for him. He did not intend to turn back now.

When they came from the north, he greeted them and asked if they had seen Comet. None had.

He stopped, again, and whistled the code until his lips got tired and his throat was dry. If Comet were within earshot, he would come. Andy knew he would.

At last, at dusk, the wind shifted and he smelled the acrid odor of campfire smoke drifting across the roadway. He slowed Jake and sat, silently waiting to hear voices.

He moved the horse in the direction of the campfire, then circled around to see to whom the camp belonged. He was careful not to expose himself to the campers, waiting to see if they were friendly or were the outlaws that had ransacked their supplies.

He rode past a small tree and someone dove from behind the trunk, grasping him around the waist and pulling him off Jake's back. They both hit the ground and tumbled. He felt as if he was in the clutches of a huge bear and began slinging his arms and legs to try to free himself. Jake ran away from the scuffle and raced for the road.

"You're that kid from the homesteader's place, ain't ya?" Grayson asked. "Sure ya are. Wait until Snake gets a look at this." The man wrapped one burly arm around Andy's waist and picked him up like he was a baby. He walked back to the campfire dangling Andy from where he held him at his side.

"Look here what I found," Grayson told the men sitting around the fire. "For once, guard duty paid off. Whatcha think, Snake? The nag he was riding got away, though."

"I told all of ya ta keep yer eyes open, didn't I? I told ya we had to be careful. If a kid like that can find us, it'd be nothin' for a lawman to get in here. You and Zeke get back out there. Keep watch for anyone trying to sneak up. You, kid, what're you doin' here?"

"I'm looking for my horse!"

"Well, as you can see, the only horses here belong to us."

"One of you took him, I know it."

"Well, you ain't got no proof. The horse ain't here, now is it?"

Andy hung his head. He knew they had stolen Comet. It had to be them. Then, he realized two of the men were missing. Tom and Slade. Wherever they were, he didn't figure Comet was far behind.

"You're going to be sorry when someone from my family catches up to me."

"Oh, you got reinforcements coming? Maybe we should tie you up and wait for them to get here? What do you think about that?"

Andy bit his lip. He wished he hadn't mentioned that someone was sure to follow him.

"Toss me that rope over there Joe," Snake told one of his men.

Joe's eyes glinted in the firelight as if he was in for some sport—

"Sure thing, Snake. If that don't do it, I got another over here. Let me know if you want it."

"Nah, he ain't as big as he thinks he is. Reckon one lariat will be enough. Turn around, kid."

When Andy didn't comply, Snake took him by his left shoulder and jerked him around facing away from him. The sudden movement caused Andy's right shoulder to ache. Now he wished he could put it back in the sling and baby it a little while longer. It sure was going to be aching something fierce once Snake got his arms pulled behind his back and tied.

He didn't know where Comet was and he wasn't likely to find out now. He felt an ache in the pit of his stomach and he wished he'd stayed home. He wished he'd listened to Trace. Trace had told him he'd come after them when the time was right. Now, he'd forced the issue and Trace surely wasn't up to taking on the whole gang by himself.

Andy worried that Trace or Ma had followed him and, in his weakened condition, Trace might die for his efforts. These outlaws probably wouldn't be above killing Ma, either.

The ache in his stomach grew stronger and he soon realized he was not only scared, he was also deeply homesick.

~ * ~

Slade ambled along some distance from the main road, leading Comet behind him, until he reached a desolate area where he could dump Tom's body and no one would find him until the buzzards began circling.

He dismounted and untied the lead rope from Comet's bridle. He coiled the rope around his hand. The tail end flipped up and Comet, wary of another sting from its end, hopped sideways.

"Hey!" Slade called out and ran at the horse with the rope still in his hand. Having suffered sharp jolts across the behind and flanks earlier in the day, Comet did not want to let anyone get close enough to him to whip the rope across his hide again.

The more Slade dodged and rushed at Comet, the more the horse avoided him until, at last, he took off for the main road, still carrying Tom across his back.

Having been forced to travel the unfamiliar path by his rider, the animal would be able to retrace his steps back to the corral where he usually received oats. And that is exactly what he did.

Remembering the mean weight of the stranger on his back, racing him out of town like there was no tomorrow was enough incentive for Comet to avoid the main street of Moriarty. He found his way to the schoolhouse. There, he nosed around the grass a bit and, when he found no humans about, gave that up and made his way back down the road toward home.

The closer he got, the more his instincts told him the trough would be full of fresh, cold water. He expected there would be grain for him at the corral. Andy would be waiting.

He picked up his pace. He was eager to reach all these things, and to dump this weight off his back and roll in the dust to rub away the flies that were irritating the welts left by the stinging rope.

~ * ~

Back at the homestead, Molly tried to console Seth and Rosie by assuring them Trace would bring Andy back.

"Yes, Comet, too," Molly answered Seth for the third time.

She couldn't know how serious Andy's predicament was. She and the two younger children had stayed at the homestead all day, waiting for someone to return. Night set in and there still was no sign of Trace, Andy, or Comet. It was as if their whole world stood still, waiting for their loved ones to return.

She urged the children to go to bed, but relented and let them stay up. It was as much for her sake as theirs—she didn't want to worry alone.

Around midnight, the sound of a horse's hooves approached and Molly shooed the children under the buckboard and grasped the shovel handle in her hands. If it were an intruder, she'd be ready. If it was one of their own, well, better safe than sorry.

She stood in the shadows until Comet approached, then rushed out with the shovel raised high, ready to slam a rider off his horse, if need be.

"Comet!" Comet had come home! Then, with the glow from the firelight, she saw a form draped across his back.

Her heart froze. *Was it Trace? Or Andy?*

She was so scared she nearly fainted.

Fourteen

Molly tossed the shovel aside and reached for the horse's mane.

"Whoa, boy." Molly spoke in a soothing voice to Comet as the horse pranced nervously at the corral gate. "Easy, Comet. Let me take a look at what you've got there." Molly grasped his bridle.

The horse lowered his head and blew air through his nostrils. He pawed the ground, anxious to get inside the corral and eat oats.

Molly looked at the body slung over his back and didn't recognize the clothes. It was too small for Trace and too big for Andy.

She patted the horse's neck, ducked under his head and went to the other side where she could get a look at the passenger's face. She cautiously pushed the horse around where the firelight would shine on the man's features.

It was a gruesome thing to have to do—to look at the face of a dead man—even if it wasn't someone she knew. There was no one there to do it but her. She had no choice.

Carefully, she turned the face toward her and the man's head moved, without resistance, in her shaking hands. She recognized him instantly. It was Tom, the young man that was one of Snake's gang members.

At first, she was angry. What did she care if another outlaw was dead? That was just one less to take advantage of someone else. She had to get him off Comet's back, though, before she could put the horse away. She could tug him off by his legs and let him fall where he may. Perhaps she should move him away from where they slept. She didn't want to frighten Seth and Rosie. When Trace got back, they could bury him or take him into the sheriff, then.

She walked Comet past the fire to move the body away from the children. They certainly didn't need to be confronted with this. Hadn't they had to deal with enough in their young lives?

As she walked Comet toward the corral she heard the slightest moan—more like a whisper in the dark. Was it the night breeze?

The hair on the back of her neck stood on end and she froze in her tracks. She didn't believe in ghosts. If the man was dead, he wouldn't make any noise. Unless Comet's movements jostled the air from his lungs, she considered the possibility. Surely, if that were going to happen, the breath would have been expelled on the way to her place. She had heard horror stories of people believed to be dead and having been buried alive.

Could it possibly be that this young man was still alive?

She steadied Comet, patting him while she went back to inspect the outlaw.

Away from the firelight, she felt for a pulse in his wrist, expecting to find the skin cold and clammy. Instead, the skin was still warm, although moist, like someone who had broken a fever.

Molly felt no heartbeat there. She was sure she had heard him make a noise. She felt for the artery in his neck and, at last, found the slightest pulse.

She had seen the bullet hole in the back of his cowhide jacket. He had lost a lot of blood, but he wasn't dead—he was nearly dead.

Molly led Comet over closer to the buckboard again.

"Rosie, Seth, I need you to help me get this man off Comet's back."

The strange words from Molly brought them scrambling from under the buckboard where they had hidden for protection. Their eyes were wide with fear, but they responded obediently.

"Now, I'll pull him off to where his feet reach the ground. You help me lower him to Trace's bedroll, carefully. We'll lay him on his side so I can look at his wound better."

Molly deftly directed the children quietly and calmly as if it were a normal thing to have a man brought into camp barely alive.

"Do you think you can save him, Ma?" Rosie asked.

"I don't know. He's lost a lot of blood. I'll get his coat and shirt off and see what we can do.

Molly saw his gun belt beneath his coat when they moved him to the ground. She unlatched the buckle to remove the holster. He wore only one gun and holstered it on the left. The man must be left-handed. Or he drew from his left with his right hand. Not that it made any difference. A gun in either hand was just as deadly. She put it aside, out of Tom's reach.

Somewhere, he must have a mother, or someone that cared about him. As long as he was still alive, she felt it was her duty to do her best to keep him that way. Certainly, she would want that much for Andy—or Trace.

After helping Molly and Rosie as much as he could, Seth sat down cross-legged nearby. He watched as Molly rolled Tom onto his right side. The pearl-handled gun, where it poked out of its tooled leather holster, fascinated him. Molly had put it where she could get it, but the man couldn't—even if he could move.

Molly rose, picked up the weapon and laid it in the buckboard. She got the kerosene lamp and lit it, then she got the hunting knife out of her supplies.

Molly positioned the lamp where she could see to clean the wound. She went to Tom and raised the back of his coat and shirt. Carefully, she started the knife blade at the center of the hems, splitting the cowhide and fabric up the back to the neck until she was able to pull the pieces apart and inspect the bullet wound.

"Get me the water bucket, please Rosie."

"I can do that, Ma," Seth said, anxious to help and too excited to go to sleep.

The pail was only half full and he had little trouble lifting it and carrying it to set it alongside the man.

Molly ripped one of Andy's muslin shirts into pieces and began to clean the blood away from the injured man's back. When she was done she could see that the bullet had lodged in the muscle alongside the backbone. With the bleeding stopped, perhaps he would regain his strength and come to. It was going to take Doc Landry to dig the bullet out, though. That was not in her line of expertise.

She would keep him warm for the night. Try to get liquids down him and hope for the best. She packed clean rags beneath his back and settled him in. She stretched his legs out and went to remove his boots to try to make him more comfortable.   .

She tugged the right boot off without a problem and set it aside. The left boot was more stubborn and she had to pull harder. She braced her heels in the dirt and tugged with both hands. At last, the boot was free from Tom's foot. Molly held it in her hands, ready to set it aside. As she moved to set it next to the other boot, something shiny fell away and dangled from one of the bootstraps.

Surprised, Molly moved closer to the lamp with the boot in her hands. She held the metal circle up. The pin on the back had been clamped through the loop of the leather bootstrap, then the metal had been dropped inside the boot, out of sight.

Molly turned the round object over.

"TEXAS" was printed in an arch on the front above an ornamental cut of a star in the metal. Below, arched in the other direction on the rim, it said "RANGER."

TEXAS RANGER. Oh, my God! No wonder he had acted so differently. What was he doing riding with an outlaw gang? Now, he was here and a Texas Ranger's life was in her hands and she knew very little about what to do for him.

Was that why he was shot? Had Snake, or one of his bunch, found out he was a lawman and tried to kill him to keep from being arrested?

Hearing a noise she looked up and quickly dropped the badge back down inside the boot. Then shoved the boots behind the wheel on the buckboard.

"What did you jump for, Ma? It was just the old hooty owl calling. You always tell me not to be afraid of no old hooty owl." Rosie moved closer to Seth.

"Yes. Yes, I do. I was thinking too hard, I guess. He startled me." Still, Molly stood up and looked about her. When she couldn't make out anything in the dark, she pulled the Ranger's pistol from its holster and went to put Comet up for the night.

"You've done your job well, Comet. Tonight, you get a double ration of oats." She walked the horse to the corral and put him inside with Big Boy.

In the morning, she would have to see about getting help for the Ranger, some way—if he was still alive.

~ * ~

Doggone that boy, anyway, Trace thought as he rode on into the night. He wished Andy had been more patient and waited until he felt better before taking off looking for Comet.

He knew the odds of finding the horse were next to none, but try to tell a kid like Andy that. He'd been stubborn, himself, at that age. Trace remembered what little childhood he could.

It seemed now as if he'd been an old man all his life. Maybe that was why he knew so little about kids. He'd never had the liberty of being one, himself. Or, perhaps, it was just the way he felt with his ribs sore and his muscles taut that made him think that way.

If I were a twelve-year-old boy in search of my most beloved possession, what would I do? Trace tried to think like Andy would.

Well, I'd have bypassed Moriarty.

Which Andy had.

I'd have gone on in the direction I thought the horse might have gone.

Which Andy, also, had.

He knew if the horse had his druthers, he'd have gone home. But, with a stranger forcing him to travel north, as the hotel owner's boy had said, he would have had no choice but to follow the rider's instructions.

Knowing that, Andy would have headed for Santa Fe.

Trace planned to ride on to Santa Fe, if he didn't find Andy before hand. Surely, Snake's bunch wouldn't be so brazen as to be hanging out in Santa Fe. They must have a camp outside town somewhere. But where?

He had been watching carefully for any sign of a campfire or any noise along the road, but to his disappointment, found nothing to lead him to where Snake, Andy, or Comet were.

~ * ~

Once Snake had Andy tied up, he began to worry that someone might sneak up on them and surprise them.

"Put that fire out! If this kid found us, anyone else can, too."

One of his men rushed to do his bidding, kicking dirt over the flames and wood. The last thing any of them wanted was to get caught. They planned to meet up with Reyes, rob the bank in Moriarty, and head back through Texas. There, they would cross the border, where the Rio Grande ran shallow, to Mexico.

Once they had filled their saddlebags with money and gotten a head start, the posse could chase them all the way to Mexico for all Snake cared. They'd be safe, and live high, south of the border.

"You. Kid. Keep your mouth shut, or I'll put a gag on you, understand?" Snake said.

Andy nodded.

The last thing he wanted was some dirty rag stuffed in his mouth. It was the only way he had to get anyone's attention. He didn't want to lose his one possibility of rescue.

"We'll have to have some target practice, fellas, if the kid don't do as he's told," Snake threatened Andy.

The campfire, mostly smothered embers, now, emitted a small wisp of smoke from beneath the pile of dirt and ashes now and then.

"Think we better break camp," Snake said, forming his plans as he went.

"We're too close to the road here. If we go on up to Santa Fe, maybe we can get lost in the crowd—or we could double back and hit the bank at Moriarty now."

"What you goin' to do with the kid?" Slade asked as he entered the camp on his return from dumping Tom.

Snake turned around abruptly.

"Don't sneak up on me like that! I shoot people for less than that. Especially when I don't recognize their voice right off. You weren't gone long. Sure you took care of that little chore of yours?"

"Yeah," Slade said. "I asked what you were going to do with the kid. We sure can't ride into Santa Fe with a young kid along. Not one that's tied up, anyway."

"I know that," Snake replied. "Guess you should have brought the horse back with you."

"How the hell was I supposed to know you'd pick up a hostage while I was gone? Besides, the fool animal took off on me," Slade said, not wanting to explain that Tom had still been across Comet's back.

Andy looked up hopefully.

Comet had escaped. He'd go home. Andy knew he would. Now, if he could get loose of these ropes, he could hide out in the trees until Snake got tired of looking for him.

"Did you see any sign of that Westerman fella along the road? Or the woman? Anybody that might have been lookin' for this kid?" Snake asked.

"No. Things were pretty quiet out there."

Andy felt his heart sink.

Maybe Trace wasn't coming for him after all. Maybe he was hurt too bad. Maybe he and Molly had decided to teach him a lesson and simply wait for his return. There was no possible way for them to know how much trouble he was in. There was no guarantee he'd have help getting out of this one. He'd been homesick before, but now he'd give anything to be back home in his bedroll beneath the buckboard.

Andy kept wiggling his hands in the ropes behind his back. With the fire out, it was nearly impossible for anyone to see what he was doing, so he worked away at the bindings, hoping they would give at some point. His right shoulder hurt worse than it had in days and he felt the ache deep within the shoulder blade. The pain was enough to nearly take his breath away, but he couldn't let Snake win. If they dragged him off to Santa Fe with them, who knew if he'd ever see his home again.

Fear spurred Andy to work more vigorously on his bindings. He tried to move beyond the pain and free himself. He couldn't wait around for someone to find him. His chances of escaping once Snake broke camp were next to none.

"Hurry up! Get your horses saddled. Anyone that's not ready to ride when I am stays behind!" Snaked snapped.

With Snake's men busy breaking camp, Andy edged farther away as he worked at the ropes.

At last, he felt the tightness give way and has arms swung free. He remained holding them behind his back as he crept ever slowly backward into the trees.

It was all scrub pine and juniper there, not high, but thick and bushy. They hadn't reached the tall timber yet, that would be on the other side of Santa Fe up in the mountains where the snow fell deep in the winter. But, no larger than he was, this stand of trees did fine. He was able to move from one clump of brush to another. He would hide behind the trunks of tree clusters until he could make his way to the road back to Moriarty. There was no need for him to go on to Santa

Fe. He hoped now, that Comet had returned home. He only hoped Jake would, too.

"Hey! Where'd the kid go?" Snake called out.

Andy broke into a run down a straight path figuring to dodge back into the bushes if he heard a horse thundering toward him in pursuit.

His heart thudded inside his chest and his lungs burned.

He jumped over the edge of the road into a gully and squatted in the dark to listen.

No one was following.

He stretched out on the weeds and lay there flat, momentarily, catching his breath and waiting for the pain in his shoulder to ease.

At last, convinced that Snake and his bunch had better things to do than look for him, he went on.

~ * ~

At daybreak, Trace rode into Santa Fe.

The town was built of tan adobe structures with brown-stained wooden ridgepoles sticking out above the walls to hold the roofs in place. The buildings were scattered about like oversized boulders, with holes through the thick walls for windows.

He passed the long building of the Governor's Palace on his right and rode on through the plaza. His eyes scanned the hitching rails for the mounts of any early risers.

The town was quiet, except for the birds singing in the nearby bushes and others bathing in the fountain, splashing water about with carefree exuberance.

Comet was nowhere in sight. Nor was Andy, but then, he hadn't expected to see the boy walking about the area. If he had come this far to find his horse, he'd be checking stables and hitching rails, just as he planned to do.

Trace approached a part of town that never slept. The saloon doors remained open day and night. Trace rode Flapjack to the hitching rail and tied him alongside several other horses.

A black-stained saddle, decorated with silver, sat atop a solid black horse in the line. The horse, larger and stronger than Comet, turned its head toward Trace when he approached. Its bridle bore the silver medallions matching those on its saddle. Two other horses, less impressive and carrying plainer tack, stood beside the black.

The horses looked familiar to Trace. Did they belong to the Mexicans that rode with Snake? Were their riders the three men that were missing the night Snake raided Molly's place?

Trace swung down slowly, to avoid jarring his sore muscles. He carried Molly's rifle with him as he went. He would have to be careful. If the bandits were inside, he would know them when he saw their faces. *But would they remember him?*

Keeping the rifle ready, Trace entered the saloon.

Two *vaqueros* lay sprawled, face down, across a card table. They were passed out, head-to-head, on top of the pasteboards.

The bartender stood behind the bar polishing glasses with a towel trying to stay awake after a long nightshift.

A third Mexican, dressed all in black and carrying a black *sombrero*, its crown encircled by a band of silver pieces, came down the stairs from the second floor. He swung his legs easily from step to step, letting his boot heels land solidly, and his spurs jingle loudly, each time to announce his approach. He rubbed his sleeve across the metal *conchos* surrounding the hat's crown, polishing them as he walked.

Trace turned his head and tugged his hat down low as he moved into a darkened corner of the saloon. He observed the man in silence as he strutted to the card table and kicked the legs on the two chairs, sending the two sleeping *vaqueros* sprawling onto the floor.

"Jose, Jesus, *hombres*, wake up!" He ordered in a thick accent.

Trace moved closer to the bar, watching the men behind him over his shoulder.

A girl leaned over the stair rail above, now, calling out to the man.

"Reyes, I will anxiously await your return."

"And I, pretty *señorita*, will bring you presents. Next time, I bring you special gift from Mexico." Reyes turned and swept his *sombrero* in a wide motion ending the arc with his hat sitting on his head.

The girl blew him a kiss.

"Quickly, *amigos*. We go," Reyes grabbed the two *vaqueros* by the back of their shirt collars and hefted them to their feet. He shoved them ahead of him as he strode out of the saloon.

The sound of Reyes' spurs faded as he moved across the uneven floor and stepped through the swinging doors.

"Who was that?" Trace asked the bartender when the three were gone.

"It's not my place to say. The men come in here, now and then. All I know is, they are return customers."

"This Reyes, as the girl called him, he wears a lot of silver decoration. I suppose that was his horse, with all the silver on it, at the rail?" He hoped the bartender would be more forthcoming with information.

"He takes care of his horse and his women," the bartender said nodding in the direction of the girl overhead. "He has a beautiful animal. Most beautiful in all Santa Fe. Shiny black with a fancy saddle. Silver buckles and coins, like most of us have never seen before. He keeps him stabled where he gets fresh water, hay, and grain." The bartender chuckled. "He likes to parade around town on him to impress the *señoritas*."

Trace nodded.

The bartender leaned forward and lowered his voice, "Let me give you a piece of advice, mister. Don't mess with him. Hear tell, anyone that does, doesn't come back—leastwise, not alive."

"Thanks. You got any coffee?"

The bartender poured him a cup and set it on the bar in front of him. Trace paid him and took the cup of steaming liquid to sit in the shadows at the nearest table, his back against the wall. If Reyes returned, he wanted to be sure he was facing him when he came through the swinging doors.

Fifteen

Andy knew it was going to take him a long time to get back home, if he didn't come up with a ride soon. He wished he had Jake to ride back, but he had lost him, too. Ma was going to really be mad.

He had no idea what schedule the stage kept along the route and even if he knew, he had no money for passage.

He trudged along in the dark until his body demanded rest and he found a spot off the road to curl up under a rock ledge and sleep for the night.

There was no rooster to awaken him when the sun rose, and as Andy came out from his groggy fog, it took a few seconds for him to remember where he was—and why.

As he became fully aware of his surroundings, he realized he had avoided recapture. His stomach rumbled for food and he wondered what he was going to do about that. He was still miles from Moriarty and farther than that from Santa Fe. Snake and his bunch were headed there. But Andy had escaped before he heard Snake state his true intentions. Andy wasn't about to try to reach that town. He was on his way home. He'd have to keep walking south.

~ * ~

Back at the homestead, Molly dozed restlessly all night, rising periodically to check on her patient. She kept a fire going in order to have hot broth available for Tom if he roused.

Tom had slipped in and out of consciousness throughout the early morning hours and when daylight finally came, he opened his eyes ever so slightly. Molly, quick to react, took a heavy bowl to the cook pot and returned with the broth.

She knelt beside him and positioned a blanket beneath his head. She cooled a spoonful of broth and slowly let it drain into Tom's mouth.

Barely able to swallow, he took only a couple of spoonfuls, then sunk back into sleep again.

Molly sighed and put the broth down. She pulled a shawl closer around her shoulders in the early dawn hour and stood up. When the children awoke, she would have to make a decision about how they were going to get Doc Landry to see the patient.

She didn't know if she dared move Tom into the buckboard. She hated to leave the children here alone with a dying man while she rode for the doctor. She dreaded sending Seth out on Comet to get help. He was so young and defenseless—what if hoodlums or wild animals approached him? Yet, she knew, her patient had to have medical aide beyond what she could provide.

She worried about Andy. Why hadn't he returned? And Trace. She knew he wouldn't give up until he found Andy and Andy, not knowing Comet had returned, wouldn't give up until he found Comet.

What should she do?

~ * ~

Trace finished his coffee at the saloon just as a commotion erupted outside in the plaza.

"*Prisa! Prisa!*" A young boy's voice called out excitedly.

Trace heard more children shouting and cheering. He moved quickly to the boardwalk in front of the saloon.

A group of children scurried along behind Reyes and his two men as they rode their horses out of town. Reyes flung candy from a broken *piñata*, flinging it behind him and his *vaqueros* as they went. The dashing young Mexican laughed uproariously as the children tumbled over each other in their attempt to gather the most candy while it lasted.

"See how the *niños* scatter like chickens pecking at grain," Reyes said to his men.

He shook the *piñata* high in the air with one hand then dug his fist deep into the hole he had smashed in the top. He turned the blue, donkey-shaped *piñata*, upside down and shook it.

"No more, *niños*. No more. Now run along. Reyes has things to do."

His two *vaqueros* were too hung-over to appreciate the chatter and noise of the children and they sagged in their saddles waiting for the frivolity to be finished.

Trace studied the man that led the little parade. His eyes settled on the silver-trimmed saddle, atop the impressive horse.

This Reyes was different. No one else in the whole territory outfitted themselves like him. He dressed himself up with silver right down to the silver-handled pistols at his hips. If his presence foretold his abilities, Trace was glad he wouldn't have to go up against him, at least for the time being.

Reyes tossed the broken *piñata* to a child standing nearby.

"Well, *niño*, were you too late to catch a treat? Here." Reyes took a silver coin from his vest pocket and tossed it to the child. The boy dropped the *piñata* and reached both hands skyward to catch the treasure.

This Reyes is a generous man, Trace thought. Not so on the night Snake's gang had plundered the Westerman ranch. But Reyes had not been the one to leave such devastation. Snake had seen to that.

Did Reyes rob then dispense his spoils to the poor Mexican people in Santa Fe?

Well, whatever he did, it wasn't his business as long as it didn't involve Comet or any threat to him or the Klings. Trace's beef with the man went back to that night on the ranch. He had been there, in the background, along with the two other riders. Trace surmised they had been hired to take the cattle back to Mexico. Even though they hadn't fired the shots that killed his parents, they had done nothing to stop Snake from killing them, either. They were as guilty in Trace's eyes as Snake was.

Trace moved to where Flapjack stood alone now, at the rail.

He mounted and rode out of town, back toward Moriarty. There was nothing more to do in Santa Fe. Reyes was on his way out, perhaps to rejoin Snake. Trace had come for Comet. Not finding him there, he would have to keep his eyes open wide for Andy, Comet, and Jake on his return.

~ * ~

Once Molly had Seth and Rosie ready for the day, she decided they would have to load Tom into the buckboard and take him to Doc Landry.

Tom was feverish and she knew the bullet would have to come out soon.

For now, Tom seemed to be holding his own and she would take plenty of water and broth and try to settle him as comfortably and as solidly as she could in the back of the wagon. If she drove carefully, she hoped she could keep from opening up the wound and starting it bleeding again.

A new dilemma arose.

Only half of the team was in the corral. Andy had rode out on Jake. Comet had come home, but having never been hitched to a buckboard, Molly couldn't use him as the second horse in the team. Trying to get Tom to town, across the horse again would probably finish him off.

The road between the homestead and Moriarty was fairly level. Big Boy might have the strength to pull the buckboard with Tom in it if she and the children took turns walking and if she pushed the rig to get it started. Big Boy would probably object to being hitched singly to one side of the doubletree. It wasn't going to be easy, but she didn't know how else they could get Tom into town to Doc Landry's office.

Molly brought Big Boy out of the corral and backed him into position. Thank goodness, Andy had taken Jake, the smaller horse. There would have been no way Jake could pull the buckboard alone.

She made sure all the tack was where it should be to avoid ensnarling the horse, and stood back to make sure it would hold.

Carefully, with the help of the children, Molly loaded Tom into the back of the buckboard. She gave the children instructions to stand back on the tailgate and she grasped Big Boy's halter tightly in her hand and tugged him forward.

At first, the horse balked. Used only as part of a team, everything was lopsided.

At last, with Molly's encouragement and the children prodding him, Big Boy began to pull the buckboard forward.

"Good boy," Molly patted the animal's head with her free hand as they began to roll.

It was slow going and Molly called a halt only occasionally to check on Tom and ease small drips of liquid into his mouth. Then, the rigorous chore of starting the wagon rolling again began to take its toll. Molly allowed the children to take turns crawling over the tailgate and resting in the rear of the wagon alongside Tom. She walked beside Big Boy carrying the reins and leading the horse by his halter.

"Careful not to disturb our passenger," she told Rosie and reminded Seth as each took their turn.

A trip that should have taken them less than an hour took several hours. Finally, they crept up alongside the blacksmith's shop.

"Josh," Molly called to the apprentice where he worked outside the shop. "Would you run ahead and tell Doc Landry we have a patient for him. The man's been shot and I'm afraid Doc's going to have to operate."

Josh dropped his tools and ran down the street. Mrs. Kling had a desperate situation on her hands and he wasn't about to slow her down.

Mr. Hughes stepped in behind the buckboard to follow. Molly sped up and soon Mr. Hughes was walking as fast as he could and Rosie and Seth were running behind them to keep up.

As Molly approached the block where Doc Landry maintained an office, she saw the doctor rush from the building with Josh beside him. Josh carried his black bag while Doc Landry hurried along drying his hands on a towel.

"Whoa, Big Boy," Molly reined the horse up in the street.

Doc Landry dropped the tailgate on the buckboard and climbed into the back to inspect the passenger.

"How long's he been this way?"

"He's been at my place since last night. He came in looking like he'd lost a lot of blood. I cleaned him up, got the bleeding stopped, and tried to get nourishment down him. I don't know how long he'd been lying across Comet's back before he reached us."

Doc turned to Josh and Mr. Hughes, "I'm going to need your help getting him inside. You were right to bring him in, Mrs. Kling. He needs that bullet dug out of him before he can start to heal. I only hope he doesn't have too much infection going on already."

Once Tom was removed to Doc Landry's office, Molly instructed Rosie and Seth to get back into the wagon.

"And stay there."

"I'm going to need an assistant," Doc told Molly. "My wife's gone to her sister's to help with the new baby."

Molly nodded.

"Josh, can you take the kids back to the blacksmith's shop with you? I don't want to leave them out front in the buckboard and risk having another runaway."

"Sure. Actually, I was just going home. How about if I take them with me? I'll check back after we have something to eat."

"That'll be fine. I'd appreciate it."

Josh left Doc and Molly to do their work and went back outside.

As he approached the buckboard, Rosie was sitting on the seat staring down the road as if looking for someone. Seth was in the back inspecting something.

"Come on kids, your Ma says you're to go with me. Are you hungry?"

Seth looked up with interest, his attention momentarily removed from the tooled leather holster with its pearl handled gun lying in the back of the wagon.

"Yeah, I am." Seth said.

"How about you, Rosie? I'll show you how I'm fixin' Trace's saddle for him."

Rosie shook her head. She was hungry but a nagging picture was forming in her mind. It was a jumble of images of both Trace and Andy and she had a foreboding of impending disaster, but she couldn't put her finger on the precise reason.

"Come on, you'll perk up when you get some food in your belly," Josh said as he lifted her down.

Molly opened the door of Doc's office and stuck her head out.

"It's all right. Go ahead. I'll come get you when I'm finished here."

Molly closed the door. Seth removed the gun from its holster. He tucked the pearl-handled pistol into his pants, the way he had seen Trace do. He scurried off the back of the buckboard before Josh could lift him down. He was careful not to get too close to Josh, in case he might see the prize he carried peeking out above his pants.

With the children safely overseen by Josh, Molly concentrated on the tasks the doctor gave her.

"There are some sterile bandages in the drawer. We need to swab down the area around his wound and lay those around the edge. I want to do everything I can to avoid any further infection."

Molly went to get the bandages while Doc carefully swabbed the area around the bullet hole with iodine.

"I haven't ever done much more than nurse a fever or help with a colicky baby, Doc. You'll have to tell me, step-by-step, what you need."

"You'll do fine. There's a tray of sterilized tools on the table, over there," Doc pointed to a small container, "I'll need those."

Tom lay face down, unconscious.

Doc probed the hole for the bullet with a metal pick.

He and Molly both heard a soft click when the two different metals touched.

"There it is. Now, all we have to do is get it out."

Molly looked at Doc in concern. She didn't know if she could watch him cut on someone without getting sick.

"There's a trick I learned a long time ago," Doc said as he worked. "If the sight of blood bothers you," he probed the tool further and reached for a delicate tweezers-like instrument. "Breathe deeply until you calm yourself inside. I don't have the luxury of making that much movement." He squeezed the tool and felt it grip the bullet. He pulled the slug out and laid it in another pan.

"This fellow might want that, now that it's outside of him."

"Doc, I've got to tell you something—in confidence." Molly looked about to be sure there was no one near the window or door. "He's a Texas Ranger. He must be working in secret or something. He had his badge hidden in his boot. I only found out when I pulled them off."

"Anybody else know?"

"I don't know if whoever shot him knew, and that's why they tried to kill him, or not. His name is Tom and he was with Snake's gang that night they rode into our camp. Trace and I thought something wasn't right because he didn't act like the rest of them. He wasn't so—mean."

"Maybe he got inside the gang to put them away."

"I guess. Maybe."

"Well, it could be Snake, or one of his men, that put that bullet in his back. Hard to say. I'll have to report this to the sheriff, though. He don't like me not telling him about bullet wounds."

"Report what?" the sheriff asked as he came through the door. He saw Tom lying on the doctor's examining table.

"A bullet wound, Sheriff."

"I heard Mrs. Kling brought someone in, that's why I came over—to see who it was and what happened."

"All I know is, his name's Tom. He was riding with the bunch that stopped by my place that night," Molly said. She looked at Doc for a sign that he wouldn't betray Tom's identity, even to the sheriff.

"He's going to take some mending, Sheriff, before he can be locked up, if that's your intention."

"Well, as soon as he's well enough, I want to talk to him. See if he knows who shot him in the back."

"I'll let you know when he's able to talk to you, Sheriff."

"No boots or gun belt? What about a coat?"

"I had to cut it off him," Molly answered, hoping he wouldn't insist on seeing Tom's boots—or gun. The gun! She had left it in the buckboard with his boots. She felt panic inside, but tried not to let her face show the emotion.

"Well, I expect he can give me any information I need when he comes around. Send someone for me, will you Doc?"

"Of course, Sheriff."

Molly followed the sheriff to the door and watched as he walked back toward his office. When he was far enough away that she thought he wouldn't be paying any attention to her, she went to the buckboard and got Tom's boots.

When she picked them up she felt the cool metal badge against her forefinger inside the left boot. She reached for the holster and quickly moved it alongside her full skirt. It was lighter than it should be.

The pearl-handled pistol was missing.

She stretched to look over the side of the buckboard to see if it had fallen out and was lying on the floorboards. She didn't want to think what might have happened to the gun. But she sensed she wouldn't find the gun there and instinct told her where it was.

She moved quickly to take Tom's things inside Doc's office. When the man healed he would need his boots and his gun. If someone had already tried to kill him, he'd need a way to protect himself if they tried it again.

"Here's his boots, Doc. Please, put them somewhere out of sight. I have to go check on the kids." Molly hung the empty leather gun belt behind a jacket on the coat rack.

"What's your rush? Josh'll see to 'em."

"I know. But I—forgot to tell them something."

She had to hurry and get Tom's fancy gun back before something terrible happened with it. Seth was too curious for his own good. Fear nearly paralyzed her as she thought about what might happen if the child did have the pistol as she suspected.

She didn't know where Josh lived.

Leaving the buckboard behind, she hurried to the blacksmith's shop. Mr. Hughes lived alongside the shop and he could tell her where to go to find Josh. She couldn't wait for Josh to bring the children back. That might be too late. She would have to find them herself.

And, if Seth didn't have the gun, then what? Then, good! Maybe it fell out of the wagon. She'd have to look for it later. For now, it was too deadly a weapon to take a chance that a five-year-old might play with it.

~ * ~

Rosie finished eating the meal Josh's mother had set in front of her. Seth had wolfed his food down and Rosie made a mental note to tell Molly he hadn't minded his manners. He'd been rude—gobbling his food then rushing outside to play with barely a thank you for Josh's ma.

"Thank you, Ma'am," Rosie said as she left the table.

"You are certainly welcome, Rosie."

Rosie was halfway to the door when the vision struck.

She stopped abruptly, but fought to keep from crying out.

"Are you all right, child?" Josh's ma asked when she saw the girl falter.

Rosie turned slowly and looked at her.

"I'm fine." She didn't want to alarm the older woman. She tried to move toward the door at a normal pace.

"Go ahead and play outside, then. Josh will take you back to Doc's office soon."

Rosie reached the front porch. There she stopped suddenly and screamed.

Seth, just as his image had appeared in her mind, stood erect, right arm extended straight out, and his left eye closed.

"Seth! You put that gun down!" Rosie shrieked.

Sixteen

Molly heard the shot ring out before she reached Josh's house.

She felt her insides turn to ice. When she broke free of the fear, she ran the rest of the way.

Rosie screamed uncontrollably. Josh's mother bent over Seth, who was lying on the ground. Josh crawled out from behind a rain barrel where he had taken refuge.

"He's dead! He's dead," Rosie screeched as Molly rushed toward the group.

Seth lay in the dirt. The pistol had landed a few inches away when it recoiled, hitting him in the head and flinging the youngster's arm backward, knocking him down. His weight had been no match for the unexpected buck of the gun.

Josh knelt down beside Seth.

"Are you hurt?"

Molly reached Josh's side and dropped to her knees.

Seth looked up at Rosie, Molly, Josh, and Josh's ma. They were all staring into his face.

"I told you not to mess with any guns," Rosie said. "The first time was an accident. This time—well, you did that on purpose!"

"I was only aiming at a post."

Seth tried to get up as Molly looked for a bullet hole or blood.

"I'm not hurt. Leave me alone." Seth began to cry as the shock of what he had done sank in. His nose ran and he swiped at it with his bare arm.

"Seth, you're lucky you didn't kill someone, or yourself!" Molly thought about leaving the gun behind when Tom was moved into the doctor's office. She knew she should have grabbed it then, but they had had their hands full. Sometimes, there were more things to keep track of than her mind had room to handle. She simply couldn't do it all by herself.

Molly felt her knees begin to shake and she wanted to cry, too. She sat there, holding Seth until they both calmed down.

Josh walked over to the pistol and picked it up. He whistled, impressed with its unique handle.

"No wonder you were curious," he told Seth. "This is a mighty beautiful piece of iron. Does it belong to the man you brought in, Mrs. Kling?"

Molly nodded, brushing Seth's hair out of his eyes with the palm of her hand.

"I should have taken it in and left it at Doc's office."

"I'll run it down there for you,"

"Thank you. The holster is in Doc's office."

Josh tucked the gun in his waistband and his mother gave him a look of disapproval.

"I'll just drop it off where it belongs, Ma."

"You know packing a gun can only get you in trouble. You get rid of that thing—fast, you hear?"

"Yes, Ma."

"I'm terribly sorry for all the trouble Seth caused," Molly told the woman.

"Fortunately, it could have been worse. You come on in and have something to eat. You look as if you could use a hot meal and maybe a cup of tea."

Tea. That would be refreshing. She hadn't tasted tea in a long time.

"Rosie, keep watch on Seth. Don't let him leave this yard and make sure he doesn't find anything else to get in trouble with."

"Yes, Ma," Rosie said darting an angry look in Seth's direction.

"You're always getting into something, you pest," Rosie told Seth as she sat down on the steps of the porch. "Ma said stay here and you do it!" Rosie picked at a blade of grass and fussed about having to watch Seth. *Where was Andy? And Trace?* Things were easier when they were around to help. Maybe it was because Seth was afraid he'd get caught messing with things he shouldn't be when they were there to keep an eye on him. Whatever the reason, she liked it better when they were home, too. She looked at the door to the house and wondered how long Ma would be inside. She sure didn't want to be stuck watching Seth too long.

~ * ~

On the outskirts of Santa Fe, Trace heard the sound of horses racing behind him. He hustled Flapjack off the road far enough into the brush to watch the riders go by and not be seen.

Reyes and his men rode south at a canter. Whether they were headed for Albuquerque or the Estancia/Moriarty area he couldn't know. If they continued south instead of turning west a few miles away from Moriarty, they could ride right through Moriarty, perhaps on their way back to Mexico.

He let them get further ahead of him, then eased Flapjack back onto the road and followed, taking care not to catch up or come upon the men unexpectedly.

He had only the rifle Molly had loaned him for protection and he felt uncomfortable going up against the three of them at close range with a long gun.

~ * ~

Andy was beginning to believe he would never reach town, much less home, when he heard the cantering horse's hooves behind him.

He ducked to hide in the brush but Reyes' eye was faster than his escape.

"Ho, *niño*," Reyes called out, pulling his horse to a stop in the dusty road. "Why you hide, *niño*? Jose!" Reyes called to one of the *vaqueros* who understood his silent order.

Andy started to run through the thick brush but José had already circled behind him. The husky *vaquero* reached down from his perch and clutched Andy by the waist of his pants to carry him back to Reyes.

Andy was humiliated. He was not a kid!

"Let me down."

"What are you doing out here alone?"

"I—I'm looking for my horse." Andy looked Reyes' mount over good. He was beautiful. Black, like Comet, only bigger and more muscular.

"It is a sad thing when a man loses his horse," Reyes said, empathizing with the boy. "Tell me, what does he look like?"

"A lot like yours," Andy said as Jose set him on his feet in front of Reyes. "Only, smaller, probably faster."

"Ho, faster? We must have a race someday, if you find your horse."

Andy didn't want to tell him he had lost Jake, as well, and kept his mouth shut.

Reyes studied the ways he could profit from his find. He could hold the boy for ransom. But, by the looks of his clothes, he didn't appear that his family had much to pay for him. He could sell him as a slave back in Mexico but it would be hard to get a good price for a young boy when the buyers preferred young women.

"Well, *niño*, what shall we do with you?"

"I just want to go home. Don't hurt me, please. There's a whole posse of people close behind me. If you shoot me, they'll hear the shot and be here before you can holster your gun."

Reyes laughed. "I don't believe you, *niño*." He pulled a long-bladed knife from a scabbard beneath his belt. "This is very quiet. No one would hear if I were to throw it." He flicked his wrist as if to release the blade.

Andy ducked instinctively.

Reyes laughed again. "Is that what you think—that Reyes Espiañata goes around hurting *niños*?" Then his eyes clouded with anger. "You offend me, little man."

"No. How should I know what you do? We've never met before."

Reyes' look softened. "Take it from me, it is not the *niños* I am after. What shall we do with him?" He asked his *vaqueros*. His horse moved anxiously at the approach of an unseen rider.

"You're ready to run, are you my friend?" Reyes asked the horse. "Put the boy up behind Jesus, Jose. Let us be on our way."

Jose again clutched the back of Andy's pants and lifted him up behind the saddle back onto Jesus' horse.

Andy smelled the scent of stale alcohol and tobacco smoke in Jesus' clothes. There was the stench of sweat mingled with the two odors—both from the horse and the man.

"What are you going to do with me?"

"We shall see," Reyes still contemplated how to dispose of his captive.

As they spurred their horses on to the south, Andy wondered if he would end up in Mexico—a slave to Reyes Espiañata.

~ * ~

Trace saw the three Mexicans pick Andy up. With only the rifle and plenty of brush for them to dodge into, he decided it was best to wait until they got out in the open to try to rescue Andy without risking getting him hurt. Farther on, the brush would drop away as they lowered in elevation and headed out into the valley toward Moriarty.

He decided to keep pace with the men ahead of him and wait for his best chance to reclaim the boy.

He settled Molly's rifle across his lap and was about to kick his heels into Flapjack's flanks when he heard a rustling in the brush nearby.

Trace picked up the rifle and spun Flapjack around, ready to fire, if necessary. He knew Snake might be out here somewhere. But, then, perhaps a range cow had broken free from a herd headed up the trail and was feeding on the brush and grass beneath the trees.

The sound of the movement was gradual and Trace listened intently. Surely, if it were something threatening it would be in a bigger hurry than it appeared to be.

Trace moved Flapjack a few feet back onto the road and used the rifle barrel to lift the branches of a tree. He looked into the thicket blocking the view alongside.

To his surprise, a horse's head poked up from behind the brush. Jake, grazing on low grasses, raised his head to chew. His reins drooped and tangled as he moved.

Trace eased Flapjack up closer, making sure it wasn't a trap, before he closed in to clutch Jake's bridle. He ran his hand down the reins, from the bit, until he had the length secure and could tug Jake behind him.

"I'm sure glad to see you, fella," he said softly so as not to draw any attention to himself if anyone else was around the area. *Had Jake been following Andy?*

"Now let's get out of here."

He hurried the horses along to get within view of the riders ahead, yet remain far enough behind to be undetected.

He knew where Andy was now, but he wasn't happy about the answer.

Snake and his bunch and Comet were the unknown factors in his search. He didn't plan on running into Snake, on this trip, if he could help it. He prepared himself, just in case. Instead of settling the rifle across his knees again, he rested it in the crook of his arm where he could grab the butt and be ready to fire at any threat.

~ * ~

Snake and the other outlaws had ridden toward Santa Fe during the night, then turned east and made camp a few miles off the road toward Las Vegas. Snake's intent was to stay hidden there a few days, then drop down to Moriarty, meet up with Reyes, and hit the Cattlemen's Bank.

He planned to take the sleepy little town by surprise. Getting the money should be as easy as gathering tarantulas along the border after a rainstorm.

~ * ~

Trace was becoming weary of riding and his injuries were aggravating him. Riding so long had not helped his healing and, when he drew a breath now and then, he felt a sharp pain in his ribs. If he didn't get some relief soon he didn't know if he could go on. Still, he fought the pain to keep Reyes and his men within earshot. He had to save Andy!

~ * ~

After what seemed too long a time to Rosie, Molly came back out of Josh's house. She said good-bye to Josh's ma and led the children back to Doc's office.

She stood them at the office door.

"Now, don't either one of you move."

"Can't we just sit here on Doc's bench, Ma?"

"Yes. But I'll have my eye on you." Molly went inside and left the door open.

"Doc, how's the patient doing?" Molly asked as she studied the quiet form on the table. She moved to the coat rack where the ranger's gun belt hung and saw that Josh had replaced the pistol. She felt better having it there, where it belonged. She was sure Tom would feel that way, too—if he ever woke up.

"I think he's going to make it." Doc turned his attention to her. "You look tired. You better go on home. You can come back in tomorrow and see how he is."

"Yes, we're going to head out. It's going to be a long trip, I'm afraid."

"Why don't you unhitch and leave your buckboard right where it is. Take my buggy. If I have to, I can ride horseback to make a call. Things have been pretty quiet lately."

"Thanks, Doc. I don't feel right doing that, though. But I think I will leave the buckboard. I'll go as far as the schoolhouse and stay for the night. I'll take Big Boy and the three of us can ride him over there."

She went over the things, in her mind, that might be a problem if she didn't go home. She had let Comet out to pasture before she left, there was plenty of water in the trough and he would stick close to the corral, she was sure. The only other problem was the chickens. They would have to roost without the coop shut. She might lose a few of them, but it couldn't be helped. She was too tired to ride the three miles or so home and Seth and Rosie were already about to fall asleep on the bench outside Doc's office. She would have to take her chances with the chickens. Perhaps the owl would keep other predators away, if he didn't decide to go inside the coop and help himself to dinner.

Molly went outside and unhitched Big Boy, then lifted Rosie and Seth onto his back before climbing onto the seat of the buckboard so she could get on the big horse ahead of them.

Doc watched from his open door.

"I'll see you in the morning, Doc."

"Ma," Rosie asked plaintively, "what if Andy comes home while we're gone?"

"Well, I guess he'll have to shut the chickens up and give Comet some grain, then," Molly said as normally as she could.

When Molly left, Doc returned to check on his patient. On his way past the coat rack he saw the pearl-handled pistol hanging there in its tooled leather holster and belt.

It was a thing of beauty. But he looked at his patient, and saw the reality. The business end of any gun could be ugly.

He didn't know what his patient was doing hanging out with Snake, but he knew he couldn't have picked a more dangerous place to be. If he ever came to perhaps he would realize that.

It would make his work a lot easier if they all just put their guns away. He had enough to do patching up broken bones and delivering babies. He much preferred that to digging bullets out of someone's flesh.

Tom remained still and pale, almost gray, on the examining table. Doc dragged a wooden kitchen chair up and sat down beside him to make sure he didn't roll off the table, if he woke up.

~ * ~

As night fell, Reyes and his men made camp along the trail, unconcerned about someone bothering them. They lit a campfire and shared jerky and water with Andy.

They used their saddles for pillows. Reyes wrapped the saddle blanket around his to protect the leather and silver. He directed Jose to let Andy wrap up in his saddle blanket for the night.

Andy lay there, thinking about what might happen to him. Should he try to sneak off? Or, should he rest for the night and ride on with these men until an opportunity arose to get away? Riding was certainly better than walking. He was still puzzling over his dilemma when he fell fast asleep.

~ * ~

Trace, aware that the men had moved off the road to make camp, stopped and tied Flapjack and Jake in the bushes. He settled down to rest and let the men go to sleep.

When it was late enough, and the moon went behind a cloud, he crept silently up to the camp.

There, he saw the three Mexicans stretched out alongside their dying campfire and Andy, sleeping, on the opposite side.

He heard the heaviest man snoring and watched as he jerked and rolled into a better position. Finally, the man settled down to an even breathing pattern like the other two.

Trace picked up small clumps of dirt and tossed them carefully at Andy. One clod bounced off Andy's chest. He flinched and brushed at his shirt as if flies were bothering him.

Trace crawled closer and changed his aim. The next chunk of dirt hit Andy in the face. He blinked but lay there taking in his surroundings and trying to figure out what kept pestering him. Sometimes, Comet would nudge him, if they were out together at night, but he couldn't make out anything that would indicate Comet was near.

"Psst!" Trace said softly.

Andy looked in the direction of the noise.

Trace raised his index finger and motioned for the boy to come to him, quietly.

He didn't have to tell him twice. Andy lifted the saddle blanket aside and, looking back over his shoulder at the three sleeping men, he crawled along the ground silently to Trace.

Trace began moving ahead of him until they were far enough away from Reyes' camp to stand up and walk quickly toward the horses.

"Am I glad to see you!" Andy said, when they had put enough distance between them and the camp not to be heard.

Trace led him to the horses.

"Jake! I'm glad to see you, too. I thought sure Ma was going to be so-o-o-o mad at me for losing you."

Trace handed Jake's reins to Andy.

"Get on. Walk him, very slowly, down the road until we get some ways past Reyes' camp. I'll signal you. When I do, ride like hell!"

Andy nodded and slung his leg up over Jake's back.

Once Trace and Andy were far enough away from Reyes and his men Trace felt they could run the horses, he turned to Andy.

"Go."

They both kicked their steeds in the flanks. They raced for Moriarty.

It was several hours past midnight when they reached the quiet town. Even the saloons were dim. The hotel where Trace had eaten breakfast a couple of mornings before was dark except for one small lamp glowing on top of the registration desk.

Trace dismounted and tied their horses in front of the hotel.

"Just as well get down, Andy. We'll try to get a room for the night. We're both too tired to go on and I hurt too much to make it the last few miles.

Trace rapped his knuckles on the glass window of the door. No one stirred. He rapped again.

Peering inside at the desk, he saw a small figure rise from behind it and come to unlock the door.

"Son, Andy and I need a room. Can you put us up for the night?"

The boy looked at him through a sleepy haze.

"Andy?"

"Yeah. Trace and I'd sure appreciate it if you could let us have a room. He's hurting awful bad."

"Sure. We've got just one left. I was just about to turn in, too."

Trace took some money from his saddlebag to give the boy. He rapidly signed the register with an illegible signature.

"Upstairs. Second room on your right," the boy said.

The hotel proprietor's son handed Trace a skeleton key. If anything, the lock would only slow someone down. All of the keys were the same and the doors were so flimsy a heavy shoulder could knock them down with little effort.

The boy looked at the clock behind him. He handed Trace the kerosene lamp.

"You might as well use this. It'll be daylight soon."

Trace carried the lamp, holding it out ahead of them to light their way along the stairs. The stairway was narrow so Andy followed Trace to the room.

Once inside, a bed barely large enough for two people filled the area with only room left over for a chest of drawers with a washbowl on top. Water sat nearby in a pitcher.

Neither Trace nor Andy were interested in cleaning up. They both dropped onto the quilt-covered mattress, without pulling the covers back. Fully clothed, they fell asleep.

~ * ~

Back at Reyes' camp, a cloudburst came by pelting rain in a narrow swath as it moved across the land.

Jose and Reyes both awoke, having no saddle blanket to shelter them from the fleeting downpour. Jesus continued to snore.

Jose moved to the campfire and poked at the embers with a stick, then threw more wood on the coals until the small limbs burst into flame. Reyes moved to the fire to warm himself and Jose glanced, sleepily, across to his saddle blanket.

"Niño!" He said. *"Niño vamoosed."*

Reyes looked to where Andy had been sleeping.

"Sí! I told him, I didn't hurt *niños*. Why he didn't believe me? Am I such a big, bad fellow? Huh, Jose?"

Jose walked over and picked up his blanket, shaking the dirt and raindrops that beaded in the oil from the horse, off the coarse material. He wrapped the blanket, like a *serape*, around his shoulders and squatted by the fire.

"We will probably find him in the daylight. He won't get far without his horse that is 'faster than mine'." Reyes laughed at Andy's faith in Comet's speed and his foolishness at trying to escape.

"Does anyone have a horse faster than Reyes?" He asked Jose.

Jose, sleep returning now that the warmth of the fire and his blanket were lulling him, answered, "Nah." He rolled away from the fire and settled into a deep slumber.

Reyes returned to his saddle and leaned with his shoulders against it, watching the fire as he became sleepy.

"We will meet again, *niño*. You and your fast horse have not seen the last of Reyes Espiañata."

Seventeen

The next morning, Trace and Andy awoke in the strange room. It was the first time in a long time that Andy had opened his eyes and seen a ceiling overhead. It took him a moment to remember where he was and why.

They had slept late. The sun was already beating in through the window at the foot of the bed.

Andy got up and washed his face and hands, then lifted the window and leaned outside. He looked up and down the street but saw no one he recognized.

Trace rolled to the edge of the bed and put his feet on the floor. He had removed his boots the night before, but nothing else. As tired and sore as he was, all he had been able to think about was getting some rest.

"Morning, Andy," he said when he saw the boy leaning out the window. "Anything out there I need to know about?"

Andy pulled his head back in.

"No, not that I can see."

"Well, let me wash up and then I'll treat you to a breakfast like you've probably never had before. The lady that runs the restaurant downstairs is a real good cook. Not that your Ma isn't, mind you."

Andy nodded. "I know the boy that let us in last night. We go to school together. Sometimes, he brings the best desserts in his lunch bucket. He shares them with me once in a while." Andy remembered the taste of fresh lemon pie and rich chocolate cake.

"He said his Ma went off to one of those places where they teach people how to cook fancy foods."

Trace and Andy went downstairs where Trace turned in the key to their room. Their only luggage was Trace's saddlebags, which were slung loosely over his shoulder, and Molly's rifle, which he checked at the desk while they went into the alcove for breakfast.

Andy had smelled the food cooking before they were all the way downstairs and his mouth watered. He was as bad as Crazy Leg was when his taste buds got aroused. He rubbed the back of his hand across his lips to make sure he wasn't drooling.

"Sure does smell good," he told Trace.

"Beats dry jerky anytime."

"Good morning, gentlemen," the proprietor said as they walked under the heavy drapes that had been pulled back to let clientele know meals were being served. "Pick a table and my wife will be right with you."

Trace selected one by a small window where he could keep an eye on the comings and goings outside on the street.

He nodded 'good morning' to an attractive patron at the next table, noticing her eastern attire.

The woman wore a full coat-styled dress with a hat to match. The parasol that went with the outfit leaned against the back of her chair.

She smiled back at Trace and Andy.

The proprietor leaned toward Trace and spoke in a low voice, "Women's underwear sales. That's what she does. The stores back East have been sending widows and women that don't have a man to support them on the road to measure the women and sell them undergarments. It's an honorable job," he said, defending the woman's position.

Trace nodded. Beyond that, he wasn't interested. It was good to know who your fellow diners were, he guessed, but, as long as they weren't outlaws, he really didn't care to know their business that much.

"Ma makes her own. And Rosie's. Leastwise what bloomers I seen her sew." Andy was surprised to see a slight tinge of red highlight Trace's cheeks.

"It's not polite to discuss women's undergarments, Andy, despite what the hotel owner said. Now, let's figure out what we're going to eat."

The woman who had waited on Trace before came to the table.

"You're the fellow that was in here looking for that horse. Did you find him?"

"No," Trace said. "Andy, here, is the one he belongs to."

"Yes, my son said it was Andy Kling's horse. It's a shame the horse is gone. My boy did what he could."

"I know," Trace said.

"That's what I been meaning to tell you, Trace. I think Comet went home. When I was at Snake's camp, I heard the one called Slade say he got away. If he did, he'd go home. I know he would."

Trace ordered hot cakes, bacon, eggs, and coffee.

"You want the same, Andy?"

"Sure."

"Only, milk for the boy, please, not coffee."

The woman left to send her son out with their drinks while she cooked their food.

When they were alone at the table again, Trace asked, "What do you mean you were at Snake's camp? You didn't say anything about that."

"I was on Jake, looking for Comet. Some big giant of a man knocked me off and dragged me into their camp. Comet wasn't there. Then this fella called Slade came in and said the horse ran off. That's why I was headed back home when I ran into Reyes and his men."

"You figured Comet would head for the corral. You're probably right, since he went home when he threw you off that night." Trace remembered the situation clearly. "How'd you get away from that bunch?"

"Snake tied me up, but I managed to get the rope loose and when it got dark, I slipped away into the trees. I didn't have time to look for Jake. All I could think about was hiding in the trees and getting away from the gang."

Andy's school friend sat a hot cup of coffee in front of Trace. He placed the milk next to Andy.

"Ma said she heard you say you think your horse went home."

The woman has good ears, Trace thought. He made no comment.

"Sure am hoping so."

"Me, too. It'd be a shame to lose him for good."

Trace poured sugar into his coffee and stirred it while Andy and the boy talked.

Once the boy left to get their food, Trace asked, "Did you get a chance to find out what Snake was up to? He's been hanging out in this area a long time. That's not like him. He usually hits and runs. I thought maybe he was going after a cattle drive along one of the trails."

"When I got back into the trees, I hid for a while until I was sure they weren't coming after me. I heard them talking about robbing a bank. Sounded like the one here in Moriarty."

"When? Do you know?"

"No. They talked about heading for Santa Fe, then doubling back here."

"Figured he was up to no good. We'll have to warn the sheriff. When they get here, we'll be waiting for them."

Trace and Andy finished their breakfast. Andy swabbed his plate with the last bite of pancake, wiping up the egg yolk with the syrup as he went. He wondered if his stomach would ever shrink back to its normal size after such a big meal. For now, he didn't care. It just felt good having the warmth and comfort of food in it.

The morning stage for Albuquerque pulled up in front of the hotel. Guests gathered their luggage and milled around beside it, waiting to load their things and climb aboard.

Jake and Flapjack moved nervously at the hitching rail as the people walked around them to reach the stagecoach stopped in the street.

The saleswoman walked past Trace and Andy and smiled again, letting her eyes linger on Trace's face.

Trace felt uneasy and rubbed the whiskers that had begun to shadow his features. It was a fleeting encounter. He would probably never see the woman again. He wondered why she had caught his attention. He wasn't looking to get involved with a strange woman right now. In a way, he was relieved when he saw her climb inside the stage to Albuquerque.

"There's Ma!" Andy said suddenly.

Trace looked in the direction Andy pointed. Molly, Rosie, and Seth rode Big Boy down the street past the stage and the restaurant window.

Trace jumped up and put some money on the table, hoping it would be more than enough to pay for their meal.

"I'll get your change, mister," the boy called out.

"No. We're in a hurry. You keep it."

Trace motioned for the hotel owner to hand him Molly's rifle as he reached the desk. Andy was already going through the front door and starting to run down the sidewalk, dodging early morning shoppers as he went.

"Ma!" Andy called out. "Ma!"

Trace was hurrying behind him now.

At last, Molly heard Andy's voice and halted Big Boy. She turned to look behind her.

"Ma, it's Andy—and Trace," Rosie said excitedly. "I told you that was Jake and Flapjack back there."

"I know, but the stage was in the way and I couldn't see to tell."

She heard Andy's voice.

She moved Big Boy over to the sidewalk, trying to remain calm even though excitement at seeing Andy running toward them, and Trace taking long strides to catch up swelled inside her. How wonderful! They appeared in fine shape and, although Trace was out of breath when they caught up to her, they looked no worse than when she'd seen them last. In fact, they seemed pretty darned good.

Despite his soreness, Trace lifted Seth and Rosie down off Big Boy. They immediately began jumping up and down around Andy and hugging him. Trace reached back up to help Molly down and when he lifted her into the air and swung her to the sidewalk, he didn't let go.

She thought he was going to kiss her again.

To her disappointment, he didn't. In the excitement of having them back, she had forgotten where she was and that public display of affection was not proper for a schoolteacher.

Trace held her in a long hug before turning her loose and letting her wrap her arms tight around Andy.

"I was so worried, Andy. Don't ever go off like that again!"

"I missed you, Ma. And Seth and Rosie."

Molly released him and he put an arm around each of his siblings.

The stagecoach started toward them and as it passed the woman from the restaurant was sitting at the open window. She lifted her gloved hand in a slight wave.

Trace waved back.

"Who was that?" Curiosity, and a twinge of jealousy, tugged at Molly.

"Just a lady that was having breakfast the same time we were." Trace looked at Molly and smiled. Had it been an opportunity lost? If he hadn't gotten involved with the Kling family, would he have reacted differently back there in the restaurant? He would never know.

"By the way, where are you headed?" Trace asked to change the subject as Molly's eyes followed the stage as it rounded a corner and disappeared.

She took Big Boy's reins and began to walk to Doc Landry's office as she explained.

"When Comet came home, he had a passenger."

"Wahoo! Comet came back?"

"Yes, Andy. He came home night before last. But he had that young fellow from Snake's bunch on him, Tom. He'd been shot in the back. I thought he was dead. He nearly was."

"But why was he shot? Sure hope it wasn't because of that fight with me," Trace said.

"We don't know who did it. Or why. I got him in here for Doc to take the bullet out the next morning."

They were nearing the doctor's office and Trace saw the buckboard sitting outside.

"That must have been quite a job to get him into the buckboard and get it here with only one horse."

"I'll tell you about that, later. Andy, please stay out here and keep your brother and sister out of trouble."

Trace and Molly went inside. The examining table was empty and Doc was coming out of a back room when they saw him.

"Morning Doc," Molly said.

"Mrs. Kling, Trace? Good to see you're back. Hope you caught up with Andy."

"He's outside with the kids," Trace answered. "Molly tells me she brought you a patient."

"Yeah, I got some help and moved him into a bed in the back room. He's doing better this morning. He came to and took some soup when the wife got home last night."

"Thank goodness," Molly said. "At first, when I saw he wasn't on the table—"

"No, he's young, healthy, and strong. I think he'll make a full recovery. I needed the table empty in case I had any other patients today. How are your injuries coming, Trace?"

"Much better today. Andy and I got in early this morning and got some sleep at the hotel. We had a good breakfast and," Trace cringed when he touched his ribs, "except for my ribs, and a sore rear end from riding so much, I'm feeling okay."

Doc, Molly and Trace walked back out to the sidewalk into the fresh air.

"Andy, why don't you go on back to the hotel and get the horses," Trace suggested now that they were where he and Molly could watch the younger kids.

"I left a note on the schoolhouse door that we wouldn't have school today," Molly said. "Figured I better get back and make sure everything is in order at the farm." She turned to Trace. "We stayed at the schoolhouse last night instead of going home."

Trace nodded, then turned to Doc Landry.

"We'll check back with you Doc. I'd like to talk to Tom when he's able."

"Sure. If you aren't around, I'll see if I can get Josh to ride out after you."

"Thanks."

"Sheriff's right interested in talking to him, too."

Trace stepped to the street to help Molly hitch Big Boy into his harness.

When Andy arrived with Jake and Flapjack, Trace backed Jake into position alongside Big Boy and finished hitching them as a team.

All of the Klings climbed into the buckboard. Andy and Molly rode up front and Seth and Rosie positioned themselves in the back.

Trace climbed onto Flapjack.

"I'll catch up with you. I have to see the sheriff before I leave town. Maybe I'll stop and see if Josh has my saddle ready. I sure could use it."

"We'll go on to the farm and take care of the animals."

Molly called to the horses, slapping the reins gently across their backs. The buckboard jolted and they moved down the street toward the end of town to turn around.

When they approached the livery, Andy saw three riders headed their way. Flashes of sunlight danced from shiny silver trim on one rider's *sombrero* and saddle.

Andy rolled over the back of the buckboard seat and crawled beneath the quilt Molly had used to cover Tom when they came to town.

Molly looked over her shoulder with concern.

"What are you doing?"

Rosie and Seth stared at the quilt in amazement.

"What's wrong with Andy?" Rosie asked.

"Ma, let those riders go by before you turn around, please. Then keep a good distance behind them."

Molly was puzzled, but assumed Andy must have a good reason to hide from the men.

She motioned for Seth and Rosie to move forward and lean against the quilt.

Reyes and his *vaqueros* approached.

"Good morning, *Señora*," Reyes called to Molly, touching his *sombrero* with his fingertips and smiling broadly.

"Good morning," she returned placidly trying to keep her eyes off the dashing man.

Andy held his breath.

Molly let the three men pass before she slowly began her turn.

Andy heard the clip-clopping of their horses and the jingle of their spurs. Gradually the sound faded.

"Stay put," Molly whispered. "They're stopping at a saloon up ahead. We have to go right past them. I'll wait until they're inside, if I can, before we go by."

Molly noticed the height of the striking *vaquero* dressed in black as he moved toward the swinging doors. He had pushed his *sombrero* off his head. It was held only by a cord around his neck and rested between his shoulder blades, exposing his hair as black and shiny as the hide of his horse. He brushed it back with his hand, then reached out to push the saloon doors open. He stood for a moment, watching Molly approach with the buckboard and smiled at her, again.

Molly ducked her head and looked away. It was flattering to be drawing his attention, but he was trouble. She sensed it and wanted no part of that. She had enough problems without encouraging a handsome *vaquero* to give her more.

She saw the decorations on the horse's bridle and saddle. She wasn't impressed with the man's outrageous preening and flaunting. He was like a peacock strutting and unashamed of it. He certainly wouldn't go unnoticed wherever he traveled.

She was glad Trace wasn't around to see her taking an interest in a man who was such a flirt with a stranger. She felt her face flush. She rarely blushed and turned her head away from the saloon to look at the other side of the street.

Too bad this attractive Mexican and Trace's friend from the restaurant hadn't crossed paths. The thought amused her. In a way, she and Trace were even, now—only he didn't know it.

Once they were past the saloon and Reyes had gone inside, Molly let the team pick up speed. She was anxious to get away from town without being followed.

At last, they were on the open road.

"You can get up, now, Andy, and tell me what that was all about."

"They picked me up on the road home, yesterday. Then, after they made camp and everybody was asleep, Trace woke me up and we took off. I don't know what they planned to do. I was just glad I didn't have to stick around and find out."

"I certainly hope you learned your lesson, young man." Chills of fright iced Molly's insides.

It's a good thing Ma doesn't know everything that happened, Andy thought as he grasped the back of the buckboard seat and climbed back up beside her.

"I did, Ma. I can hardly wait to get home and see Comet."

"You're lucky you're going home!"

Molly's anxiety over Andy's possible fate led her to speed the team along without realizing the amount of ground they were covering. They were some distance from Moriarty, now, and, preoccupied with Andy's story, she let the team continue at a rapid pace.

"There's a rider coming way back there," Rosie said, drawing Molly's attention away from giving Andy what for. Rosie pointed back toward town.

Andy turned to study the dust trail rising behind them. He sure hoped Reyes and his men hadn't decided to follow them.

Molly snapped the reins across the horses' backs to encourage them to pick up even more speed. She had nothing with which to protect herself or the children. Trace had her rifle. She should have gotten it from him when they left town. Too late for that! If it was the fancy-dressed Mexican and his men, they'd have to make a run for it.

Andy grasped the side of the buckboard seat to stay on the lurching wagon and called to Rosie and Seth.

"Hang on tight!"

Then, shouting over the noise of the team and wagon, he pleaded with Molly. "Run 'em, Ma! Run 'em as hard as you can!"

Eighteen

What's she driving like a crazy woman for? Trace wondered as he hurried to catch up to Molly and the kids. He was shocked to see the team race away when he approached.

He knew the buckboard would have to turn off the road and go down the drive to the homestead, so he headed cross-country and planned to intercept Molly before she got home.

He ran Flapjack as fast as he could go, keeping the buckboard in view.

Soon, he was gaining on it. He saw Seth and Rosie waving in the back. Molly slowed the horses, then stopped for Trace to catch up.

When the dust whipped around and engulfed all of them in its cloud Trace asked, "What was that all about? I told you I'd be right along. Why were you trying to outrun me?"

"I—we didn't expect you'd be leaving town so soon," Molly rested her arms across her knees. "Frankly, I'm glad to see you. We thought you might be someone else."

"Reyes Espiañata and his men are in town," Andy told Trace.

"Can't say as that surprises me. They were headed that way when I saw you in their camp. Did they see you?"

"No. I hid under the quilt."

"Good. Then everything is fine. We have no quarrel with those three, since they didn't restrain you when they had you in their camp.

You came with me of your own free will. I'm sure they won't want to tell the sheriff they were keeping you captive." Trace didn't want to tell the family that he suspected the three might be waiting to join up with Snake. More for him to worry about—if they were out to rob the bank, they would bear watching.

"They'll probably move on back to Mexico before long. We'll have to make sure they don't see you in the meantime."

"Yes, sir."

"How did you catch up so fast?" Molly asked. "I was so afraid it was the fellow with the silver on his hat and tack, I guess I lost my head for a minute."

"The sheriff was out of town. I stopped to see Josh and got my saddle." Trace waved a hand at his repaired equipment and Molly noticed her rifle in his scabbard. At least they had something for protection among them, now.

She hadn't told Trace about Seth's experience with Tom's pearl-handled pistol. She didn't plan to, either. She just wanted to keep all guns out of Seth's reach and the scabbard was as good a place as any to do that. He wouldn't dare mess with it on Trace's horse. Seth had learned his lesson when the horse sent him for a tumble.

They reached the house site and Molly assigned chores to the children. Andy rushed to the corral and wrapped his arms around Comet's neck. Never had horseflesh smelled so good to him.

"He must have come in from pasture, watered himself, and waited for oats," Molly said. "You better give him some."

"Yes, Ma," Andy said happily. It was good to be home. It was good to have Comet home, too.

Trace helped Molly position the buckboard and unhitch the team. Then he removed the saddle from Flapjack and walked the three animals out to pasture. Andy would bring Comet in his own good time.

Seth and Rosie were busy gathering eggs and counting chickens. When Seth reached five, Rosie took over and finished the count.

"They're all here, Ma," Rosie called back to Molly.

"Thank goodness. We can't afford to lose any."

Molly walked to the house where the walls still lay.

Trace walked up behind her.

"Figure to work on that soon. I'll have to go into town tomorrow and see if Tom is talking, yet—and see if Reyes has ridden on. But, once we get things settled back down, I'll get busy with it."

Tomorrow was Saturday. There would be no school. Trace could do what he felt he had to.

But, she was determined to get on with the house, with, or without him. She puzzled how she was going to get the walls perpendicular to the sub-floor. She would sleep on it and see if she could come up with something. She said nothing to Trace about her plans. She just knew that it was her house and it was important to her that the construction continued.

The next morning Trace went into town, leaving the Kling family to themselves.

After the chores were done, Molly asked Andy, "How are your shoulders doing?"

"Much better. The right one still hurts if I strain it, but I try not to do that."

"When you take the horses out to pasture, keep Big Boy here. I want to use him this morning."

"What for?"

"We're going to raise a house." Molly's manner was matter-of-fact as she walked away to stir beans in the cook pot.

Andy watered the horses then tugged himself up on Big Boy to ride him out to the pasture and back. Big Boy wouldn't be happy not staying with the other animals, but Andy would get there and back faster riding than leading them. He was nearly as excited as Molly was about building the house.

When he returned, Molly was standing in the middle of the four walls surveying the project.

Seth threw a stick for Crazy Leg near the buckboard. Rosie sat on the buckboard seat apologizing to Callie for having left her alone for so many hours while they were in town.

Molly had a length of rope and a hammer in her hand. She had fashioned a strap on top of the wall stringer for the front wall and threaded the rope through it.

"I want you to put the harness collar on Big Boy. Then, take the end of the rope and secure it so it can't slip off. This could be dangerous, so we'll have to be very careful. You'll have to move Big Boy out slowly and stop the second I say so. Understand?"

"Yes, Ma." He didn't want to get hurt or have Molly injured. He would do exactly as she said.

"Good."

When everything was set, Molly moved to each end of the wall and nailed a single nail through a board and into the end of the skeleton of the wall. She left the nail loose enough she could move the boards upright as the wall rose.

"Now, pull. Slowly," Molly said when she was ready.

Once the rope tightened, Andy moved Big Boy ahead one step at a time.

Gradually, the wall came up, off the sub-floor, and began to rise. Andy wanted to jump up and down with excitement, but he contained himself to keep from spooking the horse. Besides, he didn't need Seth and Rosie rushing over to see what all the commotion was about.

"Hold it there, a minute, Andy." Molly moved back to reposition the boards that served as braces.

"Now, go ahead."

The house raising was slow going, but when the wall was upright, Molly nailed the braces to the edge of the sub-floor and attached two more inside the frame of the doorway. There, she attached other braces in front of small pieces of lumber she nailed to the floor to hold them in place.

One wall of the house, the front wall, stood erect.

Molly nailed the sill plate to the sub-floor every foot or so then stopped. She stood in the doorway and grinned at Andy.

"We did it!" She said, smiling. "A crew of men could have gotten all the walls up in the amount of time it took us to do one, but we did it."

Molly and Andy repeated the procedure until they had all four walls up and braced on the ends and in the middle. On top Molly nailed pieces of lumber crosswise, on the corners, from one wall to another.

She and the three children were dancing around on the sub-floor of the house when Trace rode in that evening. Crazy Leg bounced and yipped in excitement. Rosie cradled Callie for her partner while they all celebrated.

Excited to have the house beginning to look real, Molly greeted Trace at the west door when he dismounted.

"Looks like you kept busy while I was away today. I planned to round up a crew and get the whole thing done in a day."

"I couldn't wait. You had everything lined out. All we did was put the pieces in place."

Trace held his arms out.

"May I have this dance?" He asked and whisked Molly away to an imaginary tune.

Next, it was Rosie's turn. She lowered Callie to the floor and let Trace swing her in his strong arms. She laughed gleefully as Trace swished her up into the air and back down as they spun around.

Finally, they all dropped to the floor, laughing. Crazy Leg rushed over and licked Seth's face. Callie kept her distance, grooming herself.

Molly leaned her head on Trace's chest.

"I think I'll bring the bedrolls in and sleep right here, tonight."

Trace smiled, looking up at the sky above, framed within the rim of the house's square.

"Sounds like a good idea to me."

Molly went to stir the beans and finish fixing supper, leaving the children to play in the new house.

Trace followed, letting Flapjack remain, temporarily, tied to a corner of the structure. He looked back to see that the animal was behaving himself.

"I guess I'm either getting better at handling the beast or he's given up trying to toss me off. He's actually been decent to ride lately." Trace stacked more wood on the cook fire.

"Good. What did you find out in town today?"

"Reyes and his men are still there. Tom came around. By the way, he said to thank you, many times over. He explained to the sheriff what he was doing with Snake's gang. I was there when he did."

"Oh?" Molly said, wondering if he had admitted to being a Texas Ranger.

"Yeah. Seems the Ranger Headquarters down in Waco sent him to track Snake and join up. They've been trying to stop his gang from plundering people and decided that was the only way to do it."

Molly nodded. "So, he told the sheriff he was a Texas Ranger?"

"Seems like it's no secret now that Snake thinks he's dead. He said it wasn't Snake that shot him, though. He doesn't know who it was. They were behind him in the dark. Snake would have done it, with my rifle, if someone else hadn't beat him to it."

Molly shook her head.

"Why does there have to be so much killing?"

"The land's pretty raw, yet. Until the thieves figure out they're going to get caught, we're going to have to deal with it, I guess. I told the sheriff what my interest was in Snake. He said he'd let me in on the trap when it swings shut on the gang."

"What trap?"

"Tom figures Snake will lay low for a few days. He figures he knows the bank's safe is pretty full. He figures this Sunday is probably too soon. Next Sunday, besides being the Sabbath, there's a celebration in town. Something to do with Founder's Day or something like that. Tom figures Snake will take advantage of the people's distraction to hit the bank."

"The sheriff's deputizing some men to help him take the gang if Tom's right."

"I suppose he ought to know about things like that."

"I volunteered," Trace said without any emotion in his voice.

"You volunteered?" Worry colored Molly's voice. "Won't that be dangerous?"

"Wouldn't you rather I go after him this way? I could have killed him in cold blood, like he did my folks. I could have done it a time or two, myself, and my conscience wouldn't have even bothered me. I knew you wouldn't take to that. And, I'm no vigilante, either. This way, he gets trapped and I get to see justice done."

"I'd built up my ranch, down Pecos way, so's my folks could live out their lives in comfort. Then Snake killed them and drove off the cattle to Mexico. He burned my house, my barn, and all the outbuildings, and took everything I had. I'd say I would have been justified to kill him in return."

Molly nodded. She didn't like it, but she understood. There had been a time, if someone had offered her the chance, she'd have done the same thing for her deceased husband. Being a woman and having three young children to look after, she didn't have much chance to do that.

At least, she could now own her own land, when she proved up on it. The deed would be in her name. That made her proud.

Come Monday, Molly would have to return to finish the school year out and close the school for the summer on the following Friday. She and the children would go to the celebration on Sunday. Then, she'd be free to devote all her time to raising a garden and a house. She only hoped nothing happened to change her plans. She kept her worries about Trace to herself.

The next evening, along with fresh milk and butter, Molly also brought home small green-topped onions. These she planned to fry with potatoes for the evening meal. She also brought a Farmer's Almanac and some seeds from the General Store.

It had long been a custom to plant by the phases of the moon and Molly, although she had no elders to guide her, was determined to follow that plan.

She had suspected the time was right to plant hollyhocks for her own pleasure. The directions indicated that it would take a full two years for the flowers to bloom. If she planted them now, outside the open hole for her kitchen window, when the house was finished they would be ready to bloom. In her mind's eye she could see the house complete and the hollyhocks swaying in the breeze outside the east wall where they received the morning sun and were shaded from the afternoon heat. She could picture herself in the kitchen looking out at the sunrise, over the top of the flowers, across the pasture.

When the evening meal was finished, and the chores done, Molly sat by the campfire reading the Almanac. She was happy to have things back to normal and not have to worry about where anyone was or if they were still alive. Life was meant to be this way. She looked up from her reading and saw Trace watching her from the other side of the fire.

"You've been studying that book all evening."

Molly closed the Almanac and set it aside.

"It's time to get the garden in. I couldn't work on it earlier, like Mrs. Smith, but school will be out soon, the nights are warmer. Things should grow faster. We have plenty of water. I thought I'd plant it close to the well so we wouldn't have to carry the water very far."

Trace studied the plan for the garden for a minute.

"Better plant it far enough away the fertilizer won't contaminate the well. I could make a pivot on the pipe so you could run water into a ditch alongside that would feed water along the rows."

"You could? That would be wonderful. We'll have the best garden around." Trace watched Molly react with pleasure. It didn't take much to make this woman happy. She seemed to love growing things, building things, and raising things. She was made for this place. A twinge of remorse tweaked Trace's brain.

Come next Sunday, Trace hoped he would resolve his problems with Snake. Once Snake and his bunch were in jail—or dead—Trace had no reason to stay in New Mexico beyond the time it took to finish the construction and help the family get ready for winter.

There was land of his own to get back to and take care of still. He saddened at the thought of leaving Molly and the kids. Trace had grown fond of all of them and, he finally admitted to himself, he had fallen in love with Molly.

Trace had left Texas to bring Snake to justice. He hadn't bargained for getting involved with the Kling family. Within a few days, he hoped to accomplish what he came to do. Now the question became, how was he going to be able to leave the family behind and return to a life in Texas? He knew it would be impossible to pry Molly away from her homestead—nor did he want to do so.

He still had a few days before the planned trap would be set for Snake. Who knew how that would turn out? If Snake got lucky, maybe Molly would have to bury him and he'd stay here after all. Trace shook the morbid image from his mind.

The fire popped as Trace stared into it. He looked from the flames back to Molly. He wanted to get up from where he sat, walk over to her, and take her in his arms. But, it wouldn't be fair to her to make promises he might not be able to keep. Molly was an honest woman. She deserved better than what might end up being empty promises. So, instead, Trace sat making idle conversation about the house, and the garden, until they went to bed.

Trace and Andy worked hard on the house while Molly taught school the rest of the week. The floor for the upstairs was laid, forming a flat roof above the main rooms. Trace set Andy to nailing siding along the downstairs outside walls.

Once the family had moved their bedrolls into the house, they never slept under the buckboard again. They simply rolled the bedding up during the day and shook the sawdust out of it at night before going to sleep.

Molly was busy at school filling out Completion Certificates to pass the pupils on to their next grade. The awards would be handed out at Sunday's picnic. After that, the whole summer lay ahead to complete the house and get ready for winter.

Trace and Molly had made a pact not to discuss the planned ambush on Sunday with the kids, or anyone else. Trace didn't want anyone getting in the way of flying lead. The last thing he wanted was an innocent person killed when they closed in on Snake and his gang.

His last trip to town, the sheriff had deputized him and several other men and given strict orders that some of them were to stay back at the picnic and see that no one came running to see what was happening when the shooting began. And, there would be shooting, he was sure. Trace agreed.

Trace had accepted his badge and pinned it inside his shirt pocket once he left town. He didn't want to flash it around and have Andy, or one of the others, notice it. The less curious they were, the better.

On Friday, Molly came home to report that school was officially out for the summer. The certificates were done and, on her trip into the General Store, she had seen Reyes' horse, and those of his *vaqueros*, tied up at one of the saloons again.

"That's no surprise. He's probably still waiting, like the rest of us, for Snake to show up," Trace said.

Molly had seen Tom at Doc Landry's and he was progressing slowly. He was still weak but able to sit up in a chair, now, and eat regular meals. His appetite was normal and he would be healed soon. She reported all this to Trace.

"Good," Trace said. "Maybe, when he's well, we'll have some crooks for him to take back to Texas."

Molly tensed. She knew someone had to stop Snake. If anything happened to Trace, she didn't know if she could stand it. She could forgive him a flirtatious moment with a stranger. She could deal with his wounds that would heal. But, if he was killed, she felt she would die, as well.

They were standing in the house looking out the west door toward the buckboard and the windmill.

"Trace, don't go," Molly pleaded. "Stay at the picnic with the kids and me, please."

"Molly, I can't. You know that. This is something I have to do."

"I'm so afraid for you, Trace."

Trace moved his hand from the doorframe where he had been leaning against the hole, watching the sunset cast its spiral rays across the windmill's sails. He moved his arm around Molly's shoulders. They watched Rosie and Seth playing with their pets near the buckboard and Andy checking the flow of the water into the trough where the horses were drinking.

Trace committed the tranquil picture to his memory for what might be lonelier days ahead.

Molly turned to him where they both stood in the opening for the door. She looked up and into his eyes.

"Trace, if anything happens to you, I just don't know how I'd stand it."

"Molly, don't think about that. I'll be careful. This is something I have to do. I know you, of all people, understand that."

Molly felt a tear trickle down her cheek. She did understand how he felt. But would his death compound that feeling until it was something she couldn't endure? She felt it would.

Trace lifted her chin up and saw the slow crawl of her tears. He'd never seen her cry before and, although this was like a threat before a storm, he felt a stab in his chest, like lightning striking a fence post. He would do nearly anything to keep from hurting her.

"I'm so sorry, Molly. I have to do this. Not only for me, but for you, and the kids so I'll know you'll be safe from Snake and his bunch."

He lowered his head until his lips touched hers. He was desperate to stop the flow of tears.

~ * ~

Saturday, Molly and Trace worked on the house with heavy hearts. She tried to keep her spirits up so the children wouldn't suspect anything.

Still, Rosie sensed something was wrong, but didn't know what and had not had a recent vision to tell her. It seemed her brief glimpses into the future were becoming further apart and she had to try hard not to take a normal dream as one of her spells. Fortunately, lately, most of her dreams had been pleasant ones and she could find nothing to alarm anyone.

On Sunday, the family dressed in their best clothes and climbed into the buckboard. Trace saddled Flapjack and Andy insisted on riding Comet.

"Some of the boys at school have set up a race," Andy told Molly when he was trying to persuade her to let him ride the horse instead of going with her and the smaller children in the buckboard. "They got some of the businesses in town to put up prize money. Comet can win! I know he can."

Against her better judgment, Molly relented.

"You stay out where the picnic's being held, near the school. Understand?"

"I will, except for the race. It runs east from town, then circles the schoolhouse and comes back. Is that close enough?"

"I guess," Molly said, looking to Trace for confirmation.

He nodded.

Molly drove the buckboard out of the yard and Trace and Andy followed.

"If that Reyes fellow's still in town, you steer clear of him. You hear?" Trace waited for Andy to agree.

"Yes, sir."

Little did the family know how big a day Sunday in Moriarty would prove to be.

Nineteen

When they reached town, they found red, white, and blue bunting hanging along the roofs of businesses and, at the east end of town, stretching high above the street. Letters spelling out the word "START" were attached to the center. Everything looked as if it was ready for the big celebration.

Seth and Rosie wiggled about eagerly. It looked to them, as if there was more fun to be had than they had ever seen. They could hardly contain themselves.

"Look, Ma!" Rosie called, "Isn't it beautiful?"

"Yes, Rosie." Molly wished she could feel the enthusiasm the child did, but instead, felt dread in her heart because of the risky business that lay ahead. When they reached the road to the schoolhouse, Molly reined the horses in.

"Whoa, Big Boy. Whoa, Jake."

Trace rode up alongside the wagon next to Molly.

She looked at him in silence. Surely he could see the fear in her eyes. He must know she cared more for him than she had let herself care for any other man since her husband died.

"You kids stay with your ma. Understand? No traipsing off into town. Seth? Rosie? You two mind, now."

"Trace wouldn't tell you that if he didn't think it was important." Molly waited for the two to answer him. Both nodded their heads.

"I mean it, Seth! Sometimes you wander away and give Molly a terrible fright. Today, you have to stay in her sight at all times."

"Yes, Trace."

"Take care, Trace." Molly studied his face and hoped he read her unspoken words.

"I'll be fine, Molly."

She knew he was trying to reassure her, but it wasn't working.

"If anything happens—"

Trace reached out and put his hand on her shoulder. "I'll catch up with you for the picnic, how's that?"

"Yes! Yes!" Rosie and Seth chimed together.

"Be careful in that race, Andy. Remember, winning isn't always the most important part." Trace turned Flapjack toward the sheriff's office. Molly started the wagon ahead slowly. Andy trailed along behind.

Molly turned to look back over her shoulder as Trace rode away. She felt as if he had reined his horse to the left, while they continued right, and slipped right out of her life.

She wanted to cry, then scolded herself. *You're becoming soft in your old age.* She was nearing twenty-eight and had seen enough in her lifetime to be callous. She was angry with herself for falling in love with Trace and angrier still for wanting to shed tears. *Hold onto the memories you have—and pray there are more,* she thought.

She tried to put a happy tone in her voice when she stopped the team near the tables the men had set up to hold the picnic food.

"Rosie, Seth. Look at all the room for food. Mrs. Smith is already unloading her basket. Grab what you can of our lunch and let's find a place beside her."

Rosie picked up a tablecloth that had the four corners tied together to hold sandwiches inside. Seth brought a pail filled with freshly made custard.

Andy dismounted to help, then excused himself to go sign up for the race. Seth and Rosie ran off to play with their friends, within Molly's view. Molly positioned their dishes on one of the tables.

Such an array of food was being set out! Women stood by, fanning flies away and covering plates to keep the food from being ruined by dust and insects.

"Morning, Mrs. Kling," Josh's ma called to Molly.

"Morning."

She greeted what women she knew and tried to keep the younger kids in sight.

Andy rode back toward the bunting where the race's start line was marked. Two men had set up a table and were accepting entries for the race.

Andy slid off Comet and accepted a stub of a pencil to write his and Comet's names on a piece of paper.

He was bent low, spelling carefully, when a voice spoke behind him.

"So, *niño*, you think your horse can beat mine."

Andy felt fear grip him. He straightened up and handed the clerk his entry form.

"I told you we would meet again," Reyes said with a chuckle in his voice to the two *vaqueros* that stood behind him.

Reyes pushed his *sombrero* back on his head, tilting his face so the brim still shaded his eyes. He stepped up to the table and picked up the pencil and an entry form.

"We shall see which horse is the fastest," Reyes said, winking at one of his *vaqueros*.

Andy stepped back. He wanted to jump on Comet and race away, now.

"Don't go nowhere, *niño*," Reyes said as if the tone of his voice could hold Andy where he wanted him.

One of the *vaqueros* reached out and grasped Comet's bridle, stopping Andy's retreat.

When Reyes finished filling out his form, he turned to Andy and walked alongside Comet assessing the horse's potential.

"So, this is the great race horse? I heard about the little race here, that's one reason I came to your town. I figured, if you were anywhere about, *niño*, you wouldn't be able to resist the race. I tell myself, 'if this *niño's* horse can beat mine, he would be a fine one for my sister."

"He's not for sale."

Reyes ran his hand along Comet's side and down the outside of his flank, feeling the muscle beneath.

"He is strong. You are much smaller than me and ride without a saddle." Reyes considered the differences that could give Andy an edge. His horse, larger than Comet, his own weight, and the heavy black leather and silver tack would be a greater burden for his horse to carry in the competition.

"He is much smaller than my great black. That's even better for my sister, Maria, back in Mexico. He would look quite handsome with a saddle like mine and silver decorating his bridle, don't you think, Jose? Jesus?"

Both *vaqueros* nodded. "*Sí! Sí*, Reyes," they said in unison.

"I said he's not for sale."

"No? Then how about this? I have five hundred dollars to do with as I wish. If you won't take the money for the horse—and you say he can beat me—let us make a little wager."

"What do you mean?" The promise of five hundred dollars intrigued Andy. With that amount of money they could finish the house, furnish it, and build a big barn, with money left over. But, Comet was all that he had left to remember his father by and—and he was family. Andy was torn between the amount of money Reyes offered and losing Comet.

"Well, *niño*, if your horse is so fast, you have nothing to lose. We race. If your horse wins, you get the *dinero* and keep the horse. If he loses, I'll still give you the money, but I take the horse back with me to Mexico."

Reyes snapped his fingers in the air and one of his *vaqueros* handed him a wad of bills folded in half like a small, thick book.

Andy had never seen so much money. His eyes opened wide. Oh, how the family could use the money.

Life could be so much easier for Molly if he won that cash on top of the town's small purse that was offered.

"*Mucho dinero!* Your little reward the merchants are giving, it is nothing compared to this."

Andy wanted that money so bad—but, if Comet couldn't outrun Reyes' horse, he would lose his best friend and companion. Andy swallowed hard. He felt a lump in his throat and it seemed to sink slowly into his stomach, forming a tight fist in his gut.

Other riders were registering now and a small group crowded Reyes, his men, and Andy aside.

Andy felt a heavy buzz in his head and heard himself saying, "I'll do it." It was as if the voice came out of nowhere and didn't belong to him. He had committed himself, and Comet, to a race that could end their lives together, if they lost. He didn't even want to think about the possibility of losing. His mood was somber as he waited for Reyes to give the signal for the other man to let go of Comet's bridle.

"Good! I will wait for you at the finish line."

The *vaquero* released his hold on Comet and Andy walked the horse away.

~ * ~

Trace and the other deputies took their positions on the rooftops and in the buildings throughout the town. They had no idea if, or when, Snake would appear but they could take no chances that he might. Tom had said the plan was to take the town by surprise. He also said Snake's plan was flexible. Perhaps he wouldn't show on this day.

Tom was still recuperating at Doc Landry's office. He watched as the doctor busily prepared his equipment and medical supplies for the fight. This many men confronting a band of outlaws could only mean somebody would get hurt—or die.

Molly set up her Certificates of Completion at the podium. She placed a large, broken piece of brick on top of the stack of papers to keep them from blowing away. There, she would call the names of each of her students who were finishing a grade, and hand them their pass to the next grade. While she prepared, she had a hard time keeping her mind focused and her eyes off the town's buildings in the distance.

Josh walked up beside her and she jumped at the sound of his voice.

"Mrs. Kling, I hear Andy's racing today."

She turned when she recognized the young man's voice.

"Yes. Yes, he is."

"Comet's about the fastest thing around. Sure hope he wins."

"Thank you, Josh. Andy would be right pleased, too."

"Can I help you with anything? The race is about to start, but I have a few minutes, if you need me to do something."

"No. No, thank you. It looks as if everything is about ready. I'll be going to watch the race, too."

"See you there, then." Josh turned toward the starting line.

Molly debated whether to pull Rosie and Seth away from their game of tag with the other children and decided to let them remain while she went down to Main Street to see the race begin.

As she reached the street, she saw a large cluster of men and young boys gathered around the side of the road. Mr. Hughes drew a line across the street beneath the banner with a stick.

Horses lined up behind it and riders waited for the gun to fire into the air, starting the race.

There were several bay horses on the outside, nearest her side of the street, then Comet and another black horse, then a dapple, and then a roan. All of the animals fidgeted and pranced about, anxious for the race, as their riders held them in check.

Molly looked beyond the bays to Comet and the larger black horse next to him.

The silver on the saddle sparkled in the full sunlight and she knew—the rider had to be Reyes.

Trace had told Andy to stay away from the man. But, it was a public place and the race was open to anyone with a horse. There was nothing she could do about it except to cheer Andy on.

Andy stared straight ahead, concentrating on the road before him. He knew the route well and prayed Comet wouldn't fail him.

The gun fired into the air and the horses were off.

Reyes spurred his large mount ahead and took the lead, leaving Andy and the others behind him. Comet was running second but the stronger, bigger horse was leaving him in his dust.

Reyes lay low in the saddle, close to the horse's neck to improve his speed.

Andy clung flat on Comet's back, too, but the larger animal only seemed to be putting more distance between them.

"Go, Andy!" Molly screamed encouragement.

The horses bringing up the rear disappeared around a turn. The leaders would soon be reaching the other side of the schoolhouse. Molly strained to see through the dust and the crowd that gathered to watch near the picnic tables. She wanted to run over there and see who was leading, but if she did, she would not be able to get back to the finish line in time to see who won.

She thought the race didn't mean much to Andy, the purse being so low, but she knew he would race to win no matter what the prize.

On the straightaway from the school, Comet was gaining on the big black.

Very slowly, he pulled abreast of the animal and Reyes looked over and grinned at Andy. The sun glinted off his mouth full of gold teeth.

Was he baiting him? Letting him think he had a chance, only to spur his horse on into another lead?

Andy set his chin in determination and urged Comet on.

They took the turn back toward Main Street neck and neck and Reyes spurred his mount harder. The larger horse, fast at the start, was tiring and Comet, although lighter, was showing his endurance.

"Come on, Comet," Andy called out as they made the last turn and headed for the finish line. Ahead, he could see Molly jumping up and down and shouting. He didn't have time to look to see where Reyes was. He didn't care, as long as he wasn't in front.

"Go, boy," Andy called behind Comet's ears. He sucked himself tight against Comet's back and held on.

"Let me win! Let me win!" He prayed out loud. There was too much riding on this race to lose!

Then, they whisked under the bunting past the yelling crowd. Andy was too afraid to look to see who won. He slowed Comet gradually until the horse was walking, then turned to go back to the finish line.

Reyes came toward him.

"*Niño!* Congratulations! You won."

Andy looked at him in disbelief. Then at the crowd jumping up and down and calling his name in unison.

He Won!

He would get to keep Comet, after all. Reyes' five hundred dollars were out of his mind. Relief that he wouldn't have to give up his horse washed over him like a warm rain on a summer day.

The riders on the other horses pulled their mounts away, riding them back to tie them up.

Andy and Reyes rode their sweat-frothed animals back to the finish line.

"Andy," Molly called out, reaching up to give him a big hug. "You won! I'm so glad!"

Molly released Andy and stroked Comet's neck.

Andy took the prize money from the judge, along with his congratulations, smiling as broadly as his lips would stretch.

"There's a photographer fellow, got his stuff set up over by the picnic. You ought to go get a picture of you and your horse, son," the judge said.

"Maybe I will. Thank you."

Reyes raised his hand in the air and snapped his fingers at Jose. Jose came toward him with the money and his *sombrero*.

Just then, shots rang out down the street, startling the people and the horses.

Reyes spurred his horse in the direction of the shots. His *vaqueros* mounted in quick, jerking motions, and followed. Andy was close behind.

"Andy!" Molly called after him. "Stay here!"

All Andy could think was that Trace was in trouble. He knew he had gone off to the sheriff's office, but he didn't know why.

"Go back, *niño*," Reyes called over his shoulder. "This is not your fight."

Andy paid no heed to his words and raced Comet up the street. When he approached the sheriff's office he could see men standing on top of the buildings shooting across the street toward the bank. They had six men pinned down inside the building and they continued to fire, breaking the windows and splintering the surrounding wood.

Andy slid off Comet, tossing the reins around the hitching rail as he landed. He dodged between Doc Landry's office and the building next to it, trying to stay out of the way of the bullets coming from the bank.

Reyes and his men dismounted and crept along the sidewalk, taking cover behind porch uprights and barrels as they went.

They seemed to relish trouble. Since Snake hadn't waited for them to join the party, they played along on the other side until they could figure out what to do.

Andy saw Tom come out of Doc's office, his pearl-handled gun in his left hand while he pulled a shirt on with his right.

A badge shone on the left breast of the shirt as he buttoned the cloth in front.

Andy didn't recognize the piece of metal. Most badges he had seen had been heavy tin stars. He was unable to read the emblem until Tom squatted down and duck-walked his way between the buildings.

"Texas Ranger," Andy read with awe.

"Stay out of the way, kid," Tom said when he saw Andy.

Andy nodded that he would.

Tom leaned his head around the edge of the building and studied the situation.

Over at the bank, he saw a head poke, now and then, above the hole where window glass had once been. The gang had tied their horses alongside the bank building instead of in front at the rail, apparently hoping to avoid suspicion. If they managed to shoot their way out of the mess and get to their horses, they could ride out the back behind the bank building and race away toward the south— toward the mountain—toward Texas and Mexico.

"Stay here, kid," Tom said as he moved toward a store entrance where the beveled entry offered protection.

Andy watched the battle while he tried to figure out a way to help. At last, he saw the one thing he could do, since he had no gun.

He bent low and ran across the street. Once he was out of the line of fire, beside the building and the outlaws' horses, he slipped up and untied them, then hooted and rushed them away toward the open valley.

Snake was at the back door when he saw the horses run by him.

"Damn kid," he said raising his gun to take aim at Andy.

Andy was a moving target as the guns on top of the buildings opposite the bank sent a barrage of bullets toward the bank to try to distract the outlaws and give Andy a chance to get under cover.

He dove at the nearest water trough and lay flat behind it.

Plink! Plink! He heard bullets splash into the trough and made sure to keep his head and body down lower than the trough.

"I'll get you for that, kid!" Snake called out.

Tom answered him with a shot at the corner of the building.

There was nowhere for Snake or his men to go. They certainly couldn't outrun the lawmen's bullets and now they had nothing to ride.

Andy lay low and waited for the shooting to stop.

The shots from the bank building diminished and Andy figured there must be some discussion going on as to what to do, but he dared not move.

At last, the firing stopped completely and Andy heard Trace shout, "Come out, Snake. You're out of options."

Snake saw the glint of the sun on Reyes' silver-trimmed *sombrero*.

"Dirty double-crosser," he yelled. He pointed his pistol around the back corner of the bank and fired at the light.

Sun glinted off Reyes' silver-handled pistol as he fired back.

Andy saw Snake drop to the ground and lay there.

"Hold up, Sheriff!" someone inside the bank shouted. "We're coming out."

"Throw your guns out the front. Don't try anything. You're way out-numbered."

The sound of iron clattering on the board sidewalk convinced Andy the outlaws had done as they were told. Gradually, he rose from behind the trough and crept back against the wall of the store.

There was no firing now, and Andy watched as the outlaws came out of the bank with their hands up. A couple of men came through the door while another two stepped over the low window frame. They crunched shattered glass beneath their boots on the sidewalk.

Finally, all of the outlaws were accounted for, including Snake who lay at the back of the bank.

226

The lawmen moved from the rooftops and came across the street leaving only one or two on the roof for security. Trace, Reyes, and Tom all moved across the street toward the bank.

Trace went inside the building to look at the damage while Reyes moved toward the back where he had brought Snake down.

Andy ran toward where Snake lay. He was face down with his gun in one hand and a bag of money in the other.

As Andy ran up, Snake raised his head and drew a bead on Andy.

Andy stopped running, freezing in terror.

Reyes drew his pistol and fired again.

Snake's arm jerked and his reflex pulled the trigger on his pistol. Reyes' shot threw Snake's aim off, sending the bullet flying away from Andy. Reyes had killed Snake where he lay.

"*Amigo,* you should not have tried to keep all the money for yourself. Why you not come, include us in your little fiesta, like you were supposed to? Too bad. Now you have no *dinero.*"

Jose rushed up. Reyes pulled the moneybag from Snake's fingers. He handed it to Jose, who stuffed it beneath his shirt.

Trace burst through the back door to see what had happened.

Andy stared, openmouthed.

"Are you all right, Andy? I told you to stay away!"

Andy felt his knees go weak.

Snake lay dead at his feet. It could be him lying there.

"*Niño,*" Reyes said as he reached his hand out with the five hundred dollars, "here's your money. You won it fair and square."

Andy took the wad of bills and stared at them.

"Remember, *niño*, it is only money. I can always get more," Reyes winked at his *vaquero.* "Now, if this *gringo* had been a second faster, your Mama would be crying tonight."

Reyes and his men turned and walked away.

"Come, Jose, Jesus. Let us go have some *frijoles* and tequila. Tonight we celebrate."

Trace let them go without question. He had seen the man take the money, but he figured they had done him two favors. They had saved Andy's life and they had kept him from killing Snake himself. He would consider it a reward—offered and claimed.

He had seen them with Snake and his bunch that night in Texas. But, it was his word against theirs. The sheriff had no wanted posters on them. Perhaps they had gone their separate ways from the gang. Anyway, Snake's gang would be no more. Those that still lived would end up in prison or on the end of a rope.

With any luck, Reyes and his men would return to Mexico. He hoped they stayed there. The next time, he might have to put them away.

"Andy, you best get back to Molly while we get this mess cleared up here. She needs to know you're still alive."

Andy nodded. Sticking the money into his pocket along with the prize money from the race, he went back to get Comet.

He met Doc in the street, but he was too shocked to say anything. He walked on past until he reached the hitching rail. There, he retched and threw up his breakfast. He sat down on the wooden sidewalk in a cold sweat, feeling faint.

Another shot rang out.

Andy jerked his head up.

One of the bandits had managed to get his hands on a gun and fired.

Trace? He couldn't see him anywhere. *Where was Trace?*

Twenty

When Andy finally had the courage to look in the direction of the sound of the shot, he saw Trace staring back at him with a shocked look on his face.

Tom faced Trace, with his back toward Andy. His arm was down at his side now and the pistol pointed at the ground. Smoke still curled up from the barrel and Andy knew the shot had come from his gun.

Andy stood up, knees quaking, and clung to the nearby post for what seemed like forever.

Finally, Trace turned toward Tom and uttered a feeble "thanks."

"The guy must have had a Derringer in his boot," Tom said.

"I felt the bullet whiz by my face." Trace was shaken by the incident.

"No thanks necessary. That's my job, to look for the unexpected. Unfortunately, I wasn't so smart the night I got shot."

Trace called across the street to Andy. Confusion and concern showed on Andy's face. He didn't know whether to run toward Trace or hide behind the post.

"Go on up with Molly and the kids. Everything's going to be all right." Traced reinforced his earlier directions.

Andy, shock still registering on his face, got on Comet's back to ride to the picnic area.

Near the starting line for the race, people were milling around in concern about the shots they had heard. Several deputies stood firm, keeping the townspeople from rushing up the street.

"What happened?" Someone called out as Andy approached.

"Yeah, what's going on down there?"

Andy searched the crowd for Molly. When he saw her yellow dress in the midst of the crowd he said, "It's over. All of our friends are fine. The leader of the bank robbers is dead and one of them is wounded. The rest are on their way to jail." He looked straight at Molly and said, "Trace is fine—Tom, too."

Molly sighed in relief. At last, they would no longer have to worry about Snake or his gang. Trace's job was done. Perhaps knowing the evil person was dead would give him some peace now, too.

Then Andy spoke to the crowd.

"They want us to go on with the picnic and they'll join us when the prisoners are locked up. Then, I'm sure the sheriff will make an announcement." Andy slid off Comet and dropped his feet into the dust and stood with the others.

Gradually the crowd dispersed, discussing the situation.

"You look pale, Andy. Are you all right?" Molly asked.

"Yeah. I—I've never seen someone get killed before. Hope I never do again."

Molly held him against her chest for a moment while Rosie and Seth stood at their sides.

"Rosie, Seth, come on. Let's go get some of that delicious-looking food," Molly said as cheerfully as she could.

Soon, everyone was dishing up their plates, trying to put the events of the day behind them. One of the deputies sliced slabs of beef off the hindquarter that had been slowly turning over a spit. Meat piled high on platters disappeared nearly as fast as it reached the table.

Trace and a few of the other deputies arrived to join the rest of the townspeople and Molly rushed to his side.

He solemnly put his arm around her shoulder and walked to where the family had set their plates of food on a quilt.

"I fixed a plate for you," Molly said. Despite her curiosity, she didn't want to rush him to talk.

"Thanks. I'm not real hungry."

"I'm sure. It must have been awful."

"Tom's back at Doc's office. He wasn't supposed to be in on this, but he got out there, anyway."

"It's a good thing he did," Andy said finding it difficult to keep excitement out of his voice even with the terror he had experienced.

Molly looked at Trace for an explanation.

"He had to shoot one of Snake's men. Just wounded him. Slade, it was. Seemed as if he rather enjoyed it—as if he had something personal against the fella."

"He did it to save Trace," Andy blurted out, then looked down expecting Trace to scold him.

"It's over. Tom said it's his job. He told me on the way back to Doc's office that Slade was the one that took him off to dump him. Told me whereabouts it was and that I'd probably find my rifle where Comet took off. They were going to try to finger me for Tom's death. Luckily, Comet got away and brought Tom to your place."

"Yes, it sure was lucky." Lucky both for Tom and for Trace. She was thankful Tom had been there to keep Trace from suffering the same fate he had.

"Without Tom there, Trace might have been shot in the back." Excitement, now that the danger was over, welled in Andy's voice.

Andy slid his barely touched plate of food aside.

"I'll finish it up later. I'm not very hungry either. Guess I'll go take Comet to get a drink."

"I told Tom I'd bring him a plate of food back, if you'd fix it up, Molly."

"I will. Glad to see his appetite's returned."

"Yes. Well, I suspect he deals with this sort of thing more often than I do. Hold up, there, Andy. I'll walk along with you."

Molly rose and soon returned with a plate heaped high with roast beef, potatoes, beans, and a large baking powder biscuit.

As Trace and Andy moved back down the street toward Doc Landry's office, Andy reached into his pocket and took the money out to show Trace.

"Where did you get that?"

"I did a stupid thing, I know. Reyes wanted to buy Comet, but I wouldn't sell him. Then he bet me. If his horse won, he got Comet and I got the money. If Comet won, I got to keep him and still got the money. I figured Ma sure could use it. It was a lot more than the prize money." Andy tried to explain his actions.

"That was pretty dumb. What if you'd lost?"

"I'm just thankful I didn't. And, I'll never do anything like that again. You take the money. Ma won't take it from me, I know."

"Why do you want me to take it?"

"Keep it safe. I figure there's enough there to finish the house, buy furniture and build a big barn so Comet can have his own stall. He deserves it. Maybe there'd be some left over—"

Trace laughed. "It is a lot of money, but—what makes you think Molly would take it from me?"

"I don't think she would. But, I figure, you can pick up supplies with it and, once they are there and the place is going up, I don't think she'll be too hard on us about it. Figure you can come up with some way to convince her."

Trace stuck the money in his shirt pocket behind the badge that was now pinned on the heavy denim.

"Don't you plan on telling her where it came from?"

"Not if I don't have to."

Andy watered Comet in the trough alongside the sidewalk while Trace took the dinner plate into Doc's office for Tom.

He glanced over his shoulder and saw the undertaker measuring Snake for his coffin where the outlaw lay on the ground. It gave Andy goose bumps and he looked away.

All the other men were in jail, but the memory of the shots rang in Andy's mind. He knew he would never forget that day no matter how long he lived.

Trace came back out.

"I've got one more stop to make. Then, we better get back so you can get your pass into your next grade."

They walked to the sheriff's office. Andy waited outside while Trace turned in his deputies' badge.

"If that fellow that was looking for me a few weeks back shows up again, Sheriff, I'll be out at the Klings' place for a bit longer."

"You mean that big fellow, with the Easterner suit and the single eye glass?"

"Yes, sir. The fellow with the monocle. He's been tracking me all the way from Texas. Figure I owe him an answer by now. Name's Peabody. Elroy Peabody."

"Yep, that's what he said it was. I'd forgot for a time."

"Well, if he shows up again, you can send somebody for me—or give him the directions to the Kling place, if you don't mind."

"Sure, Trace. Are you sure you don't want to keep this badge? I decided I might need a couple extra deputies in reserve—if you're interested."

"No, thanks, Sheriff. I've done what I needed to. I don't want to have to wear that again. I'll leave that kind of stuff up to you and Tom."

The sheriff picked up the tin star-shaped badge and fingered its rounded points, then dropped it into the front drawer of his desk.

"Well, if you ever change your mind, let me know."

Trace nodded and went back outside to where Andy and Comet waited.

"Now, let's go enjoy that picnic a bit before we head home." Trace laid his arm around Andy's shoulder.

The three of them, Trace with his arm resting on Andy's shoulder, Andy with Comet's reins tight in his hand, walked past the saloon where the big black horse rubbed his heels together, to disturb the heel flies, and waited for his master.

Comet could have been standing there, too, if the race had gone differently. Andy looked at Trace. Trace squeezed his shoulder lightly and dropped his arm away.

It had been a long, difficult day. Trace and Andy were ready to help Molly load up the kids and their things and head back to the comforts of home, as meager as it was.

"Hey, *niño!*" A voice rang out behind them. "I like your horse!"

Trace and Andy turned to see Reyes, leaning with both elbows drooped over the swinging bar doors, hanging as far outside as he could without falling. A tequila bottle was in one hand and a shot glass in the other.

"You watch out, *niño*. You may not have seen the last of Reyes Espiañata, yet." The Mexican laughed uproariously as if he had made the funniest joke ever.

~ * ~

The summer settled down to the more mundane activities of homesteading life. Molly and Trace were glad for the calm and a chance to concentrate on preparing for winter.

The long stretch of hot weather had dried every stem of grass and piece of brush until it was tender for a range fire. Molly worried about the possibility of a lightning strike or a misguided spark of some kind that could light the world, as they knew it, on fire.

Thank goodness Trace didn't smoke. At least she didn't have to worry about a discarded match, pipe ashes, or the remains of a cigar or cigarette.

The well still supplied plenty of water, and the windmill filled the trough and kept the garden irrigated. The hollyhocks outside Molly's new kitchen window grew to short bushes but didn't bloom.

Next year, she told herself as she watered the precious plants, next year there will be plenty of flowers and the stalks would be swaying in the breeze.

The summer moved by, and everyone concentrated on their everyday chores and the construction of the house.

The garden flourished.

The house grew.

At last, a roof sat above the second floor and the living area was ready for finish work.

The barn was raised.

Comet had a new stall, as did Big Boy, Jake, and Flapjack.

"Guess you're coming up in the world, Flapjack," Trace told the horse as he and the family inspected the stalls. "You get to sleep in a barn for the first time in a while."

"And we get to sleep in a house," Rosie said. "Even if it is still all furry lumber inside."

"One of these days," Molly said, "it will be magnificent."

Rosie and Seth ran out to play, scattering curious chickens that had been wandering toward the barn ahead of them and startling the new wiener pigs in their pen nearby.

Molly and Trace continued their conversation, enjoying the scent of raw lumber and the dry grasses used for bedding. Andy decided that perhaps it would be best for him to give them some time alone. He no longer resented the attention Molly received from Trace. He knew Trace had time for him, too.

"Well, we're nearing the end of what I can do here," Trace said, looking out across the barnyard at the house with the windmill a short distance away. "You and the kids ought to be a lot more comfortable this winter."

Molly's breath caught in her throat. She was afraid to ask the question that had been eating at her ever since the day Snake's gang was captured—*when was Trace going to say he had to leave? Had that time come?*

"Yes, we'll all be a lot better off. It was lucky that you came into our lives."

"And I've enjoyed being a part of your life. You know, I don't want to leave, Molly, but there are things I have to do. I need to go back to Texas and settle some business there."

"Why, Trace? Why can't you just stay here with us?" Even as she asked, she knew that if he had unfinished business elsewhere, he would have to go. He just wasn't the kind of man that left things undone. That was one of the traits she admired about him.

"As much as I'd like that, I just can't. There are some things that can't always be taken care of at a distance."

"When do you plan to leave?"

"In a few days."

She wanted to hug him and beg him not to go, but by now, she knew if he had something to tend to, there was no stopping him. She reached up, wrapped her arms around his neck and hugged him anyway.

"You know there'll always be a place here for you—both in my home and in my heart. Please be careful and come back. We'll all be brokenhearted if you don't."

Trace kissed her and felt her heart beating close to his. Oh, how he wanted to stay. How he wanted to make the farm pay off for her. He was a rancher, used to raising cows. Could he become a bean farmer? Did it really matter what you raised as long as you were happy?

They returned to the house and its bare stud walls. Their bedrolls were still on the floor, although now they were upstairs and in separate bedrooms. There were rough walls with no sheeting to cover the partitions, and no coverings on the floors.

Out front, since Andy had supplied enough money for the materials, Molly had her porch shading the lower floor of the house from the hot summer sun. It was an addition she had not expected for some time, but was happy to enjoy.

Each time Trace arrived with lumber or materials to work on the exterior of the house or build the barn, Molly wondered how he was paying for it. Each time, her protests were met with instructions not to worry, telling her he'd taken care of the arrangements and she could thank Andy, if she needed someone to feel obliged to for it. But a direct answer never came and finally she quit asking. She thanked her lucky stars that the house was coming along and they now had inside sleeping quarters.

That August night, the family blew out the kerosene lamp and went to bed early. Tomorrow would be another day of hard labor in the garden, in the bean field, and on the house.

Molly dozed off thinking about the vegetables that would be ready to preserve when she finished picking them in the morning.

The heat was oppressive and everyone was restlessly trying to fall asleep without sticking to their bedrolls in their own sweat.

Andy slept fitfully.

Trace lay still, contemplating his trip back to Texas. It would be a lonely one, he was sure. For not liking kids much, he had become attached to Molly's stepchildren and even found himself entertaining thoughts of having children of his own, someday. Now, he was used to the family and not content to be a solitary individual anymore.

Seth slept snuggled up against Crazy Leg, even in the heat.

Perhaps it would have been better to sleep on the main floor where the house was insulated by the upstairs and the shade of the porch kept it cooler. Molly turned in her bedroll again. Someday, she would have a real bed to sleep in. With sheets—

"Ma!" Rosie called in a whisper from the room next to Molly's. "I'm thirsty, can I have a drink?"

Rosie stared up into the open rafters, waiting for an answer.

"Go to sleep, Rosie."

"But, I'm thirsty—and I'm hot—and I can't get to sleep. I'm all sticky."

"I know. We're all uncomfortable."

Molly heard Rosie get up and move across the floor in her bare feet. As light as Rosie was, her tiny feet made a sound like a whisper as she moved to the window in search of a breeze.

She leaned against the open hole, gazing out into the darkness and trying to feel the air stir against her face.

She heard the horses whinnying to each other in the barn. It was a soft noise, barely audible from the distance where she stood.

Then, the barn door opened and she saw the minute glow of a match as someone moved inside.

"Ma?"

"Yes, Rosie. Go to sleep."

"There's someone in the barn. I just saw them go inside."

Instantly, Trace was up on his feet and struggling into his boots, bouncing on one foot while he tried to stuff the other foot into the leather top.

"Are you sure, Rosie? This isn't one of those things you see in your mind, is it?"

"No, Trace, honest. Someone just went into the barn."

Trace could see her head and shoulders above the windowsill.

"Get down, Rosie. We don't know who it might be. Get down and stay down until I tell you different."

"What is it, Trace?" Molly was up now and clutching her dress in front of her as she prepared to put it back on.

"I don't know, but I'm going to find out." He grabbed Molly's rifle from beside his bedroll. Having given up on finding his own, he kept hers handy.

He was down the stairs and out the door before Andy could come fully awake. With Trace outside, Andy hurried, groggily, to follow.

They reached the barn as one of the *vaqueros* that had ridden with Reyes Espiañata rushed around the corner leading a balking Comet.

Trace raised the rifle to shoot. If he fired, the chance of hitting Comet was greater than shooting the *vaquero* hidden by the horse's body.

Andy whistled, but the *vaquero* had his fingers wound tight in Comet's mane. The horse shook his head but could not break free of his grasp.

Andy whistled again.

Comet stopped and stiffened his legs. He tried to shake loose of the stranger's hand again.

Trace raised the rifle and took aim.

It was no use to shoot. He dared not risk hitting Comet. The target was obscured by the deepening darkness as the *vaquero* threw himself onto Comet's back and disappeared in the night.

"You stay with Molly and the kids," Trace called as he rushed toward the open barn door to free Flapjack from his stall and ride after the *vaquero*.

As Trace stepped inside, a pile of dry grass bedding inside Comet's stall burst into flame.

"Fire! Andy, get some water."

Molly was by Trace's side now. She grabbed a horse blanket from the stall and slapped at the flames.

Rosie and Seth ran into the barn.

"Go back," Trace ordered as he moved to release the team of horses and Flapjack.

The horses, terror in their eyes reflected by the firelight, ran wildly from the barn and milled around near the water trough.

Andy sloshed a bucket of water over the flames, than ran for more.

"Grab the old bucket, Rosie. You can carry that part full," Andy said. "Stay out of the way and outside the barn. I'll throw the water on the flames when I get there."

Rosie struggled to do Andy's bidding. It wasn't much, but anything would help.

They smelled burning straw and scorching chicken feathers that had fallen from the rafters where some of the hens roosted. The chickens lost more feathers as they flew furiously away, squawking as they went. They abandoned their nests to the flames and hurried toward the safety of the open barn door.

"If the barn goes, the sparks are apt to take the house, too," Trace warned Molly.

"How can we stop it?" She asked, the air in her lungs burning from the smoke and heat. Her house. Not her house. They had worked so hard and they were so close to making it a home.

"We've got to stop it here. I'll just have to go after Comet later."

Trace was using another horse blanket, now, too. He whipped vigorously at the flames smothering them as he moved, only to have new flames shoot up where fresh fuel lay on the floor.

Andy tossed buckets of water across the floor flooding the new wood as fast as he could. He took Rosie's partial bucket from her and sloshed it behind the full one he had just dumped—then ran for more while she struggled back to refill her pail.

At last, exhausted, sooty and muddy, they had the fire out.

"Thank goodness the barn was new and we didn't have the winter's hay stored in it yet," Molly said.

"Thank goodness, there wasn't too much fuel for the flames to reach," Trace agreed. "Reyes' *vaquero* must have dropped his match in Comet's stall. We'll probably never know if it was on purpose or an accident."

"I'd bet it was on purpose," Andy said coming up with another bucket and gasping to catch his breath. "Reyes wanted Comet powerfully bad. Now, I guess he's got him. We can never catch up with them and he'll take him to his sister in Mexico. What chance do we have of getting him back then?" Suddenly, Reyes' five hundred dollars didn't seem like so much to Andy. He had been foolish to believe he would be able to keep the money without Reyes getting Comet.

Molly put her arm around Andy. She knew how painful his loss must be. She felt helpless.

"In the morning, when I can see what I'm doing, I'll track them—if I have to go all the way to Mexico." Trace placed a heavy hand on Andy's shoulder.

Molly looked at him with concern.

"For tonight, we better all get some rest. There's a lot of work to do tomorrow. Andy, you have a lot of cleanup to do here. And some repair. The flames charred the stall and the horses will be too afraid to come back in if they still smell burnt wood. You'll need to clean out all the ashes and replace the damaged boards."

"But what about Comet?"

"I said I would go after him. You let me worry about that."

~ * ~

At the saloon in Moriarty the second *vaquero*, Jose, and Reyes enjoyed the companionship of two saloon girls. They attempted to dance to the slow music the musician plunked out on his guitar. When they were unable to keep the rhythm, Reyes approached the man and explained his tempo needs forcefully.

Untalented and slow, the guitarist was persuaded to step up the pace of a familiar tune. Reyes bent the tune to his foot-stomping beat.

"Ha!" Reyes called out in jubilation, tossing his *sombrero* to the floor. He stood back and watched one of the girls imitate the Mexican Hat Dance around his black *sombrero* with its heavy silver decorations.

"Ah, *señorita*, you do the dance honor. Keep it up and I will turn my *sombrero* over and let the gentlemen around the tables fill it with gold and silver for you," Reyes encouraged the dancer.

The first *vaquero*, Jesus, straight from the Kling farm, rushed in. He was breathless and excited. He took Reyes aside.

Whispering to Reyes and gesticulating with his hands he told of his recent escapade.

"What?" Reyes burst out, then motioned for Jose and headed for the door. He scooped up his hat as he went, leaving in long, full strides, without speaking.

He stood outside in the dark, looking at his great black horse and the smaller, Comet, alongside at the hitching rail. What was he to do now?

"You want to make a horse thief out of me, Jesus? I am not a horse thief!"

"But, Reyes, your sister—you said you wanted the horse for your sister. I thought, maybe, if you took her the horse and you told her who had risked their life to get it she would show just a little bit of interest in Jesus.

"You think my little sister wants to make love to a horse thief, Jesus? I don't think so. You have done a very wrong thing. The *gringo* that hangs out with the *niño* knows we were with Snake that night at his ranch. Perhaps he didn't say anything to the sheriff because I saved the young one's life. But now? You will bring the sheriff down on us."

Reyes stood contemplating what to do next.

"The boy and his friend are surely right behind you. Then what? We will have to kill them?"

"No. No, Reyes. They will be too busy fighting the fire at the barn."

"You burn their barn, too?" Reyes shrieked in disbelief. "And this is the kind of man you think my sister would want? What is wrong with you, Jesus? You drink too much tequila in Mexico? Huh? You rot your brain?" Reyes jabbed at his own head with two of his fingers.

Jesus hung his head. "I was only trying to make you and your little sister happy, Reyes. Forgive me."

"Forgive you? It will be the man and the boy that will need to forgive you, if they catch you."

"I will take the horse away. I will take him to Mexico. They will never find him there."

"For tonight, you better hide him so you don't get caught. Tomorrow, we will decide what to do."

The three men mounted their horses and, with Comet on a lead rope, headed out toward the east to cut south toward Mexico, away from Moriarty, to set up camp for the night.

"You spoil my good time, Jesus. I stayed on in this town for a celebration and you take that away from me. I don't know what I'm to do with you."

"Forgive me, Reyes. I was only trying to make you happy."

"You were only thinking about yourself and how you would court my little sister."

"Ah, but your sister is a pretty *señorita*, Reyes. Any man would do a foolish thing to win her hand."

Reyes shook his head in disbelief at Jesus—so lovesick he would risk his own neck, and that of Reyes Espiañata, to try to make an impression on a woman.

Perhaps they should have tied the horse to the hitching rail and left him there? Perhaps they should have let someone find him and be done with it. He decided to wait until morning to determine Comet's fate.

They would be fortunate if the *niño* or his friend didn't catch up to them before then.

Reyes didn't relish being hung in the United States as a horse thief—nor did he know if he could reach the border ahead of Trace.

~ * ~

As Trace lay once more, perhaps for the last time, in his bedroll in Molly's house, he thought about his desire to hold Molly in a common bed—to smell her hair, to taste her lips, to make love to her. He knew it was impractical to think that way, unless he married her. So, instead, he made plans for tomorrow.

He would leave Molly's rifle for her protection. His first stop would be Moriarty where he would replace his rifle with a set of six-guns.

Twenty-one

Early the next morning, before the rooster crowed, Trace dressed and went to get Flapjack. Molly followed quickly behind him.

"You're not going to leave on an empty stomach, are you?"

"I want to get an early start. It's probably better if I'm gone before Andy gets up."

"I'll run to the house and pack you some food. How about some cold biscuits and jerky?"

"Good. I don't want to have much weight to mess with."

"I'll have it back to you before you can get Flapjack saddled."

When Trace was ready to leave, Molly lifted a small bundle of food and held it up for him.

"Here, I want you to keep your rifle," Trace said trying to exchange it for the food she held out.

"No, you better take it."

"I'll buy a new one when I get to Moriarty."

"Take care of yourself." Molly found her words inadequate but could find no others to say to him. Going after Comet meant he might have to trail the *vaquero* all the way to Mexico. Was Trace riding out of her life forever?

Trace leaned down and kissed her forehead, like a father would an adored child.

"I wish you didn't have to go." Molly's voice trailed off as she choked back tears.

Trace turned Flapjack away and hurried down the path to the main road. The pain of leaving Molly standing there was nearly more than he could bear. He knew he must not weaken and let Comet slip away. If he didn't get an early start, there was no telling how far ahead Reyes' *vaquero* would get with Comet.

Where the trail from the house met the road Trace reined Flapjack up for a few seconds. He looked back at the farm. Scanning the dawn horizon he saw the results of his labor.

The windmill sat idle for the time being—the stillness of the early morning unable to turn the blades. The new wood of the house and barn shone brightly as the sun broke in the eastern sky. Molly stood, a small figure from this distance, waving relentlessly. Trace waved back, then kicked Flapjack's sides. The horse broke into a run in the calm warm morning air. It was going to be another hot day. Trace wanted to cover as many miles as he could before the heat came on.

In Moriarty, Trace headed first to the sheriff's office. There he found the sheriff and Tom discussing wanted posters detailing outlaws that had moved from the Texas jurisdiction.

"Sheriff. Tom," Trace greeted them as he entered the door. "Surprised to see you're still here, Tom."

"I've been trying to convince Doc Landry I've been well enough to leave for weeks now, but he just wouldn't hear of it. You're out early this morning, Trace," Tom said. "Something come up that couldn't wait?" Tom moved to the stove to refill his coffee cup. He came back with a second one for Trace, too.

"One of those *vaqueros* that's been hanging around town with Reyes came onto the place and stole Andy's horse. That's the second time someone has helped themselves to the kid's horse and he's pretty broken up over it."

The sheriff nodded.

"I was hoping we were through with that kind of stuff for a while. Guess I should have known better."

"Well, I noticed Reyes and his men were at one of the saloons yesterday. Then, they seemed to be gone this morning. Of course, if they have the horse with them, that'd make 'em all horse thieves," Tom said. "What do you figure, they headed back to Mexico?"

"Yeah, that's what I thought. If they get across the border, that'll be the end of Andy ever seeing that horse again."

"You figuring on tracking 'em?" The sheriff asked.

"Well, I don't figure you've got time to go off and leave the town unprotected. Besides, this is kind of my own problem."

The sheriff pulled his desk drawer open and flipped a badge out. "You better put this back on. That way, if you catch up to 'em, whatever you do, within reason, it'll be legal."

"I'm ready to head back to Texas," Tom said. "I'm going to let the sheriff here hold Snake's gang for the traveling judge. I've got a horse down at the livery waiting for me. I'd be happy to ride along."

"I don't care if we never see Reyes and his men around here again. If you do catch 'em before they reach the border, try to take care of it in Texas, would you?" the sheriff asked.

"I have to go buy a rifle and a couple of six-shooters," Trace told Tom. "Then I'll meet you at the livery."

"Sounds good to me. I wasn't looking forward to a long ride back alone, anyway."

Tom and Trace met up at the livery and rode through town to make sure Reyes and his men had left during the night.

"I figure there wasn't any way they'd come past the Kling place, so they wouldn't have gone directly south," Trace said.

"And, if they're headed for Mexico, they probably headed east until they came to a trail that would lead them far enough past the Kling place without having to ride through the mountains," Tom said.

"I figure they're headed toward El Paso and taking as short a route as they can across Texas to the border. Probably cross the Rio Grande where the water's shallow this time of year," Trace added.

"Well, we better take it easy. If we don't come across them soon, you could be in for several days on horseback. Not that I don't want the company."

"I have something to take care of in Texas before I come back, anyway." Trace didn't elaborate. He supposed he should have told Tom and the sheriff about Reyes having ridden with Snake in the past. He should have told them he had seen one of his men steal the bag of money at the bank. The way he saw it, it was his problem, now. He'd have to do what he could to get Comet back, and the money. Surely, by now the banker had audited his funds and realized they came up short.

They rode on in silence, watching the road and looking for the first trail to turn south.

So many horses and wagon wheels had traversed the main road that it was impossible to distinguish Reyes' horse's prints, those of his *vaqueros'* animals, or Comet's prints in the dust.

When they came to the trail leading south, it was easy to see the prints of four horses on the new path. Trace could see by their tracks that the Mexicans were in a hurry to get off the main path and onto this side trail. After inspecting the prints, Trace remounted Flapjack. He and Tom moved slowly along the new trail, ever cautious of ambush and looking for Reyes' camp from the previous night.

They came to an area where the horses' prints moved from the trail into the low dry brush and grass. Trace pulled one of his new pistols from its holster and grasped it in his right hand while he moved Flapjack forward.

Tom, his pearl-handled pistol at the ready, followed him silently.

They found an area where the four horses had been tied for the night. The grass was eaten low to the earth there, and packed tight in three places where Reyes and his men had slept.

There were no remains of a campfire.

There was no Reyes, nor either of his *vaqueros.*

"They probably got out of here early," Trace said. "Bet they left before I even reached Moriarty."

"At least we know they still have Comet with them," Tom said. "I've seen some horse thieves that would shoot the horse and leave it lay to avoid getting caught."

"And someone had sense enough not to light a campfire and catch the countryside ablaze," Trace said.

"We better step our pace up a bit." Without waiting for Trace to agree, Tom kicked his horse in its sides hard enough to cause it to bolt forward. He'd just as soon get this over with while they were still in the United States. He'd have no jurisdiction on the other side of the border, nor would Trace. Reyes and his men could flaunt Comet at them from across the Rio Grande and there wouldn't be anything they could do about it.

~ * ~

At the Kling homestead, Molly had returned to the house after watching Trace until he and Flapjack became so small they were tiny figures moving along the horizon.

Her heart ached. Would she ever see him again? Perhaps she should have been more adamant against his leaving. But she was sure, if she had argued with him to stay, her words would have become tiresome and she would have lost him that way, too. She knew she would not be happy with a shell of a man who stayed behind in body, but whose mind was on the injustices he felt he needed to right.

For a moment she remembered the night she had thought he was asking her to make love to him—and she wished she had. At least, she would have had that to hang onto in her memory. Would it have been such a sin? Now, she might never know the fullness of his love. Would Trace ever come back to her—or would he die in his search for Reyes and his men?

She walked through the unfinished downstairs of the house and heard the children stirring upstairs in their open bedrooms. The night before had been difficult and everyone was extra tired. She would let them come down to the makeshift kitchen table in their own time. After all, with Trace gone, no one was going to feel like doing much today.

"Something to eat, Andy?" Molly saw the boy come down the stairs with his clothes dirty and crumpled and his hair sticking out all over like a porcupine's quills.

"Nah. I'm going to see what the damage looks like in the daylight. Trace already out there?"

"He left at daybreak. He didn't want to wake you."

Andy nodded. He knew Trace probably hoped to avoid an argument with him over wanting to go along.

"Andy—" Molly asked, hesitating.

He stopped on his way out the front door and looked back.

"I'm not going to have a problem with you running off after him, am I?" Her mind begged that he would say 'no', but she feared the worst.

"I want to, Ma."

Molly tried to think of what she could say to keep Andy from going.

"But, I learned my lesson last time. I'll let Trace take care of things this time. It's all my fault, anyway. If I hadn't gotten mixed up with Reyes and raced him, Comet would be here where he belongs."

"You can't blame yourself, Andy. The first time, when you ran into Reyes, you were going after someone you loved. You couldn't know what would come of it. I am glad you'll stay, though. Promise me, you'll stay here."

"I will, Ma."

Although Molly was glad to hear his words, she felt heartsick at the defeated tone in his voice. She only prayed Trace would come back—with Comet.

Rosie and Seth were up now, standing in the kitchen area as they waited for Molly to fix their breakfast. Rosie stood in her bare feet and held Callie across one arm. Crazy Leg had already gone outside for his morning walk.

Molly called out after him, "You stay away from my flower bed, Crazy Leg."

She looked out the kitchen window to make sure the dog obeyed and hadn't slipped around the side of the house. She could see Andy going into the barn to get the lead rope for Big Boy and Jake to take them to pasture. He seemed a sad little figure to her and she wished there was some way to ease his pain.

"Will Trace come back, Ma?" Rosie asked, having heard the conversation between Molly and her brother.

"I hope so, Rosie. We'll just have to keep busy and pray that he does."

An hour later Andy came from the barn leading the team to pasture. He stopped and stood still gazing into the distance. "Ma!" Andy rushed toward the open kitchen window being sure to keep the horses at bay so they wouldn't eat the green leaves of Molly's hollyhocks.

"There's a rider coming down the lane."

Molly moved to get her rifle.

"You and Seth stay in here," she told Rosie.

Crazy Leg ran toward the approaching rider, barking wildly as he went.

Andy moved on around the house, taking the horses to the water trough, both to keep them out of trouble and because the rider was approaching slowly and there would be plenty of time to get back to the house before the rider arrived. Besides, Crazy Leg was giving him notice that strangers weren't welcome.

The dog darted back and forth, nipping at the heels of the rider's horse, then cowered back when the animal swung its head to look at him and take aim with a hoof.

When the man pulled up to the front of the house, he faced Molly standing square on with her feet spaced apart and her rifle aimed at his chest. Andy was standing next to her. Crazy Leg ran up and sat down on his haunches next to Andy, panting. He kept this stranger under surveillance. Together, they formed a defiant force.

"What do you want, Mister?" Molly studied the overweight hulk of a man. His body was shaped like the bow of a sailing ship. His puffed-up arms reached toward the reins where hands too tiny to seem to fit on the stumps of his arms gripped the leather straps in fear at this unwelcome greeting. He straddled a nag almost as fat as he was.

Although he wore an expensive-appearing dark suit and a businessman's hat, Molly noticed that his sleeves and pant legs hiked up from his wrists and ankles. He had the look of someone who was about to burst the seams of his fancy clothes.

"I asked you, what you wanted?" Molly repeated when the startled stranger temporarily lost his voice.

"I'm looking for a Mr. Westerman. Mr. Trace Westerman. The sheriff in town said I might find him out here."

"He's not here." Molly maintained her aim at the stranger.

The gentleman reached for his pocket.

Molly cocked her rifle.

He raised his hand away and showed her it contained only his monocle, a single lens in a silver circle that attached to a heavy silver chain. With it was a calling card.

He adjusted the monocle to his left eye and studied the card before holding his arm out toward Molly and Andy.

"I'm Elroy Peabody, Ma'am. Been looking for Mr. Westerman for some time now. I'm with the railroad. You'll see my title on this card."

Molly nodded to Andy to go get the card.

"Watch yourself. We don't know if he's who he says he is or what he wants."

Andy, with Crazy Leg guarding his side, approached the fat man cautiously. He figured, if he had to, he could break away and the man wouldn't be fast enough to catch him. He reached out and took the card from Peabody's fingers.

Andy stepped back reading the card as he moved alongside Molly.

"Says here he 'pro-procures' property for the railroad, Ma."

"Well, Mr. Westerman's not here and we've got work to do. And, this property is not for sale. Good day, Mr. Peabody."

"Can you tell me when he might return?"

"Can't say. Whatever business you got with Mr. Westerman will have to wait."

The man tipped his hat at Molly and Andy and slowly turned his horse around the other way. The animal moved as if its own weight made it difficult for it to complete the simple procedure. Peabody booted it with the heels of his shiny boots that looked as if he never went any place to get them dirty. Rider and horse pointed the other direction.

"If Mr. Westerman returns, please tell him I'm still interested. I'll be in this area for a time. Perhaps we'll meet again. Good day, Ma'am, son."

Andy hated it when a stranger called him "son". He'd almost rather be called "*niño*" by Reyes than "son" by some fat stranger that could hardly ride a horse. Besides, he was still mad that Comet was gone and he wanted, badly, to ride out after Trace and help search for him.

But, he had promised Molly that he wouldn't.

When Mr. Peabody left, Andy gave Molly his card and walked back to the water trough to finish his chore of taking the horses to pasture. He could still see Peabody moving away from the farm and hear the slow plod of the animal's hooves. It was going to be a long ride back to town for Mr. Peabody—whoever he was.

Molly uncocked the rifle and studied the card as Crazy Leg lay down in the shade of the porch to rest from his excitement. She studied the print on the card, puzzling over why the man wanted Trace. She went back inside the house.

There, Rosie was feeding Callie milk from one of her few bowls. She had set it on the kitchen floor, having been none too careful when she moved it. Small puddles of milk dotted the immediate area and Rosie called Crazy Leg to lick it up.

Callie took offense at his intrusion. She arched her back and hissed at him. He stayed far enough away from her so he could dodge a strike, should she raise her claws and swing at him.

Molly laid the card on the table. *What was Trace up to?* Surely, he didn't think she would be interested in selling out to the railroad. She had heard they could be persuasive, if they needed a piece of property for right-of-way and the owner didn't want to sell willingly.

Was Trace somehow involved with the procurement division of the railroad? Old suspicions haunted her. Why would Trace help her build up the farm, if he wanted her to sell it to the railroad? She would have to be more vigilant in protecting her interests.

Maybe she would set Andy to riding the perimeter on Jake or Big Boy, in case someone was up to something. Maybe it was time Andy learned to shoot the rifle and carry it with him on his rounds.

Twenty-two

Molly and the family continued with their daily chores: the harvesting of the garden, putting up food for the winter, picking what pinto beans they had been able to raise for market, and continuing Andy's target practice.

For the sessions with Andy and the rifle, Molly made sure Rosie and Seth remained within the safety of the house, or yard, guarded by Crazy Leg. To their disappointment, the two younger children felt banished from Andy's lessons. They heard the consistent plink of bullets hitting a scrap of tin, leftover from the windmill blades, as Andy's aim became more accurate.

"Now, just because I'm teaching you to shoot, doesn't mean you're to start carrying a gun. You know I don't approve of that. Guns are for protection, only. Remember that."

"I know, Ma." Andy gave Molly the answer he knew she wanted, but he couldn't help feeling proud of his marksmanship. He hit what he aimed at nine times out of ten. Molly called a halt to the practice.

"We can't waste bullets. Remember don't point a gun at anyone unless you intend to use it. And don't use it unless you have to. If there is danger, fire three shots into the air at an angle."

"Yes, Ma."

"And, at all times, keep it away from your brother! That child is too fond of guns. Some way, we'll have to break him of that."

~ * ~

It had been several days since Trace and Tom left Moriarty in search of Reyes and his men.

Signs they found along the way confirmed that they were on the right trail.

"We can't be far behind them," Tom said early one morning as they were barely on their way from breaking camp at dawn. He pointed out large circles of dry grass where the four horses were hobbled for the night and left to graze. The feed was poor. The grass was so brittle the animals had pulled the roots up with the blades as they tried to make a meal of their surroundings. They had wallowed the ground bare, leaving indisputable marks of their having been there in the near-barren prairie.

Tracking the horses turned into drudgery and, except for the times when they came to a town where they could replenish their supplies and refresh themselves, they endured dust and sun and hard riding.

They would have given up, but occasionally, in one of these settlements there was a saloon where they inquired about the Mexicans and learned they were a day or two behind them. If they found they were two days behind them, they hurriedly left town and spurred their horses to a quicker pace. They hoped to shorten the distance between them and Reyes and his men before they got too close to the border—before Reyes and his *vaqueros* could make a run for it.

~ * ~

The closer to the border Reyes and his men came, the more Reyes sensed Trace and the Ranger were closing the gap between them. He felt their pursuers would need to be pushing their horses hard to catch them before they reached the Rio Grande. He did not plan to be shot as a horse thief on the American side of the border when he had a palatial home and family on the Mexican side. A single man, he didn't want his mother and sister crying because he had not come home.

He had been considering what to do about the horse and Jesus for many hard, dry miles now, and he had made his decision.

Ahead, surrounded by miles of barren land, stood a single skeleton of an ancient tree. Its branches, though long dry, were thick and strong and reached out horizontally, then angled upward. When it was alive, it must have been magnificent. But what could live forever in this forsaken land that saw extreme heat and little rainfall?

Reyes slowed his horse near the tree and dropped the reins while he dismounted and squatted on the ground.

"Why we stop?" Jesus asked.

"Get down. Rest. We are but a few miles from the border."

Jesus obeyed.

Jose, always eager to take a break, swung off his horse and tied him, Comet and Jesus' horse to one of the lower branches of the tree.

When all three were on the ground, Reyes, still squatting, Jose stretched out flat on his back, and Jesus standing nearby fidgeting as if he smelled something in the wind, Reyes studied the man lying before him.

"Jose, I been thinking. And, the more I think about Jesus stealing this horse," Reyes waved his arm toward Comet, "the angrier I become. I think, maybe, I should teach him a lesson and maybe slow the lawmen down a bit so you and I can get back across the border."

Jesus looked at Reyes with a frown on his face, his eyes questioning Reyes.

Suddenly uneasy, Jose sat up and began to rise to his feet. He wondered how this would involve him.

"What are you talking about, *mi amigo*?" Jesus asked.

"For many years, the travelers along this trail have called this 'the hanging tree.'" Reyes rose to his feet and took his lariat from where it lay looped over his silver saddle horn. He ran his fingers along the rope, feeling for the loose loop to enlarge the circle. He snapped it into the air and brought it down quickly around Jesus' body, jerking it tight so that Jesus' arms were straight against his frame and pulling the rope taut at his waist.

"What are you doing, Reyes? Have I not always been loyal to you?"

"Hand me your lariat, Jose," Reyes spoke to the other man standing nearby watching and waiting to see what Reyes had in mind.

Reyes made a second circle of rope and dropped it over Jesus' body until it reached the leather of his boots at his ankles. Then he moved beneath the strongest branch on the tree and slung the other end of the rope over the heavy limb.

Slowly, Reyes pulled on the rope, then enlisted Jose's assistance until Jesus was forced to the ground and gradually dragged upside-down beneath the tree. His *sombrero* dropped to the dirt below him.

"What is wrong with you? Why are you doing this? Let me down!"

"*Amigo!*" Reyes released the rope that held Jesus' arms to his sides. He stood rewinding his lariat into its tight circle and replaced it on his saddle horn. "I told you, this will slow the *gringos* down. If you get out of it before the *gringos* find you, we'll meet again, on the other side of the border. If you don't, they'll probably put the rope around your neck instead of your boots. Just remember, I chose your boots this time."

Jesus knew it was a warning from Reyes. He should never have stolen the horse, regardless of how beautiful and rich Reyes' sister was. Now, he would never have a chance to try to win her hand. Nor would he want a brother-in-law who treated him this way.

"If you do come back—the horse stays here. We have had enough trouble with the *gringos*."

Reyes checked the reins on Comet and Jesus' horse to make sure they could not break free from their bindings. He wanted to be sure Comet would be there when Trace caught up. Jesus would have to take his chances. He looked at Jesus swinging back and forth, his arms stretching toward his feet, his hands trying to reach and untie the slipknot that cinched tighter with each movement.

Reyes ran his hand down Comet's neck, across his back, and down his rear as he moved away.

"Too bad the *niño* wouldn't sell you. My little sister would have loved you."

Reyes and Jose mounted their horses.

Reyes drew one of his silver-handled pistols.

"No, *amigo!* Please don't shoot me," Jesus called out.

Jose looked at Reyes, but held his tongue.

"The *gringos* shoot horse thieves, Jesus. And some people shoot horses." Reyes knew that if Trace and Tom were not so close, the merciful thing would be to shoot the animal rather than put it through the misery of dehydration or being eaten alive by wild animals. His sixth sense told him Trace could not be far behind them. If he shot the horse now, that would surely slow the Americans down.

He fired the pistol.

Comet jumped.

"*Adiós, amigo*." Reyes and Jose spurred their horses to make a last dash for the border.

When he looked back over his shoulder, Reyes could see Jesus dangling beneath the tree. He also saw the dust of two horses, behind them, racing toward the tree, Comet, and the dangling man.

~ * ~

Trace and Tom had kept a steady pace and now, ahead, they could barely make out the branches of the huge tree in the middle of the barren prairie.

"The Hanging Tree!" Tom called out to Trace over the sound of their own horses' hooves heavily beating the earth. "We're nearing the border."

They heard the shot ring out.

Trace and Tom pulled their horses to a halt.

Dust, from other horses, rose toward the south as they watched. Trace had no doubt it was from the horses they had been tracking, racing for the border.

"That son of a bitch," Tom said, fearing Reyes had killed Comet.

Trace clenched his jaw. Surely, a man who loved horses, as Reyes did, could not bring himself to waste a horse like Comet? But why had they heard a shot?

Again, they spurred their mounts ahead, fear gripping them now as visions of what they might find flashed through their minds.

Ahead, they could see something swaying beneath the biggest branch of the tree as they hurried toward it.

Their horses were lathered when at last, they stopped beneath the rare ancient tree.

On the ground, pieces of dry twigs lay scattered about everywhere. Overhead, shiny leather boots hung from a tight slipknot. Comet stood nearby, tied to another branch of the tree.

Comet jerked his head and whinnied.

They heard someone shouting encouragement to their horse to run as the sound of its hoof beats diminished toward the border. Jesus, barefoot from having slipped free of his boots, lay tight to the saddle and sped for Mexico.

He knew he was one lucky man. When Reyes blasted the tree limbs overhead, he had thought he was a dead man. He resolved never to cross Reyes again. Perhaps he would find another woman to worship and someone else to ride with instead of Reyes, if he got across the river to Mexico before the *gringos* caught him. If not, Reyes was probably right, they would take him back to the tree and, this time, the knot would be around his neck.

~ * ~

"Well, looks like we missed 'em," Tom said.

"Fortunately, Comet's alive." Trace inspected Comet to make sure he had no injuries. He untied him and brought him back to his own horse where he tied the lead rope to his saddle horn.

"This close to the border, they'd be across before we could get close enough to shoot at 'em," Tom continued.

"I have what I came for."

"By the looks of the rope and boots, I'd say the horse thief learned his lesson."

"You'd think so. I have a feeling that shot we heard was Reyes making sure we found the horse, whether we caught his *vaquero* or not."

"Yep. That's what I think, too. Guess unless the other fellow comes back and causes more trouble, it's best just to let them go."

The sooner Trace got out of this part of Texas, the better he'd like it.

"I'm headed back to Ranger Headquarters in Waco," Tom said. "Do you want to ride along?"

"No. Now that I have Comet back, I have other business to tend to."

"Suit yourself. Don't think either of us wants a lonely ride." Tom hoped Trace would change his mind. There were many empty miles between there and Waco.

"Sure do get used to having someone to talk to," Trace said. "But, I have things to do in another part of Texas and I best get on with it."

"I understand."

They shook hands.

"Well, good-bye, then. Maybe we'll run into each other again, somewhere," Tom said.

Trace nodded. He hoped they would.

They mounted their horses, leaving the boots hanging in the tree.

They rode along, together, a short distance until they reached a fork in the road. Tom turned in the direction of Waco. Trace turned north, toward his ranch along the Pecos, leading Comet behind him.

He was a long way from Molly, and her family in New Mexico, but he had spent many years in Texas. As hardscrabble as ranching had been there, it was home.

Twenty-three

A deep feeling of remorse overtook Trace when he reached the boundaries of his ranch on the Pecos. The pain of losing his parents was still fresh and, while Molly had eased the ache somewhat, he still missed the couple that had loved and sheltered him until he became an adult. Out of love, he had felt a commitment to make their later days comfortable. He had done his best to fulfill that promise.

Standing on a knoll, looking down at the remains of the ranch buildings, he surveyed what had once been a dream. It was a dream that had turned into a nightmare in a flash, one catastrophic night. It was a night he relived when Snake and his gang had raided the Klings' place and, again, when the *vaquero* set fire to their new barn.

To the left, on a hill beyond where the main buildings had once stood like a fortress, was the small family plot. With its unpainted graying picket fence, to keep wild pigs and other animals out, it was situated in the shade of a young tree. Inside the cribbing were two wooden headboards. From the distance, Trace read them in his memory as he had carved them—Beloved Mother and Beloved Father.

WESTERMAN.

He saw, to the right and downhill some distance, the few remaining ashes of the main house. Alongside, his own windmill creaked slowly in the nearly still air. The shaft attached to the pump handle moved gradually up and down delivering a trickle of water into a wooden trough.

He was amazed to see that, somehow, the water continued to flow, although meagerly.

Nearby, the bunkhouse stood with its uprights looking like a drunk's rotted teeth. Its blackened corners jutted skyward in defiance of the flames that had licked upward on that awful night. The barn beyond had not fared as well as Molly's had. It lay, with what walls that had not burned, flat on the ground. But something was missing.

There had been horses inside and he thought some of their skeletons might still be there. Once he had buried his parents he had planned to see that his hired hands buried the animals, but they had either quit or run off when the trouble started. As he looked toward the ashes now, he could not make out the bones of anything within the perimeter of the barn.

The coyotes or vultures must have dragged them off, he thought.

Not far from the barn, a small shack stood seemingly unscathed by the fire.

Surprise registered in Trace's mind. Everything was destroyed. He was certain. Or, had his grief been so deep that he had missed seeing the small tack shed still standing?

Excitement pulsed in his veins. Perhaps there was something to be salvaged from all this. From the distance, he started Flapjack and Comet down the knoll.

As he drew closer, he realized the siding on the tack shed was irregular and patchwork. Someone had salvaged boards from the ruins and reconstructed the storage shed. Why would anyone do that?

Squatters! Who else would go to all that trouble?

"Hold it right there, Mister," a man's voice, with just the slightest quiver, boomed out at him as he approached.

He saw the barrel of a rifle sticking out of a knothole in one of the boards and reined Flapjack to a halt.

He heard a baby crying inside the shack.

A woman shushed it.

"I don't know who you are, but you're trespassing," Trace told the stranger.

"You're the one trespassing. Now, get out of here."

Trace had no intention of leaving. This was his ranch, what was left of it, and until he decided differently, he'd stay. He looked about trying to find a common ground to talk to the man about.

"This is my ranch, whoever you are. The deed's registered at the courthouse. Those are my folks buried up on the hillside over there."

There was silence inside the shack. Then, the door slowly creaked open and the rifle barrel came through the crack first, then a young man.

"I—I didn't know. We thought it was abandoned. Figured, maybe, the Indians had raided and burned everything."

"It wasn't Indians."

"My wife was having a baby. We needed shelter. This was all I could think to do. Then, when no one showed up, we stayed on. We'll move along, Mister, just as soon as we can get our stuff together."

"You take care of the animals in the barn?"

"Yeah. The wife was afraid they'd bring disease down on us. I dug a pit off toward the pasture and hauled 'em out there and covered 'em up."

"Well, I thank you for that. I was in too much of a hurry when I left to do it myself."

The man nodded. Trace could see he was young, perhaps barely twenty. His wife joined him at the door, holding an infant in her arms. They came outside.

"We usually don't go in there 'til it cools down in the evening," the man said. "It's like a bake oven in there in the daytime."

"You had some right nice things, Mister," the woman, who Trace could see was not much more than a girl, told him. "We picked through the ashes of the house and saved what we could. Most of the dishes were broke, though. It's a shame."

"You're welcome to take anything we found," the man said, anxious not to provoke Trace.

"Sure do appreciate being able to stay here for a spell, Mister," the man went on.

"Trace. Trace Westerman. You can call me Trace."

"Westerman? That's the name on the headboards up in the cemetery," the girl said.

"Like I said, they're my folks."

"I've been taking wildflowers up to the graves, once I was able to."

Trace dismounted and led the horses over to the watering trough. The young man followed.

"Sure hope you aren't mad, Mr. Westerman—Trace. I mean, we needed someplace to stay real quick."

"No. It doesn't matter. Everything's mostly destroyed, anyway."

"There's a couple of cows, over yonder, and a calf. I been seein' they were watered and kept them from wandering off. We been eating what wild game I could shoot and what provisions we had with us. Didn't eat any of your cows."

Trace laughed.

"I'm surprised there's even that many left. I wouldn't have known if you had made a meal of one of them."

"You're welcome to eat with us tonight," the girl said, "if you're planning to stay."

"I'm staying. At least tonight."

Trace walked through the debris of the buildings. He saw nothing worth picking up and remembered that the young woman had said they had retrieved what few things were salvageable. He'd look at those before he left.

"I'll show you where the cows are, if you like," the young man said.

"Sure. You got a name?"

"Oh, yeah. Sorry, Trace. I was so shook up when you came up on us like that, I plumb forgot to introduce myself. I'm Bill and my wife's, Miranda. We just had our baby, little Billy, two weeks ago."

"A son. That's nice."

"You can ride the black horse. It belongs to a friend of mine."

"Thanks. We have an old worn out nag that pulls our small buggy. Everything we own fits in it. I'm trying to find a place I can get hired on somewhere as a ranch hand."

Bill led the way to the dry pasture where the cows grazed.

Sure enough, there was his T-bar-W brand on the hip of both animals and none on the new heifer that clung close to one of the cows.

"I herd 'em in and let 'em hang around the water trough in the afternoon." Bill said. "If they get thirsty enough, they'll come in on their own."

Trace nodded. He looked out across the land. As far as he could see it was his.

They herded the cattle ahead of them back to the trough. When they dismounted, Miranda had the meal cooking on the battered wood stove. She had dragged a rocker outside and sat in the shade of the shed rocking the baby.

Trace was surprised the rocker had survived the inferno.

"Figure the house must have had a porch," Bill said.

Trace nodded.

"It was my ma's favorite place to be in the evening, sitting in that rocker, on the front porch."

"It must have got knocked off the porch and fell far enough away to avoid the flames," Bill said.

"I'm glad to see someone's enjoying it. My ma would be happy about that. She hated to see anything go to waste."

"Miranda and little Billy use it all the time. They sure like it."

They ate their meal while the baby slept in a scorched drawer that Trace recognized as having belonged to a chest in the bunkhouse.

Miranda swatted flies away from the top of the drawer. The insects buzzed in a swarm to where they found fresh grease spots the diners left on the rickety table.

When they flew too near the plates Miranda swept her hand vigorously above the food to shoo them away.

"The food is delicious, Miranda. I haven't had a hot meal in a while. It feels good to sit down off a horse and enjoy it for a bit."

"Miranda's a right good cook," Bill said proudly. "A good mother, too."

"I can see that."

Trace wanted to tell them about his mother, but the wounds were too fresh. He decided he'd save his words for when he walked up the hill tomorrow to where she and his father now lay.

"I reckon I'll toss my bedroll down out here somewhere tonight," Trace said.

"Mighty glad to have the company," Bill said. "It gets a might lonely out here."

Trace could have told him of a time when the ranch bustled with activity and it was a great place to work. The Westermans were fair to work for and paid a good wage.

There wasn't time to get lonesome when the ranch was at full capacity and cowboys were busy with branding or moving the cattle. It was a good place. Maybe someday it would be again.

The next morning, Trace arose early and walked to the small plot on the hill while what little dew had touched the ground clung in beads on dry grass stems.

When he reached the fence, with its enclosed headboards, he noted that Miranda had, as she said, kept fresh wildflowers on the graves and tended the plot so no weeds grew inside.

She was like the daughter-in-law his ma had never had. And, now, a tiny babe was carried to the site when Miranda came. He felt sad that he had never married and given his parents grandchildren—that he had never experienced the joy of watching a child of his own grow and gaze at the world through eyes of wonder.

Trace stood for a few moments mentally saying things he knew his ma would like to hear. There were tears in his eyes when he turned and walked back down to the burned-out dream that would take a lot of work to resurrect.

"Morning, Trace," Miranda said as she went to the well with one of his Mother's colorful pitchers to fetch water for the start of the day.

"'Goin' to be a scorcher, today."

Trace looked at the sky. She was right. Already the oppressive feeling of heat that should be saved for midday was upon them.

Bill joined Miranda outside the shack.

"Morning."

Trace returned the greeting.

"I'll be moving on today. I reckon I'll take the one cow with the calf along. I'll give you a Bill of Sale for the other one—for looking after my land and what was left of my herd."

"But, Mr. Westerman, we been using your land without your permission," Miranda said. "You don't owe us anything."

"I know. But, well, you did some things that needed doing and I figure one cow and a calf is going to be hard enough to move along the trail."

"We thank you, Trace," Bill said. "I don't take much to being called a 'squatter.' Maybe, with the Bill of Sale for the cow, folks will see things a little different. Like you said, maybe they'll see me more as a caretaker."

"You can stay on here for a while, if you like." Given a few weeks or months, perhaps the couple would be better on their feet and able to fend against the world on their own.

"You want to look through the stuff we got out of the ashes?" Miranda asked.

Trace had almost forgotten they had discussed that possibility earlier.

"No. Anything I'd want would have gone up in the fire. I can't take glassware with me."

Miranda nodded. She understood and, having found only unreadable scorched pages of books and papers all that remained was some pottery, the damaged cook stove they used despite its warped sides and uneven top, and the rocking chair.

She glanced toward the rocker.

"I don't want to haul that across a horse, so you can keep it, too. Ma'd be pleased for you to have it."

"Thank you. Some nights that's the only thing that settles little Billy down. It's as if he feels the love that old rocker's held, you know?"

"I know."

"Anyway, as far as I'm concerned, you can stay as long as you want. The railroad expansion is coming through here. I plan to sell the property to them for a right of way to run their trains on. What happens when the railroad people take over is up to them. Maybe, if you can raise the money, they'll sell you a little piece, once they get the right-of-way they want. I intend to try to withhold this parcel with the graves on it." Trace considered his plans for the future.

"Shoot, maybe I can just give it to you. I ain't ever coming back." Trace cringed at the sound of the word "ain't" and heard the echo of Molly's voice correcting him." He smiled to himself, then went on. "What's left ought to be enough land to satisfy the railroad people."

Bill looked at Miranda with disbelief in his eyes.

"You mean it, Mr. Westerman—Trace?" Bill asked.

"I sure do. I know Miranda will look after the graves and that'll be a big weight off my mind. I was going to sell all of it to the railroad, anyway, until I got here and saw the graves again. When I get where I'm going, I'll mail you a deed—free and clear." It was a moment's decision on Trace's part. *What the heck, sometimes even squatters ought to get a break,* he thought. The railroad acquisition agents didn't always see to it that the real landowners got what they deserved. Maybe it was a chance for him to make up for some of the stories he had heard about ranchers and farmers being run off their property for the railroad workers to lay wooden ties and steel tracks across their land.

"Sure do appreciate it, Trace," Bill said. "Before I met Miranda, my family got ran off their land by the railroad. Maybe it's only fair Miranda and little Billy and me get a piece of theirs. Boy, howdy! I never thought I'd see the day we'd be landowners!"

Trace saddled Flapjack. With a good supply of fresh water and a food bundle Miranda had made up for him, he mounted the horse and split the cows apart from the other one. He herded the cow and calf ahead of him, and led Comet, as he left the ranch for what he figured would be the last time.

Too much pain remained on that hill, behind where the ranch house had sat, for him. Miranda, Bill and the baby brought new hope to the place. He looked back and waved at the couple grinning broadly in front of the shack. He wished he'd had one of those photography fellows there to take a picture of the new landowners bursting with pride. It was a pretty picture.

"So long, Trace," they called after him.

"So long." Trace looked, for the last time, at the picket fence on the hill beneath the shade of the tree.

"So long, Ma. So long, Pa." Trace turned and rode down the drive, away from the T-bar-W ranch.

He never looked back.

Twenty-four

To Molly, it seemed as if Trace had been gone away forever. Sometimes, she had to convince herself that his being there with them during the spring and summer had not been merely a dream. Had the stirrings within her heart and, in fact, her whole body been only a strong desire for a man to love? Had she imagined him? And then, in those moments, she would remind herself to look about and see all that Trace had helped them build and know the gnawing hunger in her belly was not from want of food, but from her need to love and be loved. Her strong sense of knowing that Trace was someone she could share her life with convinced her that they could live as partners— each satisfying the other's needs. Yet she felt they could trust one another enough to be apart and not be tempted by others.

Everywhere Molly looked there were things to remind her of Trace. She gazed about the open partitions of the bedrooms in the house and thought about how far they had come. Since meeting Trace Westerman, they had come from crawling beneath the buckboard for protection from the elements and enemies, to being secure within a wonderful, albeit unfinished, house. As she studied the open spaces with framing between them she envisioned the finished walls and ceilings that would, one day, provide privacy for each of them.

She looked out the south window and saw the field of beans maturing toward their final harvest. When she walked to the kitchen window, she saw her hollyhocks filling the small patch of dirt they were allowed. Beyond, the chickens scratched by the barn door.

Near the barn, the pigs squealed in their pen and, when they dared let them out and block them from the bean field, they took joy in eradicating any stray snake they came upon out there. They seemed to be competing with Crazy Leg to clear the land of the unwanted creatures.

Yes, they had come a long way, she thought, and, yet, she felt an emptiness she would not have known had Trace not appeared that day on her rocks.

She smiled to herself. How he must have thought her daft to be ready and willing, to shoot a stranger over the rocks. How could he have known how much they meant to her? How they were the basis of her very beginning of a new life for herself and the children. What was Trace doing now? Would he ever return? Or had she lost the man who meant so much to all of them?

It was the first part of September, shortly before she was to start teaching school again. Molly sat in the shade on the front porch. The weather had not cooled and rain had been elusive, so the best relief to be had was under the shade of the porch roof.

With Rosie and Seth's help, Molly shelled pinto beans to sell to the General Store. They had been at the chore most of the day and into the early afternoon, taking breaks now and then to refresh themselves. It was tedious work, but the money would be welcome and, having set aside their own supply of dry beans, Molly could think of nothing better to do with the rest.

Molly gathered her long apron up into a carrier and poured the newly shelled beans into a nearby gunnysack. She returned to her seat where she loaded more pods into her lap. She had just settled back down to work on the next arduous batch with her aching fingers when she heard the shots.

Seth, having taken a break to go to the outhouse, came running out at the sound of the gunshots. He let the door bang behind him and ran toward the house fastening one strap on his overalls while the other strap flapped in the breeze as he ran toward Molly and safety.

Molly recognized the repeat of her own rifle as it cracked again. Two shots! She jumped up from the box where she sat and sent beans scattering toward where Rosie sat on the porch deck. The chickens rushed to peck up the runaway beans.

"What is it, Ma?" Seth asked, more excited than afraid.

"I don't know."

"Ma! Ma!" Andy shouted, his words mingled with the sound of Big Boy's hooves pounding the ground.

Andy had been out patrolling the property line, as she had asked him to do. He must have run into some sort of trouble. Over the last few months, she had learned to expect nothing but the worst.

"You kids get into the house and stay there!"

They obeyed without question, knowing that it was better to be out of the way when trouble started than to get caught in the middle of it.

Rosie, frightened, began to cry and ran toward the door.

"When are you going to teach me to shoot, Ma?" Seth demanded. He added defiantly, "I'd give 'em what for."

"Into the house, I said." Molly shooed him with her apron like he had seen her do the chickens when they got into the garden. "And fasten your pants."

Before Seth had crossed the threshold, they heard Andy call out again.

"Ma! It's Trace. He's coming in!"

Trace! Molly remembered she had heard only two shots, not three. Three shots in the air meant danger, her rational mind reminded her as her excitement spun her into a flurry of decisions.

What should she do? Should she try to calm herself and greet him with dignity when he finally reached the house? Should she rush inside and brush her hair and wash her face—maybe put on a better dress? She tried to push the wrinkles out of the skirt she wore with her hands.

"Trace! Trace!" Seth and Rosie were jumping up and down and shouting.

Molly grabbed the porch rail and spun off the porch to the ground for a better look.

She couldn't see Trace, but Andy was running Big Boy across the pasture. He waved the rifle in the air and let out several hoots as he raced toward the house.

When he skidded Big Boy to a stop, the dust billowed over the porch and Molly and the little kids coughed and waved the dust cloud away from their faces. The chickens scattered, squawking and losing feathers as they flew away.

Andy was so out of breath he could hardly talk.

Molly waited impatiently for him to speak.

"It's Trace, Ma. He's coming. He's leading Comet and herding a cow and a calf. I saw him from the corner line. I waved and called to him but he was too far away to hear me. He'll be riding down the main road to our drive soon."

Molly pulled her apron off and tossed it over the pile of beans left to shell.

Andy turned Big Boy around and headed out the drive toward the main road, running the horse. Molly was envious that Andy would reach Trace long before any of the rest of them. She wanted to fly to Trace's arms, but reality held her to the ground.

Rosie and Seth ran behind Andy. Crazy Leg joined in the fun in spite of the dust cloud Big Boy stirred in his face.

Molly's feet took over her mind and she began to run, too. Excitement replaced the ache in her heart. At that moment, she felt as if she could run all the way to town, if she had to do so. At least, she could meet Trace long before he'd reach the house.

As they ran, they could see Andy already stopping Big Boy.

The two horses were side-by-side. Andy greeted Trace waving his arms with excitement until he finally settled for a quick handshake. Trace handed him Comet's lead rope and Andy moved quickly to greet his horse. Trace pressed Flapjack on toward the homestead, herding the cow and calf ahead of them.

His pace and slump in the saddle told Molly he was tired. He'd probably been pushing himself hard to get back.

When Seth and Rosie reached him, he hefted both of them up onto Flapjack. It was clear he was glad to see them. Rosie sat across his legs and hugged his neck. Seth sat in front of the saddle. He held his head high as if things didn't get any better than this.

How was Trace going to greet her when she got there? Would he shake her hand like he had Andy's? Or could she hope for more?

It seemed the distance between them was taking forever to close. She felt as if she would never reach him. She wished she could run as fast as the youngsters or, at least, not feel as if her legs were going to give out or her heart was going to explode. She ran, instead, like an older person too tired to keep up. She was reaching the end of her endurance and slowed her pace so she would, at least, have breath enough to greet him when they met.

And then, he was there looking down from his perch in the saddle. He studied her as if he had thought he'd never see her again. They stared into each others' eyes. Then, they both moved at once. Trace shifted Rosie off his lap and dismounted swiftly to land both feet solidly on the firm soil of the homestead.

Molly threw herself into his arms.

At last, Trace released her from his embrace and held her at arm's length, looking into her eyes and studying her face as if she had only been a figment of his imagination until then.

"I've missed you so much," Molly said.

"And I've missed you. too. You'll never know how much!" He remembered the lonely nights along the trail when he could only hold her in his mind and pray that everything would be all right—that they were all safe and would still welcome him when he returned.

He kissed her gently, at first, then more hungrily before restraining himself in front of the children.

The cow and calf, having gotten the scent of water at the trough, rushed past the couple blocking their way. The calf bumped Trace's leg as she followed her mother toward water.

Trace turned in surprise as the calf's abrupt rush interrupted their embrace.

"I pushed them hard trying to get here before dark—trying to get back here before you changed your mind about having me hanging around," Trace half-joked, wanting reassurance that Molly felt as he did.

Molly slipped her arms around his chest and pulled herself tight against his shirt. "I prayed every night that you'd come back to me."

"I love you, Molly. I couldn't tell you that before. I had some things to take care of before I could ask you to love me in return.

Now, I have one last thing to do, simple as it is, and I'll be free to make a new life."

"And, I love you," Molly said without hesitation. "I've loved you for a long time, now, but I didn't know if you could ever be happy with a person like me."

"A person like you?" Trace thought about her stubbornness to build the house, her determination to make a life for her and her taken-on family. While, at first, he had judged her to be willful and hazardous, he now loved these traits. He knew she would take care of her family against all odds. And so would he.

He kissed her tenderly.

"I love you just the way you are."

Molly hugged him. How lucky she was to have this man back in her life.

"Molly, I have to see a Mr. Peabody as soon as I can track him down—"

Molly broke his words off with a frightened look.

"No, I'm not leaving again. I've been told he's been looking for me. I don't plan on going any farther than Moriarty. One thing I have to do is to get rid of this badge—for good, I hope. The other thing is to sell my holdings in Texas."

"Then, you didn't send him here to buy me out?"

"Buy you out? Why would I do that?"

"I don't know, but after you left this Peabody fellow showed up. We didn't know what he wanted. Some of the men working for the railroad have done some strange things to get their right-of-ways. You weren't here. I was scared. I guess I sort of started questioning your motives."

Trace took Molly's hand and walked her slowly toward the house.

"Molly, I want you to marry me."

Molly stopped abruptly and looked at Trace in amazement. This man she had come to love so much was actually asking her to be his wife.

"After I accused you of trying to negotiate with the railroad to sell my place? You're asking me to marry you?"

"Yes. I realize I've been close-mouthed about my business. I thought you had enough to worry about. I figured there wasn't any point in concerning you any more with my dealings."

"But, what about the kids? When we first met, you didn't like kids very much."

"Well, I've had a change of heart there. Guess I've grown kind of used to these three. I wouldn't mind having some of our own to go with them."

Molly blushed, then smiled at him. She had dared to dream that they would marry and now that dream was coming true. She could hardly believe her ears.

"Yes, Trace. Of course I'll marry you." She turned to him and buried her face in his shirt so he wouldn't see the tears of happiness welling up into her eyes.

Trace led Flapjack, with Rosie sitting in the saddle and Seth in front of it, toward the house as they walked. When they reached the front yard, Trace dropped the reins and lifted the children down.

Rosie, having overheard their conversation began chanting in a singsong voice as she ran toward the porch.

"Trace and Molly are getting married. Callie, where are you?" Rosie called for the cat, planning to dress her in flour sacks and pretend she was a bride.

Seth looked after her as if he didn't understand how getting married was anything to get excited about—he didn't care if they got married or not, as long as Trace hung around here. Life had been better with the man there. Maybe he'd even teach him how to shoot—one day, if Molly wouldn't.

Seth hurried to catch up to Rosie and see what the game she was about to play was all about.

"I hope we didn't mess things up for you with Mr. Peabody, Trace. Not knowing who he was—we ran him off."

Trace looked at her, amused. He knew there would be a story behind her comment and he waited to hear it.

"This fat man on a fat old nag came into the yard one day. He left a card. It's in the kitchen. He said to give it to you when you returned."

"A fat man with a monocle?"

"Yes. His calling card said Elroy Peabody on it. Had something to do with the railroad. I never did trust the railroad men. Once they set their mind to getting your property for their trains to run across, they never leave a person alone. As I told you, I thought they wanted my land. So, I taught Andy to shoot and set him to patrolling the property lines. If they want this land, they'll get a fight!"

"That I don't doubt." Trace chuckled. He imagined Mr. Peabody hadn't argued much with Molly and her rifle. "You can rest easy. I didn't bring the railroad down on you. They want my land in Texas. And, they can have it—for the right price. Most of it, anyway."

"What do you mean most of it?" Was he going to hold onto a parcel to return to?

"I gave a young couple a bit of it, that's all. They needed a place to live and I wanted to know I wouldn't be leaving my folks behind in a forgotten plot."

Trace told Molly the story of Bill and Miranda.

"It was nothing," he finished, "I was glad to do it."

Molly thought about where she might have been at Miranda's age, had she not married a man with three children already. She had wanted a first love that she could share the thrill of having their first child with, but became involved with a man who was stable, honest, and needed a mother for the children he already had. She had set her dream aside, hoping to fill her life with someone else's children until she might have some of her own. Then, when her husband had been killed before they had known that joy, she found that not many men were willing to take on a woman with three children already at home.

She had set herself to be content raising her stepchildren, believing she would never know a child of her own flesh and blood to love along with the others.

She would never have given up her stepchildren. Still, she felt there was love enough in her heart for more.

Trace noticed her gazing out across the pasture, lost in her thoughts. "Is there a problem?"

"It's nothing. I'm just happy you're back."

"Well, I'd better help Andy find a place for the cow and calf so they don't eat up your garden."

~ * ~

A few days later, Molly and all three children were back at school during the daytime. Trace was left to himself to work on the place and do chores.

As he tried to stretch a particularly stubborn piece of wire to make a fence for the cow, Spot, and her calf that Rosie had named Missy, he heard Crazy Leg growl nearby then break into a bark, and run for the drive.

Trace straightened his back and sheltered his eyes with his hand to see who was entering the property.

Plodding along was Elroy Peabody, looking from one side to the other in order to make sure Andy or Molly weren't about to attack.

Trace laid his tools aside and walked toward the yard.

"Mr. Westerman?" Elroy Peabody called out.

"You must be Peabody. I'm surprised you showed yourself again, after tangling with Molly."

"I wouldn't have, 'cept the railroad wants that land of yours badly and I heard she taught at the schoolhouse during the day. I was hoping you'd gotten back and would be here alone."

Crazy Leg nipped at the horse's heels and the horse moved about trying to keep him off.

"Crazy Leg! Stop that!" Trace called to the dog.

"Get down, Mr. Peabody. Come on up to the porch where there's some shade. Don't know when this hot weather's ever going to break," Trace was casual.

The fat man hefted himself off his animal and the horse seemed visibly relieved.

Crazy Leg lay down in the shade, alongside the porch, and guarded against the chickens climbing the steps.

"What can I do for you, Peabody?" Trace asked, trying not to be anxious about unloading his property along the Pecos.

"I've got the money in the bank at Moriarty for your land. You sign this Quit Claim Deed and it's all yours."

"Well, I've given some of it away." Trace hoped that wouldn't change the deal.

"We need that south parcel in particular. We'd take it all, but as long as we get the piece we need, I don't reckon it makes much difference. We'd just sell it off later, anyway." Peabody pulled his monocle from his pocket to look over the sheaf of papers in his hand. He handed one paper to Trace.

"Good! Then we have a deal as long as you meet my price." Trace looked at the promissory note detailing the amount. "The description on the deed will have to change. You can get your surveyors out there as soon as you want. I told the people living there to expect someone from the railroad to survey their parcel. I expect a fair deal for them, Mr. Peabody."

"They'll get whatever you promised them. You have my word on that. You mark off the portion on the map and we'll see to it it's theirs—all proper and legal."

"Good. That's all I ask."

"Right pleased to do business with you, Mr. Westerman," Peabody said with relief. He'd had tougher struggles with landowners in the past than with this willing seller.

"You can transfer the money to my account when you have the legal descriptions ready and the deeds for me to sign. I set one up after Snake and his gang tried to rob the bank. The banker was right pleased to accommodate me. I don't have any reason to keep cash on hand out here." He hoped Peabody would pass the word along that there was nothing of value to try to rob the Kling farm over.

"I heard tell the woman that lives here and, now, her boy, are both pretty good shots. Last time I came out here I thought I might find out. Anyway, with you back, that makes three good shots. I don't think any one's going to come around here uninvited again."

"They best not."

"The word's out in town. This is no place to mess with. That's why I was so cautious coming out." Peabody mounted his nag and turned away from the house.

"Well, good day to you. I'll take care of the business at the bank. You can come in and pick up your copy of the paperwork when it's ready." Peabody fingered his monocle, then replaced it in his jacket pocket.

Trace nodded. "Good day to you, too."

Dealing with railroad men left a bad taste in Trace's mouth. Trace had work to do and signing papers took time away from things he felt were more important, right now—like getting prepared for winter.

That night, when Molly and the kids returned from school, Trace was eager to tell Molly about having completed the deal with the railroad. He forced himself to wait until the younger children were in bed and Andy was putting Spot and Missy in the barn.

Molly cleared away the dishes from dinner. Trace helped her load them into the dishpan filled with water and lye soap.

She turned to wipe her wet hands on her apron and came toe-to-toe with Trace.

"Oh, I'm sorry. I didn't mean to bump into you."

Trace chuckled and grinned at her.

"You didn't. I blocked your way. I want to talk to you." He took her hands in his and sat her down on an empty wooden crate that served as a temporary kitchen chair.

"Molly, I finished up my business today."

"You mean with Peabody?"

"Yep. He heard you were busy teaching and took a chance on coming out without getting shot."

"Really, Trace. I wasn't going to shoot him."

"He didn't know that. Anyway, we made an agreement and, when I sign the papers, I'll no longer own a cattle ranch in Texas."

"Oh, Trace. I'm sorry. I know that place meant a lot to you."

"It did, at one time. But, now you and the kids mean more. Molly, I want you to marry me this Saturday. Will you?"

Trace pulled another crate forward and sat down in front of Molly. "Saturday?"

"We can go into town and get the Justice of the Peace to do the ceremony. Doc would be my best man, I'm sure. What do you say?"

"Trace! It's—it's so fast. It seems like we were just talking about it and now, here we are only a few days away from getting married." Molly was stunned. She had looked happily forward to the day they would be man and wife, but now that it was about to happen she felt like she was caught up in a whirlwind and her mind wouldn't release her from its old pattern of worry.

"Are you sure? Not many men would want to marry a woman with three kids—"

"Of course, I'm sure," Trace said. "Have you ever known me to back away from something I thought was right?"

"No, it's just—hard to believe that it's really happening." Molly swung her arms around Trace's neck and hugged him. "Trace, it's wonderful!"

"Saturday it is, then."

"We have to tell the kids."

"First thing in the morning." Trace swept her off her feet in a joyous hug.

~ * ~

On Saturday, the family and Doc Landry met at the office of the Justice of the Peace.

Molly was in her least-worn dress. Seth wore a hand-me-down suit that had been Andy's and had seen better days. He also wore a new white straw hat that Trace had bought that morning at the General Store. True to his word, Trace had replaced the original band with one made from rattlesnake skin. The rattles were fixed into an upright position on the right front. Seth stood proudly—every inch of his small frame supporting the new hat. Rosie wore her best school dress. Trace was tall and lean in his freshly washed shirt and pants. His badge was at the sheriff's office where he planned on leaving it when they finished their business and left town. He was determined nothing would spoil this day.

When Trace kissed his bride and the group went back outside, the sheriff, and a good share of Molly's students and their parents, was there to wish them well.

Trace helped Molly into the buckboard. The kids scampered aboard and settled in the back.

Andy looked out over the group of his classmates and waved. He saw Rebecca Waite in the crowd, looking demure and pretty in a dress her mother had sewn. He'd observed her a lot in class, lately, and wondered, now, as he caught her eye and she looked down and blushed, if his affection for her might be returned. It made him feel giddy inside. This man and woman thing was complicated. He liked the way it made him feel, but he didn't quite know what to do with those sensations, yet. He wondered how many years he would have to wait until he'd be old enough to court.

Rosie jabbed Andy in the ribs.

"I saw you looking at Becky! You're sweet on her, aren't you? I'm going to tell her at school Monday. Becky's got a beau."

"Don't you dare say a word to her, Rosie."

"Why not? If I still had my headaches, maybe I could tell your future. How'd you like that, huh?"

"But, you don't. You hain't had a spell in a long time."

"Haven't." Molly corrected Andy, automatically, as she wove her arm through Trace's crooked elbow and smiled up at him.

"Rosie, you leave Andy alone, you hear?" Trace said. "It's hard enough for a man to let a woman know how he feels. Besides, someday, it'll be your turn to have a beau and Seth will probably be teasing you."

Molly looked back at the children pestering each other. If that was the worst they got, they had no problem at all.

The ride back to the farm seemed to have a whole new perspective to it for Molly. She hadn't been so happy or content in a number of years and she planned to make the most of her new life.

Twenty-five

Three springs later, Andy was courting Rebecca Waite. There were no immediate plans for a wedding, since both of them were still quite young. With stable home lives, neither saw the necessity to rush into setting up a household of their own.

Trace made life at the farm educational and interesting for Andy. He felt confident, one day, he would be able to work his own farm, then he would be ready to take a wife.

For now, he helped Molly and Trace keep the farm in shape, saw to it that Crazy Leg behaved himself when he got too ambitious about running someone off the land, and tried to help keep Rosie and Seth in line. Andy even took charge, occasionally, of little Eula Mae. Molly had given birth to her eight months before—the family called her Emmy, for short. Trace and Molly had agreed to name her after his mother. Rosie insisted Eula was too hard to say, so everyone settled on Emmy.

But then, watching Emmy was a pleasure to Andy. He enjoyed watching Trace and Molly cuddle the baby each had thought they'd never have.

She was a healthy, beautiful child that the whole family adored.

The hollyhocks outside the kitchen window had bloomed the second year, re-seeded, and bloomed again. From her now-finished kitchen, Molly could look out the window and enjoy the thicket of multicolored blooms.

Molly scooped Emmy up off the floor and carried her outside to show her the ballerina flowers and teach her the name of each color. Callie threaded herself between Molly's ankles as she held the baby before the blooms and watched her reach for the brightest flower.

Many changes had taken place in a few short years. Molly could hear Trace hammering on something in the barn. She saw Seth following Andy as he led the newly acquired milk cow out to pasture with the horses. Crazy Leg hurried behind them, moving a little slower these days. Arthritis, Molly figured. With his misshapen leg, she had expected it would set in one day. But, the dog had a lot of good days left in him. He was as much a part of the family as anyone else.

Emmy was leaning down, now, grasping for Callie's tail that twitched across the front of Molly's skirt.

Rosie came up behind Molly in search of her pet.

"There you are," Rosie called to Callie as she wrapped her arms around the cat's rotund belly. She held her for a second, letting Emmy pat Callie's fur with her chubby hand.

And, life goes on, Molly thought. Who could have guessed that a widowed schoolteacher with three stepchildren could threaten to shoot a man over a silly thing like some rocks, and end up marrying him? But then, who would have ever dreamed she'd be a homesteader, either?

"Someday, you girls will be able to be, and do, anything you want." She hugged Emmy and Rosie close. "Don't ever let anyone tell you that you can't."

The hammering in the barn stopped and Molly saw Trace coming toward them. He carried a newly completed cradle in his hands for their second child Molly was now carrying. He hoped it would be a son. He had been too busy to make a special bed for Emmy before she was born. He regretted that she had been, temporarily, relegated to the wicker laundry basket. He smiled with pride in their direction and held the handiwork up for their approval.

Molly smiled at him and basked in her own happiness.

"And, sometimes," Molly told the girls softly, "the best thing to be is yourself."

Meet Mary Jean Kelso

Mary Jean Kelso's other books include: *A Virginia City Mystery, Abducted!, Sierra Summer and Goodbye, Bodie. Goodbye is Forever* (a reprint of *A Virginia City Mystery)*, is due out in March 2006 through Wings ePress. A longtime photojournalist, her work has been printed in numerous magazines and newspapers. She served as Associate Editor for several pharmaceutical magazines before concentrating on fiction.